CAN I GET
an *Amen*
AGAIN

CAN I GET an Amen AGAIN.

JANICE SIMS • KIM LOUISE
NATALIE DUNBAR
NATHASHA BROOKS-HARRIS

ARABESQUE®

SiM

CAN I GET AN AMEN AGAIN

Copyright © 2007 by Harlequin Enterprises S.A.

ISBN-13: 978-0-373-83067-1
ISBN-10:   0-373-83067-X

The publisher acknowledges the copyright holders
of the individual works as follows:

BROWN-EYED HANDSOME MAN
Copyright © 2007 by Janice Sims

THE REAL THING
Copyright © 2007 by Kim Louise Whiteside

MY PROMISE TO YOU
Copyright © 2007 by Natalie Dunbar

A CHANGE IS GONNA COME
Copyright © 2007 by Nathasha Brooks-Harris

www.kimanipress.com

Printed in U.S.A.

CONTENTS

BROWN-EYED HANDSOME MAN

Janice Sims

For the women of A.A.W.W.K: Ask A Woman Who Knows. Gwen, Melanie, Dera and Leslie. Because you know that "the end" is not always the end. And although we have very little control over what life chooses to send our way, we CAN choose how we react to it. Hence, we tend to be lemonade-makers.

I'd like to thank our general manager, Linda Gill,
for asking us to do another *Amen,* and our editor, Evette Porter,
for doing her usual wonderful job.

Doing the first anthology, *Can I Get an Amen,*
was a positive experience due to the company I got to keep:
Nathasha Brooks-Harris, Natalie Dunbar and Kim Louise.

Here we go again, ladies!

CHAPTER 1

"That's what he gets for marrying a woman more than twenty years his junior."

Gena Boudreau, the woman the speaker was referring to, paused with her hand on the door that led to the kitchen. The voice belonged to her recently deceased husband's sister, Cynthia, who had driven from New Orleans to attend his funeral. Gena supposed she should be grateful Cynthia had shown up. Taylor's two grown children had not.

Still, Cynthia's comment made Gena heartsick. She'd always known Cynthia didn't like her, but it was beyond cruel for her to say something so mean-spirited about a brother whom she had supposedly loved. Taylor had always been kind to Cynthia.

She knew it had to be Cynthia's grief talking. Pain made you say awful things. Things you instantly regretted. She took a deep breath and pushed the door open.

Cynthia and the woman to whom she'd been speaking, a stranger to Gena, gasped in surprise. Cynthia lowered her eyes, shame evident in them. The other woman did not look down. She narrowed her eyes, her expression cold and accusing. "Here's the widow," she said derisively while walking toward Gena. Petite and shapely, she was in her late forties. Her hair was stylishly cut, and her black dress equally so.

"You don't know me," she said when she was standing directly in front of Gena. "Taylor and I were seeing each other when you entered the picture. He dropped me for you." Hatred permeated every inch of her body. She fairly bristled with it. An evil smile spread across her attractive face. "I told him then that he would die without me, and I was right." Her eyes sparkled with glee at the knowledge.

Gena calmly turned to Cynthia. "Is this woman a friend of yours?"

At least four inches taller than the stranger, Gena looked over her head at Cynthia, demanding a reasonable explanation for the woman's presence on the most devastating day of her life.

Cynthia grabbed the other woman by the arm. "Come on, Karen, you promised you wouldn't make a scene."

"You *brought* her here?" Gena asked incredulously.

"We've been friends for over thirty years. I thought she and Taylor were going to be married one day. Then *you* stole him!" Cynthia wasn't in the least repentant.

Gena didn't feel as if she had to explain herself to Cynthia, or anyone else, where Taylor was concerned. When she'd met him, two years previously, he'd told her he was single and unattached. In fact, she'd met him when he was a heart patient at the hospital in New Orleans where Gena worked as a registered nurse. After Taylor was released, with a clean bill of health, she thought, and the promise of a long, full life if he took care of himself, he had asked her out and she'd accepted. It was true, Taylor was twenty-two years older than she was, but he had also been handsome, charming, and enormously confident. Theirs was a whirlwind romance, and up until his death they'd been deeply in love. Now these women were trying to diminish that love. Turn it into something sordid.

"Taylor never mentioned you," Gena said, her voice steady in spite of the anger that seethed beneath the surface. "No, I don't know you. And you don't know me. Taylor spent two weeks in the hospital after his heart attack, and I never saw you visit him."

"I was out of town," Karen said. "I would have rushed back if anyone had seen fit to inform me." This time her eyes skewered Cynthia accusingly.

"Taylor told me not to contact you," Cynthia said in her defense. "He obviously already had his eyes on that one."

Gena was getting tired of being looked at as if she were a piece of trash. She was taller, stronger, younger than either of these women, and the way she was feeling right now—stressed out, brokenhearted, wound tighter than a steel coil—she was perilously close to wiping the floor with both of them. She hadn't been brought up on the tough streets of New Orleans for nothing.

"I'm not havin' this conversation," she told them through clenched teeth. Tears sprang to her eyes. "You come here, on the saddest day of my life, to accuse me of stealing Taylor away from you? Are you crazy?" The last three words were shouted as she chose the largest carving knife from the wood block on the counter and tapped the flat side of the blade in the palm of her hand. "I'm a grieving widow. I could go ballistic any minute. Go slam out of my mind and do something in a fugue state that I won't even remember doing once it's over."

Indeed, she did look unhinged. Her brown eyes blazed. Her nostrils flared, and her lips were drawn back from her teeth in a snarl. Release in the form of a double murder seemed preferable to thinking about Taylor lying cold in his grave.

Cynthia and Karen slowly backed toward the swinging doors, their eyes on the knife in her hand. "You've got a houseful of people," Cynthia said reasonably. "You're the one who would be crazy to try anything."

Gena smiled as she advanced. "The more witnesses, the better. If I kill you both in front of them, no one would believe I hadn't gone temporarily insane. I'll hire very talented lawyers who will make certain that things go like this—I'll spend some time in a psychiatric facility. They'll eventually determine that it was aberrant behavior. I'm no harm to anyone else. And I'll be back home in a matter of months. Best of all, I'll have the satisfaction of never seeing you two witches ever again!"

"You're a nurse," Cynthia reminded her desperately. "You're supposed to be a healer. You couldn't harm another human being."

Karen was cowering behind her, primed to leap for the door should Gena start lashing out with the knife. She hadn't foreseen this sort of reaction from Gena. Cynthia had told her that Gena was a mild-mannered mouse of a woman whom Taylor had married for her youth and beauty. Rich men traded their worldly goods for trophy wives all the time. Karen simply wanted to have her say, exact a kind of revenge for the shoddy manner in which Taylor had treated her, and go back home feeling justified. She hadn't expected her life to be threatened!

"Right now," Gena told her, still tapping the knife in the palm of her hand as she continued to walk toward the women, "you don't look particularly human to me. You look like a couple of rabid dogs. And the humanitarian thing to do with rabid dogs is to put them down." She raised the knife menacingly. Cynthia and Karen shot through the swinging doors, with Karen screaming, "Somebody call the law, she done lost her damn mind!"

The doors flapped closed behind them and Gena dissolved in gales of laughter. She put the knife back in its slot in the wooden block on the counter, and after composing herself she walked out to the expansive living room with its two-story ceiling where more than a hundred people were standing about enjoying a buffet and conversing. Or they had been before Cynthia and Karen had interrupted them with screams of terror.

Everyone looked in Gena's direction when she entered the room. She smiled graciously, the epitome of the brave widow with a backbone of steel.

Maybelle Carmichael, her neighbor for the past two years, immediately came forward and placed a comforting hand on her arm. She looked back at Cynthia and Karen, who were surrounded by concerned guests and gesticulating wildly. "What's going on, child?" Maybelle asked.

Gena met her eyes and said sincerely, "I have no idea, Mrs. Carmichael." She always referred to Maybelle in this way because of their age difference. Gena was thirty-four. Maybelle was in her seventies. "But I think it has something to do with the fact that I threatened to cut their throats for coming here today and disrespecting my husband. The tall one is Taylor's younger sister, Cynthia. The short one is his ex-girlfriend."

Maybelle harrumphed as she cast a severe eye on the two women. "Came to cause some mess, huh?"

"Yes, ma'am."

As a woman who had buried more than one husband, Maybelle Carmichael knew how to handle troublemakers on that most depressing of days. She turned and addressed two young men, their suit jackets stretching over bulging muscles.

"Cleotus, Leroy, I want you to escort those two ladies outside and make sure they know the way out of town. They're upsetting Gena, and this is not a day for heaping stress upon stress."

"Yes, ma'am," said Cleotus, the bigger of the two. He'd known Maybelle Carmichael all of his twenty-three years. She'd pulled his ear for talking in church when he was a kid, and helped him get into college on a football scholarship when he was a teenager. Now he was the assistant coach at Red Oaks High School. Leroy was his teenaged cousin, and where Cleotus led, Leroy followed.

Cynthia and Karen soon found themselves respectfully asked to leave the premises by two gentle giants. They did not lay a hand on the women. When they got outside, they held their car doors open for them and firmly shut the doors. Then they stood and watched as

Cynthia started the car and pulled out of the parking lot that the lawn made.

They did not go back inside until her car was completely out of sight.

Maybelle and Gena were watching from the living room window. As the red taillights of Cynthia's car faded in the dusky afternoon shadows, Maybelle reached for Gena's hand. "Come with me, sweetheart. You and I need to have a chat."

Maybelle led her through the other guests and upstairs to the master bedroom. Once inside she closed and locked the door. "Sit down," she said, gesturing to a chair in the seating group of the large room. Gena sat on the edge of the chair. Maybelle sat across from her and pulled her chair closer to Gena's so that their knees were nearly touching.

"What's going on in your head, Gena?" Maybelle asked softly, looking deeply into Gena's eyes. Gena could hardly bear the intensity of Maybelle's gaze. She wasn't ready to talk about what was actually bothering her. It might sound ridiculous to anyone who hadn't experienced what she'd been through in the past few days. Her grievances might appear selfish considering the fact that Taylor was dead and she was still breathing. You had to forgive the dead all their trespasses, didn't you? After all, they'd already suffered the worst punishment visited upon mankind, death itself.

Ashamed for thinking what she was thinking, Gena lowered her eyes.

"Look at me, Gena Boudreau," Maybelle said sharply. "Is it regret? Is it deep sorrow? Is it anger or rage? It's not uncommon for a widow to be angry with her husband for dying, you know. I was mad at my husbands when they left me. Heck, I would go to the cemetery and cuss them out for dying on me. Every time I got married I fooled myself into thinking that it was going to be forever. That we were going to grow old together. I'm winding up growing old by myself!"

Gena found herself crying again. She was angry with herself for crying so much for a man who didn't deserve her tears. "He lied to me!"

Maybelle sat back on her chair and crossed her legs. Now they were getting somewhere. "What did he lie about?"

"Everything," Gena said with a deep sigh. "Okay, maybe not everything. He really was a successful business-man. But we got married under false pretenses. He told me he had a clean bill of health. After the heart attack, he went on a restricted diet and an exercise regimen. Both things I helped him with. There were times when he appeared exhausted to me when he shouldn't have been. I would question him and he'd say it was because he'd had an especially hard workout. Nothing to worry about. But the fact was, Mrs. Carmichael, he was dying. When the doctor released him from the hospital after the heart attack, he knew he had only a few months to live."

"But he lived two years after his heart attack," Maybelle reminded her.

"I was a fanatic about taking care of him. But that's beside the point. He knew he was dying and he chose not to tell me, to forewarn me so that I would be prepared for what happened."

Maybelle gasped, something she rarely did because not many things shocked her after nearly eighty years on earth. "You mean he died…"

"During sex," Gena answered softly. "Can you imagine the horror? It happened in an instant. One second he was fine, and the next he had collapsed on top of me. The air expelled from his lungs, and he was dead. I gave him mouth-to-mouth. I massaged his heart. I knew what to do. I did it automatically. Thank God those skills came to me automatically, because one part of my mind was in the grip of sheer panic. I couldn't bring him around. I'd dialed 911 just before I began working on him. They got here in less than six minutes. I knew that because while I was trying to get him to breathe I was watching the clock on the nightstand. They were going to catch hell if they took their time. I was like a madwoman. One of the paramedics had to pull me off him so they could get to work on him. They pronounced him dead in the ambulance."

Maybelle was shaking her head sympathetically. That was an awful last memory for any wife. She took both Gena's hands in hers and squeezed them reassuringly. "Honey, I know that to your ears this is going to sound like a platitude, but *this too shall pass*. Right now the memory is sharp. Your emotions are high, and it feels as if you may never get over the trauma of Taylor dying the way he did. But time will soften the memory. Maybe Taylor didn't tell you he was dying because he didn't want you coddling him. A man should have the right to die as he wishes. Most of us don't get the chance to choose. You can look at it as your final gift to him. Instead of lingering in a hospital with tubes coming out of every orifice of his body, he died in the arms of the woman he loved. Don't look at the horror of it. Look at the peace you gave him. The joy you gave him for two years when the doctor said he only had a few months to live. That's what you need to focus on, child. The positive, not the negative."

Most of Maybelle's words were lost on Gena. She tried to concentrate, but the loud images in her mind drowned out Maybelle's voice. That night was still crystal clear.

She and Taylor had showered together and patted each other dry with warm, fluffy towels. Then they'd kissed all the way to the bed. Taylor might have been in his late fifties, but his sexual drive was never a matter for concern. Their sex life had been exciting and fulfilling. She was reminded of the saying her mother and aunts used to repeat about the benefits of being an older man's lover: Older lovers actually cared about a woman's pleasure, whereas young men cared only for their own.

Taylor was like that, a wonderful, giving lover. Perhaps she shouldn't have been as enthusiastic that night, but they'd both been hungry for each other, and she'd given him her all. During the course of the evening she'd had two orgasms. He'd held back just for her and when he was about to experience his first, he collapsed.

Therefore, no matter what Maybelle said to Gena, she only heard part of it because she held the quiet conviction that she'd been the cause of Taylor's death. Yes, he had been guilty of withholding important information about his health. But she was the one who had pushed him beyond his limit.

He'd died giving her pleasure.

How could she put a positive spin on *that,* as Mrs. Carmichael suggested?

In her mind, she was the black widow of Red Oaks, Georgia. However, her lethal weapon of choice wasn't any of the customary ones chosen by the average murderous wife such as poison, or a gun, or a knife.

She killed with sex.

CHAPTER 2

Eight years later

"Get a move on, Lily!" Nathan "Nate" Lincoln bellowed from the foot of the stairs. "We have to be there by seven."

He heard a protracted groan from his sixteen-year-old daughter, then the sound of a heavy work boot hitting the hardwood floor of her bedroom. It was August, and Lily would have preferred to sleep late on her summer vacation. Her father, however, had other ideas; he'd taken her on as his apprentice in his home-repair business.

By the time Lily got downstairs Nate had the cereal, milk, and orange juice on the table and had prepared sandwiches for their lunch. Lily yawned so widely as she dragged herself into the kitchen that Nate was afraid her jaw might lock.

"What have I told you about staying up late watching TV?"

Pouting, Lily sat on a chair and began pouring cereal into a bowl. She was tall and slim with golden brown skin, a headful of curly jet-black hair, and whiskey-colored eyes. The eyes were exactly like her dad's. The skin and hair were genetically somewhere between her dad and the mother she'd never known. Her dad had kept photos of her mom, though, and she knew that her nose and mouth were kind of shaped like Charity's, too. She'd always called her mom by her first name. She saw no reason to waste respect on a woman who'd abandoned them when she was barely two weeks old.

Talk about a disappointment in the mother department!

"I wasn't watching TV, Dad, I was talking to Chloe."

Nate had a habit of raising his brows when he couldn't believe what he was hearing. He did it quite a lot in Lily's presence. "Am I mistaken, or isn't Chloe in Florida on vacation with her family?"

"Yeah, but she has lots of free minutes on her cell phone after eight o'clock."

"How long did you talk?"

Lily wrinkled her nose, something she did whenever she didn't want to answer her father. She didn't lie to him, though. "Four hours."

"Four hours!"

"Dad, that vein is popping out of your forehead again," Lily said softly. Smiling, she lowered her head and shoveled the cereal into her mouth. If he asked another question she would require at least a minute to chew and swallow before replying. That would hopefully give her time enough to think up an adequate explanation for that four-hour phone marathon.

Nate surprised her, however, by sighing deeply and burying his nose in the paper while he ate his cereal. She heard him mumble a couple of times during their meal. Something about "teenagers."

Across town, in a stately home on a hill, Miss Edna Strawder rolled over in bed and hit the snooze button. The mistress of the house had been up for at least an hour. *She* was the housekeeper and didn't have to rise for another fifteen minutes. By the time she got out of bed, showered, and went downstairs to start breakfast her employer would have run five miles, showered, and dressed for her Ladies Auxiliary meeting. She closed her eyes. Even thinking about everything that woman did in the course of a day made her tired. Drifting back off to sleep, she tried not to think about it.

When she got downstairs, the first thing she saw as she strolled into the kitchen was a large, beautifully wrapped gift, sitting on the table. Next to it was a gorgeous bouquet of yellow tulips and lavender tulips, her favorite flowers in her favorite colors.

Tears immediately sprang to her eyes. Miss Gena hadn't forgotten. Today was the tenth anniversary of her employment with the Boudreau family. Well, now it was just Miss Gena, but when they'd hired her, Mr. Taylor had been alive.

Her heart skipped a beat.

Come to think of it, this year would have been Miss Gena's and Mr. Taylor's tenth wedding anniversary if he had lived, God rest his soul! It would be best not to remind Miss Gena of that when she came downstairs.

A short, stout woman, Miss Edna walked over to the table and removed the lid from the bow-festooned box. Inside were two beautiful dresses. Miss Gena had exquisite taste and never forgot her size. She withdrew one from the box and held it up against her. She loved the smell of new clothes. Even more than that, she loved receiving presents. She had never married. Had never had children, and most of her family lived in Mississippi. There were few people she bought gifts for, or who bought gifts for her. She never failed to feel excitement when someone thought enough of her to actually go out and buy something especially for her.

Of course, Miss Gena, ever practical, was not the kind of employer who stopped at giving her employee trinkets or pretty things as compensation for service. No, she made certain that Miss Edna's retirement account was generous, and also advised her about investments. After Mr. Taylor had died, Miss Gena had become somewhat of a whiz at finances. Miss Edna remembered when Mr. Taylor's son and daughter had tried to cut Miss Gena out of the family electronics business. A multimillionaire, Mr Taylor had left one-quarter of the business to Miss Gena.

For months the son and daughter, who were both officers in the company, chose to leave Miss Gena out of any communications concerning the business. Finally, Miss Gena had grown tired of their shenanigans and gone to New Orleans to confront them. Miss Gena had never told Edna exactly what she'd said in the board meeting, but from then on she had been apprised of everything that went on in the boardroom. A few years ago, the son and daughter had wanted to sell the company for a bundle of money, but even then they had to get Miss Gena's permission to do it. Miss Gena had agonized over the decision to sell for weeks before giving her consent. They'd all come out of it a great deal richer and now Miss Gena, no longer a businesswoman, devoted her time and energies to the community.

Miss Edna admired the other dress before gently folding both and returning them to the box. "Then you like them?" said Gena from behind her.

Miss Edna wiped tears from her cheeks as she smiled at Gena. "They're beautiful. I'll be the belle of Red Oaks Christian Fellowship."

"You're already the prettiest unattached woman there," Gena told her as she poured herself a cup of coffee that she'd set to perking before going upstairs to shower after her run. "Listen, Miss Edna, don't you dare cook anything or do a lick of work today. I can fend for myself and the house can go a day without being dusted or vacuumed. Go do something nice for yourself."

Miss Edna considered it. They were getting ready for a revival at Red Oaks Christian Fellowship Church, and she was sure the ladies could use her help with something or other. All she had to do was phone Maybelle Carmichael to get the lowdown. That wouldn't exactly be like taking the day off, but the companionship of the other ladies in the church was like a vacation to her.

"I could go over to the church grounds where they're erecting the tent for the revival meeting," she said thoughtfully.

"Tell Mrs. Carmichael I said hello," Gena said.

She and Maybelle were close friends and neighbors, but she was not a member of her church. She didn't attend church anywhere. She supposed if she did attend, it would be Red Oaks Christian Fellowship since she knew a lot of good people who went there. They set a fine example. However, deep down Gena found it hard to have complete faith in a God who would take Taylor from her in such a manner. It was unreasonable to feel that way, she knew. Still, she couldn't shake the feeling.

Maybelle had tried to tell her over the years that God was not the architect of bad things happening to good people. God got the blame for so much nowadays, Maybelle would say, when it was really Satan the devil behind all the suffering of mankind. And don't forget that mankind brought a whole lot of suffering on themselves. God didn't start wars, for example. Gena, however, could not reason something with her head that her heart didn't feel. If God were truly up there concerned about us, why didn't He do something about our suffering? Maybelle explained that God was merciful in many ways. He provided us with a planet to live on. It wasn't His fault if we polluted it. He gave us life and free choice. Would we be happier with a God who dictated to us how to live? And enforced it? The world would definitely be a more perfect place. There would be no wars, no starving children in Third World countries, or in our own country for that matter; we'd all live forever without sickness or pain. That, Maybelle, often told her, was promised in the Book of Revelation. But humans were not meant to be treated as slaves, with no free will. God knew we needed to make up our own minds about our lives. Surely Adam and Eve illustrated that fact when they could not live in a perfect paradise without questioning the Almighty's rules and regulations. They set the precedent; now we had to live with the consequences.

Gena laughed suddenly, remembering Maybelle's words: "If you want to blame somebody for Taylor's death, blame your first father and mother, Adam and Eve. They're the ones who got us into this mess!"

"What?" asked Miss Edna, wondering what had struck Gena as funny.

"Nothing," said Gena. "It was just something Mrs. Carmichael told me a long time ago."

Miss Edna laughed too. "That woman's something else, ain't she?"

"That, she is," Gena agreed. She glanced down at her watch. "Oh, look at the time. I have to run. Have a wonderful day, Miss Edna. And happy tenth anniversary!"

Her big brown eyes suddenly held a sad aspect in their depths. Miss Edna knew she must have been thinking about Mr. Taylor. She grinned, though, spun on her heel, and walked purposefully toward the garage door adjacent to the kitchen.

"Aaaruhhh!" came a mournful bark as Cary Grant careened around the corner so swiftly that when he tried to slow down on all four paws he wound up sliding the rest of the way into the room on his backside, and into Gena's legs.

Cary Grant was Gena's two-year-old russet-coated Labrador. So named because of his gentlemanly demeanor. He would steal her shoes and hide them, but he would not gnaw on them.

He loved to go places. Hence his desperate behavior.

Laughing, Gena bent to rub his handsome head. "You can't go this time, baby. I'll take you for a long walk when I get back home."

Miss Edna firmly grasped him by the collar. "He can go with me," she offered. "The ladies love him."

It was true. Cary Grant was such a handsome brute that the females all melted when Miss Edna took him for walks in the park with several other ladies who attended Red Oaks Christian Fellowship. And Cary Grant loved the attention. He went from one lady to the next, the scamp, accepting belly rubs and scratches underneath his chin.

"You really don't mind? He has his moments of rebellion." Gena wanted Miss Edna's day to be free of worry.

"It'll be fun for both of us," Miss Edna assured her.

"All right, then, I'm gone," Gena said, closing the garage door after her.

Miss Edna looked sternly down at Cary Grant. "Now, if that good-looking Mr. Butler is at the church today, don't you go growling at him like you usually do."

Cary Grant peered up at her and whined as if to say he wasn't aware of any bad behavior on his part toward a Mr. Butler. He wasn't even sure he *knew* a Mr. Butler.

"All right, then," said Miss Edna, taking the expression in his eyes to mean that he had agreed to her terms. "Let me get a little breakfast in my stomach before we go."

Laughter bubbled up. She was getting as crazy as Miss Gena, talking to a dog as if he could understand her!

Gena drove a golden 1990 Volvo 740 GLE around town. It was seventeen years old, but it suited her needs, which were to have safe, reliable transportation and a car that didn't make people gawk. She knew her reputation in Red Oaks: the rich widow on the hill. She also knew that most people speculated on just how rich she was. Her home, a white brick mansion on a hundred acres, made them believe she was rolling in dough.

The car confused them. Her motto was *never give them what they expect*.

She parked the car and got out to run up the steps of the community center, wearing sunglasses and looking fit and lithe in jeans, a bright emerald short-sleeved cotton shirt, and Reeboks.

The temperature was already in the high seventies, and she feared it would be ninety by noon. Such was August in their part of Georgia. Landlocked, they didn't get the breezes Savannah enjoyed. Savannah was one of her favorite places to visit within driving distance. Sometimes she and Cary Grant would drive there for the weekend.

She smiled as she pulled the door open. How pitiful was her love life when she was going on weekends with her dog? Still, she didn't mind being single. In fact, she found a strange kind of comfort in it because even though she was president of the Ladies Auxiliary and donated her time to several other charitable organizations—and this certainly illustrated her commitment to caring for the world—she stopped short of risking her heart.

Eight years ago, she'd lost her husband. Two years prior to that, she'd lost her mother. She'd never known her father, nor did she know where he was, so there was no risk of being devastated by the news of his death.

She loved her mother's sisters, two aunts who lived near New Orleans. She visited them once a year. She wasn't as emotionally attached to her aunts and the rest of her family as she had been to her mother or her husband, though. Her heart was safe. And she liked it that way. Sometimes she did wonder if it was a cowardly act to go through life guarding against loving too deeply.

Luckily, she hadn't met anyone who even came close to making her lose her mind like the woman in her favorite Chuck Berry song, "Brown-Eyed Handsome Man." The woman whom the song was about would do anything for the man she loved. Completely ignoring the fact that he was a Lothario and an ex-convict.

Gena couldn't imagine herself that wild about *any* man.

"Gena!"

Gena, only two doors away from her destination, a conference room on the second floor, smiled when she heard that deep, masculine voice. Speaking of handsome men, a fine specimen was jogging toward her right now. Cleotus Riley. Okay, she wasn't a *dead* woman. She simply wasn't a cradle robber or a Mrs. Robinson. Cleotus was a good eleven years younger.

Gena's heart turned over at the sight of his square-jawed face. This was proof that in spite of her resolve to stay unattached she was not, however, incapable of being moved by a man's beauty.

He wore a gray summer suit with a white shirt and dark gray tie. Gena suspected he was also bound for a meeting in the community center. "Cleotus, what a way to start the day," Gena teased, her dark brown eyes sweeping over his muscular body.

They stood a few feet apart, giving one another admiring glances. Over the years they'd come to the understanding that Gena was never going to go out with him, but it was all right to flirt outrageously every chance they got.

Cleotus secretly harbored the hope that she'd one day give in. He'd fallen in love with her eight years ago, the first time he'd laid eyes on her. She'd been married then, though. She and Taylor were regular supporters of the high school football team. They attended all of the home games. Cleotus found that the highlight of every game for him was seeing her beautiful face in the stands. She, on the other hand, saw him as a kid, and that hadn't changed.

"The Athletic Association is meeting this morning. I'll be finished by eleven," he told her hopefully. "How about you?"

"Sorry, it's election time. We'll be in there until doomsday." At least it felt like the elections took that long. Her term was at an end, and this year she wasn't going to throw her hat into the ring. She was sure Marveen Sanders would be glad to hear it. Marveen had lost to her the past three years.

Cleotus screwed up his handsome, chestnut-brown face in a frown. "Too bad. I wanted to take you to lunch."

"A free lunch?" Gena joked. "I'll make an excuse and get out of there by twelve."

Cleotus smiled, which only made him more irresistible. "It's a date."

Gena wiggled a finger at him as she turned to continue

down the corridor to her conference room. "Now, don't start that foolishness again. This is a friendly lunch between friends."

He laughed shortly as his eyes took in how delectable she looked in those jeans. "Call it what you want to. Which room will you be in? I'll be waiting outside at twelve."

"Two thirty-two," she told him over her shoulder. "See you."

"You sure will," Cleotus said under his breath. He sighed regretfully. Why couldn't he get her to see that her embargo on taking their relationship further was ridiculous and unfair? Penalizing him because he was younger was so hypocritical of Gena when she'd married a man almost twice her age!

CHAPTER 3

"Furthermore, I foresee a bright future for the Ladies Auxiliary under my direction," Marveen Sanders said as she stood behind the podium flipping yet another page in the folder that held her seemingly endless campaign speech.

"Can't she foresee it a little faster?" Gayle Jackson whispered near Gena's ear.

Gena wondered why they had never put a time limit on campaign speeches during these interminable election meetings. Many of the one-hundred-plus members were looking weary, some downright hostile, because of Marveen's long-windedness.

"Have you ever known Marveen to waste a minute in the spotlight?" asked Alexandra Cartwright-Kyles. Both Gena and Gayle shook their heads in the negative. They were likely to be there another hour before Marveen gave out for loss of breath.

Gayle and Alex were best friends. Gayle ran her family's bakery, while Alex and her husband, Jared, were owners of a construction/landscaping business. Both women were happily married, a state they fervently wished on Gena.

Between the two of them and Mrs. Maybelle Carmichael, Gena had rejected about ten men they'd sicced on her. Okay, "tried to fix her up with" was a more generous way of describing their matchmaking efforts. They meant well. Her friends always did.

Gena's stomach growled. She glanced at her watch. It was nearly twelve. When she looked up at Marveen, who appeared to have gotten her second wind, she realized she would have to do something she had never done in all the years of her membership in the Ladies Auxiliary; she was going to have to interrupt the meeting. She wouldn't have had to do it if she had drawn the longer straw prior to the meeting, but Marveen had lucked out and had won the right to make her speech first. All Gena was going to say was that she was not going to seek reelection. Relinquishing her duties would give her more time to devote to the hospice. And Marveen would win by default.

Gena rose, thinking that what she was about to do was an act of mercy.

"Excuse me, Marveen…"

Marveen's light brown eyes narrowed. She self-consciously wiped the sweat from the fuzzy area above her top lip. "Yes, Gena?"

"I apologize for interrupting you, Madam President." Gena simply smiled at her then, allowing what she'd said to sink in.

Marveen's eyes stretched in shock, and then she let out a whoop. Grinning from ear to ear, she said, "Are you sure?"

"Yes, I am. Three years is long enough for this battle-weary incumbent." She quickly went up on the stage and shook Marveen's hand. Marveen hugged her.

The other ladies applauded and started chanting, "Gena, Gena!" possibly wanting her to make a farewell speech. Gena addressed them with "No, no, I've bored you all enough with my long, drawn-out monologues over the years. I'm just going to say one thing. It's been a pleasure serving you and this fine community and I'm going to miss working so closely with the scholarship recipients. They've really made us proud."

The main function of the Ladies Auxiliary was to provide scholarships for deserving students. They didn't simply award money, but provided career counseling and kept in touch with the students once they were in college.

Alexandra's sister, Vicky, who was a resident at an Atlanta hospital, had benefited from the program, as well as more than fifty other Red Oaks High School students.

As Gena walked down the aisle she was met with hugs, pats on the back, and assorted comments like "Job well done, Madam President."

Alex and Gayle waited for her at the door. Gayle had gotten her purse off her chair to save her from having to double-back for it.

Handing her the shoulder bag, Gayle said, "Short and sweet."

Gena smiled. "I aim to please."

The three of them stepped into the corridor, closing the door behind them. Cleotus had been sitting on a bench across the hall. He got to his feet when he saw Gena coming out of room 232.

Watching his approach, Alex grinned and said, "A date, no less."

"It's not a date," Gena disavowed softly. "He's a dear, sweet boy who invited me to lunch, that's all."

Gayle disagreed. "He's a dream walking, that's what *he* is. One of those night dreams that leave you all hot and bothered."

Gena was happy that Cleotus wasn't yet within hearing range. "Stop that now, ladies. You're going to embarrass him."

Alex and Gayle refrained from ogling Cleotus, although, he, Alex, and Gayle had gone to the same school and he was, quite frankly, used to being ogled by them. As star fullback on the football team, he'd been very popular with the ladies.

He'd been a senior when those two had been wild and crazy freshmen. He bet Gena didn't know that Alex had been a cheerleader who had lost the bottom half of her uniform while doing a cartwheel at a game, and the school photographer had conveniently snapped the momentous occasion. He still felt embarrassed for her.

Nor that Gayle, a seasoned athlete, had once challenged the captain of the boys' track team to a race and had won, getting her picture in the local paper.

He admired Alex for her bravery. She hadn't missed one day of school following the wardrobe malfunction. And he admired Gayle for her self-confidence.

As far as he was concerned, their husbands were lucky men.

He beamed at them now. "Gayle, Alex, it's good to see you two!"

"Same here," said Alex. She patted her distended belly.

"Although I'm afraid you're seeing a bit more of me than you're used to seeing."

Cleotus chuckled. "Alexandra, you've never looked lovelier."

"His mama taught him right," Gayle said, grinning.

The two women took turns hugging him tightly.

"Enjoy your lunch," Alex said to Gena and Cleotus as she and Gayle prepared to leave. "We both have to get to work."

They hurried toward the stairs.

Cleotus turned to Gena, who had been enjoying his exchange with Alex and Gayle. It was even more apparent to her now that Cleotus needed a younger woman to focus on. His eyes had lit up at the sight of Alex's big belly. The man wanted children, plain and simple. And she was far too old at forty-two to be entertaining the notion of giving birth. Even if she *did* take his advances seriously. Which she didn't.

She continued to look up at him speculatively as they began walking toward the stairs. She hoped they had a wonderful lunch together, something worth remembering because after today she was not going to share any more friendly meals with him.

She felt she wasn't being fair to Cleotus. By continuing a flirtatious relationship with him she was only giving him false hope. His attention should be elsewhere. On a young woman who could give him children.

She hooked her arm through his as they took the stairs and she smiled at him. For the present she was going to enjoy his company.

* * *

"I'm glad you forgot to bring the sandwiches," Lily said, enjoying her cheeseburger. "If I had to eat one more bologna sandwich for lunch, I was going to kill Oscar Mayer."

Nate laughed softly. As always, Lily was exaggerating. He didn't prepare bologna sandwiches for their lunches every day. Sometimes he made peanut butter and jelly.

"So, sue me if I'm not a chef. I do the best I can. You know, you're welcome to make the sandwiches yourself."

Lily was a worse cook than he was. *If only,* she thought, *I'd had a mom to teach me.* She would never have said that out loud. Her dad had enough guilt to carry around for not having given her a worthwhile mother. She knew that because every woman he dated who he later discovered didn't want children was swiftly dropped. He wanted someone who could be a good example for Lily. He would accept nothing less.

That's why Lily would be happy when she graduated in a couple of years and went to college. Then her dad would be free to date whomever he pleased. She wouldn't be at home, so she wouldn't need a mother, although, knowing him, he would still think she needed a mother well into her old age.

She laughed briefly at the image of him in his eighties and still trying to find the perfect mother for her. He was weird, but she loved him.

Lily looked up and realized that her dad's attention was riveted on a woman sitting at a table a few feet away with a big, good-looking guy in a suit. She scrutinized her. The woman was laughing at something the guy had said. Her large brown eyes were animated. She threw her head back and her long, thick black hair fell beguilingly down her back. Lily noticed things like that because she was a writer. Love poems mostly. Andre Thomas, a boy in her advanced algebra class, had inspired a sonnet or two. So she knew about attraction. Her dad definitely liked what he saw.

The woman was pretty in a not-made-up way. Lily gave her points for not spackling on the makeup. When she grinned, dimples popped into her cheeks, and her teeth were perfect. But anybody could have perfect teeth with the help of the right orthodontist.

Lily had recently had braces taken off her own teeth, thank God. They'd been the clear kind, but still, some boys had looked at her like she was an alien life-form. Her dad said it was her imagination. But she didn't have to imagine the fact that after they'd been removed boys had started asking her out left and right. Dates that she had to turn down because her dad didn't allow her to go on dates yet. Group dates, yes. When there was adult super-vision. She sighed. College was her only hope.

"She's pretty."

Her dad casually glanced at her, smiling charmingly as if he hadn't been caught red-handed staring at a strange woman. Lily was just glad that they were sitting at a booth in the back, and the woman's table was in the center of the room. Unless someone clued her in that she was being observed she'd never know it.

"What woman?"

"You know the one I'm talking about. Green blouse, long black hair."

"Are you finished eating?" asked her dad, stealing one of her fries. "We still have a good five-hour job at the Harrison house. We start a new job tomorrow morning."

"I might be sick tomorrow morning," Lily said. "Heat stroke. How can you stand to be out in the sun all day?"

"You get used to it. Besides, there's a chance we'll be inside tomorrow."

Lily didn't believe him for a minute. "Really? What are we repairing tomorrow?"

"A front porch."

Lily threw a fry at him. It fell onto Nate's plate. He picked it up and ate it.

Lily shook her head at his antics. She didn't know where he put all the food he ate. He should be fat, but somehow he worked it off every day. He was a little over six feet tall with muscular arms, legs, chest, and a flat belly. Lots of women thought he was dreamy, including Chloe, and she was only sixteen.

His gaze had drifted back to the woman. Lily followed his line of sight. This time the woman wasn't laughing. From the expression on her face, the man she was with was saying something very disagreeable. Lily couldn't hear a word of his speech, but he was gesturing wildly, almost violently. The woman was staring up at him with shock and surprise written all over her face. Lily wished she could hear what the man was saying.

Her curiosity swiftly fled when her dad tensed and went to get out of his seat, obviously intending to go to the woman's rescue. Lily latched on to his arm. "Daddy, no. He's leaving. Look!"

Indeed, the man had turned his back on the woman at the center table and stormed off.

Nate relaxed and settled back onto his seat in the booth. Lily picked up her sweet tea and took a big swallow, her throat suddenly parched. What exactly had her dad thought he was going to do? That guy had to be two inches taller and twenty pounds heavier than he was. It did give her an idea, though. That was the first time her dad had shown an interest in a woman in a long time. If she could somehow find someone who could sustain that interest, maybe, just maybe, her summer could be saved. With his attention divided and not solely on her, there was the possibility that when Chloe came back from her vacation in Florida next week they could actually plan some fun activities together.

At this rate all she'd have to show for her summer vacation would be callus-covered palms and a lower body weight due to having sweated nearly to death in this heat.

Nate still wanted to go over to Gena Boudreau's table and ask if she was okay. He knew who she was because he'd been seeing her jogging around town for years. As far as he knew, she never changed her route. If he was doing work at a house on her route he could be assured that she would pass it at practically the same time each morning.

One morning the owner of the house that he was putting a new roof on saw him watching her.

"Don't get your hopes up," the man had said. "That's Gena Boudreau, the richest woman in town. Her husband left her loaded." He'd laughed. "But there's no harm in looking, huh? I know she makes *my* mornings worth getting up for."

Nate had immediately recognized the name Boudreau. He remembered the huge spread in the paper when Taylor Boudreau had died of a heart attack. The paper had listed his age at fifty-six. Nate had assumed his widow was nearer his age.

Later, he'd heard the rumor that Taylor Boudreau had died in his wife's arms. Nate's heart had gone out to Gena. If it were true, it had to have been a nightmare for her.

Being a realist, he didn't fantasize about approaching her and asking her out. The richest woman in town would have no need for a Mr. Fix-it.

Gena sat at the table for ten minutes or longer after Cleotus left in a huff. She felt like crying, but held the tears in check. Eyes and ears were everywhere in Red Oaks. In a matter of minutes word would have it that Cleotus had broken off their affair (because there's always an affair) in Marge's Café and left her bawling like a baby.

So she sipped her water and composed herself.

She'd told him she wasn't even going to flirt with him anymore. He should find a nice girl and get married. Why waste his time on a woman who was so set in her ways she'd probably never get married again, let alone to a man eleven years younger?

He'd taken it all in stride until she had said, "I know some incredible young women who would love to go out with you."

He'd become incensed at the idea of her fixing him up with someone else. "If you don't want me, that's fine, I'll get over it. But don't treat my feelings for you as if they're so trivial that you can sit there and think of women who are more suitable for me. Give me a break!"

His dark brown eyes flashed angrily. "I feel sorry for you, Gena. You sit up there in your house on the hill pretending as if you don't need anything, or anyone. When inside you crave love like everybody else. Don't tell me," and his voice got much lower, so low that she had to strain to hear, "that you don't want me in your bed at night, because I know you do. You're simply too much of a coward to allow anything good to happen to you. Ten years, Gena! I've been in love with you for a decade. But it's over, I'm done with you now. I'm too young for you? That's a laugh! You're not mature enough for *me,* because I need a woman, not a mouse!"

Gena's emotions were in turmoil. All these years she had clung to the hope that Cleotus's feelings for her were about as deep as a puddle. That he'd simply enjoyed their harmless flirtation. Nothing he'd said a few minutes ago had shocked her more than his admission of love. She didn't want anyone to love her. He was wrong when he said she craved love. She despised love. All it did was rip your heart out and leave you bleeding to death.

She got up. Glancing down, she saw that Cleotus had left enough money for the bill plus a generous tip. He had definitely washed his hands of her, not even wanting to be indebted to her for a meal.

As she walked across the crowded restaurant, she convinced herself that what she had done was for the best. She'd just have to live with the fact that someone who had possibly loved her now hated her.

When she finally made it to her car, she got in, started it, turned on the air full-blast, and sat in the parking lot, crying. Sometime later, she drove home, still sniffling, wondering if what Cleotus had said about her having lost the ability to believe in good things happening to her was true.

She didn't believe in fairy tales. Good fortune didn't simply fall out of the sky. Not in her experience. You worked for good fortune. The only time something good and unexpected had happened to her was when she'd met Taylor and fallen in love with him.

And that had ended badly.

So perhaps Cleotus had a point: It *was* hard for her to believe in anything good simply *happening* to her.

CHAPTER 4

When Gena and Taylor had had their home designed more than ten years ago, Taylor had insisted on having an ornate fence installed around the property. At the time, Gena had thought the added security unnecessary in a town the size of Red Oaks. It was ostentatious and off-putting. An alarm system would be sufficient for safety.

Taylor had won that argument. Now Gena was glad he had when she saw who was outside the gate when she returned home following that dreadful confrontation with Cleotus.

Cynthia Boudreau-Williams. Otherwise known as the sister-in-law from hell.

She'd been good enough not to block the driveway and had parked her car, a battered Ford LTD, on the side of the road. She was leaning against the land ship of a car, waving and smiling at Gena as though she showed up on her doorstep every day.

Gena started to drive right past her, use the remote to open the gate, go in, and shut it behind her, but thought better of it. Knowing Cynthia, she'd race through the opening before she could get it shut again.

Besides, if she didn't stop and talk to her she'd never

find out why she'd come. And she was dying to know why the woman was on her property after an eight-year cessation of communications. Not a phone call or a Christmas card...nothing!

She wasn't going to let her inside, though. They could talk in the driveway.

Gena parked the Volvo and got out. The heat slapped her in the face, and she wondered how long Cynthia had been waiting for her. She saw that the windows of the LTD were all down. Cynthia wore a pair of white cropped pants, a turquoise sleeveless T, and green flip-flops. It was the flip-flops that made Gena look at her with less cynical eyes.

Gena had never known her to wear something as casual as flip-flops. Normally, she would wear three-inch heels with cropped pants. Cynthia had once ridiculed her for wearing white after Labor Day. "As Taylor's wife, you must be presentable at all times, Missy," she'd said. Gena had hated it when she called her Missy. Cynthia had said the word so condescendingly.

At any rate, nothing short of a disaster would make Cynthia leave home dressed the way she was. Gena removed her sunglasses as they began walking toward each other. "I don't believe my eyes. Cynthia! What brings *you* here?"

Cynthia laughed nervously. Her eyes darted from side to side as though she was expecting somebody to jump up behind her and yell, "Boo!" at any second. When she focused on Gena again, she cleared her throat and said, "Can't I visit my brother's wife?"

The defensiveness in her voice made Gena pause in her tracks. She didn't look right. Her face was drawn. Yes, she was eight years older. She had to be in her mid-fifties by now and she'd lost weight. But there was something else about her, something desperate.

"I haven't seen you in a long time," Gena said, keeping her voice friendly. "I'm sure you can understand why this is such a surprise."

Cynthia's mouth trembled as she attempted a smile. "What do you want me to say, Gena, that I lost everything in Katrina and have never been able to recover anything? That I've been living out of my car for the past year, and now I'm down to my last twenty dollars?"

She must have read disbelief in Gena's expression, because her tone took on a hard edge as she continued. "I know that must be hard for you to believe. Katrina happened practically two years ago. Everybody should be back on track by now. But that's not true of a lot of people who were affected by the storm. I was comfortable before Katrina. I owned a business. Owned my house. Paid my taxes. I was the model citizen. Now I'm one of the walking poor. Because I was nicely middle class, I didn't qualify for a government loan. I went through my savings in no time. I'm fifty-five years old. Nobody wants to hire a fifty-five-year-old!"

Hot tears ran down her cheeks. "If I had anywhere else to go, do you think I would have come to you? I know you hate me, especially after what Karen and I did on the day you buried Taylor. I would hate me, too. I was in so much pain that day. Taylor was the only one in my family who loved me, warts and all. The thought of never seeing him again made me act ugly." She looked Gena straight

in the eye. "I know that's no excuse, but it's the truth."
Her legs wobbled as she turned to head back to her car.

Gena was in a quandary. On the one hand, she didn't
know whether she could trust Cynthia in her home.
Perhaps she'd waited eight years to get back at her for
pulling a knife on her. On the other hand, Cynthia was
Taylor's sister, and if she was truly destitute, Taylor would
want her to help.

More importantly, she could not look into Cynthia's
eyes and see the pain and suffering in their depths without
wanting to offer solace.

"Cynthia, wait a minute!"

Cynthia stopped walking, but it was as if she hadn't the
strength to turn around and face her, so Gena went to her
and placed an arm about her shoulders. Cynthia collapsed
against her as if human contact was something she hadn't
experienced in a very long time. Gena led her to her car
where she opened the passenger door and helped her in.
Running around to the driver's side, she got in, threw the
gear into Drive, and pressed the gate's remote.

As the gate slid open, she said, "We'll collect your car
later. It'll be good to have a houseguest. There's nobody
but me, Miss Edna, and Cary Grant."

"Cary Grant?" Cynthia said, puzzled. She wiped her
tears with the back of her hand.

"That's my dog."

Cynthia laughed. "Oh God, I thought you were just
hooked on the actor's movies."

"I am," Gena said. "That's one of the two reasons I
called him that."

"What's the other reason?"

"He's never used my shoes as chew toys."

"I admire that in a dog."

Gena laughed. "Me, too. Anyway, I figure it's the mark of a gentlemanly dog not to gnaw on his mistress's shoes. And in films, Cary Grant is the ultimate gentleman."

"That actually makes sense," Cynthia admitted.

"A twisted kind of sense," Gena said. "But, as you'll soon find out, I'm a twisted kind of girl."

Gena decided not to put the car in the garage right away. She wanted to take Cynthia into the house through the front door and get her situated in one of the guest rooms as soon as possible. If Cynthia had been in the heat all day, she was undoubtedly in need of rest and a refreshing shower.

Before they got out of the car, though, Cynthia reached over and placed her hand atop Gena's. "Thank you for not turning me away, Gena."

"I don't turn family away, Cynthia," Gena said gently.

Cynthia's touch had been cold and clammy even though the day was hot and dry. It had made Gena wonder after her health. Taylor had had poor circulation due to his heart problem. As a nurse, she knew poor circulation was usually the reason someone had cold hands like Cynthia's. Cynthia must have had to endure terrible conditions during the year she'd lived in her car.

Gena resolved to broach the subject of a medical exam after Cynthia had settled in.

Miss Edna came home so excited about the revival that the moment she and Cary Grant came in through the garage door and saw Gena preparing a meal in the kitchen, she started talking. "Oh, Miss Gena, the revival's going to be the best we've ever had. Invitations are going out over radio, TV, and in the newspaper. We've even got a Web site inviting folks to come out and partake of the word of God."

Cary Grant went over to Gena and rubbed his head against her leg. Gena wiped her wet hands on a dish towel and gave him a sliver of the pot roast she'd prepared. He didn't get fed from the table often. She knew it wasn't healthy for him. But he enjoyed the treats when she offered them. "Were you a good boy for Miss Edna today?"

Miss Edna was pouring herself a glass of water. "Yes and no. Yes, he was a good boy when it came to the ladies. But he growled at Mr. Bishop and bared his teeth."

Gena laughed. "Maybe he's trying to tell you something about Mr. Bishop."

Miss Edna sat down at the table. She saw that Gena had set the table for three people. It wasn't unusual for Gena to cook. She enjoyed cooking. But it was very unusual for her to have guests for dinner. "Are you having someone over for dinner tonight?"

Gena joined Miss Edna at the table. "We've got a houseguest. She arrived a couple of hours ago."

"I didn't know you were expecting anyone," Miss Edna said, trying not to sound slightly panicked. She liked to be prepared when they had guests. There was the guest room to freshen up, the grocery list to do, making adjustments based on the guest's preferences, and myriad other things when there was another person in the house.

"I know," Gena said, keeping her voice low. "I didn't know she was coming, either. It's Taylor's sister, Cynthia. She went through Katrina, Miss Edna, and life hasn't been easy for her since then."

Miss Edna was all sympathy. Her pretty face crumpled in a frown. "Oh, God bless her. Don't you worry, Miss Gena, I'll do everything in my power to make her feel welcome. You don't have to say another word."

When Cynthia came down, showered and shampooed, and looking and feeling much better, Gena introduced her to Miss Edna, after which the three of them sat down to a meal of pot roast, new potatoes, green beans, garden salad, and dinner rolls.

Gena filled their glasses with sweet iced tea before sitting down. "Cynthia, we'd just as well tell you how we do things around here over dinner so your day will run more smoothly tomorrow."

She drank some tea before continuing. "I'm usually up by seven and jogging. I run five days a week. I give my body a rest on the weekend. Miss Edna comes down and starts breakfast around eight-thirty."

"What do you like for breakfast, dear?" Miss Edna asked as she speared a tender green bean and put it in her mouth.

"Oh, I don't want to be a bother," Cynthia said. "I'm not fussy."

"No food allergies?" Miss Edna wanted to know.

"I'm lactose intolerant," Cynthia said.

"Then do you use soy milk, or take supplements?" asked Gena.

"I used to take supplements," Cynthia replied. She

balled up her mouth. Before her life had been torn asunder, she'd been able to afford supplements.

"The reason I asked is I use soy products myself," Gena said lightly.

"She'll even eat tofu," Miss Edna put in. "The blandest food known to man."

"It's supposed to be able to take on the flavors of other foods," Gena said, defending her eating habits. "Besides, it's very good for you."

"It might be good for you," said Miss Edna. "But it tastes like paste. Even Cary Grant won't eat it."

Cynthia burst out laughing. The tears started flowing again, but this time they were tears of joy. Gena and Miss Edna joined in.

"She's right," Gena said between laughs. "Tofu is incredibly bad. It's even bad fried. And what southerner doesn't like fried *anything?*"

Miss Edna wiped the tears from the corners of her eyes with the linen napkin. "Now, what were we talking about? Oh yeah, the schedule, such as it is."

"Things are pretty relaxed around here," Gena said. "Dinner is catch as catch can. Miss Edna does most of the cooking. But I'll do it occasionally."

"I love to cook," Cynthia offered.

"Wonderful," said Miss Edna. "We get to eat someone else's cooking for a change." And her smile was so warm that Cynthia relaxed fully for the first time that day. Maybe things were looking up.

After the meal, Miss Edna insisted on cleaning the kitchen since Gena had done the cooking. Cynthia offered to help, so Gena left the two women in the kitchen while she went outside to the back porch. The night was warm and humid. She could hear the cicadas rubbing their legs together, a sound that always made her think of Taylor at this time of night.

The porch was screened-in so she didn't have to worry about mosquitoes. Several went to their deaths on the two electrified traps hanging on opposite corners of the porch. There was a satisfying buzz after each execution.

Sitting down on the chaise, she whispered, "Taylor, your sister's gonna stay awhile."

She lay back on the chaise and closed her eyes. If only she and Taylor had had children. It was her biggest regret. She tried to tell herself that it was probably for the best that they hadn't had any, because now that child would be without a father. But deep down, she knew that she would have been able to raise a child alone. Women did it all the time.

She must have fallen asleep there, because the next thing she knew, Cynthia was sticking her head through the door saying, "Miss Edna said you were out here. I'm going to bed. I just wanted to say good-night."

"Good night, Cynthia. Sleep well," Gena replied, smiling.

Cynthia smiled back and left.

That night, they both cried themselves to sleep. Gena because of all the things she regretted not doing in her life. Cynthia because of the kindness she'd been shown that day.

It was so quiet on Sinclair Street that Nate heard her footfalls when she was a block away. He squinted in the sunshine, trying to make out her approaching figure. Lily, beside him holding a board in place while he was supposed to use the nail gun to secure it, looked up, too.

Knowing Lily was watching him watch Gena Boudreau, Nate returned his attention to his work. "Hold that steady, Lily."

Lily smirked. By the time her dad had finished firing nails into the board, the jogger had passed the Anderson house. Today was her lucky day. The jogger was the same woman they'd seen in Madge's Café yesterday. Her father had gone mindless over her, yet again. His interest was unmistakable. The only thing for her to do was to be ready for the woman tomorrow morning.

She was going to leave the clodhoppers she was wearing home tomorrow and wear her athletic shoes. When the mystery woman came by, she was going to start running alongside her, and by the time they reached the end of Sinclair Street, she would have secured a date for her father with her.

One of the good things about being sixteen years old was, she got to believe in the inevitability of success as opposed to failure. Life hadn't yet taught her that there was a fifty percent chance that things were not going to go her way.

She was stoked!

CHAPTER 5

"Get a move on, Dad. What's the holdup, huh? We've got to be there by seven!"

Nate could clearly hear Lily's voice through the bathroom door while he was taking a quick shower. What had gotten into her? Rushing *him* to get to work? Either she had been replaced by a pod-person overnight, or she was up to something.

His bet was on the latter option.

Glancing up at the clock on the wall as he stepped from the shower stall, he saw that he had more than forty minutes until seven. He stood in front of the bathroom mirror with a towel wrapped around his lower body. Rubbing his jaw, he decided he could use a shave. He had to wipe the condensation from the mirror before generously lathering up. Why was he shaving? It wasn't as if anyone was going to notice, especially not the one person he wanted to look his way: Gena Boudreau. He was foolish to fantasize about her but, obviously, couldn't help himself.

She interested him on many levels. Of course, he was physically attracted to her. He was a healthy male animal and she was beautiful. Not unnaturally beautiful like some of those supermodels in the magazines Lily liked to peruse. He hoped to God that she wasn't comparing herself to those women. Nobody really looked like that, not even the models themselves, without a lot of help from makeup artists and skillful photographers. Gena had a healthy glow about her. Her skin was medium brown and had golden undertones. He could tell when she'd been out in the sun a lot because it got even more golden brown. She had an hourglass figure that no amount of jogging had been able to eradicate. He knew some joggers whose muscles got stringy and their behinds bony, but Gena had nicely rounded buns and while her arms and legs showed some musculature, she hadn't lost her feminine curves.

He was a runner himself. Had been since high school. He knew why she loved it. Other than being in love, there was no high like it. Once you reached a certain point in your run the endorphins kicked in and a kind of euphoria enveloped your brain, causing you to feel as if all was right with the world. You can get hooked on running.

He did it to stay in shape and to help with pent-up sexual desires that he hadn't been satisfying lately. Maybe Gena did it for the same reasons. In which case it would be interesting if...

Lily pounded on the bathroom door. "Dad, what are you doing in there? I've already made breakfast *and* prepared the bologna sandwiches!"

Startled, Nate cut himself while shaving. "Doggone it, Lily, I'm trying to shave in here. Get away from the door!"

He heard her sigh loudly and stomp down the stairs. He chuckled and finished his shave. Something was definitely up.

Five minutes later he walked into the kitchen with several pieces of toilet paper covering the nicks on his face. Lily looked at him as if he had grown a second head.

"You're not going outside like that, are you?"

Nate sat down and poured cereal into his bowl. "Hopefully I will have stopped bleeding by the time we get ready to go."

Lily sat down to finish her own cereal, but Nate couldn't help noticing how fidgety she was this morning. Underneath the table, her leg was jumping to beat the band. Fortunately, she wasn't having a seizure. It was simply a nervous habit.

She was also eating way too fast. Usually a fastidious diner, she was shoveling the cereal into her mouth at such a rate, milk was dribbling onto her chin.

"Lily, wipe your chin, and sit up straight. Do you eat like that when you're away from home? I might not have been able to teach you all the manners a mom could have taught you, but come on, I taught you better than that!"

Lily hastily wiped her chin and sat up on her chair. "Sorry, it's just that we're going to be late if we don't rush."

"Late for what?"

"For work!" What if she started out earlier this morning? she thought. What if she was running by the Anderson house right now?

"Dad, I thought you'd be proud of me. You've instilled

the work ethic in me. That's on your list of things to do as a parent, right?"

Nate smiled and shook his head. "That, and to one day drive you to the college of your choice and *leave* you there."

Lily snorted with delight. "That's definitely on my list of things to do as a daughter."

They finished their cereal in silence, then rinsed their bowls, glasses, and cutlery before heading out the back door. "Don't forget the sandwiches," Nate said.

Lily held up the cooler. "Got 'em."

Gena had slept fitfully. She kept imagining Cynthia sneaking into her room and stabbing her in her sleep. Okay, so those weren't exactly Christian thoughts, but she'd be lying to herself if she said she completely trusted Cynthia not to be trying to run a con on her. Did that make her cynical, or careful?

Chalk it up to years of animosity on Cynthia's part. Gena had made a sincere effort to become friends with her, mostly because Taylor wanted them all to get along, but Cynthia had made it clear throughout their marriage that she wasn't good enough for Taylor and she'd never consider her an equal or a friend.

Now things had changed and it was going to take a long time for Cynthia to earn her trust, if ever. She was human, after all. That didn't mean she would withdraw her offer of shelter and three square meals a day until Cynthia was back on her feet.

She was simply going to watch her back.

Even though she wasn't feeling as energetic as she

usually felt at six in the morning, Gena put on her athletic gear and hit the road.

When she started out, she wore a thin jacket because the temperature was in the low seventies. But as she reached mile three she removed the jacket and tied it around her waist. Gena's house was two miles on the outskirts of town. She would run the two miles, jog around the park in downtown Red Oaks, and head back home. For half a mile, upon leaving the house, she was jogging downhill. Therefore, on her return, when she was more fatigued, her heart got a good workout because she would be running uphill.

She passed a road crew on the way into Red Oaks. As always the fellas yelled catcalls, confident that should any of them get her in a secluded place she would be his for the taking. She totally ignored them. One guy yelled, "Hey, baby, what you runnin' for? You already look good enough to raise a man from the dead!"

The other fellas guffawed loudly and slapped their thighs with their hard hats. Another guy who must have been the foreman yelled, "Get back to work, you slackers!"

Grumbling, they did so.

Gena smiled with satisfaction and jogged on.

A little while later, she was jogging through a residential neighborhood when a feminine voice called, "Hey, lady, wait up!"

Gena didn't slow down, although, looking out of the corner of her eye, she saw that the person accosting her was a teenaged girl a few inches shorter and more slightly built than she was, and not a mugger. "Hey, yourself," she said, still jogging.

The girl kept pace. "Hi, I'm Lily, Lily Lincoln. I know, it lacks imagination, but I like it."

Gena saved her breath.

"Um, don't you get tired of running?"

Gena laughed shortly. "No."

"You're not much of a conversationalist, are you?"

"Talking and jogging don't go well together."

"Okay, I'll do the talking. As I said, my name is Lily Lincoln. I'm sixteen, and that guy you saw back there, the guy with the great biceps and abs, is my dad, Nathan. Everybody calls him Nate. Anyway, my dad had this bright idea of making, I mean 'taking' me on as his apprentice in his home-repair business this summer."

"Good for you."

"Good for me? Are you serious? I haven't been able to do anything fun with my friends all summer. What he needs is to get out and have some fun himself. Then maybe he'll remember how it was to be a teenager, and get off *my* case."

Gena didn't know what this brown-skinned young lady with the sparkling brown eyes was getting at, but she was delighted with her. She liked her spirit. If you want something, go for it. She wanted something from Gena. The question was, what?

"What has your dad having a little fun got to do with me?"

"You could go out with him."

Gena laughed. "Did he put you up to this?"

"No!" Lily denied hotly. "He'd kill me if he knew I was trying to set him up. He hates being set up."

"So do I."

"Well, you already have one thing in common."

Gena smiled. This girl was a charmer who knew how to roll with the punches.

"Lily!" an agitated male voice yelled in the distance.

"I think that's your dad now," Gena said.

Lily made a last-ditch effort. "Look, he works hard, owns a successful business. He built our house, for God's sake. How many men can you say have done that?"

"None that I know of," Gena said.

"I know that's right!" Lily's breath was starting to get short. "So, what do you say? When you jog by the house where we're working tomorrow, and he gets up the nerve to say something to you, would you not blow him off right away?"

"What makes you think I'd blow him off?"

"My dad's good-looking and everything, but he's a little rusty when it comes to dating. I can't remember the last time he brought somebody home. He has this thing about their having to be suitable stepmother material. He's funny that way. But I like you already. Maybe you two would hit it off. Want to give it a shot?"

Gena was surprised when she heard Lily's father running after them and closing in, too. Lily was right, he was a hunk. Tall, muscular, square-jawed, and all male, he looked like he could run a marathon. "Okay, I'll see you tomorrow morning."

That's all Lily needed to hear. She stopped in her tracks and waved Gena off. "Thank God," she said. "You were about to *kill* me!"

Gena laughed and picked up the pace.

Nate was incensed when he caught up with Lily. "What are you up to? Talking to Gena Boudreau?"

Lily realized she had not gotten the woman's name. She grinned up at her dad. "You know her name!"

"Probably half the people in town know her name."

They began walking back to the Anderson house, which was four blocks away.

"Why, is she notorious or something? Did she spend time in prison? Win the lottery? Kill her husband?"

Nate laughed. "You know that big house on the hill we pass every morning coming into town? The one you're always saying you'd like to get a look inside?"

"Yeah, so?"

"So, she lives in that house. What were you talking to her about?"

"Uh, I was just asking her about running." It wasn't a blatant lie. "I'm thinking of joining the track team next semester." That was a whopper.

Nate liked the sound of that. Lily had never shown an interest in sports. He'd always wanted her to be more athletic. Her pursuits were all intellectual. He couldn't gripe about that because she got straight As. He was proud of her. But everyone should be physically active. How she stayed so slim with her huge appetite was a mystery to him. But when she got older and her metabolism slowed down, she'd regret not being more active. "That's good," he commended her. "I'm glad somebody was able to inspire you."

"Uh, Dad," Lily rushed on. "Did you find that lady…Miss Boudreau…attractive?"

"She's not hard on the eyes," he said casually. "But I don't think she'd be interested in a guy like me, Lily, so don't get any ideas."

Lily glared at him. "Are you saying that you're not good enough for her?" Her hackles were up now. "Because if you are, don't be ridiculous! She'd be lucky to get you. You'd be a great catch for anybody. Besides, she's nice. She let me ask her all kinds of questions and didn't look down her nose at me. Tomorrow morning I want you to say hello to her when she passes."

Nate laughed. "You do, huh?"

"That's an order, Dad."

"I'm the one who gives the orders in this outfit."

"Okay, I'm pleading with you, then. She's nice. She'll stop and talk to you."

Nate considered Gena for a moment. He thought of all the times she'd jogged past him without looking up at him once as if she were in her own world and that world did not include him. He thought of all the times he'd imagined walking over to her, stopping her, and saying, "Look at me. I'm right here, and I think you're wonderful."

He blew air between full lips. He really had it bad for that woman. It wouldn't kill him to give it a try. It wouldn't be the first time, or the last, a pretty woman told him to step off.

"All right, but I'm not putting on airs or anything. If she doesn't like me the way I am, then so be it." He smiled at Lily. "Now, get back to work or we'll be here *two* more days instead of one."

Lily attacked her job with added vigor. She couldn't believe her plan was coming together so well.

Later that day, after a great deal of cajoling on her part, Gena convinced Cynthia to take her long-standing doctor's appointment and get a physical. As they sat next to one another in Dr. Trinette Brown's waiting room, Gena sensed Cynthia's nervousness.

She'd been trying to read last September's issue of *Essence,* but the strong pull of nervous energy coming off Cynthia kept distracting her. Glancing at Cynthia's profile, she said, "You know, you and Taylor looked an awful lot alike."

Cynthia immediately smiled, thinking of her brother. "Everybody used to say that."

She turned toward Gena. "When we were real little people used to ask if we were twins. There was a time when we were the same height. You know girls sometimes grow faster than little boys. I was two years younger. Taylor hated that I was as tall as he was." She laughed shortly, recalling how much she'd adored her brother from the start. She would follow him everywhere in the Quarter. Their father had been a prominent physician and their mother an accomplished pianist. She played and sang nightly in a club on Bourbon Street. Both were gone now. In fact, Cynthia had no family except her niece and nephew, Taylor's children. And neither of them had any familial love in them thanks to their bitter mother, Lani, who had tried to take their father for everything in the divorce. Before Taylor's death, they were little more than strangers to their father. Cynthia didn't know where they were today.

"Were you two very close as children?" Gena asked.

"I often felt as if he was the only one who understood me," Cynthia confessed. "We grew apart when we became adults. I was spoiled and stubborn and full of myself, not wanting to listen to anything he or my parents told me. I married Jay, my first husband, just to spite them. They told me he was a drunk and a gambler and I didn't want to hear it. Within six months he'd gotten in a fight over winnings in a card game and somebody shot him to death. They never found the guy who did it."

"That must have been a terrible time for you," Gena said sympathetically.

Cynthia pursed her lips, as if to say, *that's life*. "I still hadn't learned my lesson. I moved back in with my parents and started dating a doctor, someone my father had taken under his wing. Everyone thought he was perfect husband material. So when he asked me to marry him, I jumped at the chance to start again. I was only twenty-two, I wanted a home and a family. George, that was his name, and I were so happy together. Then one morning I heard him coughing uncontrollably in the bathroom. I got up to see if I could help. There was blood in the sink. Come to find out, he had third-stage lung cancer. George smoked like a chimney, but everybody smoked back then. Much more than people do these days. He died three months later. After that, I decided that marriage wasn't for me. I went to live with my parents again. It was a good thing, because my mother got sick. I nursed her until she died. And then my father got sick and I nursed him until he died. People were always saying,

'Cynthia is the most selfless woman.' In reality I was bitter and cold inside. All the losses made me stop believing in good things happening. My parents left me the house and I turned it into a bed-and-breakfast. You know, you've been there."

"It was a beautiful house, Cynthia."

She smiled regretfully. "Yes. When I lost my business, I also lost the family home."

"I'm sorry," Gena said sincerely.

Cynthia squeezed her hand. "That's very kind of you." She sniffed. "I have a lot to apologize for."

"Oh no," Gena began, about to say that there was nothing to apologize for.

But Cynthia was adamant. "Oh yes, I do. I was the perfect b-word to you. First of all, after Lani divorced Taylor, he and I got closer. I introduced him to Karen, and I thought the two of them were destined to be together. Karen and I had been friends since sixth grade. Then you came along and I hated you upon meeting you. It wasn't anything you had done. It was what you represented, someone else to take Taylor away from me. You see, with Karen I knew that I would always have a place in their lives should they ever get married. Taylor surprised me and Karen when he married you and moved to Red Oaks."

Gena sat quietly soaking all of it in. She wanted to know something else.

"Did you know Taylor was dying when he married me?"

The shocked expression in Cynthia's eyes told her she didn't. "Oh God, poor Taylor. No wonder he did what he did. He wanted to experience some happiness before he died. He really loved you, and he risked everything for you." Tears rolled down her cheeks.

Tears immediately sprang to Gena's eyes, too. "He didn't tell me, either."

Cynthia impulsively threw her arms around Gena. "I'm sorry, child, so sorry."

The nurse found them that way when she came to the door and called Cynthia's name. Luckily, Gena and Cynthia were the only occupants of the waiting room so there was no one there to witness their emotional breakdown.

Cynthia rose reluctantly and followed the nurse back to an examination room.

Gena wiped her tears with a tissue from the box on the end table in the waiting room and picked up last September's issue of *Essence* once again.

But there was nothing in it as satisfying as her conversation with Cynthia had been.

CHAPTER 6

It was with a bit of trepidation that Gena set off on her jog the next morning.

She was worried that conspiring with Lily to set her dad, Nathan, up with her might be construed as the act of a desperate woman. In fact, she was not desperate; she'd just lost her mind for a hot minute. Lily had been so charming, and so genuinely interested in seeing her dad going out again and having fun, that Gena had seen no conceivable reason to refuse her.

But what if Nathan Lincoln didn't rise to the bait? Gena tended to intimidate most men here in Red Oaks. Once they learned she had more money than they'd earn in a lifetime they slunk off. Unless it was the money they were interested in. In which case they pursued her all the more vigorously. She had yet to meet that mythological hero, a man with whom she shared a mutual attraction and who wanted her solely for herself.

She breathed in the fresh morning air and ran down the hill to the main road that led into town. As she was about to cross the road, she saw a Dalmatian darting in and out of morning traffic. She immediately recognized the dog. It belonged to a neighbor who lived about half a mile up the road, Mrs. Cox. Mrs. Cox was recovering from a stroke and had recently been forced to hire a live-in caregiver. Someone must have left a door unsecured, giving the Dalmatian the opportunity to run away.

Gena ran a bit faster. Maybe she could grab it by the collar and take it back home before it got more lost than it already was.

Mrs. Cox had obviously raised it as a house pet. It didn't appear to be used to being let off its leash, especially near a busy highway. Confused, and frightened, it ran out into traffic pell-mell.

Suddenly there was a resounding thud. Gena choked back a scream as she saw the Dalmatian soar ten feet into the air and land in the middle of the blacktop. The car that had hit it kept going. Drivers' horns blared in protest as they avoided the injured dog.

Gena couldn't imagine hitting a creature the size of the Dalmatian without being aware that her car had collided with something. The driver obviously knew it had hit the dog and either didn't care or was afraid of the repercussions and had chosen to flee the scene. Gena had been focusing on the dog so intently that she hadn't thought to get the car's license plate number.

Other cars drove around the body of the Dalmatian. Gena quickly retrieved her cell phone from her fanny pack and dialed the house. Miss Edna answered.

"Miss Edna, I'm at the bottom of the hill. Someone just ran over Mrs. Cox's Dalmatian. It's still alive, but it's in bad shape. I'm going to need you to get Cary Grant's muzzle and drive down here."

"I'm on the way!" Miss Edna said without hesitation. She knew Emily Cox. The poor woman had not fully recovered from a stroke she'd suffered six months ago. Now this. She loved that flighty dog. Doobie, for that was the dog's name, was not known for his intelligence. Miss Edna had seen it in the park chasing squirrels and actually running headlong into trees when the squirrels scampered up them to escape him.

At the house, Miss Edna put the phone in its cradle in the kitchen. Cynthia was sitting at the table enjoying a cup of coffee. "I've got to go out, Miss Cynthia. Miss Gena saw a neighbor's dog get hit by a car while she was running and she needs me to bring her the car and a muzzle so she can take it to the vet."

Cynthia, who was already dressed for the day in jeans and a white short-sleeve blouse, got up from the table, alert and ready to help. "I'll go with you."

"Okay, then, meet me in the garage."

A couple of minutes later, Miss Edna was behind the wheel of Gena's Volvo with Cynthia riding shotgun.

In the meantime, Gena was in the middle of the road talking soothingly to Doobie, who was whining pitifully and still trying to hitch his way across the road. A broken hip prevented his going anywhere.

Miss Edna and Cynthia arrived and parked across the street. They got out and ran over to Gena. "Here's the muzzle," Miss Edna said breathlessly.

Taking it, Gena knew she had to approach Doobie cautiously. Even though he wasn't normally a vicious dog, any animal, when hurt, would bite. Having had to corral Cary Grant for vet visits, she was used to un-cooperative dogs, though, and approached Doobie from behind, caught him off guard, and put the muzzle on him.

She gently picked him up. Miss Edna and Cynthia ran ahead to open the back door of the Volvo. With Doobie securely on the backseat, Gena went around to the other side and got in the back with him. Miss Edna drove to the veterinarian's office.

Ten minutes later, the three women were sitting in the waiting room hoping for a positive prognosis from Dr. Ben Everett, a tall, angular gentleman in his fifties.

"I can't believe some people," complained Miss Edna. "You mean the driver just kept going?"

Gena nodded. "Didn't even look back. He was probably late for work."

"What are we going to do if he dies?" Miss Edna asked worriedly. "Emily doesn't need any more stress, poor thing."

"She won't be contacted until we know if he's going to live or die," Gena said.

After an hour, Gena told Miss Edna and Cynthia to go. She would call them when she needed a ride home.

They had gotten to the vet's office at around eight. Fifteen minutes past noon Dr. Everett came out to speak with Gena. His face was grim. When he shook his head in the negative, Gena knew that Doobie had not survived.

"I'm sorry, Gena, but his internal injuries were too severe. His hip was shattered, as well. His quality of life would have been very poor even if he had lived."

Gena felt helpless. She hadn't even known Doobie.

Didn't know his mistress well, either, but the thought of another life having been snuffed out utterly depressed her.

It was just a dog, she told herself, a poor dumb animal. She still wanted to blubber like a baby. Dr. Everett smiled at her compassionately. "I'll go see Mrs. Cox. You go home, Gena. You've had a stressful morning. Tell Cary Grant I said hi."

Numb, Gena nodded, smiled wanly, and left the office.

Outside, she phoned Miss Edna and asked her to come pick her up. It was now ninety degrees out and she didn't relish having to walk the three miles home.

It was then, when she thought of having to walk home, that she remembered with regret her promise to Lily Lincoln. She would just have to explain in the morning.

Lily had clung to hope until noon. Then she figured anyone with half a brain wouldn't go jogging in ninety-degree weather. Gena Boudreau struck her as someone with more than half a brain. Therefore, she wasn't coming.

Lily glanced at her dad, who was too busy putting the finishing touches on the Andersons' porch to worry about whether Gena Boudreau was going to jog past the house or not.

He'd shaved again this morning. And he'd worn a new shirt. A short-sleeve denim shirt that looked really good on him. To Lily his making an extra effort meant that he had anticipated his meeting with Gena Boudreau this morning.

Her own disappointment at being stood up meant very little to her. But the thought of Gena Boudreau rejecting her father made her mad. Maybe she had a good excuse.

Maybe she didn't. At any rate, she might never see her again to hear it. They would not be here tomorrow morning. The Anderson project was finished.

"You're upset," Miss Edna said the moment she saw Gena's face when she went to pick her up with both Cynthia and Cary Grant along for the ride.

Gena got in the back and Cary Grant immediately jumped into her lap and licked her face. She hugged him. Miss Edna always knew when she needed comforting, and Cary Grant was the only male who was allowed to do that.

"Life just seems so pointless sometimes," she said resignedly.

"What you need to do is go to the revival with us Saturday night. Miss Cynthia is coming. Let's us all go," said Miss Edna cheerfully. Sometimes, when she got really excited, her homespun sayings came tumbling out. Hence the "let's us all go" phrase. Gena secretly loved it when she sounded like a character straight out of *The Color Purple*.

"Some good singing and preaching might cheer you up," Cynthia put in. "I know I could use some spiritual food right about now."

"Are you hungry, Miss Gena?" Miss Edna asked hopefully.

Gena knew she was asking if she was hungry for God's word, and not lunch.

She was remembering what Cleotus had angrily accused her of: that she didn't let happiness into her life. What were his exact words? "You're simply too much of a coward to allow anything good to happen to you."

She wasn't anybody's coward. If God was indeed trying to give her something good, then she was going to let go, and *let* Him.

"All right," she said. "I'll go on Saturday night. But if people start foaming at the mouth and doing cartwheels down the aisle, I'm outta there!"

Miss Edna and Cynthia laughed heartily.

It was a beautiful summer night. Gena could actually smell the Georgia pines on the air. The buzz of what sounded like hundreds of revival attendees could be heard inside the tent, but she, Miss Edna, and Cynthia hadn't gone inside yet. She glanced up as they entered the temporary edifice, if you could call a tent a building. The height of the tent rose two stories. There was an enormous stage with two levels, the pulpit on the first level and the choir stand on the second, a bit higher than the pulpit.

They must have been about ready to begin the program, because the choir members were taking their places and a tall, bald, handsome man in his forties with caramel-colored skin was standing behind the pulpit. Gena assumed he was the Reverend Terrance Paul Avery. Both Mrs. Carmichael and Miss Edna had told her what a wonderful minister he was. They extolled his personal life as well, saying he was happily married with five children, all of whom were active in the church. To them, no one set a finer example.

He stepped up to the microphone. "Welcome, brothers and sisters." He waved the stragglers who were hanging around the back of the tent forward. "Come on in, there's plenty of room up front where the Lord can see you better."

Folks laughed.

Gena, Miss Edna, and Cynthia found seats in the middle of the tent. The temperature was controlled by huge air-conditioning units outside and fans suspended from the ceiling. Gena imagined it was nothing like the tents of old in which folks sweltered and attempted to cool off by using cardboard fans generously donated to the church by the local funeral home.

Reverend Avery motioned to the choir director, who signaled the choir to begin. Their voices rose in a heartfelt rendition of "Just as I Am." Gena knew the song well; it was one of her mother's favorites. She found herself thinking of her mother and how much she missed her. She wondered if she would have been as good a mother to her children as her mother had been to her. Poor, uneducated, and abandoned by the father of her child, her mother had still managed to raise Gena to be a hardworking, independent woman.

The choir concluded the song and Reverend Avery spoke. "Revival," he said, his deep voice resonating. "The dictionary has several meanings for the word. A renewed interest in a subject. To bring something back to life, and back to its full strength. Beloved, we are in *need* of a revival. Wake up! Wake up your hearts! Wake up your minds. Be here *now!* Because if you're not wide awake, then God is gonna catch you sleeping! And we don't want to be caught sleeping. We need to be wakeful soldiers of God."

"Amen!" cried several attendees.

During the sermon, Gena watched the faces of some of the people around her. They all appeared to be soaking in what the Reverend was saying. Rapt was the way she would describe their expressions. She felt ashamed for having expected to find false piety in their countenances instead. Perhaps they were looking for something bigger than themselves just as she was. Hoping to find some meaning in a life that often didn't make sense.

She observed the faces of her companions and saw that they were also riveted. She resolved to give the experience a chance. Skeptical though she was, she would try to keep an open mind.

"Some of us aren't living life, we're letting life pass us by. We live in a rut, a routine that never changes. Like mice in a maze, we go about our days on a set course afraid to vary the course because we'll get a shock. Well, sometimes, beloved, we need a shock to the system. God didn't make this beautiful planet for you to walk by a garden and not marvel at the wonder of it. God didn't make other human beings for you to ignore them, to not even look into their faces and see the miracle of individuality He wrought in every last one of them. And He didn't instill in you the need to know Him personally for you to forget that fact because your life is so busy that you don't have time for Him. Be honest with yourself. Don't you find that something is missing in your life? No amount of money, no amount of material possessions, no amount of intimacy with the opposite sex, is going to be as fulfilling to you as a personal relationship with God. He knows that, and you know it. Yet the disbelieving among you will endlessly try to fill that void with everything else except God. Beloved, I'm here to tell you that only God can fill that space inside you."

Gena felt he was speaking directly to her. For the past

eight years she had stayed so busy literally running, metaphorically running, volunteering, directing people's lives in her capacity as president of the Ladies Auxiliary, that she had suppressed any spiritual needs she might have had. She'd been too busy blaming God for taking Taylor away from her to acknowledge that she needed His love. She needed His direction.

Something her mother used to say popped into her head: *Honey, your arms are too short to box with God.* She couldn't remember where her mother had gotten the saying but right here, right now, sitting in a revival tent on a Saturday night, she knew exactly what she'd meant. It was pure idiocy to fight God. Any weapon you used against Him would be woefully inadequate.

The realization that she had unfairly blamed God for letting Taylor die freed something inside her. She smiled, and she continued to smile as if she had a secret until the sermon ended, and the choir performed two rousing hymns, and the people started filing out of the tent.

As she and Miss Edna and Cynthia rose to get in the aisle, Miss Edna said, "Well, Miss Gena, what did you think of Reverend Avery's sermon?"

"You were right," Gena said simply. "He's a wonderful speaker."

Miss Edna grinned widely. "I told you so!"

There was a reception on the lawn after the service. Lights had been strung and gospel music was piped through speakers. The ladies had spread several tables with cold drinks and various pastries. Folks stood around socializing as they partook of the repast.

Those who needed to use the restrooms were obliged to walk the few yards to the church next door. Gena left Miss Edna and Cynthia chatting with other church ladies while she walked over to the church.

Luckily, she was among the first to get in line at the entrance to the ladies' room. Six women later, she was in a stall. Relieved, she came out to wash her hands and was startled when someone screeched at her. Lily Lincoln stood at the sink washing her hands. Gena figured she'd come out of a stall after she'd gone into one of them.

Lily's reflection in the mirror glared at Gena. "Don't you run off, Miss Gena Boudreau. I have a few things I need to say to you."

The other three ladies in the restroom hurried out after washing their hands.

"Lily!" Gena cried, delighted to see her again.

Lily dried her hands, angrily snatching paper towels from the holder. "You lied to me," she accused, feeling rightfully indignant.

Gena calmly washed and dried her hands as she spoke. "No, I didn't lie to you. When I was jogging I saw a dog get hit by a car, and by the time I'd taken him to the vet and waited to see if he'd be okay or not it was after twelve. It was way too hot for my run so I decided to see if I could catch you and your dad the next morning. But when I got there neither of you were around."

Lily sighed with relief. "We finished that job the day before." She smiled at Lily. "I'm so glad you didn't just decide not to show up!"

Gena marveled at the odds of seeing Lily at the revival. "Do you attend this church?"

Lily shook her head in the negative. "Nah, but my aunt Maya does. She invited me and Dad. I bribed Dad into coming. I'm sorry to say my spiritual upbringing has been sorely neglected."

Gena laughed. "Do you talk like that all the time? Like an English teacher?"

Lily laughed too. "I'm what my teachers refer to as advanced beyond my years." Her sparkling brown eyes perused Gena's face. "Do you attend this church?"

"No, my, um, friend invited me."

"A male friend?"

"No, a female friend."

Lily perked up. "Then you wouldn't mind coming with me to meet my dad?"

Knots of anxiety suddenly appeared in Gena's stomach, but she followed Lily out of the restroom and across the lawn anyway. Lily talked en route. "This is *so* cool. My dad is not going to believe you're here. When you didn't show up the other day we figured we'd never see you again."

A few yards away, Nate was standing underneath a red oak chatting with his sister, Maya, a tall, stout woman in her early thirties with a boisterous laugh that could be heard ringing out right now.

He happened to look in their direction as they approached and suddenly felt inadequate in his shirtsleeves even though most of the men in attendance were not wearing jackets on this warm summer night.

Maya, ever curious, looked up too. "Who is that with Lily?"

"Gena Boudreau," Nate answered, and cleared his throat. Even saying her name made his voice crack. How was he going to hold an intelligent conversation with her if his voice kept going in and out?

"Ooh," said Maya in anticipation of the imminent introductions. "I always wondered what she was like up close and personal."

"Maya, behave yourself," Nate ordered.

His sister was fun loving and always meant well. But sometimes she would say anything that came to her mind, and tonight he needed to make a good impression on Gena if he ever wanted to see her again. And he did.

"Dad!" Lily exclaimed. "Look who's here, Miss Boudreau."

To Nate's utter relief his voice didn't crack when he said as he shook her hand, "A pleasure, Mrs. Boudreau."

Gena noticed that he had not forgotten to respect her husband when he'd addressed her. Most folks, like Lily had a moment ago, simply called her Miss Boudreau. It was a southern habit to refer to ladies, married or otherwise, as Miss. She didn't mind it. However, she always heard the difference whenever anyone bothered to call her Mrs.

Her mind was grasping at mundane trivialities in order to stamp down the rush of excitement she'd felt upon putting her hand in his. He was the epitome of masculinity. Big, strong hands, a solid, muscular form that made her want to trip and fall just so he would catch her. One look into his brown eyes and her determination to be detached fled.

Say something, girl! she thought furiously.

"It's a pleasure to meet you," she croaked, and cleared her throat immediately afterward. She felt her face flush and was helpless to control it.

Maya smiled knowingly. Her brother had it bad. Miss Gena Boudreau was also bitten. Maya couldn't wait to see where it would lead.

Lily introduced her next, and she pumped Gena's hand. "I'm so glad you could come tonight, Miss Boudreau. Are you here with a member of the congregation?"

"Yes, Miss Edna Strawder."

"Ah, Sister Strawder. I know her well. A lovely woman."

Lily wasn't about to let her aunt monopolize the conversation. "Auntie, would you show me the baptismal pool? You said they were setting it up this afternoon for tomorrow night."

"Okay, sugar," Maya said. She smiled at Gena. "Excuse us."

In his sister's and daughter's absence, Nate joked, "Lily's not too subtle, is she?"

"About as subtle as getting hit by a train," Gena agreed. They laughed.

Nate liked the sound of her laughter. He liked the sound of her voice, period. It was deep and sensual. He felt like he could hear her emotions in her tone. Perhaps he was being overly sensitive, because he had discovered that while he had thought that from a distance she was a pretty woman, up close she was stunning.

He was experiencing sensory overload. Her skin's scent was delicious. That was the only way he could describe it. The warmth of her skin coupled with the light, flowery cologne she wore was so enticing he wanted to lean in and sniff her. Of course, he restrained himself.

She was wearing a simple sleeveless summer cotton dress in white that buttoned down the front, and matching sandals. Her hair was drawn away from her face in a casually upswept style as though she hadn't really given it much thought, but the effect was very becoming. It displayed her graceful neck. And the neckline of the dress, which didn't dip too far down, gave him a tantalizing glimpse of her beautifully formed shoulders.

This was bad, really bad. Gena Boudreau in the flesh was everything he'd always dreamed she would be. He spotted an empty bench underneath one of the red oaks.

"Would you like to sit down?"

I should sit down before I fall down, Gena thought gratefully. "Yes, thank you."

After they were seated, Nate said, "I suppose Lily pestered you into meeting me."

"I wouldn't have come if I hadn't wanted to," Gena told him truthfully.

Nate was relieved to hear that. "Good." He looked at her intensely. "Don't take this the wrong way, but I've watched you jog around Red Oaks for years. I always wanted to strike up a conversation with you, but I figured I was not the type of man you'd want to talk to."

"That's not fair, is it?"

"What?"

"Assuming that you know the type of man I would want to talk to."

He smiled. "No, it isn't fair. But is it accurate?"

Gena saw where Lily had gotten her charm. His question could have been antagonistic, but his intonation had had a hopeful cadence to it. He was asking her if he had a chance with her.

She chose her words carefully. "Lily says you don't date much. You'll only see someone who you believe would make her a good stepmother. She also said that you're hardworking and a wonderful dad. That definitely sounds like a man I'd like to talk to."

His smile was devastating. It made her quiver inside. She wondered if God was having a good laugh at her expense. Thirty minutes ago, she was giving her mind over to all things spiritual, and now that she'd met Nate Lincoln, she was consumed with lust.

What was happening up in heaven? Had God made a wager with a lower angel? Let's see whether Gena Boudreau can make good on her promise to herself to become closer to You. Or if I put temptation in her way, will she succumb to it?

It wasn't unprecedented. God and Satan had made a wager about whether or not God's faithful servant Job would remain faithful to God if everything dear to him was snatched away leaving him poor, sick, and grieving for his loved ones.

Job proved faithful to the end.

Sitting on that bench beside Nate Lincoln underneath a summer sky, Gena was not at all sure she'd be able to resist temptation.

CHAPTER 7

The world around them receded into the background as Gena sat beside Nate. His lovely baritone, the volume low and intimate, induced her to listen more closely. She'd asked him what it had been like to raise Lily.

He'd smiled thoughtfully. "I think we've kind of raised each other. When Charity, that's her birth mother, got pregnant with her, I was so happy. I was twenty-eight at the time and ready for children. Charity and I had been married for nearly two years. We'd been trying to get pregnant since we got married, so I was beginning to think something was wrong with either me or her. I should have known by her reaction when she found out she was pregnant that something was up, but I didn't pay strict attention. Turns out she was disappointed. She'd been on the pill, but had slipped up. While I thought we had been trying to conceive, she was doing everything she could to prevent a pregnancy. At least she didn't have an abortion. Days after giving birth, she left me, saying she just wasn't ready to settle down. Taking care of a baby was too much responsibility. We were living in Santa Monica then. I was doing well in construction."

He took a deep breath and sighed, remembering the

shock of being left alone with a helpless week-old child. "I literally freaked out. I knew I couldn't raise Lily by myself, so I came back home to Red Oaks where I'd be surrounded by family. My mother and sister were lifesavers. I didn't half know how to change a diaper, but I learned. Soon, Lily and I bonded and I couldn't bear to be away from her for any length of time. My mother would keep her during the day while I worked, and at the end of the day I couldn't wait to get home to see her. We've had our rough times, but on the whole I highly recommend parenthood."

"What about her mother? Does she ever see her?"

Nate shook his head in the negative. "Charity occasionally writes but Lily doesn't respond. She's still too angry. I think one day she'll want to meet her. We all want to know where we came from."

"She's fiercely devoted to you," Gena said.

"The feeling's mutual." He smiled at her. "Now tell me all about yourself."

Gena laughed shortly. "Don't tell me you're the only person in Red Oaks who hasn't heard about the widow on the hill."

"That's how you think the town sees you?"

"I've actually overheard people call me that at charity events, in supermarkets, even once at a friend's house for dinner. So I know that's what they call me."

"Well, forget about them. Tell me about the real Gena Boudreau."

Gena was quiet. Who was the real Gena Boudreau? She felt as if she'd been lost somewhere along the way. "I really don't know that woman," she surprised herself by saying. "Sometimes I think I'm defined by my actions. My husband died eight years ago and I've kept busy by working in the community and jogging. So I guess I *am* the widow on the hill."

"But what are your dreams? Where do you want to be a year from now?"

"When my husband was alive, I wanted children and I wanted to found a hospice here in town because there wasn't one, and we needed it. I've known people who made the transition alone in their homes without family or friends around them. No one should die alone. Since Taylor passed, I've founded the hospice, but I never got around to remarrying and having children. I think that's my biggest regret."

Nate knew about the hospice. He'd read an article in the local paper about it when it had opened three years ago. Gena had named it after her husband, the Taylor Boudreau Care Facility. He'd visited friends and family there and found it to be a warm, caring, comfortable place where the patients were pampered by the staff.

Nate smiled warmly. "Gena... May I call you Gena?"

"Of course."

"Gena, you're a strong, vital woman. It's not too late to have children."

Gena laughed softly. "Nate, how old do you think I am?"

He squinted at her. His smile never wavered. "Thirty-six?"

"How old are you?"

"Forty-four."

Thank you, God, she thought. "I'm forty-two."

"You don't look it. As if I know what forty-two looks like on a sister. Y'all tend to age gracefully."

Gena flashed him a smile. "That's a nice way of putting it. But, seriously, Nate, I think my childbearing years are over."

"Nonsense, anybody who runs practically every day like you do would breeze through a pregnancy."

"Okay," Gena said, enjoying their chat and feeling brave. "Let's say that my body *could* withstand the pressure. There's still the matter of finding the right man to become the father of my child. By the time I find him, I'll be a wizened old lady."

Nate moved a bit closer to her on the bench and lowered his voice considerably. "I've always wanted to have more children."

Gena was shocked down to her toes. Imagine his saying something like that, and on church grounds! She could not have misjudged his meaning. He was volunteering to father a child with her.

"I just met you," she hissed.

Nate threw back his head in laughter. "Gotcha!"

Gena hauled off and punched him hard on the upper arm. "You beast!"

He couldn't stop laughing. "I had you going there, didn't I? No, Gena, as much as it will disappoint you I am not offering to be your baby's daddy. I would, however, love to take you out to dinner one night soon."

She accepted.

A week later, Gena stood in front of the full-length mirror in her suite wondering if the dress she had on was too provocative for a first date. Miss Edna was in her closet looking for her strappy white sandals to go with it. Gena had insisted she didn't need help, but Miss Edna was more excited about the date than she was. Having found the sandals, she came back into the bedroom. "You've got to admit, Miss Gena, that was a good revival. You found the Lord *and* a man on the same night!"

Gena smiled at her reflection. She did look happy. Okay, she looked like the cat who ate the canary, satisfied and a little wicked. She and Nate had been burning up the phone lines all week. There was no subject that man felt embarrassed discussing. She'd learned so many intimate things about him that she could have sworn she'd known him all her life instead of seven days. And he was so easy to talk to she'd spilled her guts to him.

He'd mentioned seeing her with Cleotus at Madge's Café that day and she'd even told him exactly what she and Cleotus had been talking about. "You're too much woman for a boy anyway," he'd said. "I, for one, am glad you decided not to see him again. If you'd been involved with him, you'd never have agreed to go out with me."

"Selfish," she'd accused him lightly.

"You bet I am," he'd agreed.

Now she turned in front of the mirror observing the way the white wrap dress clung to her curves. V-necked, it could be adjusted to plunge or not to plunge. She chose not to plunge tonight.

Smiling, she faced Miss Edna. "Okay, what do you think?"

Miss Edna's eyes were animated. "He's gonna have to pick his jaw up off the floor."

"I'm so nervous," Gena said breathlessly.

"You should be," stated Miss Edna. "It's been quite a while since you went out on a date. Sometime in 2005, wasn't it?"

"Has it been that long?"

"Just remember," Miss Edna advised. "You don't kiss on the first date and if he asks you back to his place for coffee, refuse."

"Let me see if I can remember that," Gena joked. "We can make love but we can't kiss. And if he asks me back to his place for cocoa, I can go. Got it."

"Joke if you want to," said Miss Edna. "But seeds like to grow when you put 'em in fertile earth, and your earth is as fertile as it gets. Eight years without one birth control pill. *You* do the math."

Gena was slipping into her sandals. "You're so funny, Miss Edna. I have no intention of making love to Nate tonight. It's only our first date."

"From the look of you two sitting on that bench the other night, this ain't the first date. It's the second. You had already reached a certain level of intimacy by the time you parted. And those phone calls have been hot and heavy. Just watch yourself. Nate ain't no boy, he's a man, and men like him know what pleases a woman."

There was a knock at the door. "Come in!" Gena called.

Cynthia stuck her head in. Earlier that week she'd signed up for an introductory computer science course at the junior college. Every night since then she'd been holed up in her room reading the textbooks in anticipation of her class starting in September.

Gena was impressed by her industriousness.

"Your date's here," she said now, grinning. "And he looks very handsome."

"Thanks, Cynthia." She wondered if Cynthia felt awkward coming to tell her deceased brother's widow that her date had arrived. Life certainly had gotten surreal lately. She went and got her purse. "All right, ladies. Hope you both have a good evening."

Nate was waiting in the foyer at the bottom of the stairs. When he heard her footfalls, he turned, and their eyes met. His heart thudded. She was a vision. Those dimples were working overtime, and all he wanted to do was pull her into his arms and kiss those juicy lips of hers.

But they didn't know each other that well yet.

Gena's eyes swept over him in his well-cut navy blue suit. A summer fabric, it fell just right, accentuating the masculine lines of his body from his broad shoulders to his long muscular legs. His clean-shaven face had broken into the most seductive grin upon seeing her that she'd fairly melted on the stairs. Miss Edna was right. This was a man to be reckoned with. He didn't have to do anything to entice her, just be himself.

Gena moved forward and they grasped hands as though they were going to formally shake. Instead, he pulled her close and planted a kiss high on her left cheek.

She inhaled the wonderful scent of him as his lips touched her skin. Felt the strength of him through her fingertips as her hand rested in his. "Gena," he said, longing evident in his tone. The rumble of his voice seemed to reverberate in the pit of her stomach. She was acutely aware of his longing. Her body yearned to be closer to his.

"Nate," she said softly. To his ears his name on her lips sounded like happiness personified. Their eyes met and held. For what seemed like long moments, they gazed at each other.

Then he inhaled, she inhaled, and both released simultaneously. Gena felt as if she had just made love to him, not simply said hello.

Her pleasure points were tingling like mad. "Welcome to my home," she managed.

Nate looked around him appreciatively. "It's everything I imagined it would be. Italianate, isn't it?"

"Yes, it is. Taylor wanted it to look like an Italian villa on a hill. We went to Italy on our honeymoon and he fell in love with some of the old houses we saw."

As they walked to the door Nate asked, "That was your preference, too?"

Gena didn't want to say that she had wanted something more traditionally southern. It was a beautiful house, and that might have sounded ungrateful. She liked to exile to the far reaches of her mind the negative characteristics Taylor had displayed, like being a know-it-all and throwing his weight around because he had been more than twenty years her senior.

"It grew on me," she said. *Sort of like a wart on my nose,* she silently added. "Where are we going tonight?"

"The Big House," he said. "Have you ever been there?"

An African-American couple had transformed a

Colonial mansion formerly owned by slaveholders into a smart eatery; hence the tongue-in-cheek name. "A few times," she said. "They make delicious soul food."

They were outside now. Nate placed his hand beneath her elbow as they walked down the front steps then he opened the passenger-side door of the Ford F-150, his company truck.

Gena had never been in a truck before. She had to step up into its high cab. Nate jogged around to the driver's side and got in. The late-model truck had clearly been detailed inside and out. It had that freshly washed smell. Gena instantly loved it.

"How is Lily?"

Nate laughed softly as he put the truck in gear. "She's in hog heaven. Her best friend, Chloe, is back from a family vacation, and tonight the two of them are going to the movies and then out for pizza with friends."

Gena smiled, remembering Lily's plea to her to go out with her father so that she might have a social life. "That's great. Give her my best when you see her again."

"She'll probably pounce on me as soon as I get home tonight. She was thrilled that you'd said yes when I asked you to dinner. She likes you a lot."

"I like her, too. How can you not? She's so smart and full of life. You must have done something right."

Nate chuckled. "If you call winging it doing something right, then I guess I did. She's starting to make some of her own decisions now. I'll have to step back and let her succeed or fail. That's hard to do."

"Yeah, I imagine it is hard to sit back and let your child

learn from her mistakes. I don't know if I could do it. I'd probably jump in and save her at the last minute."

"Only if it were something life-threatening, or soul-shattering," Nate said. "And let's not forget that there are some things in life that will blindside the most diligent parent. Sometimes we can only be there to help pick up the pieces."

Gena felt that she would gladly have borne all of the heartache associated with raising a child if only she'd been blessed with one. "You're right. Being a parent is the hardest job on earth."

"I don't know," Nate joked. "Being a roofer ain't no walk in the park either. You can die of heat stroke up there."

Gena laughed. "You've been a roofer?"

"Yeah, when I was in my early twenties. Some guys take to it and can withstand the elements. It only made me work harder toward my contractor's license. I had to get off that roof. And you, what was the hardest job you've ever done?"

"Mmm," said Gena thoughtfully. "I've been a dish-washer at a restaurant, I've peeled shrimp, shucked oysters, worked as a maid at a hotel, babysat children and the elderly. But I think the hardest job I've ever had was being on the custodial staff of a hospital. You get to clean up blood, feces, all kinds of bodily secretions. It was awful. Not exactly strenuous, but if you had a weak stomach, which I did, sometimes you wouldn't be able to eat anything without feeling nauseated for days afterward."

Nate was frankly amazed by the menial jobs she'd had in the past. "Then you were not born with a silver spoon in your mouth."

"Nah, not I. My mother and I never had much in the way of material possessions. She raised me alone. I've never met my father. She couldn't give me the best of everything, but what she did give me was a lot of love and the ability to think for myself. I worked my way through nursing school. When I met Taylor I'd recently gotten my master's degree, and had been promoted to head nurse of the cardiology department. That's how we met, he had a heart attack and recovered in my unit."

Nate was silent as he drove. All of this was unfolding rapidly in his mind. Had she known her husband only had a few years left when she had married him? He was ashamed of the turn his thoughts had taken. Would she have married a man who was dying so that she could inherit his money? By her own admission she had been brought up with very few material comforts. She'd had to work hard for everything she'd achieved prior to meeting Boudreau. It would be tempting for any woman, however moralistic, to say yes to marriage with a man who promised her the moon.

In Boudreau's case, the moon, the stars, and the sun. In that same article in which Nate had read about his recent death, his net worth was estimated to be in the tens of millions.

He couldn't put Gena in the category of an Anna Nicole Smith, though, because at least Gena had done something constructive, like opening the hospice, with her inheritance. And she was a pillar of the community. Plus, it wasn't as if she was flashing bling all over the place. She drove a car older than his daughter, for God's sake!

He stopped trying to analyze her. She was an enigma, and he'd leave it at that. His gut told him that she was wonderful, and that was good enough for him.

"I loved him, you know," Gena said quietly. "It's funny. If I'd been closer to his age no one would have wondered if I actually loved him. But because I was in my early thirties and he was in his early fifties when we married, people speculated about my sincerity and his sanity." She laughed. "I think I would still have married him even if he *had* told me he was dying when he asked me. That's how much I loved him."

That revelation rocked Nate. "I'm sorry," he said, his voice full of sympathy. "His death must have shaken you."

Gena had to quickly rummage in her purse to find a tissue before mascara streaked her face. She tilted her chin upward as she dabbed beneath both eyes. "I feel like I should forewarn you that I come with a truckload of neuroses."

"He died in your arms," Nate stated softly.

Gena stared at him. "Where did you hear that?"

"A friend of mine was one of the paramedics who responded to your call that night. He told me in confidence, Gena. He isn't the type of person to spread idle gossip. But we were having drinks one night and I told him I had a crush on you. How I always saw you running by as if nothing ever bothered you. That's when he told me he was certain you weren't that carefree and how he'd had to fight you to get you to stop trying to resuscitate your husband so that they could get to work on him. He said you were hysterical at the thought of losing him." Now, remembering what his friend had told him, Nate was doubly ashamed for even entertaining the notion of Gena being a gold digger.

They were at the supper club now. Nate parked, but because it was a warm, humid night he left the truck running in order to take advantage of the air-conditioning.

"Say something," he urged her.

"What is there left to say?" Gena asked tightly. "You've known from the beginning that my husband died while in the throes of passion. It will come as no surprise to you that I haven't had sex since then."

She was mistaken. It did surprise Nate. He opened his mouth to say something and clamped it shut again. He tried to come up with a reason why she would have avoided intimacy with anyone for eight years. Only one came to mind: She didn't believe in sex before marriage. No husband, no sex. That made sense to him.

Gena, however, disabused him of that theory with "And it's not because I'm frigid. I still have those desires. It's just that I can't risk killing someone else."

Nate laughed shortly. "You're not serious?"

She gave him a sharp look.

"You *are* serious!" Somehow he didn't feel like laughing anymore. He turned on the seat and grasped her firmly by the shoulders. "Look here, Gena, you didn't kill Taylor. He had a bad heart. He was willing to take the risk of dying in your arms when he married you. Personally, I can't imagine a more wonderful way to go."

Gena simply stared at him with her mouth partly open in amazement. By now she was used to his making outrageous comments, but this one took the prize. "You're not going to get the chance!" she said huffily.

Nate smiled. "Let's see about that."

Since the beginning of time there have been kisses that aroused, enticed, and generally wreaked havoc with one's senses. There have been kisses that were so maddeningly intense that they left you drained of all resistance. And there have been kisses that were only meant to send a message of chaste devotion. This kiss wasn't like any of those. This kiss left nothing to the imagination. Its intent was to possess fully. To chip away at years of ill-conceived abstinence. To reawaken or, in fact, establish a stronghold of wanton desire.

His mouth, clean and sweet, descended on hers with utter command. She could only sigh with satisfaction and taste pleasure that she never knew existed. Her arms went around his neck. His hand held her head at the base of her neck. Although he'd initiated the kiss, he knew when to withhold, knew when to increase, knew exactly what amount of pressure would please her most. At first he thought she liked it gentle, but soon learned she liked it a little rough when she playfully nipped him. He only smiled and redoubled his efforts. He couldn't get enough of her.

Breathlessly, they finally parted. Eyes clouded with lust, he said as he gently rubbed his thumb across her bottom lip, "Gena, you *give* life to a man. You don't take it away."

CHAPTER 8

"Dad was right, you never change your route," Lily said as she began jogging alongside Gena early one Monday morning in October. She had driven to the Anderson house in the compact car her dad had bought her for her seventeenth birthday in September, parked on the street, and waited until she spotted Gena.

"Good morning, Lily," Gena said, smiling at her.

Lily had known Gena wouldn't stop jogging just to talk, so she'd worn her athletic shoes. Plus, she and Chloe had started getting in shape by jogging past the football field where the team practiced for two to three hours after school every day. She had a big crush on the quarterback, Sean Winfield.

"Good morning," she answered equally cheerfully. "I wanted to invite you to Dad's surprise birthday party this Friday night. It starts at eight."

Gena and Nate had been dating for nearly two months. She had met his mother and several other family members. She'd gone to his house for dinner. He'd made sure that she and Lily got to spend time together. The three of them had gone to the movies and Gena had been touched when

Lily asked her to go shopping with her for her school clothes in September.

Still, she didn't want to horn in on a family celebration. "Are you sure your dad would want me there? A birthday is a very personal thing."

Lily laughed at Gena's question. Her startlingly alive brown eyes danced. "You're joking, right? If it were left up to Dad, you'd be living with us by now! He's crazy about you. Don't you know that?"

Gena couldn't help smiling. She felt the same way about Nate. In the past two months her life had changed drastically. She was, like Reverend Avery had said in the first sermon she'd ever heard him deliver, *fully awake!* She savored life. Every day was a gift now instead of another reason to groan and moan and carry on about life being a pain in the butt and ultimately pointless. She knew what the point was: God wanted us to be as happy as possible before we died. He wanted us to be happy and He wanted us to make others happy. A simple philosophy, but it was what fired her enthusiasm.

"I'll be there," she told Lily.

"Splendid," said Lily, sounding like a prim little old lady instead of an eleventh grader. Satisfied, she made to leave.

"Wait a minute," Gena said. "How should I dress? Should I bring a gift? And if so, what? I don't know your dad's sizes or anything."

Lily laughed. "Believe me, once Dad sees you he isn't going to care what you're wearing or if you have a gift with you. Wear jeans. And forget about a gift. Just bring yourself. Bye now!" She turned and jogged back to her car.

Gena continued running toward the city's park.

* * *

After a day of making the rounds—meeting with the Red Oaks High School principal, Mrs. Millicent Riley, about scholarship-worthy eleventh and twelfth graders; going over the hospice's budget with the administrator, Mrs. Jane Britton; and visiting several of the patients— Gena was emotionally drained when she returned home at seven that evening.

Miss Edna and Cynthia were in the kitchen putting the final touches on dinner.

As Gena came through the garage door, Cary Grant ran to greet her. Paws all up on her blouse and tongue licking her face, he was delighted to see her. Laughing, Gena got down on one knee in her tailored slacks and hugged him. "Somebody thinks I've been neglecting him," she said lightly. She looked up at Miss Edna and Cynthia. "Evenin', ladies, how was your day?"

"Evenin', Miss Gena," Miss Edna said, smiling. She turned back around to stir the savory chili in the huge Dutch oven on the stove top. "My day was going pretty well until I went to the market to pick up a few things for this chili and spotted Mr. Bishop with his arm around Miss Liz Green. By the look on his face, he was surprised to see me. And seeing the look on his face, Miss Liz Green knew something was up and confronted him right there in the produce section. By the time she was finished with him I don't know which was greener, the cucumbers or Mr. Bishop's face." She giggled. "That's the last time he dates two women who go to the same church! That tired Casanova!"

Gena shook her head sympathetically. "Cary Grant tried to tell you he was up to no good."

"Yes, he did," Miss Edna agreed. "Next time I'm going to listen to him."

Cynthia laughed as she set the table. "Maybe I ought to bring the gentleman I met in my computer science class around to meet him."

Cary Grant sat amongst them, turning his handsome head to regard one woman, then the next as though he were holding court. Gena didn't like assigning human qualities to him because, after all, he was a dog, but sometimes she could swear he knew when they were talking about him.

"What's he like?" she asked Cynthia as she went to the fridge for a bottle of water. She immediately drank half of it and peered at Cynthia, awaiting her reply.

"Oh, he's in his late fifties, very distinguished, with no holes in his salt-n'-pepper Afro yet."

Miss Edna and Gena laughed at her description.

Cynthia, who had picked up a few pounds since she'd been living with them, looked very pretty in a pale blue silk blouse and a pair of jeans. She'd recently had her black hair with silver streaks in it cut short, and it was becoming on her. "He's a widower with three grown children, all living out of the state. His ex-wife, too. Out of the state, I mean. He says he'd never consider moving. Georgia's in his blood. When I told him I'd lived in five states he looked at me as if I were a sophisticated globe-trotter, or something." She met Gena's gaze. "Could I be falling in love?"

Gena laughed shortly. "Why're you asking me?"

Miss Edna answered that one. "Because in this house

you're the authority on the subject, seeing as how you're in love."

Gena pretended to be aghast. "What makes you say that?"

Miss Edna balled up her mouth, something she did when she was irritated.

"Gena Boudreau, you've never lied to me that I know of. Don't you start now. I've seen you when you're in love with a man, remember? I know how you behave, and you're acting crazy, girl!"

Gena *had* to hear this. "How am I acting crazy?"

Miss Edna began ticking off a long list on her fingers. "You walk around here with your head in the clouds. You're glowing. You haven't paid this much attention to your appearance in ages. Now, you've never been a slob but you've never been what I would call a clotheshorse, either. These days you don't leave the house without your clothes hittin' on all the right places. Afraid, I guess, that you're going to run into Nate during your busy day in town."

Cynthia hadn't chimed in, but she was nodding in agreement with Miss Edna. "Mmm-huh," she said.

Gena laughed. "Okay, I'm busted. I do like to dress for Nate. I love seeing that certain look in his eyes when he likes what he sees."

"He'd like what he saw even if you were naked," Cynthia said. She howled with laughter when she realized what she'd said. So did Gena and Miss Edna. "I didn't mean that," she exclaimed. "What I meant was… Well, you know what I meant!"

After Gena had wiped the tears from her eyes, she said, "He hasn't had that honor yet."

The other two women abruptly stopped laughing. There were astonished expressions on their faces. "Really?" Miss Edna said incredulously.

Gena sat down at the table. Suddenly, the mood was somber. "I've made a lot of progress since meeting Nate, but I haven't gotten over that particular phobia yet."

Miss Edna and Cynthia were both aware of how Taylor had died. They encouraged Gena to move forward at her own pace. So while they were surprised that she and Nate had not made love yet (because it was so obvious that she was in love with him), they were not particularly shocked that she'd chosen not to take that step.

Miss Edna went to place a comforting hand on Gena's shoulder. "You've got all the time in the world."

Lily ushered Nate into the bathroom for his shower the instant he got home from work on Friday night. She had made reservations at the Big House for his birthday, she told him, and she was paying.

Nate was tired. He would have preferred to stay home and watch ESPN. But even when she was very small Lily had always taken pride in doing something special for his birthday. Now that she was a "mature woman" as she put it, and had a part-time job in the food court at the mall, she was going to treat him. He didn't have the heart to beg off.

What Lily actually had planned was a surprise party right there in their home. While he was in the shower, a small army of men, women, and children decorated the great room. The women, Nate's mother, Marian, his sister,

Maya, and assorted aunts and cousins and friends, brought the food into the kitchen through the back door.

Organization being second nature to the women in his family, they had things set up within minutes. The other guests began arriving at seven-thirty. The sign on the door advised them not to ring the bell but to go on in.

Gena arrived at seven forty-five wearing jeans, a lovely purple off-the-shoulder long-sleeve cotton blouse, and a pair of sexy black patent leather sandals. Her wavy black hair fell down her back. She knew Lily had said she didn't need to bring a gift, but she nonetheless had something special for him in her purse.

Lily met her in the foyer with her finger to her lips. "We're staying quiet because Dad hasn't come downstairs yet. Come on, everybody's in the great room."

Their home, a large two-story southern-style bungalow with a wraparound porch, sat on twenty acres about a mile from Gena's house. Nate had built it himself with the help of his family. Like everything they did, everyone had pitched in. Gena had never been a part of a family like his. She found herself falling in love with all of them. Even his uncle Jimmy, who told the most ribald jokes she'd ever heard and laughed louder than anyone else when he got to the punch line.

Lily left her at the entrance to the great room. "I'm going to get Dad. See you later." Since Lily hadn't offered to take her purse, Gena slipped the long strap over her head.

As soon as she stepped into the room, she found herself surrounded by people. "Hey, Gena," called Maya, coming to give her a quick hug.

Gena hugged her back. "Good to see you, Maya. You look gorgeous."

"Thanks, so do you!" As usual she wore a colored tunic over slacks. This time the tunic was in several bright jewel colors, and the slacks were slim and black. Her husband, Eric, was more casual in a Georgia State jersey and jeans. "Hey, Gena." He sounded like Michael Clark Duncan. "Good to see you, Eric," Gena greeted him.

"Gena!" someone yelled from across the room.

Gena craned her neck. It was Uncle Jimmy.

"Gena, have you heard the one about the three nuns who were walking through an alley late at night when some thugs jumped them?" he breathlessly said upon reaching her side.

"No, I haven't," Gena said somewhat cautiously.

Not much taller than she, and thin, Uncle Jimmy had a fragile air about him except when he was telling a joke. Then he was liberally infused with vitality.

"The older nun says to the younger ones, 'Run, sisters. I'm old. I'll sacrifice myself to save you.' But the younger nuns said, 'No, sister, we're young and strong. You run and we'll stay and fight them off.' One of the thugs gets frustrated that the nuns are talking among themselves when they should be cowering in fright. 'Shut up,' he says. 'We—'"

Suddenly Maya yelled near her ear, "Surprise!" Gena spun on her heel as the sound was amplified by fifty voices. Nate stood in the doorway, a mixture of joy and surprise on his face. Gena's heartbeat picked up its pace at the sight of him. He looked straight at her and fairly devoured her with his eyes. But Lily was behind him urging him into the room to be enveloped in the arms of his family.

They sang "Happy Birthday" to him, whereupon one of the aunts rolled out the birthday cake, already lit up with forty-five candles, on a tea trolley. He blew them out, and everybody started chanting, "Speech, speech!"

Nate grinned. All of the people in the world that he loved were here, including Gena.

He held Lily in the crook of his arm as he spoke: "You got me, baby girl," he said to her. He looked at his friends and family. "She told me she was taking me to dinner at a restaurant. I was going to make her pay for the prime rib, but this is much, much better! Thank you all for coming."

He kissed Lily's cheek. She kissed his, and then left his side to go join Chloe and some cousins on the patio where Chloe already had the stereo blasting the latest rap sensation's CD.

He made a beeline for Gena, but was waylaid by his mother. She was a tall, handsome woman in her sixties who wore her coal-black hair with silver streaks in a chignon. He didn't think she'd ever cut her thick, lustrous hair. The subtle fragrance of ginger surrounded him when he put his arms around her. He bent and kissed her silken cheek.

"Thank you, Mama, I know Lily left the food preparation up to you."

Marian smiled up at him. "Honey, these days I just give directions and your sister and cousins do the cooking." She squeezed him for good measure, then moved out of his embrace. "Go on and get her now. I know that's where you were headed."

Nate didn't even try to deny it. "Maybe I shouldn't be such a fool for love."

His mother rolled her eyes. "I say it's about time you were. I didn't see you with Charity, remember? I'm enjoying watching my son fall in love. She's a nice girl."

Nate looked across the room at Gena, who was laughing at something his uncle Jimmy had said, probably one of his bad jokes. "If she'd have me, Mama, I'd marry her."

His mother frowned. "What do you mean by *if?* Have you asked and she turned you down?" Nate saw the indignation on her face and laughed softly. The women in his family thought he could do no wrong. All of them had bonded when he'd come home seventeen years ago with an infant in tow and admitted he needed their help. Now they were proprietary about him. And would defend him at the drop of a hat. He, of course, would die for any of them.

"No, I haven't built up the courage yet."

His mother smiled, relieved. "Don't wait too long," she advised. "You're already forty-five. If you're going to give me more grandchildren, you need to get on the ball!"

"You've already got five grandchildren," Nate joked. "Isn't that enough?"

"No!" was her emphatic response. "I can always love some more." With that, she abandoned him in favor of his father, who was standing a few feet away holding his cup underneath the mouth of a bottle of whiskey as a nephew poured the potent potable.

Nate hurried across the room to rescue Gena from Uncle Jimmy. If he knew his mother, and he did, she was about to raise bloody hell. His father had recently been told by his doctor to stop drinking hard liquor.

If he was quick, he and Gena could be in the gazebo out back before the stuff hit the fan. For maximum enjoyment of a family gathering, you had to know when to beat a hasty retreat.

He didn't give Gena time enough to say anything. He simply walked up to her and Uncle Jimmy and said, "You don't mind if I steal Gena, do you, Unc? There's something I need to talk to her about."

Looking confused and not a little put out by the interruption, Uncle Jimmy sputtered, "Oh, okay, Nate." He was about to say something else, but Nate and Gena were gone before he could form the words.

"We're going some place private," he told Gena as he pulled her along.

Nate felt like a soldier trying to sneak out of enemy territory. There were people everywhere. He tried to go through the family room's door that was on the side of the house where the gazebo stood, but there were about ten guests in that room with the TV tuned to a sports channel. He thought of the kitchen, but there would undoubtedly be someone in there dishing up food. They hadn't started serving the meal yet.

Then he remembered the front door. With luck the hallway and the foyer would be empty of guests. Everyone had probably arrived by now.

"I don't think there is anywhere private," Gena said with laughter bubbling up.

"If anyone's in the gazebo, I'll politely ask them to

leave," said Nate through gritted teeth. His tone was un-necessarily rough due to his desire to be alone with her.

"If you bark at them like that, I'm sure they'll be happy to."

They came to the foyer. The coast was clear, and they made a mad dash for the front door. Nate eased it closed behind them, and they ran down the steps and around the house. Gena was glad she hadn't worn stilettos. Her heels were not impeding her movement.

Tense with longing, Nate could not wait until they reached the gazebo, approximately forty feet away. He pulled her into his arms and held her close to his heart. "Lily knew just what to get me for my birthday."

Gena smiled up at him. "I'm glad you like it."

"Oh, I do. Very much." Then he bent his head and hungrily kissed her mouth.

Gena gave a soft sigh and met his passion with her own. It had only been a few days since she'd seen him, and they were planning to go out tomorrow night, but the separation had still been painful.

As for Nate, he knew he was in love. To be honest, he had loved her from afar for so long that their finally getting together had felt right from the beginning. The moment he had sat down with her on the bench under-neath the red oak tree after the revival he had known his life would never be the same.

Breaking off the kiss, he looked intently into her eyes. "I want you, Gena."

Gena was still aroused from his kiss. At that moment making love to him seemed like the most natural, and logical, next step in their relationship. Her arms encircled his waist. "I want you, too."

"Well, then, let's get out of here." Nate didn't want to waste any more time. As far as he was concerned, they'd already wasted years.

Gena held back. Suddenly, images of Lily standing at Nate's grave, her once animated eyes cold and dead with grief, flooded her mind. *I won't take a father away from his child*, she thought. *Don't be ridiculous, Gena*, she reasoned. *Nate is not Taylor. He's younger, his heart is sound. Sex is not going to kill him!* But, reason as she might, she could not shake her fears.

Jerking her hand free of his grasp, Gena cried, "I can't do it, Nate. As much as I want you, I can't go through with it." Backing away from him, she added, "I'm sorry." She turned and walked swiftly around the house in the direction of the spot where she'd parked her car. Nate ran after her. "Gena, we need to talk about this!"

"There's nothing to talk about," she shouted over her shoulder, walking so fast now her shoulder bag was bouncing against her hip. It was when her mind focused on her shoulder bag that she remembered the birthday gift she'd brought with her. It was still in her purse.

She couldn't give it to him now. Almost running, she reached the car and hastily unlocked the driver's-side door. Nate came and stood between her and the door, preventing her from opening it. Gena tried to physically push him out of the way, but he outweighed her by at least eighty pounds. All muscle.

Frustrated and breathing hard, she glared at him. "You can't make me talk to you if I don't want to."

"Stop being childish," he said evenly.

He waited until she had calmed down and was breathing normally. Then he spoke calmly and slowly so that she would understand him perfectly. "I'm in love with you, Gena. And I want to marry you." He paused.

Gena supposed he expected her to have another mental breakdown, and was giving her a reasonable amount of time to compose herself. His words had had the opposite effect on her, however. She was stunned into silence.

One part of her rejoiced. He loved her and wanted to spend the rest of his life with her. Another part was screaming in horror. *No, this is a nightmare. It's history repeating itself. If I marry him, I'll have to bury another husband. No way!*

She looked up at him, at those wide-spaced beautiful brown eyes, that rugged, all-male jawline. She loved him so much all she wanted to do was hold him close.

And that, to her mind, was the best reason *not* to marry him. She loved him too much!

Perhaps thinking that she was ready for another dose of reality, Nate continued. "I want to marry you and bring you here to live with me and Lily. I want to make love to you every day. I want to make love to you so often that having a child together will be inevitable. That's how much I love you, Gena." He paused again. "Marry me."

Gena threw her arms around his neck and repeatedly kissed his cheeks, his forehead, his smooth-shaven chin.

"I love you, too." Tears sprang to her eyes. "That's why I can't see you anymore."

Nate laughed harshly as he removed her arms from about his neck and stepped aside. If she wanted to go, she was free to do so. He watched as she reached for the door's handle.

"Just answer this question before you go."

Blinking back tears, Gena turned to face him. "What?"

"Where is your faith?"

Trembling with emotion, Gena wiped her tears with the pads of her fingers. She looked at him askance. "My faith?"

"Yeah, that thing you recently recovered. You go to church every Sunday now. You've said you no longer blame God for taking Taylor in the manner he was taken. You say that you feel God's presence in your life. If that's all true, then why do you still believe that He would allow another man that you love to die in your arms? Faith without works is dead. Even I, heathen that I am, know that much. Faith untested is not faith at all. And at the first sign of a test of your faith, you prove that you have none." He laughed shortly. "You can take this two ways. This could be the most desperate rap ever by a man who simply wants to get you into bed. Or it could be a sincere plea from the man who loves you, for you to see reason and let go of your fears. Which do you believe it is?"

Gena stood looking at him for a long time.

Nate watched her with an enigmatic smile and his arms akimbo. He would not press her further. The decision had to be hers. She had to step up and accept the challenge of loving him completely or go home alone to an empty house. She'd told him earlier in the week that her little family, including Cary Grant, were taking a road trip to Savannah this weekend. They'd left this morning.

Suddenly, venting her frustration, she growled deep in her throat and grabbed him by the collar. "Follow me home, Nathan Lincoln, but if you die on me I'll never forgive you!"

CHAPTER 9

Nate didn't have to be asked twice. Once he saw Gena safely into her car he sprinted around to the front of the house where he'd parked the truck, praying all the way that none of the party guests had blocked him in.

Luckily they'd been thoughtful enough to park on the grass instead of in the driveway.

He went straight to the driver's-side door, bent down, reached underneath the truck's body, and retrieved a magnetized metal container no bigger than a matchbox.

He kept an extra key there in case he locked himself out. He definitely did not want to go back into the house. Someone would see him, and he'd have to make up a plausible excuse for leaving the party.

He felt a little guilty for sneaking off like this, but it wasn't as if he was going to spend the night at Gena's. This was a small town, and people gossiped. More importantly he had always been circumspect about intimate relationships around Lily. His manner of teaching morals was not "do as I say." It was his responsibility to set an example. That's why he kept his sex life private. He never spent the night with anyone. Conversely, he did not invite women to spend the night at his house, either. He knew single parents who did that around their children and he sincerely believed it was a mistake to do so. Half of the time kids didn't necessarily hear what you said to them. They were too busy observing your actions.

After he backed out of the driveway he saw that Gena had waited for him at the turnoff to his house. She pulled onto the highway when she saw the headlights of his truck, and he pulled out behind her.

At the house, she parked on the circular drive and got out. She waited while Nate did the same. Once she saw him step from the cab of the truck, she ran and leaped into his arms. Nate gratefully held her hard against him. He'd feared that on the drive over she might have changed her mind.

They kissed lingeringly. She grinned at him after they came up for air. "Let's go inside before I chicken out."

Arms about each other's waists, they walked up the steps. Gena unlocked the double doors and disengaged the alarm. Nate closed and locked the doors behind them.

Tossing her shoulder bag onto a straight-back chair in the foyer, Gena said, "Just in case you're wondering, I moved out of the bedroom Taylor and I used several years ago. It's a sewing room now."

"It never crossed my mind," Nate said with a smile. He went to her and kissed the side of her neck. And it hadn't. Taylor had been gone for eight years. If his ghost was still skulking somewhere in these rooms it was going to be exorcised tonight!

Gena sighed with pleasure as he worked his way up to her earlobe and sucked it.

Her warm skin smelled of exotic spices. He pulled away

and began undressing her, beginning with her shirt, which was a pullover. Gena raised her arms and wriggled out of it. The shirt went on the chair with the shoulder bag. She backed farther into the house as his talented hands made short work of removing her bra.

Heavy breasts spilled into his hands. Breasts with wholly natural contours. He could not have been more delighted. Gena, however, feeling suddenly self-conscious, placed a hand over each nipple. Thank God for sports bras. But at forty-two, her girls didn't exactly salute the sun anymore.

Nate firmly pried her hands from her chest. "You're beautiful, Gena."

He pushed her against the wall, raised her hands above her head, and kissed her inhibitions away. Gena gave him a saucy grin when he finally raised his head again.

Nate felt something on his crotch, and realized that Gena's right hand was grasping him through his khaki slacks. He'd grown hard during that kiss. Well, harder. He'd had an erection since they'd kissed in his yard minutes ago.

"Can you make it upstairs?" she naughtily asked him, referring to the bulge in his pants. "Because I'll be waiting for you in the second bedroom on the left."

With that, she pushed out of his embrace and ran in the direction of the stairs.

Nate wasted no time getting out of his clothes. He left them, along with his shoes and socks, in a pile at the bottom of the stairs. Then he took the stairs two at a time.

He paused on the landing. What was he thinking? He'd

left the condom in his wallet, and his wallet was in his slacks. He turned around and went and got it.

By the time he pushed the door of bedroom number two open Gena was standing next to the bed without a stitch of clothing on. Nate's heartbeat quickened at the sight of her. Full breasts, a tapered waist, flaring hips with a nicely rounded bottom. He couldn't comprehend why she would want to hide all that beauty from him. She had a woman's body, voluptuous in the right places and soft or firm in others. Her legs and thighs were conditioned from running, as were her buttocks, but her belly, which to him was the center of a woman, was not rippled but flat and soft the way he liked it.

While he was enjoying the view, Gena was also getting her fill. Hard work had wrought a hard body. His arms, chest, legs, thighs, and stomach all had well-defined musculature. She watched him walk toward her. Yes, he even had those indentations on the sides of his butt that appeared with years of conditioning. Good Lord, she didn't know how her poor little runner's body was going to react when a body like that touched it. It would probably faint dead away.

She lowered her gaze to his manhood. Okay, if the body didn't do her in, *that* would definitely finish her off. It was without a doubt the biggest… She didn't finish her thought because Nate put his tongue down her throat, after which her thought processes became kind of befuddled.

"Mmm," she moaned as he backed her toward the bed.

She tried to slow his progress by digging her feet in, but only succeeded in having that killer body pressed more firmly against her softness, which, in turn, further inflamed her. In panic mode now because, after all, it had been eight years since anyone had gotten this close to her, she turned her head, breaking off the kiss, and cried, "Condoms! I don't have any!"

"I have one." His arms tightened around her.

"One! What if it breaks?"

"It's brand-new. It's not going to break."

"Yeah, but what if it does?"

"We'll worry about that if it happens," he said firmly.

She remembered what Miss Edna had said about her having gone eight years without using birth control pills and about her womb being fertile soil just waiting for the right seed to come along.

Get a grip, Gena, she thought desperately. *You're buggin'*.

It was either get a grip, or live in fear of intimacy for the rest of her life. She could not bear to be afraid a moment longer, so she said, "Screw it," and pushed Nate onto the bed.

"Screw?" said Nate, smiling at her crude language. "I didn't know that word was in your vocabulary."

"Well, now you know," she said as she bent to kiss him.

She rained hot, passionate kisses down his chin, onto his chest, his stomach, and farther still, until Nate stopped her. He didn't want to come too quickly.

Turning her over, he returned the favor, kissing her face, her neck, giving special attention to her breasts, nipples, and savoring the feel of the soft skin on her belly against his mouth. When he reached her mound he gently opened her legs.

Gena didn't even tense, she was so relaxed by now. His tongue spread the lips of her vagina and skillfully manipulated the tender flesh there. Gena felt as though she would cry with the want of release before he finally sent her senses reeling. She moaned and writhed. Nate did not raise his head until she had come down from the orgasm. Until she sighed with fulfillment.

He then rose and put on the condom, knelt again, gathered her up in his arms, and placed his engorged penis at the mouth of her vagina. He waited for her. Gena looked into his gorgeous whiskey-colored eyes. She smiled at him and pushed. He moved slowly. She was tight, as he'd expected. The friction just about did him in. But he got control and slowly, with delicious deliberation, entered her.

He felt her vaginal muscles contract around him. He went deeper. Gena pushed. He began a rhythmic dance to which she responded in kind. As their arousal grew, his coming to a peak, and hers slowly building again after her earlier climax, they continued to look deeply into each other's eyes. Their breath mingled. Gena felt as though he were giving her an infusion of his spirit. Nate wanted nothing more than to see that wonder-filled expression in her eyes for the rest of their lives.

As his thrusts gained in momentum, so did hers. She started panting softly when she discovered that another climax was approaching. Nate moaned, the sound causing ripples of pleasure to shoot directly to Gena's clitoris. She began to throb down there but wanted to hold on until Nate came. She marveled at his control, thinking that the average man would have climaxed right after she had a few minutes ago. How long ago? She didn't know. Time was irrelevant when you were connecting this well with another human being. All that mattered was how much he was giving of himself, and he was giving his all.

Suddenly, he bent his head and took her nipple between his teeth. The bud, already sensitive, seemed to explode with pleasure. Gena climaxed with a fierceness she'd never known before. Nate followed close behind, fairly roaring when his release came. His breath came in short intervals as he collapsed on top of her. Rolling off her, he pulled her close to his side. Smiling happily, they peered into each other's eyes.

"I'm still here," Nate joked.

Gena laughed. "The curse has been lifted." She kissed his chin and rolled away from him. "I need to get something from downstairs." She rose, and Nate followed her with his eyes.

"I'll just use your bathroom while you're gone."

Gena went into the adjoining bathroom, grabbed her robe from the hook behind the door, and smiled at him. "Help yourself. I'll bring your clothes back up with me."

She hurried from the room. He swung his legs off the bed and got to his feet.

By the time she got back, he was in the shower. She neatly placed his clothes on the bed, his shoes on the floor nearby, and went to join him.

Disrobing as she entered the bathroom, she said, "I'm coming in."

"Come on, there's room enough for four people in here," Nate joked.

Gena paused long enough to put on a shower cap, then stepped into the stall. "I like lots of space. I get claustrophobic." The large bathroom had a shower on one side of the room and a sunken tub on the opposite end. "I love being in water. I think I was a mermaid in another life."

Nate's eyes swept over her lissome form. "I can see it."

Gena blushed and changed the subject. "Think they've missed you yet?"

"More than likely. Come back with me and we'll pretend we were outside talking the whole time."

"Sounds like a plan."

They were silent while they soaped each other's bodies and rinsed under the lukewarm spray. As Nate was toweling her dry, he asked, "Do you think you could be happy living in my house after all of this?"

Gena smiled at him. "I've never been in love with this place. It was really Taylor's dream house, not mine. I adore your house. If I'd had my way I would have built a house similar to it."

"But you didn't have your way." Nate looked deeply in her eyes. "Gena, I can't promise you'll always have your way if you married me. But I would definitely value your input and I would expect you to help me make decisions. I'm telling you from the jump, though, that in a lot of respects I'm traditional. I *want* to take care of you. That means you would have to be happy living in my house where I pay the bills. I don't need or want your money. I would insist on a prenuptial agreement if you decided to marry me, because I have no designs on what you accumulated with Taylor or since he's been gone. Are we clear?"

Gena had a few stipulations of her own. "That's fine with me," she began. "I don't need a mansion or a housekeeper. But you have to realize that I have certain responsibilities. I want to continue volunteering with the Ladies Auxiliary and I will continue to oversee the running of the hospice. Okay, so you don't want my money. I never thought you did. But being rich is not the kind of thing you can totally ignore. I'm not an extravagant person who has to have the latest designer clothing or drive the most expensive car. You know what I drive. But there may be times when I want to splurge on something, and I wouldn't want you getting bent out of shape when I do. Plus, I may want to give Lily a gift every now and then. Like a trip to any place in the world after she graduates from college."

Nate laughed. "Just don't start spoiling her right away. I've got her so that she knows the value of a dollar. I'd like her to keep thinking that way well into adulthood."

"Deal," Gena said.

Nate smiled broadly. "Okay, then, will you marry me?"

"Yes!" she cried, throwing her arms around his neck and kissing him soundly.

Afterward, they went into the adjoining bedroom to put on their clothes. While Nate was buttoning his denim shirt, Gena removed his birthday gift from her purse and walked over to him. "Happy birthday," she said, handing him the box that was about the size of a hardback book.

He opened it and smiled. Inside was a portrait of Gena in an ornate wooden frame.

"For your nightstand," she said.

Nate considered Gena, herself, to be his greatest birthday gift. But the portrait ran a close second. "I love it," he said, pulling her into his arms. "And I love *you*."

"I love you, too," Gena said.

It was late when Miss Edna, Cynthia, and Cary Grant returned from Savannah on Sunday night, so Gena didn't get the chance to tell them the news. However, on Monday morning just after they all sat down at the kitchen table, Gena told them, "Nate and I are getting married."

Miss Edna had been about to put a piece of buttered toast in her mouth. She dropped the toast and sprang to her feet, going to hug Gena tightly. "I knew it! I knew the first time I saw you two together that there was something special going on. Congratulations, Miss Gena. I'm so happy for you."

Cynthia also hugged her, but her enthusiasm was tempered by her own reality. If Gena was getting married, there would be no place in her home for an ex-sister-in-law.

She could show nothing less than gratitude for Gena's happiness, though. She hugged her and said, "No one deserves happiness more, Gena."

Gena held her at arm's length. "Thank you, Cynthia." She smiled at Miss Edna. "Thank you both. Now, let's sit down because I have something I'd like to run by you. Just an idea I've been kicking around."

Her eyes were alive with excitement when she began. "I'm going to be moving in with Nate and Lily." She met Miss Edna's eyes. "That means I won't be needing your services, Miss Edna." She saw the astonished expression in Miss Edna's eyes. "So I'm going to start your pension right away, and give you a nice severance package, as well. Enough so that you'll never have to worry about finances again. You've been like a surrogate mother to me, and I think it's the least I can do."

Miss Edna had tears in her eyes. "Miss Gena, I don't know how to thank you."

"You don't have to," Gena said, reaching across the table and squeezing her hand.

Now it was Cynthia's turn.

Cynthia swallowed hard. She had grown to love Gena over the weeks she'd spent in her house. She hoped she wasn't going to be cut off from her the way her niece and nephew had cut her out of their lives. Gena was the closest thing to family she had left. Eight years ago, she would never have thought she would feel that way.

Gena smiled warmly before addressing her. "Cynthia, when I was married to Taylor I never thought you and I would become friends."

"I know I was a bitch," Cynthia said with regret.

Gena went on as if she hadn't heard that comment. "But since you've been here I've come to know you and, well, I like you. And I consider you a friend."

Grateful tears pooled in Cynthia's eyes. "I consider you a friend, too."

Gena blinked back tears. "So I was trying to think of a way you could become that independent business-woman you had been before Katrina, and it occurred to me that you could turn this house into a bed-and-breakfast. As far as I know, Red Oaks doesn't have one yet, and we get tourists through here all the time."

Cynthia's eyes stretched in shock and disbelief. "What?"

"I think Taylor would want you to have the house. I'll sign it over to you lock, stock, and barrel. Then you'll only have to worry about maintenance and yearly property taxes. You're hardworking and smart. You'll make that easily."

Cynthia grabbed Gena around the neck and, crying, hugged her so tightly she practically cut off her air supply. "Oh my God! I'll make you proud of me, Gena. You'll see, this place will be a huge success."

Miss Edna grinned happily. "You're gonna need a head housekeeper, aren't you?"

Cynthia let go of Gena and regarded Miss Edna. She smiled. "I will, yes. Are you applying for the job?"

"You bet I am!" Miss Edna smiled at Gena. "I'm too young to retire. I'd bore myself to death within a year."

Gena sat down to enjoy her breakfast, pleased with the outcome. She watched as Cynthia and Miss Edna put their heads together, already planning the opening of the bed-and-breakfast.

Gena and Nate were married at Red Oaks Christian Fellowship on a sunny afternoon in December. They honeymooned on Harbour Island of the Eleuthera Island Group in the Bahamas where they spent a week on a private beach with pink sand and crystal-clear water.

Three months after their return Gena learned she was pregnant. Everyone was overjoyed by the news except Lily, who groused that she was too old to have a baby sister or a brother. However, when the baby, a girl, arrived she doted on her more than anyone else.

Looking at their life together, Gena supposed that things could have turned out differently. Fortunately, for her, though, they didn't.

THE REAL THING

Kim Louise

To Retonya Lasley

Thank you to all my family and friends who keep encouraging me. Kofi Folson. Kenneth Maroney. Michael Maroney. John Bernardi. Beth and Diana at The Bookworm. Cortney at The Meeting Place. My Bozell family.

A special thanks to the wonderful women who share the pages of this anthology with me. Janice, Natalie and Nathasha. I'm honored to be in your presence.

CHAPTER 1

Just when she thought her professional life couldn't get any worse, Justine Graves's boss kept talking.

"...response was forty-two percent less than the projected eighteen percent increase in sales, customer interest, and Web hits. My recommendation is to pull the three remaining spots, retest with the numbers we have, and use those stats to create a course of action."

Well, at least he was tactful. He could have said Justine's idea to profile Value-Mart employees was a rousing failure. Not only did the campaign fall, but it seemed as though Value-Mart's sales had decreased since the start of the ads. Her credibility with her ad agency was in serious jeopardy.

Harold Arturo, director of marketing for Value-Mart, steepled his fingers and stared at the ceiling. "We've only seen half of the ads run. Isn't that right?"

"That's right," Cort Waite said.

"I say we move forward."

"Harold—"

"I believe in the vision," Harold said and glanced at Justine.

Ever since Justine started working on the Value-Mart account, she and Harold had taken to each other like loving relatives. He reminded her of her father. They could be brothers, she'd often thought. The idea had even crossed her mind to get them together for dinner one day. She'd just never made the time.

"I know the vision of our president like I know my own name. I was there when he created it. He believes in people. His people. And Justine understands that." He paused for a minute to let that sink in. "Let's give her concept the full opportunity it deserves."

If Justine hadn't been in a boardroom full of executives, she might have been tearful. But she knew better. In this environment, her composure served her best. That and her intelligence and determination. If Harold was determined to see her vision through to the end, she would put in long days, work in the field, and check stats hourly if she had to, to give the "We Are You" campaign every chance of success.

She would also find some special way of thanking Harold. He deserved it for being in her corner all the way.

Cort glanced at Justine. "I know this is your baby, but I also know you are fair and objective. Should we shoot this project and put it out of its misery or should we shout 'clear' and bring down the paddles?"

Justine smiled with a renewed sense of determination. "Clear!" she shouted.

Her enthusiasm must have caught on. The executives around the table smiled with her and nodded at the decision.

"Cleanup on aisle twelve."

Markos Raineau frowned as the muscles in his stomach

tightened with frustration. That voice was way too sultry to be that of a Value-Mart employee.

It was also too familiar.

He got up from his desk in the manager's office and headed straight for aisle twelve.

Who'd she bribe this time? he wondered, taking long, deliberate strides.

Markos thought that by putting some distance between him and Sabrina, she'd cool off. Be less aggressive. He'd heard that adage about absence making the heart grow fonder. He'd hoped that it would work in his case.

It hadn't.

The distance and days had only helped him realize one thing. He didn't love Sabrina. And if he probed for the deeper truth, he didn't like her much either. She'd just been so…easy. Right there, all the time. Like low-hanging fruit. He just had to reach out a little and there she was. Smiling, pawing with big dreams and wide legs. Something about her, no, everything about her, was too accessible. Lately, he'd started to realize that if Sabrina didn't respect herself, she couldn't possibly respect him.

Lettuce and cabbage blurred into cold cereal, smeared into shampoo and lotion. Health and hygiene. It figured, he said to himself as he turned into aisle twelve. Sabrina stood smack dab in the middle of the condom and lubrication section.

Markos's frustration tipped toward anger.

"Sabrina, I understand you want to get my attention, but this isn't the way to do it."

"Oh yeah? You're here, aren't you?" She stood with

arms outstretched. Everything about her was loose. Hair. Lips. Dress. Hips.

"Only to tell you that at one time, I thought your intercom announcements were sexy, but I was wrong. They aren't."

As a manager, he should have known better than to allow Sabrina to flirt with him on the job, but something about her had been so damned alluring. And that something had gotten the best of his better judgment.

He wouldn't let that happen again.

"You've been hiding from me. Why?"

"I haven't been hiding. Why don't we have dinner and talk about it?"

He didn't have time for foolishness. He was at work. Another thing that Sabrina didn't respect.

She slithered up to him, trying to put her arms around his neck. Instead, he grabbed her wrists and held them at her side.

"Can't you take a break now?" she pleaded.

Markos glanced behind Sabrina to see one of his employees pretending to look for a product. It was the fourth employee he'd seen at the edge of the aisle since he'd gotten there. His relationship with Sabrina was spilling over into his professional life in a less than productive manner. He couldn't allow it to continue one minute more.

"Sabrina, I thought I would be able to talk to you about this privately, but it doesn't look like it's going to happen that way."

She stepped back and eyed him with suspicion.

"Our relationship isn't working. For either of us, I think, but definitely not for me."

"Say what?" she said, blinking hard and planting a hand on her hip.

"I think you'll make a deserving man very happy. But I'm not that man. I'm sorry."

"You sure as hell are!" she shouted. "I can't believe you are breaking up with me like this."

"Trust me. I can't believe it either."

"But why?"

The last thing Markos wanted was a scene. And if he was honest and said, "Baby, you just don't do it for me," he knew there would be one. So he simply said, "I'm just not in the right place for a relationship." Or this conversation, he thought, hoping she would leave now.

"You could have mentioned that before you slept with me."

Sabrina's remark snapped the thread of Markos's frustration. He smiled despite the anger boiling inside him. "Let me walk you out," he said.

Sabrina looked like she could spit. "Don't even," she said, whisking past him. A trail of way too much perfume wafted past him in her wake. He turned away from it, turned away from her, and headed back to his office.

Just as he reached his desk, an all too familiar voice came over the loudspeaker again. A lot less sultry this time.

"Attention, Value-Mart shoppers. Store manager Markos Raineau is a…"

He gritted his teeth at the foulness of her words, picked up the phone on his desk, and dialed security.

"Please make sure that woman gets out of the store quickly and safely," he said.

When Markos hung up the phone, he considered putting a watch out on Sabrina. Just in case she decided to come back to the store for more of her crazy antics. He didn't, though. He decided to give Sabrina the benefit of his doubt. She was upset, but she wasn't crazy. One thing was for sure, it was time for him to put some distance between himself and dating. He hadn't been successful in that arena lately, and Sabrina was a shining example of that fact.

It was time that he concentrated on his job. Value-Mart was on the verge of closing a few stores. His being among them. They just couldn't compete with Wal-Mart and Target.

He was a loyal Value-Mart employee. It was the first place he worked after graduating from college. When he couldn't find a job anywhere else, Value-Mart had hired him and one year later, he'd submitted an application for the management training program. Ten years later he was manager of his own store and regional liaison for three others.

It was becoming very clear to him that no matter what he did, he didn't fully understand women. Retail, on the other hand, he knew as if he'd invented it.

Six months ago, he'd been selected by the regional leadership team to be part of an advertising campaign, geared toward putting a more human feel to Value-Mart. "Not just prices, but people," he'd said into the cameras. Those spots were just beginning to air in the area. He hoped they were helping. It was the first of a long list of things he'd planned to commit himself to in order to save the company that had saved him.

Dating, and all that went along with that, would just have to wait.

* * *

Spots five and six had bombed miserably. Justine sighed at the numbers as she sat behind her desk contemplating next week's update meeting. They hadn't pulled the plug at the last meeting, but there was no avoiding it this time.

She shook her head knowing that there was no way the last spot could make up for the failure of the previous five.

But because of Harold's insistence, they had let the campaign run its course. At least she'd have that. She'd never had to wonder what would have happened if all six Value-Mart spots had aired on television.

The preliminary report for the last spot was due tomorrow. She had her assistant, Craig Daniels, collecting the data. In-store traffic reports were added to phone calls, faxes, e-mails, and Web site hits to determine impact and influence.

Justine had assigned that task to Craig so she could focus on recovery. On how to bounce back from a major campaign that had lost as much money as it cost to create.

She'd just typed a third idea into the project planner on her computer when Craig came briskly into her office.

A quick entry like that could only mean one of two things: something really, really good or really, really bad. The way things had been going, Justine could only imagine it was the latter.

"What is it, Craig?" she said, not wanting to waste time.

"I want a raise," he said. The man's long, lean features and bright smile made him look like a lighted match.

Justine's muscles released the tension they'd held since Craig walked in.

"Thank God. I thought you were in here about We Are You."

He took the seat across from her desk. "Oh, I am. And that's why I need the raise."

"I don't get it," she said.

Craig placed the stack of papers he had in his hands in front of her.

"What's this?" she asked, flipping through the seven spreadsheet pages.

"The stats for the last spot."

At first she was still unclear and then the light dawned in her mind.

"That's why I need the raise. If you want me to crunch *these* numbers, you better come up with a bonus plan or something. I'm good, but what the hell is happening here?"

Justine looked at the numbers again. They were outrageously high in every category. Stats this off-the-chart couldn't possibly be real, could they?

"Is this a computer error?" she asked.

"That was the first thing I checked into."

"So they're real."

"They're real."

Justine closed her eyes and said a *thank you* prayer. Someone was smiling on her. Spot six might not save the day, but at least the campaign would end on a positive note and in a powerful place.

"I had Nancy call our contact at Value-Mart. They are faxing over some of the hard data right now. I told her to bring it in when it comes."

"I can't believe it," Justine said, switching programs on

her computer. She accessed the We Are You file on the shared drive and opened the Manager Spot.

The video program launched on her computer and the man she remembered as Markos Raineau graced the screen.

She'd insisted that they save this spot for last for a reason. Just like the anchor on a relay race, Justine knew this was the strongest commercial. Not only was the writing and editing better, but there was something about Markos. He was personable, honest, compelling, and quite possibly the most handsome man she'd ever seen. Justine knew that if he appealed to the mass audience the way he appealed to her, his spot would be a great way to close the campaign.

"Damn, he's fine!" Nancy said, approaching the side of Justine's desk. She dropped a one-inch stack of papers on her desk and leaned in.

"Play it again, Jus," Nancy said as the commercial came to an end. The woman's fake hair and fake nails never outshadowing her genuine attitude.

Justine ignored her colleague's playful request and flipped through the stack of faxes and e-mails.

It only took a few seconds for her to figure out the documents were all from women and the women wanted one thing: Markos.

Is he single?

Is he married?

Is he involved?

Is he attached?

Is he straight?

Her hopefulness decreased somewhat. "These responses aren't about Value-Mart. They're about—"

"My main man Markos!" Nancy said, beaming.

She still hadn't taken a seat. She looked too geeked up and excited.

Markos wasn't *that* fine, was he? Justine took another flip through the stack of responses.

Maybe he was.

"Well, don't just sit there. Let me see them," Craig demanded.

Justine handed over the stack and watched intently as Craig flipped through.

"This guy is Mack of the year," he said. "Forget Value-Mart. You better put your stock in him!"

"That's the last straw," Justine said. "I'm ready to concede defeat on this one."

She turned back to her computer, saddened and frustrated. "Why don't you two compile what you can, and I'll put the finishing touches on plans B, C, and D?"

Craig got up while Nancy headed for the door. "Do you still want an activity report tomorrow?"

"Yes. Let's see this thing through till the end," Justine said.

Craig nodded. "Sounds good."

He headed out of her office with Nancy not far behind. She paused at the door. "So, is he single?" she asked.

"Go check for more faxes please," Justine responded.

Nancy left her a smile and headed out.

Justine paused for a moment before returning to her work. The numbers on the spreadsheet were some of the highest for any campaign ever. She couldn't help herself. She played the spot again, remembering the first time she'd seen Markos.

Tall and thick. Shoulder-length locks. Skin the color of espresso with smoldering eyes and a smile that could stop traffic. Upon their introduction, heat had immediately rushed to her face and her eyes had immediately traveled to his ring finger. She had been no different than the hundreds of women who'd written, called, and faxed their question.

He was definitely worth inquiring about.

Justine wished she could have predicted this reaction. She probably would have figured out some way to leverage that anticipated response.

Glancing at her backup plans, she wondered if it was too late.

If there was one thing Justine knew, it was her own mind. If she sat still for a few minutes, maybe drank another cup of coffee, she'd figure out a way to leverage this boon and partially salvage the account.

It was just a matter of time.

CHAPTER 2

They'd made Markos bring the mailbags with him. All eight of them. Markos had piled them in the back of his Jeep as if they'd been luggage and he was going on a long trip.

But they weren't luggage. They were letters. Bags of them. And the only trip he was going on was across town to the Value-Mart Regional Office Building to meet with representatives of Basco & Graves Ad Agency.

As Marko approached a stoplight in downtown Red Oaks, his mind could not wrap itself around the fact that the commercial, which he'd been volunteered for, had not only done well but had surpassed the previous spots by like a go-zillion. At least that's the figure his boss had used when he'd spoken to him about it.

Markos wished that Nigel Watts was with him now to meet with the ad people. Unfortunately, he wouldn't be able to join them until lunchtime.

So for the first hour, Markos would be alone, unless Phil Banister from Value-Mart could make it. He was flying in from corporate for the meeting, but his flight had been delayed. He would be landing just as the meeting got started at ten.

It figured. And that had been the story of his retail life.

Stepping in when the regional directors were: away, unavailable, ill, MIA, hungover, or just plan unable to do what needed to be done. He'd made a name and a track record for himself by making the hard decisions when no one else wanted to. It had gotten him a reputation in Value-Mart Industries and made him one of the most experienced regional managers on staff.

His rise within the company hadn't come smoothly, though. Not everyone was pleased with his decisions and his impatience to let things come "in time." Value-Mart was an old industry. Old and set in its ways. It moved at a trimethodon's pace. Markos knew his quick actions had seemed to some like he was the Tasmanian Devil. But companies like Wal-Mart and Target were walking all over his company, and he wasn't going down without a fight. So the fact that his spot was doing well was music to his ears. Even as misguided as they were, the women who'd suddenly taken an interest in him had also taken an interest in Value-Mart. Sales were up. And whatever this meeting was about, Markos would make it clear that he was in it to win it. If that meant making another commercial, or whatever, he'd do it.

On Fifth and Vine, where the old warehouses had all been torn down and replaced by high-tech office buildings, the corporate headquarters of Value-Mart Industries sat sandwiched between two glass information-age monoliths. A throwback to a simpler time, VMI held court in the oldest building in the area. Markos entered the brick parking garage, and parked his Jeep in the space reserved for management. He grabbed one of the mailbags and headed toward the lobby.

Inside, the office building belied its exterior. Although not on a grand scale, the ten-story building held a comforting and velvety grace. Upscale all the way.

Markos signed in at the front desk and made his way to the fifth floor and the office of Broderick Stansfield. At Value-Mart, Rick Stansfield was God, or at least the employees seemed to think so. No matter what it was, from sales figures to sales campaigns, Rick made it happen. You needed numbers, Rick got them for you. He was the go-to guy for...everything. His official title was director of process improvement. But the reality was, Rick had his hands in every part of the business and was the catalyst for any positive, lasting, sustained change the company had for the past ten years. He was a visionary and a motivator. No one reported to him, but he reported to everyone. Whenever Markos thought about what Rick did, he thought about Tom Hanks in *Big*.

Markos was an attractive man. Even he knew that. He'd noticed his ability to bring out the blush in women when he was in high school. Over the years, he'd become accustomed to it. Come to appreciate it. Come to think of it as normal, as just something that happened, like the sun coming up every morning. But since the commercial, it was like whatever appeal he had with women had increased by a factor of eighteen. The looks he got now were bold and much more thorough. Even in the office building, as he made his way to Rick's office, the women literally stopped in their tracks to watch him. And a low buzz of whispers followed him as he walked.

"Love your commercial," one woman said as she passed.

Damn, Markos thought. Bold, but definitely not beautiful.

He turned the corner, hefted the bag onto his shoulder, and stopped at Rick's office door.

A man and a woman were already seated across from Rick in the only available seats in the office.

Markos cleared his throat. "You ready for me?" he asked.

"Hey!" Rick said and rose from his seat.

He walked around his desk with his long arm extended. Markos took the man's hand and the two shook vigorously.

"Now, there's the man of the hour!"

Markos couldn't help but smile at the man's exuberance.

"Come on in." Rick motioned to the individuals seated across from his desk.

"Markos, this is Justin Graves. President of Olmec Broadcasting."

Markos extended his hand to the older gentleman. The man was tall and thin. His close-cropped hair was completely gray. He had wise eyes, a firm handshake, and looked as though he hadn't bought a suit off the rack in forty years.

"Mr. Raineau," he said.

The fact that the man knew his last name was not lost on Markos. "Mr. Graves," Markos returned.

Rick took a step toward the woman sitting next to Justin. She had the same wise eyes. No mistaking that they were related.

"And this is Justine Graves, president of Basco and Graves Advertising."

Now, she's *beautiful,* Markos thought, remembering. He extended his hand.

"Good to see you again, Mr. Raineau," she said.

Her voice was deep, rich, and sounded remarkably like the man's. Father? Markos wondered.

"And you," Markos responded, and meant it. The only part of the commercial shoot he'd liked was the view of Justine Graves. The shoot hadn't been "fun" as his family and friends had imagined. It had been work. Very hard work. If Markos had ever romanticized actors and the jobs they did, he'd let go of those notions after the first hour of taping. He'd stick to what he did best, straight-up supply and demand, product to people, retail.

Suddenly, flashbacks of cameras filming him from all angles flooded his memory. And...*action! Take one. Take two. Take twenty-five. This time with feeling. Make the camera believe it.* On second thought, he'd take back what he said. He'd resist doing another commercial with every ounce of energy he had. By the time he'd left the shoot, his face itched from the makeup, his eyes were dry from all the lights, his throat was sore from all the talking, and he thought he'd never be able to get his lines out of his head for as long as he lived. He repeated them so often, he didn't know if he'd ever be able to say anything but those lines. If that was acting, Markos would be a happy audience member for the rest of his life.

Markos dropped the mailbag on the floor.

"Is *that* the mail?" Justine asked, smiling.

"Yeah," Markos said. "There are more like this in my car."

Justine slammed her fist into her hand and grinned at the man Markos believed was her father. "I knew it!"

A feeling of unease crept through Markos. "What's this meeting about exactly?" he asked.

Rick looked to Justin, to Justine, and then to Markos. "Well, I wanted to wait until the marketing team was here, but they'll just have to catch up. Come on. Let's go to the conference room."

The four of them headed toward Value-Mart's state-of-the-art conference room and media center.

Before they even entered the conference room, Markos felt as though he had to make his intentions clear. "Rick, if this is about another commercial—"

"Not even," Rick assured him.

Justine smiled in a way that bothered Markos. The smile said she knew exactly what was going on. Everybody did. And he was being kept in the dark deliberately.

"Hey, Markos!"

The call came from a woman in a large corner cubicle. He could never remember her name. It was either Mirna or Marny. Heck, maybe it was Mildred. He was bad with names, but good with figures. And her figure was one he remembered. They'd had a good time at a bad hotel seven years ago.

"Hey, M!" he said, hoping to cover his bases. He gave her a smile and flashed the eyes women were always commenting on.

"It's Beverly!" she called. "Remember? Bev-er-ly!" She smiled back at him as though he hadn't flubbed her name.

Damn. I'm terrible.

"In here," Rick said.

The massive two-hundred-seat conference room had

been cordoned off. The piece of room they entered had all of the features and none of the size. The movable walls had been put in place to resize the room to accommodate twenty or fewer employees. Perfect for their meeting if the members of the marketing team arrived before the big reveal.

Justine checked out the equipment for a moment and then said, "It will only take me a minute to set up."

The men took their seats. The unease in Markos turned into frustration. "Rick—"

Rick held up his hand. "Just hold on, Bubba. You're gonna love this."

Markos shook his head. Rick had to know he seriously doubted his words.

"So, Mr. Raineau, how long have you been in retail?"

"All my life," Markos said. "At least it feels like it."

Justin smiled. "I can tell you mean that in a good way."

"Absolutely. Everyone has a purpose, Mr. Graves. I believe mine is to find out what people want and make sure they get it."

"Hmmm," Justine said. "I'm glad to hear you say that."

"Ready?" Rick asked.

"Ready," Justine said.

Rick got up, killed the lights, and retook his seat. "I've put together a presentation to show you the preliminary results of the We Are You campaign."

For the next five minutes, Markos sat through an electronic slide show of charts, graphs, numbers, and figures concerning the campaign. The numbers were dismal and after the first minute, Markos found himself fighting sleep.

Then Justine clicked a button on her laptop and his commercial came to life on the screen in front of them.

He'd only seen the darn thing once. All the other times it had come on television, he'd turned away—reluctant to see how the editor used the worst takes and spliced together a testimony to Value-Mart and their devotion to their customers.

After his commercial, more figures. These numbers were different, better. Dramatically better. And after that, another click.

"Hi. My name is Shondra Lewis. I just wanted to know if someone there could tell me about that Markos guy. I mean...is he really a Value-Mart manager? And does he have a wife?"

Markos could not hide his shock. "There are phone calls?"

Justine played sound file after sound file. All women. All wanting the same thing.

Him.

"This is crazy!" he said finally.

Two calls were flattering. Two more interesting. Two more disconcerting. And the rest, just plain off the chain.

"I think you are, what they call, a hit," Justin said.

"A *big* hit," Justine corrected. "And that's why we're here. We want to strike while the iron is hot and leverage your popularity into something spectacular."

If Markos had reservations about doing a commercial before, he really had them now after hearing those women. Images of ten, fifteen, fifty Sabrinas and Bev-er-lys with their hands on their hips in his store saying, "Why haven't you called me?" flashed before Markos's eyes. Nothing like that had happened, but already he felt the impact of the commercial was out of hand.

Justine smiled broadly. "You are single, aren't you?"

"Who's asking?" Markos said, feigning nervousness.

Justin and Rick chuckled.

"Me," Justine replied.

"Well, in that case, yes."

Markos saw the woman let out a tremendous sigh.

"Remember what you said about giving people what they want?"

"Yes," Markos said, dragging out the word cautiously.

"Well, my father and I are here to do exactly that. We want to give the people you."

"Come again?" Markos said.

"A TV show!" Rick shouted. "Can you believe that? A freakin' TV show. They want to build the whole thing around you and all the women who want to get to know you."

Markos felt as if someone had set him adrift on a tiny raft with no rations and days to go before he would reach the shore. "You have got to be kidding."

"Not at all," Justin said.

"Markos Raineau...if everything goes right...Olmec Broadcasting and Basco and Graves are going to find you a woman!"

CHAPTER 3

Damn, I'm good, Justine thought. *I'm talking to this man like he's just a regular human being instead of the finest man I've ever seen.*

From the precious moment that Markos walked into Rick's office, Justine had the overpowering urge to fan herself...between her legs. This brotha was some kinda hot. Only...was he a brotha? He looked like he had some African descent in him, but it wasn't in there alone. There was some Polynesian, Hawaiian, Pacific island kinda stuff up in there, too. Her curious nature couldn't wait to find out what it was.

If there was one thing about Justine, she had a way of finding out any information she needed to know about anything.

Her attraction to the man was getting the best of her. He looked as though he was packing up to leave the meeting and she hadn't said anything to stop him.

"Hey, Markos, what's, what's going on? What are you doing?"

He stood. All six-one, two hundred pounds of him, she surmised. "You all are talkin' crazy."

"Mr. Raineau—"

"Markos!" they called after him.

"Tell Nigel and Phil that I went back to the store, would you?"

He headed toward the door. Baby boy got back, Justine thought. Then she realized that that baby boy held the key to her struggling business. He was the last straw. Once that straw walked out on the project, the camel's back would be broken.

And so would Justine's company. Broken in a way that no one could repair.

"Mr. Raineau, please," she said. Her plea stopped him at the conference room door. He turned slowly. The fluorescent light flashing in his eyes made him seem magical. Almost not real. Just a 3-D work of art for women to drool over and rub themselves against.

"Yes?" he said.

"Please," she said, thinking about her disintegrating business. "Please just listen to what I have to say. Stay for the proposal, at least. Give your colleagues a chance to arrive."

She waited. He waited. He hadn't left yet.

"Then if you still think it's a crazy idea, well, then…" She took a deep breath and conjured the confidence she needed to finish that thought. "Then we won't pressure you to do anything you really are dead set against."

He took his time looking into the faces of everyone in the conference room. The expression on his face looked as though he still could not believe what he was seeing and hearing.

"You all really want to do this? A television show?"

"Yes."

"A local show?" he asked, looking a little less tense.

"National," Justine's father said.

Rick went to Markos's side and took the duffel bag from him. "Sit down, buddy. Hear us out."

Markos shook his head as if he were trying to shake off a hangover. Without another word, he took his seat.

Justine let go a deep, long sigh. *Make this good,* she told herself.

She continued with her presentation, showing the preliminary proposal for a reality series called *That Value-Mart Guy*. She'd gotten the title from the plethora of e-mails that the company had received that started, "I'm writing to find out more about that Value-Mart guy I saw on television."

Justine spoke in her best saleswoman voice and enthusiasm. She mustered all her energy and did her best to make the idea sound like the greatest thing since *The Real World*—the show that gave birth to the entire reality TV craze.

All the while, she kept her brown eyes on Markos. He was as stoic as a granite wall. He sat and stared. Barely breathing. Barely blinking. But the intensity in his eyes was unmistakable. He was indeed taking it all in. But so far, his rigid posture led her to believe that despite her best efforts, she hadn't said anything to convince him to do the show.

When Nigel and Phil finally came into the meeting, Justine thought she might have some more leverage. They'd been briefed about the project and for the most part were on board with at least considering the idea. And Justine had done her homework. She'd found out that

Value-Mart and her own company had something in common. They were both on the verge of going extinct. Both companies needed something drastic, something powerful—hell, a miracle to pull them out of the hole they'd slid into. The proper execution of her idea could be the boon both companies needed to recover. At the very least, if they did the show and neither company was saved, they would at least go out with a bang.

"Even with a few snags in the project plan, we could be ready to shoot within three months," Justine said in conclusion. The culmination, of course, would be if one of the women on the show actually managed to catch the man's true interest.

Always prepared, Justine opened her portfolio and took the handout packets that summarized her presentation. She handed them out to everyone. The men flipped through the pages with some interest. All except Markos, who'd been silent the entire time.

Not being one to beat around the bush, Justine plunged ahead. "Well?" she asked. "What do you think?"

She knew she should have been asking the higher-ups. The ones with the money and power to greenlight her idea. But she'd directed her query to Markos—the nucleus of the whole thing.

It felt to Justine like the entire world was holding its breath. Despite her energy and enthusiasm, Justine held her breath, too, and waited for a response from Markos. Not wanting to get her hopes up, she braced herself for the "Hell no" she hoped wouldn't come. What she got instead shocked not only her, but everyone in the room.

Markos laughed. And not just a jovial vibrant laugh. His laughter was raucous, loudly boisterous. He started packing up again, and this time Justine could tell there was no stopping him.

He gathered his things—Mont Blanc pen, leather portfolio, PDA, and handout packet—and kept right on laughing.

"Mr. Raineau," her father began, but it was no use. He waved off the comment and then wiped the tears from his eyes.

"You, you all, have a nice day," Markos said between chuckles and headed quickly out of the conference room door.

Everyone stared at each other for a moment, not knowing quite what to do. Then Phil leaned forward, took a sip of the Starbucks coffee he came in with, and said, "I for one think it's an exceptional idea. However, three months seems a bit long to wait. Any chance we can get this thing rolling in, say…three weeks?"

"Do you think legal will be ready by then?" Nigel asked.

"Leave them to me," Phil said.

Confusion rose inside Justine and she took a seat next to her father. Suddenly, her feet were killing her and all she wanted to do was get the heck out of her panty hose and unsnap her push-up bra. "Did I miss something here? I don't think Markos is interested."

"But, my dear, Justine, is it?" Phil asked.

She nodded.

"*We* are interested. Now, we've read over your contract, Mr. Graves. As we speak, they are poring over the pages and preparing their counteroffer. But let me assure you, this is something we're prepared to move forward with."

Justine shook her head. Did they not just see Markos laugh his way out of the meeting?

Nigel leaned over and touched her on the forearm. "In other words, Justine, we're ready on the business end."

Justine's father looked her in the eye. "This was your idea, sweetheart. And it's a good one. Are you willing to see it through?"

Justine realized that all the men in the room were looking to her to get Markos on board. Rarely did Justine turn away from a challenge. And even if it hadn't come down to her, she would have taken on the challenge anyway. There was too much at stake for her not to break out all the stops to see her dream come to life. If the man, handsome though he might be, turned her down after that, then it just wasn't meant to be. But until then, she was going to give this project everything she had.

"Give me a week," Justine said.

That was last Friday. By Tuesday, Justine was starting to get worried. She'd called, e-mailed, and even faxed Markos. He'd ignored her like she was a dead fly on a windowsill. She'd even gone to the store and staked out his office. But Markos was a smart man. He'd obviously trained his staff well at ways in which to keep her away from him.

After four days, Justine started to wonder if Markos was some kind of coward. He hadn't responded to her in any way.

Justine was starting to wonder about the wisdom of her

actions. She'd started to focus all of her creative energy on the reality TV project. She wondered remotely what business she was missing out on by devoting so much time to getting a response from Markos.

But that business couldn't save her. Markos could.

As she walked around the store, she noted that it was small in terms of superstore size. But it had everything you would expect from a superstore. One-stop shopping. From pedicures to Pedialite. From Vienna sausage to Viagra. You could get it at Value-Mart. It was like a little village or castle you never had to leave.

One thing that surprised her was the age of the clientele. It seemed to be women and men—mostly women—over the age of forty. While they certainly were the power centers of the country—holding the vast majority of the United States' wealth, according to Justine's marketing sources—studies showed that more and more consumers in that age bracket were turning to the Internet and online shopping networks to get their goods. That trend could account for the decline in Value-Mart's sales.

The ad featuring Markos had been a success on more than just the human interest level. It had generated interest in a whole new generation of consumers. It made Justine even more proud of her work. Now if she could just take her work to the next level.

Maybe I should just ride up on his house after work, she thought.

Somewhere in the contract files, she had to have Markos's address. She pulled out her BlackBerry and was about to call Nancy for the information when the man himself strode in the front door of the store.

He slowed his pace when he saw her.

"Your people are well trained," she said.

"They better be," he responded.

There was no time to take it slow with this man. And something about him told her he would appreciate the quick, straight truth. "I've come to change your mind."

He gave her an appraising look. Head to toe. Nice and slow. She guessed he was trying to figure out who she thought she was.

The man had no idea.

She was a woman used to getting exactly what she wanted. Although she believed Markos was a man to be reckoned with, she was in every way up to the challenge.

"I thought I made my decision clear when I walked out of that meeting."

"Have you thought about what this could mean for your company?"

"Yes."

"And?"

"And the execs want me to do it, but they're leaving the final decision to me."

"What kind of man wouldn't want his own television show—with a dozen or so beautiful women vying for his attention?"

"This kind," he said and maneuvered around her.

"Markos, wait!" she said, hearing the desperation in her voice. She caught up with him as he went through a huge set of double doors and headed toward back offices.

"Don't you realize you could save your company?"

He turned to her, his strikingly sexy eyes bearing down on her so heavily she felt their weight. "I have every intention of helping to save this company, but my plan has nothing to do with reality television." He spat the words out like bitter seeds.

"Now, really, Ms. Graves. I've been out of the office for almost a week. I have a lot of catching up to do."

His words ricocheted in her head. Out of the office.

"You've been out of the office?"

He picked up a stack of mail a foot thick, frowned, and rifled through it. "Yes."

"I've been trying to contact you for that long. I thought you were avoiding me."

His eyes took on that smoldering look again. The one like when they first met. "I would never try to avoid you, Justine."

Hmm, she thought. *I think he's flirting. Not only do I like it, but maybe I can use that to my advantage.*

"Markos, I'm going to be very forward here and ask you out. Let me take you to dinner. We'll talk some more about the project. I'll answer every question you have. And if you still aren't on board after that, then at least I can say I did everything I could to persuade you."

His eyebrow rose. She knew what he was thinking.

"Everything within reason, Mis-ter Raineau."

He smiled then and licked the most kiss-a-luscious pair of lips Justine had ever seen. Just that action alone made her want to rush home and check the batteries of a device that hadn't seen use in a long, long time.

She couldn't keep her eyes off his lips and the way they moved when he spoke. Spoke!

"I'm sorry, what?" she said, chiding herself for spacing out.

"I said, I accept."

Justine warmed inside. "Good."

"I like Italian, Persian, Indian, Japanese, and southern."

"What? No Mexican?"

"No Mexican."

"Darn. That cancels out Señor Matias. How about Ahmad's?"

"Sounds good. Pick me up at seven." Markos retrieved the Mont Blanc pen from his shirt pocket and wrote his address on the back of his business card.

Justine smiled. "Get ready to be wined and dined."

His eyes flashed in a way that sent her soul into sensual meltdown. "I'm always ready for that, Ms. Graves."

CHAPTER 4

"Okay. You really have to stop looking at me like that."

"Sorry. When I find a woman attractive, it shows in my eyes. I've tried to control it over the years, but these caramel browns of mine always tell the truth, no matter how I might try to camouflage the situation."

"That must get you into all kinda trouble."

"All the time," he said. His smile was almost as deadly and devastating as his eyes.

They made it through soup, salad, and most of their meal without a single word about the TV show. They'd talked about themselves instead.

They both lived in Red Oaks, Georgia. Both came from small families. Both put themselves through college. And they both wanted to be millionaires by the time they were forty.

"So, your business. It's called Basco and Graves. Who's Basco?"

"Basco is Averil Basco. My best friend at one time. When we decided to go into business together, everyone we knew said 'Don't do it. It will ruin your friendship.' Our response was 'They don't know us like we know us. We can *do* this.'

"And we did it for a while. Business wasn't booming but it was all right. Promising, you know?

"We'd just made it over that three-year milestone and a major client that we had went out of business. So, that coupled with a slumping economy had Basco and Graves with a fight on its hands. But instead of sticking it out, Averil decided she wanted out of the business."

"Did you buy her out?"

"Yeah. I've been trying to keep my baby afloat ever since."

Markos sat back in his chair and eyed Justine with suspicion. "So this is a rescue mission."

"What do you mean?"

"Don't do that. Don't go stupid. We've been having a good time tonight. Don't mess it up. Just be honest. This isn't about your excitement about the project, or me, or bolstering Value-Mart. This is about your company having one foot in the grave."

"Markos—"

"If you deny it, I'll get up from this table and never speak to you again. Now tell the truth. This dinner tonight is nothing more than you bending over your company, administering mouth to mouth."

Justine looked into Markos's eyes. The smoldering attraction she'd seen there not ten minutes ago had vanished, replaced by suspicion and distaste.

She wanted a lot from Markos, and for that he deserved the truth.

"Mostly. Yes. I'm here because I want to save my company."

Justine wasn't a crier, but a lump formed in her throat

nevertheless. "Every morning, before I go to the office, I play that song 'Survivor' by Destiny's Child and I sing my can't-carry-a-tune ass off. I've had a real easy life, Mr. Raineau. My dad's a media executive and my mom is a chemist for Pfizer. This company is the first thing I've ever done on my own. And I want it to live and breathe and be alive. Right now, it's on life support. It needs..." She paused for a moment to keep the tears back. "It needs an organ transplant. And you are the right type, Markos. I need you—my company needs you."

Markos studied the woman, the determination in her face, the tension in her body, the sadness in her voice, and had to admit he was moved.

He thought back to when he first saw her. It was during the shooting of the commercial. She'd kept herself out of the way, yet still managed to add her creative input to the process. Every time they took a break, he'd noticed her talking to the director and coordinator. Mentioning things to the photographer. Hair and makeup people. And it wasn't intrusive. It was subtle, but impactful. He thought the shoot was better because of it.

Yes. He'd noticed her. He was certain every man there had noticed her. She was something to look at. Sultry eyes, sweet smile. Gently sloping features. Great hips. The kind of woman men imagined naked immediately and then plotted ways of getting her that way.

So far, Markos had invented at least seventy-five scenarios and he was working on number seventy-six at the moment.

Justine straightened in the chair and lifted her chin. The

move was subtle and Markos liked it. Never let 'em see you sweat. She wasn't about to show how vulnerable she was. But he could tell anyway. Something about Justine was so easy for him to read. As if her emotions were transparent to him or that she'd allowed him to see inside her. Either way, Markos thought that she was sexy as hell. If she kept that up, what he was about to agree to would make it difficult for him to keep his eyes and hands off her.

Justine rose and smoothed the wrinkles out of her skirt. "I understand silence, Markos. I thank you for your time, though."

She turned to leave and Markos stood quickly.

"Hold on," he said. "One thing you'd better learn about me fast is not to make assumptions. Some people are easy to read, but me...not so much."

"Are you saying you'll do it?"

Markos took a deep breath, wondering just exactly what he was getting into. "I am."

The smile that rose in her came from deep inside her. By the time it reached her face, her mouth, it was on full beam. He'd never seen a woman bloom like that right before his very eyes. Fascinating. She was radiant.

"Markos!" she said, extending her hand. "It will be great. We'll keep it professional. Not at all hokey. And we'll find you someone. Someone special. Someone you'll be happy to have."

Markos wasn't the least bit interested in finding someone special. After Sabrina, he needed a long break from relationships. And he had no illusions about finding true love on a reality television show. It was all for ratings, advertising, and promotion. It was all about money and that was the only real thing about them. He did believe, though, that he might be able to help his company *and* Justine's. Accomplishing that might be worth enduring the outrageous notion of being on television.

"You come with the deal, right?" he asked against his better judgment.

"Excuse me?"

"You. You're going to be on set during this?"

"Well, maybe to start."

"So you're just going to feed me to the television lions and walk away?"

Her face flushed, warming the red undertones in her skin. "No! I wouldn't do that. Of course I would visit the set periodically, just to make sure things are going well."

"So how important is this?"

"Very."

"Then I think you should be there the whole time."

"Why does it matter to you?"

Markos hesitated. He wondered if he should be truthful and tell her that the only reason he'd consented to the show was her. Her conviction, her emotion, her passion, and because he hadn't been able to have one thought independent of her face, her sultry voice, or the mouth he'd imagined setting into for a long luxurious kiss.

He scraped together his composure.

"Justine, I'm going to level with you." He persuaded her to retake her seat. The perfume she wore should have been called Sex in a Bottle. It made him want to forget where he was.

"The only reason I'm doing this is you. Not the attention, not my business or yours."

Her eyes widened. "Markos, I don't know how to respond to that."

"I'm not asking you to. I just want my motives to be clear."

She looked as though she'd just become ten years younger. "And those would be?"

"That when this thing is over you will let me take you away for a weekend. Aspen or Barbados."

The look in her eyes made him feel cocky and self-assured. "You won't be sorry."

"You talk a good game, Mr. Raineau."

"And I can back up every inch of it."

Justine ignored his borderline crass remark. She'd gotten what she wanted. She was happy. By the time the show was over, she'd know what kind of man she was dealing with and whether he was worthy of going away with. Her finely tuned instincts told her that he was and that he meant what he'd said about doing it for her. She'd felt his eyes hot against her skin more than once. She knew he was attracted. Truth was, she was feeling him just as strongly. But she knew where her loyalties were. To her company and her client and her father. She couldn't—she wouldn't—do anything to mess that up.

"What about the last woman standing?"

"Don't worry. I'll make it good for the ratings."

Justine nodded.

She studied him for a moment and thought she saw a slight smile beneath his delicious-looking lips and groomed mustache.

"Is there anything else?" he asked.

"No," she said, strangely wishing there were. It had been a while since a man had looked at her the way Markos did. Not just with lust or carnal attraction. There was something deeper and more respectfully longing in his eyes. And she liked it.

"As soon as we're ready, someone from my staff will call you."

He nodded.

She looked down and remembered her dessert sitting in front of her. She didn't look up. She just started eating.

"Barbados," he said.

Justine concealed her smile by licking her lips and taking a sip of coffee. But it wasn't the beverage making her hot.

Lord, but this man is fine. It would be a piece of cake finding twelve women who'd like to become romantically involved with him.

Justine decided to make sure that Markos had his pick of the best of the best. As she thought more about it, a sadness inside her made her wish that she wasn't in charge of the project. Seeing him just might make her crazy enough to apply for one of the contestant slots.

But that was crazy and she was determined. Nothing would jeopardize her or her intentions. Nothing!

CHAPTER 5

"Next!" Justine yelled. *My God,* she thought. *Aren't there* any *decent single women in the world?*

"What was wrong with her?" Bernie Singer asked. Bernie was the executive producer for the show and had graciously allowed Justine to be part of the selection committee.

"She's too, too..." Justine didn't even have the words to describe how wrong the woman was.

"She would have added conflict and interest, Justine."

"That's what you said about the last one."

"And the one before that. But you keep vetoing the ones who will ensure ratings."

Justine was the tiebreaker. Two people from Olmec Broadcasting and two marketing professionals from Value-Mart were also in the decision-making team. Whenever there was a split decision, Justine got to add her two cents and so far her two cents had added up to thousands of dollars in revenue—lost revenue, according to the marketing folks and the producers.

Value-Mart had turned their conference room into an audition center.

Casting calls had gone out across all the reality TV information Web sites and quite a few local media outlets.

The response was double what they'd predicted. Based on experience with other shows, they expected one thousand applications. When just over two thousand came to the station, Justine's father hired additional staff just to handle the overflow.

"I thought we were looking for a certain feel," Justine said.

"What we're looking for is a moneymaker, and we won't have one if you keep letting in all the sweetbread types and shutting down the hoochies."

"Look, Markos is a good man. He deserves a good woman. Shenaynay and all her ghetto-fabulous cousins just don't fit the bill."

"What do you care? I thought you were in this to save your business."

Justine clamped her mouth shut to keep from calling the young producer out of his name. "I'm in this because it's a good idea. A good idea that I happened to come up with."

"So what's your problem?"

"My problem is all these women you all seem to want are just all wrong. At least for Markos."

"And you know that because..."

Justine started at the sound of that voice and turned toward the direction it came from. Markos strolled into the conference room looking so deliciously luscious in a tan body shirt and Dockers that Justine forgot her name, where she was, and what she was doing.

Her father came in beside Markos wearing a suit and his classic Graves smile. "I thought we needed a sixth opinion. So I called in the man himself. I know it's not customary to allow the talent to have a say in the selection process, but I decided to make an exception in this case, because my daughter seems determined to make choosing the seven women difficult."

Markos strode over to the seat next to her and sat down. He smelled divine, like he'd just stepped out of the shower and was still wet and slightly soapy.

"So, gentlemen. Fill me in. Who've we got so far?"

"Justine, since you seem hell-bent on taking this thing over, why don't you bring Markos up to speed?" Bernie insisted.

Justine opened the file in the middle of the table and removed the eight-by-ten head shots of the three women they'd selected. She briefed him on their backgrounds and summarized how well they did on their interviews and screen tests.

He stared at her and listened closely to what she had to say. He nodded, seemingly taking it all in.

"How many more are there to see today?" he asked.

"Eight," Bernie said.

"I'm ready when you all are."

"I just want to be honest with you, Mr. Raineau. We will take your opinions and suggestions into consideration, but the ultimate decision goes to the green-lighters upstairs."

"I understand," he said. And he did. Markos had no doubt that the nods would go to whoever the network thought would generate the most ratings. He was just glad that he had been asked to come in at all. Hopefully, he could bring some sensibility to the choices.

He still didn't quite understand what was going on

with Justine and why she was so disagreeable. She must have gotten up on the wrong side of the bed. Maybe her man made her mad this morning. Didn't give her any. Or more likely, didn't give her any more. She seemed like the kind of woman who wasn't easily satisfied. Which could also account for the problem.

"We want attractive, diverse, and interesting," Bernie said.

Markos smiled. "In other words, eye candy, polarized, and confrontational."

"You learn fast, Mr. Raineau."

Markos nodded. "I've been around the block a few times."

He slid a glance in Justine's direction. She seemed unaffected by his remark, but the hint of warmth growing just below the surface of her cheeks told him otherwise.

His instincts hadn't been wrong. There was an attraction between them. It wasn't one-sided, thank God.

Well, this ought to be interesting, he thought. Justine, helping to select women for him to—

"Hey," Markos called, getting Justine's attention. "What's the prize for this thing? An expensive date? Weekend getaway?"

"Marriage," Bernie said, without breaking his cool.

"Marriage!" Markos and Justine echoed.

"Yes. Didn't you get your memos? We've retitled the show *Marrying Markos*. We're lining up plans for a five-star wedding to take place as the last episode."

Markos stood. "Whoa, whoa. I didn't agree to anything like that."

"Sure you did," Phil chimed in. "Read your contract. There's an 'other duties as assigned' clause."

Nigel's eyes sparkled with mischief. "Of course, we can't control what you do once the show's over. I mean, honestly, I don't know any of those reality show marriages that have lasted twenty-four hours past the last taping. So...there's that."

Markos ran a hand down the front of his face. He was going to kill his sister. Such a hotshot lawyer. She'd reviewed the paperwork for him and told him it was okay to sign. But she'd been trying to get him married for years. She probably read the changes in the contract and kept her mouth shut.

Yep, he was going to kill her or at least shake her until her teeth rattled.

"Y-y-you can't be serious. I mean, this man didn't know anything about the change. Hell, I didn't know anything about the change and this whole show was my idea! How can you do this?"

Markos touched Justine's arm. "Slow your role, little mama. It's cool. We'll figure it out."

"But," she began, seemingly in some sort of a panic.

"What other changes did you make?" Markos asked.

"We reduced the number of women from twelve to seven. We just couldn't get the dollars for any more weeks than it would take to whittle down the seven. Sorry."

"Don't be," Markos said. He smiled for the first time since he'd arrived. That was the best news he'd heard since the whole reality TV mess started.

Justine seemed pleased with the idea as well.

"Only seven, huh?"

She didn't even bother to hide her delight.

Damn, Markos thought. *It's like we're already dating.* This woman was relieved that the competition had been narrowed down already.

That word, *competition,* stuck in his mind and wouldn't budge. He wondered if Justine saw herself as competing for his attention. Well, one thing was for certain. He couldn't wait to find out.

"So," he said, cracking his knuckles and getting comfortable in the chair. "Let's get 'er done!"

The next woman came into the room, escorted by a dorky-looking kid who couldn't have been out of college yet.

After the barrage of prepared questions the network and agency came up with, like "Tell us about yourself. What was it about Markos that made you enter the contest? How do you plan to win?" Markos decided to ask a few questions of his own. Questions that weren't on the list.

"Why are you single?"

"I'm sorry?" the woman asked, blinking nervously.

"I assume you're single. You're obviously beautiful and intelligent. So, what's up?"

Bernie seemed impressed. He smiled and picked up his pen to write her response.

"Because the last man I dated was a freakin' jerk and I hope he rots in hell!"

"Thank you," Markos said. "We'll be in touch."

The woman nodded, stood, and left the room quickly.

Justine turned to him, her eyes firing accusations before she even spoke. "So, what was wrong with her?"

"Man hater," he said.

"Just because she had a bad experience with a guy?"

"No," he said and turned so he could get a better look at her beautiful face. "Because a guy had a bad experience with *her*."

Justine frowned.

"Trust me. Men can tell."

"Are you here to help or hinder?"

"Look, there's only one reason why a woman her age is single. She's toxic to men. Otherwise, she'd have one."

"That's not true. I'm older than she is, and I'm single."

He just stared at her and let the implications of her words hang in the air. He wasn't about to touch that with any kind of pole, six-foot or otherwise.

"You don't even know me," she proclaimed.

He got serious then and lowered his voice so only the two of them could hear. "But I'd like to."

"Next!" she called as if she were calling for relief and escape.

The intern escorted in Tamera Sullivan, the next woman on the list according to his agenda. Markos liked her immediately. She wore a pantsuit that made her legs look incredibly long. Her brown hair was thick, curly, and hung just below her shoulders. And the best part wasn't the slow curves of her body, it was her sweet face. She looked as though she'd never told a lie, sped through a yellow light, or fudged the weight on her driver's license in her entire life.

"Hello," she said in a voice as innocent as she appeared.

Someone like her would make this madness of a reality TV show bearable.

"I want her," Markos said.

Justine turned to him with the dirtiest look on her face. "Can we interview her first?"

"Knock yourself out, but I want her on the show."

After a few uncomfortable seconds, Justine spoke up. "Ms. Sullivan?"

"Yes?"

"Would you care to have a seat?"

"Actually, I'd just as soon stand. I took a lot of time pressing this suit. I managed to keep it wrinkle-free getting over here, and if I can I'd like to keep it that way."

"Welcome to the show!" Markos said.

Bernie fidgeted in his seat. "Ms. Sullivan, let's be clear that although we will take Mr. Raineau's wishes into consideration, the final decision rests with the network."

"I understand," she said, speaking directly to Bernie. Then she turned to Markos and her smile brightened the room. "I appreciate you wanting me. I guess I must want you, too, or else why would I be here?"

"Uh-uh," Justine mumbled under her breath.

"Don't knock it," Markos said.

"I'm knockin' it," Justine replied.

While Markos and Justine listened, Bernie took the time to ask the questions on the list. Tamera answered every question with poise and a quiet honor.

"Well, that's it, Ms. Sullivan. Thank—"

"Hold on," Justine said. "Just one more question."

She stole a sideways glance at Markos and then turned back to Tamera. "Why are you single?"

Tamera, whose body had been an artistry of fluidity and grace, stiffened. Her smile disappeared and she simply stared in Justine's direction.

After a few moments, Justine broke the silence. "Do you need me to repeat the question?"

Markos thought Justine was bordering on rude, but he had to admit, he wondered as much.

"No, ma'am," she said. That's when Markos saw the tears.

They made her eyes appear even more round and doelike. Suddenly, she was as vulnerable as an abandoned child.

"I'm single because…well, Rick…that's my husband." She stopped, took a deep breath. "*Was* my husband. See, he wasn't wearing his seat belt…and—"

"Thank you, Tamera," Markos said. He turned to Justine, who looked as sick and sad as he felt. He was angry with her nonetheless. No, angry was too strong a word. Just disappointed.

A single tear tracked down Tamera's face. At that, Markos got up from his chair and was at her side instantly. "I'll walk you out," he said.

Before he could get Tamera out the door good, Bernie, the eager producer, said to the cameraman, "Gus, tell me you got that!"

"I got it, boss!"

Justine stood in front of the large lit mirror in the women's restroom and didn't recognize herself. On the outside, she looked the same. Her mother's eyes and cheekbones. Her father's mouth. But inside... She was a foggy mix of adrenaline and hesitation.

She wanted the television opportunity more than anything. But she'd been a bear to just about all of the women who'd auditioned and especially to Markos. She hadn't been able to say one pleasant word to him since he sat down at her side. His eagerness and bubbly helpfulness rubbed her in all the wrong ways. He was just way too cooperative for her taste. And when he'd rushed to the side of that brown Pollyanna...well, didn't that just beat all?

"Hey, you all right?"

Justine looked up from where she'd leaned against the sink as if she expected her breakfast to reverse gears.

"Yeah," she said, turning on the cold water. "I think I just need some chocolate. Or maybe it's PMS."

"Oh, it's PMS. Perfect Man Sittin' next to ya."

Justine laughed even though she didn't want to. Nancy had the quickest wit in the South.

"Is he makin' you nervous or somethin'?"

Justine wet her hands and pressed her palms against her face. She closed her eyes and held her hands in place for a moment, shutting out the light.

"I'm just anxious. I want this to go so well. No," she said and removed her hands. "I *need* this to go well."

Nancy patted Justine on the shoulder, pulled a paper towel from the dispenser, and handed it to her. "It will, sweetie. It will."

Justine nodded, but she wasn't quite as confident as she pretended to be. The project had already started off slufooted—with her and Markos in a tug of war for who was best for the show.

Justine wished she could blame him for being difficult. Truth was, she was the unreasonable one.

And for the life of her new TV show, she couldn't figure out why.

Justine heard a growl. She didn't know if it was her stomach or her spirit. But she did know she was truly frustrated with herself and fed up with her feelings. With her reaction. Every woman who looked at Markos the way she wanted to made Justine want to give her a right cross and say, "Eyes off. He's mine!"

One day, she would work on getting her jealousy under control. But not now.

"All right," she said, drying her hands and her face. "I'm going to make this show a success if I have to put in twenty-four-hour days for the next three months!"

Bernie perked upwhen she repeated that remark to him as if someone had poked him in the behind with a sharp needle. "No way. Are you kidding? We're going to fast-track this thing. The production team is putting together a schedule that starts in two weeks."

"Two weeks!" Both Justine and Markos sounded stunned by the quick planning.

"I didn't know a show could move that fast," she said.

"It can when we want to get a jump on a good thing. You know, capitalize on the popularity of the commercial spots."

At first Markos was glad that he would get the whole thing over with. Then a possible conflict came to his mind.

"In two weeks, my church has our yearly revival. It's a tradition with me. I never miss it."

Bernie stroked his chin pensively. Thoughtfully. "Churchgoin' man, huh?"

"That's right."

"Maybe that can work to our advantage." Bernie stood. Paced. Ignored everyone else in the room. "How long is your revival?"

"A week."

Bernie stopped and smiled so broadly, Markos felt uncomfortable.

"Mr. Raineau, how would you like a date for every night of the revival?"

Markos smiled then. He'd love a date, but not the one he was sure Bernie planned.

"What's on your mind?" Markos asked.

CHAPTER 6

At first the idea of fewer women sounded to Markos like a shortened filming time. But that incident with Justine let him know that no matter how many women were involved, the process was going to be a long one.

Was it his imagination, or was she blocking every woman who auditioned? She's too nice. She's not nice enough. She's ghetto. She's too bourgeois. And if a woman was beautiful, intelligent, well spoken, and good-humored—and Markos had to admit there were precious few of them—look out! They were Justine's enemy numbers one through infinity.

There was a simple explanation.

Justine was jealous.

She'd more or less acted lukewarm at his Barbados offer, but she didn't want anyone else to get close enough to go.

He was flattered. Her constant rejection of each woman stroked his ego with delicate, soft hands. It felt damn good. But at the same time, it was annoying as hell.

The first and last straw was the incident with Tamera. That had started the ball rolling in the wrong direction and left a bad taste in Markos's mouth.

But exactly two weeks later, Markos had to smile. It was

lights, camera, action up in the tent. And although quite a few folks made sure to express their *con-soin* about reality all up in the revival, members showed up in their best best. When it came right down to it, *Ebony Fashion* didn't have anything on Red Oaks Christian Fellowship.

The crews tried to be as unobtrusive as possible, but no matter how far to the edges of the tent they stayed, their cables were everywhere. Men were taking wives and intend-eds by the arm to navigate the skein of cords and wires.

Markos scanned the throng for Justine. He didn't want to admit why, but after a while in her company, he'd taken a cool liking to the way the side of her lip lifted when she was frustrated or stressed or just plain pissed. And he really liked the way her eyes squinted when she thought one of the contestants was getting too fresh or too friendly. Even when the cameras stopped rolling, she never did. So far, Justine had done everything except throw her body between him and the seven lucky contestants.

Yeah, yeah. The girl had it bad. And who was to say that he didn't either? Somehow, he planned to sneak her away from all this media business and give her the kiss her lips told him she needed. After that, who knew what would happen?"

Every muscle in Markos's body froze in place, or rather heat-fused into place. The woman looked hotter than cayenne pepper. Way too hot to be in a church. Satan walking among saints. The looks she got from petition-ers were nothing compared to the look he knew he was tossing her way. Pure animal appreciation.

Her curvy hips led her through row after row of chairs.

Threading carefully. Superheating his body temperature. Not hoish, but just a bit on the scandalous side. The likes of which Red Oaks had never seen.

"Markos," she said.

Heat pooled to all of the hot spots on his body. "I need to talk to you about that dress."

She cocked her head. "Yes?"

"Do you have one in red? 'Cause red's my favorite color."

"I'll see what I can do."

An usher approached and *whispered* in Justine's ear, "Sister, you are twistin' like DNA up in here. Go 'head witcha baad self!"

Justine smiled.

A collage of music was being piped in through speakers Markos couldn't see. Mary Mary. The Blind Boys of Alabama. Smokey Norfil. Kirk Franklin. Someone was trying to please everyone. Markos didn't have to wonder who Justine was trying to please.

"What's up, Ms. Graves? Everything all set?"

"So far, so good. The girls are on their way from the hotel as we speak."

"Good," he said and caught a flicker of emotion in Justine's eyes.

From their actions already, Markos could tell that more than a few of the women hadn't been in a church in quite some time, if ever. "It will do them some good to be in the Lord's presence."

Justine's eyes narrowed with inappropriate hunger. "Amen."

The show's producer/director made his way over then.

Unlike the crew dressed in T-shirts, cargo pants, and Birkenstocks, Bernie came suited up. With his cream suit, tie, gold cross, and cream wing tips, he was the blackest white man Markos had ever met.

"My man," he said, extending his hand. The two shook, bumped shoulders, and stepped back. Even with his headset on, he looked like he belonged in the church.

"You have a good day?"

"Yes," Markos lied. He'd spent the day trying to lead a normal life in Red Oaks, going grocery shopping, mailing his cable bill. When the assistant producer had suggested that he allow someone from the show to run those errands, Markos had balked. But what was normally an hour-and-a-half trip had taken three. He'd autographed so many postcards, store receipts, bill envelopes, and body parts, he knew carpal tunnel was just one signature away.

At that moment, the woman who would have been his girl Monday sauntered past, brushing him with her train of fake hair. "Hey, Markos."

He watched her walk, wondering how many pounds that much hair weighed and thinking back to his marathon autographing session. "Next time I'll take you up on your offer."

"Thought so," she said.

Justine glanced from the woman to Bernie to Markos, boiling with discomfort.

"Look, I gotta go...check on some things."

"Okay."

"Later, Ms. Graves."

* * *

Justine's emotions baked and crusted over like her mother's mac-and-cheese casserole. She wished she could wonder why she felt so jealous. But she didn't have to wonder. It was Markos, her feelings for him, and the fact that she didn't know how to handle so many women who wanted his attention, including her. She marched down the aisle, all eyes on her and the shameful orange flame of a dress she wore. It painted a bright and sensual S down her body and she knew she looked good in it.

Not at all professional but it got the job done. Markos had made a good show of keeping his hands to himself, but his eyes and attention had been all hers. Because of the show, she couldn't have the man, but she could certainly have his focus.

The promise of that thought brought a heat that rose from the pit of her stomach to her face. She thought of Loretta Devine in *Waiting to Exhale. He's watching me walk*. She turned back out of curiosity and sure enough, back straight, suit draped like a million dollars, diamond smile, and enough muscles to make Mr. Universe jealous, Markos was watching.

Humph, she thought, turning so that he couldn't see her sly smile. Those contestants didn't stand a chance.

"Good evenin', Ms. Graves," came a strong female voice.

Justine turned around to see an older woman, nearly a head shorter than her, dressed to the nines in a camel-colored suit. All Justine could think to say was, "You *go*, Miss Old Thing!" She wanted to offer her two snaps up, but the piercing look coming at her from the woman let Justine know she'd better keep her finger snappin' to herself.

"Hello," she said, realizing the woman had called her name, but she didn't remember ever having met.

The woman extended a well-groomed and sweetly aged hand. "I'm Mother Maybelle."

The two shook hands. No arthritis, Justine thought, pulling back her hand.

Church mother, she mused. Probably wanted to meddle. Well, Justine didn't have a minute extra. She was busy trying to dig up some dirt. "Nice to meet you, Mother Maybelle. Will you excuse me?"

The older woman nodded but kept a level gaze on Justine. "I don't excuse everything or everybody. That's a failing in me I pray on. *But*, God excuses *all*. All we've done and all we're about to do."

Justine nodded and smiled, wondering if the woman had gotten inside her head somehow and saw what she was planning.

"Aren't you supposed to be somewhere counting down the minutes to the show?"

Justine started at Nancy's words. Her nerves ricocheted in her body. She'd been caught. Like a kid with her hand in the Chips Ahoy bag.

"Aren't you supposed to be taking care of business at the office?"

"Yeah," Nancy said, stepping into the church meeting room. "But my boss is out, so I can get away with murder."

Justine continued clicking her mouse and adjusted her body to shield Nancy from her flat screen. The big room with the long shiny wooden table and ten comfortable chairs shrank with every second Nancy stood in the doorway.

"What are you doing in here?" she asked, stepping forward.

Justine couldn't click fast enough, and thanks to the lightweight pop-up blocker on the church's computer, she couldn't get rid of the evidence fast enough.

"Justine?" Nancy questioned, leaning in close enough for Justine to smell her signature perfume Premonition.

"I'm just trying to get ahead of the competition. You know some other store is bound to—"

Nancy threw a petite hand to a round hip. "That ain't what you doing. Looks like you're checkin' up on somebody."

Justine shuffled the papers in front of her, suddenly realizing how stupid and desperate she'd gotten and also wishing that the woman would just leave so she could finish what she started.

"Ooh!"

"Shh!" Justine said, feeling the sting of embarrassment in her stomach. She'd been busted.

"I thought the production company already ran background checks on the girls."

"They did. I was just, just..."

"Trying to dig up some dirt."

Justine put her head in her hands. "I'm terrible. I saw all those voluptuous women and I panicked. Why couldn't I have met Markos before this?"

"You did, silly. And when he flirted with you, you didn't give him the time of day.

"Look, girl, you need to shut this down right now," Nancy said, reaching over and using the quick keys to close the Internet search engine.

"I don't know what I was thinking."

"Neither do I. You know my cousin is a skip tracer. If any of these girls pick their noses when no one is looking, she can find out and give you a computer printout of the whole thing."

Justine put her head back into her hands. This couldn't be happening. She really couldn't go through with something like that.

Could she?

The first evening of the tent revival went off without one single hitch. Markos and Suki, the first contestant, met before the service, sat together during the service, and went out to dinner after.

Justine watched the whole thing on the monitor, reluctant to look on directly as the man who made her spirit crazy "got to know" a potential wife.

"Ugh!" she said, involuntarily.

"What?" one of the assistants responded.

"Nothing," Justine had grumbled.

Toward the end of dinner, they allowed the other contestants to join them and between most of the women, a full verbal battle royal ensued.

The camera crew caught every "heifer," "skank," and "toad-faced bee-otch" leveled.

All Justine caught was a big stomachache and hoped that Nancy's cousin worked fast.

The next day, Justine awoke to the sound of her phone ringing off the hook. She flopped over in bed. Stared at her alarm clock. Seven a.m.

Who in the world would be calling her at this hour? Barely on the edge of consciousness. Was there a ringing? Who? What?

Shoot!

Justine rose up just enough to reach over to the night-stand and snatch the receiver from its base.

"This better be good," she said, voice thick with sleep.

As she listened to Nancy prattle on the way she could and often did, she realized that it wasn't good. It was *real* good.

CHAPTER 7

She told herself she was doing the show, her agency, and especially Markos a favor. Two of the women in the show were not who they claimed to be, and if exposing that brought drama, it would probably bring ratings, too. It would also weed out two women who didn't deserve to be on the show and certainly didn't deserve to have Markos.

Justine was doing the right thing.

"You're being obscure today."

Markos came up behind her. His voice reached her first. Soothed the nerves that had her stomach clenched like a fist since she awoke.

"I've sort of made this conference room my home away from home," she said, without turning. She knew if she took her eyes away from the computer or the day's agenda, the soft golden walls, or the massive wooden cross hanging on the wall directly in front of her, she'd be in danger of flirting or touching the man who was not hers to touch.

"I expected a repeat of yesterday. I thought you would have ordered me around half a dozen times by now."

She clicked the window of her e-mail closed before he could come any closer.

"Are they looking for me?" Justine asked, sensing his

approach. She allowed her mind the luxury of a fantasy. One in which she was the only woman in Markos's reality. Since he'd agreed to the show, he'd handled the whole thing with dignity, confidence, and duty to his company. She liked that. Admired it. She believed he'd bring those same sensibilities to any relationship he had—or would have in the future.

Her fantasy grew more vivid. She imagined Markos walking up behind her, placing his hands on her shoulders, massaging away the tension she carried there all day, and telling her he'd asked to be relieved from the contract he'd signed. That he'd found the woman he wanted to be with. That—

Markos took the seat beside her and she finally turned to acknowledge his presence.

"So, what's up?"

Each word came like a blow to her confidence. He couldn't know. There was no way.

"What's up with what?" she asked, trying unsuccessfully to keep the shakiness out of her voice.

Markos took a deep breath. "This is cliché as I don't know what, but from the second I laid eyes on you, you felt so familiar to me. And just from watching you—and I have been watching you—I know you're not the kind to sequester herself in a room alone unless something is up. So…what is it?"

Markos's dark brown eyes grew soft, curious, and all too sexy.

Impure thoughts! she admonished herself. No impure thoughts in the church.

She decided to save herself by telling the truth.

"I'm worried about the show. This is a big client for me." The *only* client, her mind corrected. She ignored her inner voice and continued, turning toward Markos.

"I've got a lot riding on this. Like my entire agency business and two people who are counting on me for jobs. So if this doesn't go right, I'm letting several people down."

"Including yourself."

She nodded. "Including myself."

"Don't think too hard about it. Reality shows are the hottest thing since fire—and…maybe you."

Justine smiled at his offhanded compliment.

"I'm going to do what I can to make this thing work. Trust me," he said, then covered her hand with his.

The touch of his hand came alive inside her. Awakened something beautiful and sweet. She gazed into his eyes. They were already twinkling with heat.

He felt it, too.

Maybe her fantasy was wrong. Maybe she should be the one to insist they call the whole thing off. Could she find a way to smooth things over with Value-Mart? With Olmec Broadcasting? Would she get sued?

One touch from Markos's hand, one gentle stroke, and she was ready to throw good sense, and her lingerie, out the window.

He had a way of turning up the volume on all of her senses. She could see him without looking. Feel him without touching. He was almost too handsome to look at. And the way light danced in his eyes told her that he knew it. But not in a conceited way. Just in a way in which he knew the effect he had on women and liked it. Enjoyed flirting with it.

His confident and playful smile made her feel beautiful and appreciated. As if he saw her, the way she was. Not just on the outside with her—gotta please the client—hair, makeup, top-of-the-line coordinates, Chico's chic, and attitude. But the part she never shared. The part of her that was sometimes sad and often lonely. The part that was humanly flawed and searching for love.

And he accepted her lock, stock, and imperfections.

She felt more comfortable around him than she did around anyone she'd ever known. His demeanor set her at ease. Markos was yoga only without all the poses. Meditation without the mantra. With a man like Markos at her side, there was no client Justine couldn't win.

His touch woke her soul and made her tingle like chocolate espresso. Flooded her body with awareness. He'd added another sun to her sky. Aware of her body and his and how delicious they would feel pressed together. She moistened and ached with the fantasy. The day was exciting in more ways than Justine could count.

"Markos," she began, unsure and afraid of what she was about to say.

"Yes?" he said. The bass in his voice made her spine tingle.

"I think—"

"Justine!"

The door to the conference room banged open against the golden wall. A frantic Bernie all but ran inside.

"Thank Buddah—" He stole a look at the large wooden cross. "I mean, *Jesus,* I found you. We've got an emergency."

* * *

The commotion in the hallway confused Justine for a moment until she saw Nancy approaching fast with a smile on her face and a newspaper in her hand.

People Justine didn't recognize with cameras and notepads choked the church hallway. At their first glimpse at Markos, the crowd moved like an oncoming ocean wave, a clamor of questions rising in great tides.

Cameras flashed like strobes, blinding Justine and making her draw closer to Markos.

"Markos!"

"Mr. Raineau!"

"How do you feel about having a stripper as a potential wife?"

Justine's good feelings dissolved into horrible guilt.

Markos stepped directly into the sea of reporters with mics and cameras outstretched. Not a shred of fear or hesitation from him.

"I'll tell you how I feel about you disrespecting my church. I'll tell you how I feel about pariahs in the house of the Lord. Anything else, you'll have to wait."

Markos reached out, took Justine by the hand, and led her away from the group of journalists. Reporters trailed behind them.

"How did they find us?"

"I don't know."

"Where are the producers? Where'd Bernie go?"

"I don't know," she said, hearing her nerves shake the words out.

"What the hell is going on here?"

"I—I…" Justine stammered. She could barely respond with the answer to that question blaring loud and clear in her mind.

I paid someone to dig into the contestants' pasts. So far, she's uncovered a pole dancer and a woman who left her fiancé at the altar to try out for the show. This is just the first domino to fall.

But instead, Markos made a mad dash out of the church with her in full tow.

"I'd say that went well, wouldn't you?"

Nancy stood in the women's restroom of Red Oaks Church looking serenely smug and self-righteous wearing a brick-red pantsuit and a cheesy grin. Justine paced in front of the empty stalls.

"I guess," she said almost too softly to be heard.

"You guess? One down, six to go."

"Yeah. Except I feel awful."

"Why? She was a stripper. Probably has a closet full of clear heels and shelves of honey dust. Is that really who you think Markos deserves? Plus, now that the ho is out of the closet, ratings for the show are going to blow straight up."

Justine shook her head, trying to keep her friend and colleague's words from seeping in. But in the emptiness of the lavatory, the words bounced like strong echoes and seeped inside.

"Maybe," she said. "But no more."

"Too late. I think Sheila's fiancé is on the way here."

Justine took a deep breath. It was too late to undo what

she'd already done, but at least her less than savory behavior didn't have to go any further. She'd stop it before it got out of hand. "Okay, but really. No more. That's it."

"All right, damn!"

"Hey! We're in a church."

"Sorry. But I knew you were going to spoil the drama."

"This is not a soap opera, Nancy. This is people's lives."

"It's reality TV, which is as close to a soap opera as you can get."

Justine didn't have an answer for that, but being in a church, she had a response. She would pray that she'd done the right thing and for the swift end to revival week. The sooner they wrapped up the show, the sooner she'd be able to find out what impact the series had on her agency and the quicker she could begin to get Markos Raineau out of her system. Her feelings for him were mucking up her judgment. And her carefully planned lifestyle needed clarity, the kind of clarity she hadn't had since the moment she shot the first commercial for Value-Mart.

Justine stopped pacing, turned, and faced Nancy. "I need a Mary J. promise from you."

Nancy rolled her eyes wildly and sucked her teeth loudly. "I promise...no more drama."

"Good. I'm going to try and salvage tonight's taping. You behave yourself."

"Me!" Nancy implored.

But Justine was already hurrying out the door, so fast that she ran smack into Tamera and knocked her onto the lush rose carpet with a thud.

"Oh no, I'm sorry, Tamera. Here," she said, extending her hand. "Let me help you up."

Tamera's shoulder-length hair fell away from the sides of her face, revealing eyes that flashed a monstrous glare. Then in a second, the glare was gone, replaced by a stiff smile and the turn of her head. "That's okay, Jasmine."

Tamera blinked meekly, gathered her legs under her and stood.

Justine drew back her hand. "Are you all right?"

The woman smoothed the pink ruffled blouse and matching skirt she wore. The woman sure was fond of pink.

"Yes," she said, stretching out the *s*. "Excuse me."

Justine watched her for a moment, wondering where she could possibly be going when the tent was at the opposite end of the church.

She couldn't worry about that. Tamera was a grown woman. She would find her way.

As Justine hurried outside, she hoped that she would as well.

Bernie tried to take credit for the entire evening. From Reverend Avery's introduction of the guest minister, to the choir's joyful noise, and the rapturous praise from petitioners. He especially tried to take credit for the filming of the evening with Sheila Carmichael close and snug against Markos's side pretending to be so full of the Holy Spirit that the church nurse had to rush over and tend to her as she fell out repeatedly each time the guest minister said the name Jesus.

But the best part of the evening went to Markos, who, as Justine stood back and watched, had successfully corralled the small media swarm around the morning's events—Suki's pole dancing revelation and subsequent leaving of the show. The producers predicted that the show's ratings would double as a result. But Markos's confrontation with the press that morning put them in check and increased Justine's level of respect for him tenfold.

On evening two of the weeklong series, Justine decided to hang back and observe. Relax a little instead of being so keyed up and apprehensive. Something else that had changed since she'd met Markos. And she kept that relaxed feeling. All the way through the revival service and afterward when it was time for the crew to follow Markos and date number two to dinner until...

"Sheila!"

The crowd filed out into the parking lot. The best-dressed folks in three counties. Most went about their business, ignoring the cameras and taking the spirit of the gospel home with them. But a few hung back, hearing the call of the man approaching from the side of the church, looking desperate and profoundly sad.

"Sheila!" he called again.

Church security and security from the production company took notice and moved closer to the man. Sheila halted with Markos at her side right before getting into the car ready and waiting to take them to the restaurant. Markos and Shelia almost looked like a couple headed home after a good dose of gospel. Their fast comfort sent a cold shiver of unease through Justine's body. Markos's periodic glances at her throughout the sermon and quick wink afterward did little to dislodge the image of the woman who looked surgically sutured to his arm since the cameras started rolling. Only the voice of the man scurrying up the sidewalk served to pry an inch of space between the two.

"Jasper? How did you find me?"

He walked up before security could stop him, with wire-frame glasses, knit vest, Hush Puppies, and wide eyes. He looked like a schoolteacher wired on caffeine.

"I got a freakin' phone call! Now, what is going on? Is this where you've been all this time?"

Sheila stepped back. Markos threw up his hands, and three members of the security crew surrounded the man. The cameras kept rolling.

A few of the revival attendees did a quickstep to their cars while others hung back and gawked, having front row seats to what looked like an impending disaster.

Nancy all but skipped up to Justine's side.

"I think I'm going to be ill," Justine said.

Nancy elbowed Justine. "Not now, girl. This is getting good!"

"What? Are you married?" Markos asked with way too much concern in his voice for Justine's taste.

Sheila lowered her head just a bit. "Fiancé," she said.

The oohs and oh Lawds from the crowd came in a chorus that rivaled that of the Red Oaks choir.

"Keep rolling!" Bernie instructed the camera men and women. "We'll edit later."

Markos took a step away from Sheila, frustration

turning his handsome face into a tight grimace. "Unbelievable," he said.

Markos stared at the woman who was busy looking from him to Jasper and back.

"All right, then," Markos said, running a hand through his loose locks. "No big decision here. Bernie, let's not prolong this any further. It's a no."

"No?" she said, bottom lip quivering as she stood between the two men.

"Sheila, come home," Jasper pleaded.

Sheila looked into the nearest camera, the emotions of her fifteen minutes of fame glistening in her eyes. The crowd grew silent and Justine's heart slowed. "I'm sorry, Markos," she said, in a tone that sounded overacted and dramatic.

Nancy nudged Justine once again. Justine got the message. The Young and the Ridiculous right before their eyes. Sheila ran toward Jasper, past the security guys, and flung herself into his arms.

A few parishioners had the nerve to cheer. Although Justine felt a pang of relief, she didn't let it show. Just kept her eyes on Markos, who did everything but hide his emotions.

"First a pole dancer, then a fiancé." He stormed off toward the limo that had been waiting to take him and his lady for the evening to an expensive restaurant. "What's next?" he grumbled.

Justine ached to run to Markos. Just as Sheila had run to Jasper. She wanted to hold and comfort him. Tell him to hang in there. And let him know that she would do everything in her power to make sure the series went smoother. But that would cause an even greater stir—one that could possibly change the nature of the show and jeopardize everything they were both trying to accomplish.

Some things were bigger than personal desires. As Justine watched Markos getting into the limo and the cameras following after him, she was glad that she hadn't gone any further with investigating the women. She and Nancy had caused enough trouble. It was time for things on the show to get back to normal.

Justine looked at the remaining five women. They all seemed pleased that two women had been eliminated. Contentment was written in large letters all over their faces. They all looked like little girls who'd just discovered that Ken was real and waiting for them. All except Tamera. She'd come off as the most innocent of them all, but the look on her face said she was everything but. The expression put Justine on alert. Her smile was crooked. Wicked. When one of the camera crew turned her camera in the women's direction, Tamera's smile changed and became demure. Coy.

Justine swallowed dryly. The woman was up to something. Only God knew what it was, but Justine made a promise to herself to find out.

CHAPTER 8

Markos hadn't done much of anything for the past two days except smile and make handsome for four to six cameras and make small talk with two beautiful women, yet that small task had exhausted him.

Why? he wondered, but the answer was already teetering on the edge of his mind. He'd been working the whole time—working to keep Justine out of his thoughts. Working to keep his eyes from ravaging her body. Working to keep his hands from pulling her close. Working to keep his libido in check.

Markos didn't think he'd ever worked that hard at anything in his life—even being regional manager for the third largest retail store in the country.

Justine... It didn't matter what she said to him. Every phrase sounded like "Markos, I want you."

Markos squeezed the tube of Axel shower gel into the center of the flour-white washcloth and scrubbed. He washed in quick hard circles hoping to rinse away more than the day's sweat. He wanted to remove poor choices like Sabrina and bad decisions like Bev-er-ly. He'd love to see his feelings for Justine swirl like a discarded question down the shower drain.

He turned the showerhead. The water struck his skin in tiny hard pellets. He was being selfish. He knew that. Thinking more of himself than of Value-Mart or his church. There was a committee. One designed to donate part of the revival proceeds to a local organization that helped at-risk boys. There was also a task force at his job designed to analyze the results of Value-Mart's foray into reality TV and to decide if they would try it again next year.

Markos stood still under the pummeling water. Allowed the soap and buildup to drain off his body and decided to volunteer for both groups. He could use the experience and the exposure. Most of all, he could use the distraction from Justine and the five women left in the competition who could even begin to come close to the prize Justine represented.

"Now, if I was really lookin' for a wifey," he said, pulling back the shower curtain to a steam-filled bathroom, "Justine would definitely be in the running."

The knock on his hotel room brought a long groan. Markos had managed to put off the taping of his *reaction* to the women who'd *left* the show. Gus, the camera guy he'd kinda bonded with, told him they'd be back later.

Markos wrapped a thick white towel around his waist and headed to the door.

God is good, his mind whispered as he stood still damp with nothing between him and the woman of his lust but a hotel towel.

"Justine," he said with way too much relief in his voice. "I thought you were the camera crew."

"Sorry, Markos. I just…well…I can come back."

"No!" he said, stepping aside so she could enter. "I'm glad you're not the crew."

She came in looking as sexy as ever. Her long legs were stuffed into a pair of faded blue jeans set off by a bright white tank top. The alluring scent of her perfume trailed behind her. Markos sniffed the air like a hound dog on a hunt and hoped letting her into his suite was a good idea.

She strode past him, some of that cocky self-assuredness missing from her stride.

What did she want?

"Wow!" she said, staring at the flowers.

Markos had to admit, he did a double take every time he entered his suite and saw them. The living area was quickly turning into a floral shop. His nose had done him a great job of blocking out the overwhelming fragrance.

"Let me give you the tour," he said.

"Carnations from Toni. Roses from Zara. This mixed arrangement is from Faith and Candice."

He shook his head at the unbelievability. "And I have enough chocolate to last for the next three or four years."

"They are really going for it," Justine replied, dipping her head toward the roses sitting in a large pewter vase on the wet bar.

"You don't know the half of it. I'm too much of a gentleman to mention the other things they've sent."

Justine straightened and stiffened. "Like what?"

Markos flipped through the items in his mind. Naked photos. DVD stripteases. A CD audio recording of multiple orgasms with Toni calling out his name over and over and—

"Is it *that* bad?" Justine asked.

"Worse," he said, promising himself that he would listen to the CD only one more time. After that, out with the trash!

Justine sauntered over to the mums and carnations. Fingered a shiny green leaf. "Must be overwhelming having so many women throwing themselves at you."

"Not really," Markos said, following behind her. "Most men have had this kind of fantasy in their heads since puberty. I've been rehearsing for years."

She turned to him. The eyes he could stare into for hours stared into his. "Is that so?"

"Pretty much."

He moved away before the spell of her lovely face took his soul and he gave her a taste of his more recent fantasies.

"So, what's on you mind?" he asked, and gestured for her to have a seat on the sofa.

At his question, she took a seat. To be safe, he stood across from her next to a stiff high-backed chair that belied its look of comfort and waited. Justine's confident features softened. She seemed hesitant and almost lost.

Markos imagined the worst that could happen and decided to start there. "They're canceling the show," he said.

"No! Absolutely not. That's not it at all."

Markos wasn't sure if he was relieved because he still had an opportunity to help his church and his store or because he still had time he could spend getting to know Justine.

"Then what?" This time he decided to imagine the best that could happen. "You've decided to give your body what it wants and so you came to see big papa."

Justine folded her lips and covered her mouth with her

hand. But the loud and boisterous laugh couldn't be stifled by that mere gesture.

"Okay, look," she said. "You are kinda cute. But don't get me wrong, I'm here on business. And I have something important to tell you."

"You found out who sabotaged Suki and Sheila."

"What makes you think it's sabotage?"

"Are you kidding? These women are treacherous. Just yesterday, I got—never mind." He couldn't complete that thought and tell her about the panties, worn at that, that came FedEx for him from Zara. "Bernie won't have to bother with much direction. These women are going to stoop to new reality TV lows, and it's too bad they feel they have to do that."

"Why?" she asked.

"'Cause I'm a simple guy."

Justine took long and meticulous inventory of the man standing in the middle of the most expensive suite in the hotel wearing only a white towel and a smile knowing full well he was about as complex as they came.

Just the vision of him—damp, dark skin, roguish smile, and predatory gaze—was enough to make her forget that she'd come to his room to confess that she'd been the one to sabotage the two women. She wanted to tell Markos about it before she went to the producers and confessed her misdeeds. But the longer she looked at Markos and the longer he looked back, the further that thought and her intentions slid away from her mind.

"So, what brings you to my room?" he asked, approaching.

He must have sensed some of what was in her head. Read her thoughts somehow. Or maybe she was just so damned obvious that he was doing what any healthy man would do.

But he wasn't just any man. He was Markos Raineau. The man she'd been fighting herself to ignore since the whole bloody business about the *Marrying Markos* series first began.

"You," she said honestly, a sensual chill rippling from her toes to the moist space between her legs, through her heart, and pulsing in her head. "You're on my mind."

"That's good." He stopped beside the sofa. So close. If she wanted to, she could reach up and one gentle tug of the towel and it would fall free. And oh how she wanted to.

Mischief danced in his eyes. Dared her to follow through with her thought.

Instead of stopping herself and being the good ad exec, she reached out and did exactly as her mind insisted.

Magnificent. The only word that came to mind. Markos's body was the most marvelous piece of human anatomy she'd ever seen. What kind of workout regime must he keep up in order to have hard, ultratight muscles from head to heel? Every ripple and contour of his body called to her hands.

He was a sculpted figure of shoulders and biceps, washboard abs, and log-sized thighs. Skin stretched tight, muscles straining beneath espresso-rich skin. Skin that smelled as much like Markos the man as it did the soap he just used. Justine gazed slowly up the length of his body, drunk with arousal.

She grew feverish with desire.

She shook her head no. She was about to make a very bad mistake. "Markos, I—"

"Me too, Justine," he said, taking her hands that were already headed toward his body. Defying her better judgment.

She rose slowly. Leaned in. Couldn't get to his body fast enough. Couldn't press against his hard, hot flesh quick enough.

"Umm," he said, pulling her closer.

Justine breathed out a long breath. It was as if she'd been holding it since they met. Keeping it inside since the second a silly voice in her head said *He's the one. The one you've passed over all other men for.* From the moment she shoved that absurd thought aside and ignored it, every time it snuck back. Times like right now.

All Justine wanted to do was stay right where she was and be held by this strong, intelligent, and wildly handsome man. Well, that and make wild, reckless, swinging-from-the-chandelier love with him.

Her heart beat so fast and strong, her whole body pulsed.

Markos ran his hands against her back, her sides. Pulled her closer.

"I wanna do you slow," he whispered. His voice went deep and huskily into her ear. He brushed his lips against the nook of her neck and made her quiver. "But...maybe later."

All of her hope and anticipation left her body, and her knees weakened. Markos held her steady, his hands still roaming.

"Right now I don't have that kinda restraint," he said.

Relief flooded every ounce of her body. *Thank you, Jesus,* she thought and then suddenly pulled back.

"Wait," she said. "You're a Christian. What about being saved and born again?"

He pulled back a bit and looked her dead in the eye. "That's between me and God."

The next thing Justine knew, Markos had picked her up and was headed toward the California king bed in the bedroom.

She held on tight, her fantasy come true. She wouldn't do a thing to stop it. Not even wake up if it was a dream.

CHAPTER 9

"Whew!" Markos kissed Justine's sweaty forehead and rolled off her body. A rush of cool air hit her hot, sated body in all the places where Markos had just been lying, caressing, pumping in and out of her wilder than her imagination could fathom. Every second, minute, hour a treasure and a thrill of ecstasy. They'd spent one long night of entwined desires.

Justine's body was schizo with pleasure. She didn't know whether to jump up and run a marathon or sleep for a week. Good sexin' always made her domestic. Gave her urges to knit sweaters, bake biscuits from scratch. But this, this kind of lovin' made her think about meeting parents, joint bank accounts, and baby bonnets. In the afterglow of a night of ravenous passion, she tried to shake off the wifey thoughts, but the suckers wouldn't go away.

Markos slid closer to her. Covered her leg with one of his own. Made a trail in the sweat on her chest with his finger. "Sorry," he said. "I kept thinking 'This time I'll go slow' but your body wouldn't let me."

"Oh, blame it on me!"

"Why shouldn't I?"

Markos smiled and kept sliding his fingers across her

skin. He couldn't stop touching her. Couldn't stop looking at her. Inhaling her scent. Now that he wasn't inside her, he felt disconnected from the world. He willed his body to recover quickly once again. He had to have one more dose of her sweetness before facing another day of cameras, interviews, and desperate women who wanted fifteen minutes of fame and a piece of him they didn't even understand.

"What now?" Justine asked.

Markos stiffened. There was so much at stake. They couldn't cancel the show just because he had an all-night, mind-blowing, addicting tryst with the ad exec for the series.

He had to see the show through to the end. Except that proposing marriage part. Suddenly he wasn't down for that. He wondered what the producers would do if they found out that he had no intention of marrying any of the contestants from the show. Proposing...yes. Friendship. That is, if there was one among them that respected herself enough to keep her dignity throughout the series.

"The show must go on, right?" he asked. Although Justine hadn't moved physically, he'd felt her shift. She pulled back from him. Way back. Like a spiritual walking away.

"Don't," he said and stopped his playful massage of her chest. He bent and kissed her lips still swollen from their passion. "You know, like I know, we're in the middle of something."

She took a deep breath and started to look away. He wouldn't let her and caught her chin before she could turn fully.

"Now is not a good time for us to explore what this

means. There's too much at stake. We've both got businesses to think of, right? Right?" *Convince me,* his mind said. *Make me know I'm doing the right thing by sticking to my guns—by sticking to the show—and not throwing everything away because eight hours of passion have made me crazy.*

Justine smiled then. The smile almost reached her eyes. "Remember those rumors about Angelina Jolie and Brad Pitt disappearing for days when they were supposed to be filming *Mr. and Mrs. Smith*?"

Markos pushed aside a stray lock of hair that had fallen against her face. "Uh, no. Not really."

"Well, anyway, I was just wondering. What would happen if we—"

Damn, her voice, he thought, swallowing her words with his mouth. Kissing her the way he wanted to all night but was too selfish to. Slow and deep. Lingering long in her sweet mouth. So damn good. Felt like he'd been kissing her mouth for days. Loving her for years. Holding her all his life.

He dragged himself away from her lips only to descend upon her chin, her jaw, her neck and shoulders. Teasing and tasting. Taking it easy this time. Not trying to grind her into the bed.

"So, you wanna disappear for a while?" He slid a hand under her leg, stroked it, and pulled it up around his waist.

She nodded quickly and parted her lips, panting while his hand slid a lazy path up her body headed for heaven.

"We'd have to get another room," he said, kissing her shoulder, flicking a nipple erect with his tongue.

"Yes," she said, pulling closer. "Under another name."

"Like Smith?" he asked, tugging her breast gently with his mouth, pulling a moan from her whole body.

"Yes!" she said, pushing him over and straddling him.

His arousal tightened like steel.

"We're going to need another one of these," she said, reaching toward the nightstand and the Trojans scattered on top.

When the phone rang, it startled them both and Justine dropped the condom. It fell between the side table and the bed. Their eyes locked. The phone rang again.

It was just enough to bring them both back to their senses. Once again, Markos felt Justine pulling away. This time, he let her go with every intention of finishing what they started when the time was right.

When the time was better.

Justine climbed off him, butter-brown body lithe and beautiful still stirring his insides.

"Duty calls," she said with a half smile.

"How about a rain check?"

The scowl on her face told him that was the wrong thing to ask.

"A rain check?"

Markos reached for both Justine and the phone. On one side his fingers grasped the cool plastic of the receiver, on the other recirculated hotel air as Justine slid to the edge of the bed and began gathering her things.

The temperature in the room chilled with her every movement. Markos shuddered and brought the phone to his ear.

"Hello?" he answered.

"Markos, there's been an accident. Toni Davenport is on her way to the hospital. We've got a car downstairs waiting to take you to Carter General."

Markos shot up in the bed. "I'll be right there!"

The Egyptians during the time of Moses probably thought they'd seen the worst run of curses and plagues. Justine believed that *Marrying Markos* would give them a run for their money.

After Toni tripped over camera cables and broke three toes, Faith got food poisoning, Zara was caught in bed with one of the bellmen, *and* Candice.

In the end, the congregation of Red Oaks ended up saying prayers for the contestants instead of welcoming them into the congregation. With only one contestant left, things couldn't have worked out better for Justine if she'd sabotaged them herself.

After four days of one disaster after another, Nancy was still laughing at Toni's mishap that landed her in the hospital with her left foot wrapped in an Ace bandage.

Justine stared out the window of the church conference room wondering about Markos and trying to ignore her friend. But it was hard. Nancy had set up her laptop at the desk and had been glued to YouTube for over an hour.

"I can't *believe* they got this up so fast. Girl, it's too funny!"

Somehow, Toni's slip and fall had been uploaded to the popular Web site and was one of the highest-rated slapstick videos on the site. Nancy kept playing it over and over, laughing at the top of her voice.

Justine turned suddenly uneasy. "Nan, you didn't have anything to do with that, did you?"

Her assistant and friend stared up from the flat screen, eyes wide with surprise. "Me? How could you think that I—"

"Because I wouldn't put it past you."

Nancy feigned hurt feelings. "I'm shocked."

"Nan…"

"Okay. I wouldn't put it past me either, but *trust*, I didn't do it. I wish I did, but no. It wasn't me."

Justine searched Nan's face for any hint of deception and found none. She was relieved. "All right."

"Feel better?"

"Yes."

"You'll feel great after you look at this fall again. Homegirl fell *hard!*"

While Nancy amused herself at her laptop, Justine found it hard to take pleasure in the woman's misfortune. Not only did she feel sorry for the woman, but she felt bad about the show, which with so many unfortunate events was fast becoming underwhelming. If it weren't for the fact that Markos and Tamera were getting along so well, Justine figured the whole thing would have been canceled days ago.

But the producers had fallen in love with the "last woman standing" turn the show had taken and were milking it for every cent a sponsor might spend.

Markos and Tamera had breakfast together, lunch, and dinner. They attended the revival and went on long walks. They seemed like the perfect couple—at least in the dailies.

The time and distance had been good for Justine. It had given her the opportunity to regroup. She had to admit to herself that she'd lost herself in Markos's arms. The strong confident "I'm Every Woman" she'd come to be had mellowed and morphed into someone she didn't recognize. A woman dependent on a man to make her happy.

And she wasn't about to go out like some needy young thing.

Settling into the Markos and Tamera routine had given her her schedule back. Early morning meetings with the production staff. Conference calls with the client in the afternoon. Evening wrap-ups with Nancy and Craig. Life was good, wasn't it?

Nancy's laughter cut through Justine's daily review. "You know they're putting this on the *Reality Rewind* show!"

Justine put her BlackBerry away and stared at her friend and colleague. "You are so wrong. Why are you so fascinated with that woman's fall?"

"Girl, it's like the accident you can't turn away from. Like Madea's family reunion when Madea beat the stew out of that little girl. It's wrong. You know it's wrong. And it's funny as hell, too! Justine, I could watch this woman fall every day for the next ten years and laugh like a fool every single time."

Justine walked up behind where Nancy sat at the desk. The state-of-the-art laptop Justine's company paid for was stuck on YouTube. Nan clicked Play for what had to be the tenth time that morning.

Right on cue, Toni Davenport, diva extraordinaire, came strutting into the tent. Her breasts and hips aimed acutely at Markos, she exaggerated her sway even more the closer she got to him.

And then it happened. Her foot turned over like Naomi Campbell on the catwalk and the woman went down. First she flew up, legs wide in the air, lavender thong exposed for all to see, and then she smacked down on all that behind. The expression on her face was priceless. Like the ground had knocked the slut out of her and all that was left was a confused woman who just had a side of extra stupid and couldn't tell you her name or the day of the week and couldn't tell her butt from a billy club.

The video ended right before the pain sank in, and from what Justine had heard, Toni howled and whined like a spoiled adolescent.

Nancy grabbed her stomach and bent. "Oh Jesus! But that's funny!"

"Play it again," Justine ordered, a sick feeling settling into her stomach.

"See? I told you it's addicting!"

Nancy clicked the Play button and Toni was once again strutting, flying, and falling. This time Justine paid less attention to the woman and more to the cables she tripped over, especially the one that moved just as she started to get her big bad strut on.

"Did you see that!" Justine asked.

"Girl, I've been seein' it for days. You're the one who didn't want to watch it!"

"No, no! Play it again and watch right here." Justine pointed to the place on the floor where the cables were lying at the beginning of the video.

Another review of the footage confirmed her suspicions.

"Oh my God," Nancy said.

Justine didn't think either of them would find the footage funny after that. What they would find is the person at the other end of the cord, but Justine didn't think it would take much.

Her gut told her that little miss sweet and innocent Tamera was actually anything but.

Suddenly all her care for her client, her ratings, and her business went out the window. There was a skank in their midst and Justine was going to expose who it was.

CHAPTER 10

By Saturday evening, the Red Oaks revival had surpassed anything Justine could have imagined. Each day more and people had attended until standing room only would have been a comfortable way to describe the attendance. That evening, the tent was swollen with people. It was as if everyone had waited until the last minute expecting to see something spectacular. Well, if Justine had anything to do with it, the Holy Spirit wouldn't be the only thing descending upon parishioners that evening. According to her plan, security guards, and maybe even a cop or two, would be all over Tamera like Tiny Lester on a neck bone.

After she and Nancy retraced the steps of everything that had happened that week, Justine discovered that she wasn't the only one with an elimination agenda. Tamera had picked up where she and Nan had left off and managed to get all the remaining girls "out of the way" so that she would have Markos all to herself. Immediately following the service, Justine planned a private screening in Pastor Avery's office for Markos, Tamera, and the producers of the show. After all this time of Gus hanging around with his camera, Justine had finally found a good use for the video whiz. He'd spent the better part of the previous evening enhancing the footage from the fall and revealing a devious Tamera crouching behind equipment boxes, camera cable in hand. It didn't take Justine long after that to connect Tamera to the other mishaps in the series and make a case against the woman. She only hoped Markos hadn't made the mistake of falling for her. That would put a damper on the situation for Justine in more ways than one.

Despite everything, Faith, Zara, and Toni managed to make it to the revival that evening. They were determined to see things through to the end and were hoping against hope that even though they'd been out of commission and had to tape some of their segments from hospital rooms, they wanted to win. No matter what.

Among the sea of attendees, some of whom made women on *America's Next Top Model* look poor and homeless, Tamera and Markos sat so close they looked hugged up. Cuddled. Like he'd already made up his mind and couldn't see straight because of it.

Justine turned away from the sight with a sharp twinge in her side. She groaned. She really had been out of sorts since the moment she'd left Markos's bed only a few days ago. She'd tried to go on as if she was a strong, independent woman. But the truth was, she actually might have something in common with the women who'd tried out for the show.

She wanted Markos, too.

But unlike her, Tamera and the rest were willing to do whatever it took, even make themselves look like fools to get the man of their dreams. What had she been willing to do?

Nancy came walking up to Justine just as the choir started singing "I Can't Make This Journey Alone." Justine swayed with the emotion the song stirred in her despite the fact that before that week, it had been years since she'd been inside a church.

"It's all set," Nancy said.

After they realized that Tamera was behind so much drama on the set, Nancy was furious and had wanted to confront the woman immediately. It took everything in Justine's professional nature to calm Nancy down and to persuade her that the best thing to do was the right thing. Collect all the evidence and present it with backup—in the form of people who could properly escort Ms. Devious Thing from the series set.

To that end, Justine kept Nancy busy helping to put together the details on the meeting while Justine herself kept an eye on Tamera, making sure she didn't try anything else.

"I can't wait to expose that heifer!" Nancy said.

"Shhh!" Justine said, hoping her friend would not cause a commotion at the end of the revival.

"Sorry, girl. It's just that she pissed me off."

Justine couldn't believe her ears and couldn't believe the self-righteous way in which Nancy was leaning against a post.

"Don't act like we didn't do the same thing with Suki and Sheila," Justine said.

"That was different. They were straight-up wrong with all the dirt and bones in their closet. But what ol' girl did was uncalled for. She ran a game on some hoochies that were just doing what they do best…be hoochies. They weren't lying or trying to cheat. Just trying to get over and have a nice, handsome, successful man pay them some attention for maybe the first and only time in their lives."

She turned her head proudly and started clapping with the rest of the congregation. "No harm in that."

Justine clapped as well. The choir was really full of the spirit that evening. Praises to God rose higher than they had all that week. Even Justine, who had focused solely on her objective of serving her client and keeping Markos in her peripheral vision, was forced to take notice and acknowledge God's Holy Spirit among them.

As the choir raised their voices into an encore of the song, Tamera got up from her spot that was practically on Markos's lap, and headed in their direction.

"Here this heifer comes now," Nancy said none too quietly.

"You know what? You need to chill."

"But she's a skank ho actin' like Little Bo Peep in this m—uh…piece."

"Nan!"

"I'm just sayin'. Somebody needs to set her ass straight."

Justine shook her head. "You are too foul in this tent."

"And you aren't fowl enough!"

Tamera approached, fanning like she was having a hot flash. "Praise the Lord, ladies."

Nancy stared at Tamera as if the woman had just grown a faceful of hair. "What!"

Justine grabbed Nancy's arm. "Praise the Lord, Tamera. Are you enjoying the service?"

Tamera must have gotten real comfortable and believed she had the contest on lock. "Not really. It's a little overdone, wouldn't you say?"

"I think as devious as you are, you ought to be glad that you didn't disintegrate into a pillar of salt the moment you stepped inside this tent."

Justine felt a dark cloud overhead, even in the midst of jubilation in the tent. Energy drained from her body like through a sieve. Nancy was threatening to ruin her entire plan.

Tamera stepped closer. Her eyes turned cold and she tossed them an icy smile. "Under another circumstance, in another place—not so holy—I'd call you out, boo. But because I respect Markos and the house of the Lord I won't go there."

"Nah, nah! You crazy heifer! Go there!" Nancy stepped to her and looked like she was ready to break her foot off in Tamera's behind. "I *want* you to go there. Please…*go* there."

Tamera stepped up—unabashed and unafraid. Before she could say anything, Justine stepped between the two women who were about to turn the spring revival into Wrestlemania. "Ladies, please." Believing that Pandora's box had been opened, she felt her goal now was damage control. "Why don't we take this outside?"

By now the three women had attracted the attention of the surrounding parishioners. Justine wanted to make it out before the camera crew realized that Tamera might not be just going to the ladies' room.

"Bless the Lord. Bless the Lord," came a familiar voice. Justine turned to see Mother Maybelle approaching with all the vim and vigor of someone one-third her age.

Justine wasn't a fool. The church mother was on her way over to make sure the evening's service was not disrespected any more than it already was with a six-person camera crew and a director roaming around.

"Bless the Lord," the three younger women repeated. Something about the church mother demanded respect, and Justine was grateful that the feuding women had sense enough to rely on their home training and dial back their hostility.

Justine noticed Gus staring at them. Darn. The man didn't miss much.

"We were just headed out, Mother Maybelle."

"So I see. Well, since you goin', take this with you. Flesh and blood cannot inherit the kingdom of God, nor does corruption inherit incorruption."

She put her hand on Justine's forearm. "Now, you all oughta go somewhere and make real good friends with the truth."

"We will," Justine said.

"God bless you," Mother Maybelle said and headed back to the front row of chairs where she came from. She maneuvered around parishioners still in the throes of the spirit, unaware of the cold snap of tension in the rear of the tent.

Before they could draw any more attention to themselves, they went outside.

They almost made it inside the church. Almost. But Gus and his camera followed behind them before they could get inside the building.

Anger blazed up like a bright flare inside Justine. "What do you have? A sixth sense?"

"Sixth, seventh, and eighth when it comes to drama. That's why they pay me the big bucks. Now, just pretend like I'm not here."

"There's nothing to see, Gus. Just a meeting in the ladies' room, okay?" she said, putting on a brave smile and a calm tone to convince the nosy cameraman that there was nothing to see.

"Sounds good to me," he said, refusing to be dissuaded.

"Actually, there is something to see," Tamera insisted and pushed up the jacket sleeves of her baby-pink suit.

Gus adjusted the lens on his camera. Justine knew he'd trained a close-up on Tamera.

"Tamera!" another familiar voice called from behind them. The sound made Justine tingle with anticipation. She turned to see Markos closing in on them with another camera operator trailing behind him.

Justine swallowed the huge lump forming in her throat. Things were getting out of hand. Nothing was going the way she'd planned.

"What's going on?" Markos asked, catching up with them. Lights from the street just beginning to come on made his coffee complexion glow with concern.

No one said anything.

"Is someone going to answer my question?" Markos asked, irritation setting his words on edge.

"Well, I didn't want to do this in front of you, but Markos, sweetie, Sister Graves and her sister friend here have been busy setting up contestants for failure. It started with Suki and continued with Sheila and now that I'm the only one left, they're trying to sabotage me, too."

"What?"

"Um," Gus said and stepped in for an even closer close-up.

"You whack tramp!" Nancy shouted and stepped toward the woman who wore the fresh face of innocence like it was painted on with Sharpie permanent markers.

"Tamera, you don't have to lie on Justine," Markos said.

"Lie! I don't have to lie. Ask her what she did to expose Suki."

Markos frowned. "Tamera…"

"Ask her!"

For Justine, time stopped right then. It stopped and waited for her to decide which path she was going to take.

She wanted to tell Markos that she had absolutely nothing to do with Suki's disgrace. But Mother Maybelle's admonishment rang loudly in her mind.

She held back Nancy, but decided to set the truth free.

"Markos…" she said, forgetting everything except the closeness they shared and reaching toward him. "I'm sorry."

He frowned and took half a step backward. "Sorry for what?"

"Justine—" Nancy began.

"Nan," she said in response. "We have to come clean now."

"Meaning what? That you've been playing dirty?" Markos asked.

Tamera took that time to move in for the kill. "Markos, I didn't think it was my place to expose them, but—"

Nancy strained against Justine's hold. A few people

late for the beginning of that evening's service stopped to stare at the spectacle. The red light on Gus's camera never faltered. And now cameras three through six were joining them in the parking lot, followed closely by the rest of the contestants.

"You're the one who needs to be exposed. Markos, Justine has something to show you," Nancy said.

But he didn't listen to her. It was as if he'd stopped listening altogether.

He stared at Justine with disappointment heavy on his handsome face. "I thought the contestants were the desperate ones." Markos shook his head. Ran a hand down the middle of his face. "You all seem to be so big on drama. So here's some for ya...I'm going for a walk," he said, staring straight into Gus's camera. "When I come back, I'll announce my choice."

Markos stormed off, his long legs creating a great distance between him and Gus, who struggled to capture his grand exit on tape. Tamera giggled like an adolescent and headed confidently back toward the tent.

Justine slowly released her hold on Nancy. Nancy adjusted her blouse and cleared her throat. "Well, that went well," she said, jokingly. But Justine was far from being in a joking mood.

In fact, she was sick with the realization that Markos was more than just a one-night stand. Much more. But in his eyes, she'd become just another woman desperate to get his attention even if that meant disgracing herself. And she had no idea what she could do to change that.

CHAPTER 11

News of the drama in the parking lot swept the revival like it had three sets of wings and a pair of Rollerblades. It was all Reverend Avery could do to keep the congregation's attention on the holy word and not the final word issued by Markos.

As bad as Justine felt about the whole thing, Bernie was on cloud nine and a half. After Markos stormed off, Bernie had reviewed the footage and decided that was the best part of the series so far. He declared it was a great buildup to the end of the show. He guaranteed the revelations would have audiences on the edge of their seats.

Bernie had wasted no time communicating his confidence in the show to the network and Value-Mart. No sooner had Justine gotten off her BlackBerry with the client than her father had called telling her how proud he was and letting her know he was on the way over.

Bernie boasted that *Marrying Markos* was destined to be as big a success as *The Flavor of Love*. He had spent the last thirty minutes looking for Markos wondering if making a decision at this point was even a good idea. He believed they might be able to spin into another season in light of all the deception coming out. He wanted to stage a great cliffhanger.

But Markos Raineau was nowhere to be found.

And neither was Justine's sanity. She'd spent the last hour pacing outside the tent and strangely enough praying that Markos would come back and she could explain and confess everything to him. But seconds had become minutes and far too many of them had passed. Justine started to wonder if Markos really would come back like he said.

A sickening wave of fear welled up in Justine's belly. What if she never got the chance to make this right? What if she never got the chance to set things straight with the man to whom she'd given so much more than her body? Suddenly, all of Justine's well-ordered life and her business didn't mean nearly as much as owning up to the relationship she wanted to repair between her and Markos. Even if they were never intimate again, his opinion of her was important. And his respect meant even more.

She wanted them both and knew that she wouldn't feel right until she had them.

Or they had her.

"Justine," Nancy said. She hadn't left her friend's side the entire time. "Don't you think you should wait inside with everyone else?"

"No. That's exactly what I don't want. I don't want to be like everyone else."

"Then what do you want?" Nancy asked.

Justine took a deep breath and prepared her words, but her answer was coming in the distance.

Markos. She saw him at least three blocks away. She'd recognize that powerful stride from any distance.

His stride was so self-assured, Justine found the confidence attractive. A man who knew how to handle things, the way he'd handled the press and everything about life as a reality TV star since the series began. Utterly and compellingly attractive. Justine struggled to keep her composure but sighed like a schoolgirl nonetheless.

He'd come back. But what to say?

Justine had had plenty of time to figure that out, and now that the chance was upon her, she found herself at a loss for words that would even begin to explain how crazy and rash she'd been. No words would describe that. But then again, there were three words that might.

I'm in love, she said loud and clear in her head. *And the man I love is about to propose to someone else.*

Markos strode back to the church more determined than ever to set things right.

When he'd left only a few short hours ago, he'd gone with a bitter taste in his mouth and a heavy thought on his soul. The woman he'd admired most throughout the whole ordeal of this reality TV show, the woman he'd come to think of as the levelheaded one, the one who had it together, was just as shady as the contestants he so despised.

Even more so.

The farther he'd walked away, the more bitter the taste grew, making him want to forget all about the intimacy he'd shared with Justine and how he'd never felt like more of a man than the night they'd spent together and how his mind had grabbed on fiercely to the idea of them being intimate again and again, no matter the outcome of the show.

But the thought of her being just like the others had turned his stomach. Sickened him in a way that pushed him away to collect his thoughts and reorder his mind.

If it hadn't been for Gus, Markos might have spent the better part of the next few months resenting Justine in the worst way.

But Gus had shown him the tape of the fall and it all made sense.

He came closer. Less than a block now, realizing that the producers had wanted drama and they damn sure were about to get it.

Markos's pulse raced and his pace quickened. For the first time since the production company started filming, he was genuinely excited about the series.

"It's time!" Bernie shouted, director to the very end.

Markos didn't wait for Bernie to say "action" or for the cameras to set up. He was ready to say his piece. "Listen up."

He took charge with quiet assurance, standing between Justine and the series contestants approaching from the tent. He'd managed to stay away just long enough to miss the entire service. A small part of the congregation trickled out and began milling in the background with the exception of Mother Maybelle, who'd walked right up in the midst of the filming.

"Markos," Bernie began, still trying to reel in the show and stage for effect, "why don't you address the women?

Tell them what you liked and didn't like about each one before you announce your choice?"

"Because that would take too long. I can't wait to begin my life with the woman I've selected."

Out of the corner of his eye, Markos caught a glimpse of Tamera beaming like she'd just swallowed a 200-watt lightbulb. Where she was going, he figured that smugness would fade quicker than she could blink.

"I do want to say this. The experience of being on this show and going from a guy managing a few stores to practically a household name has taught me that in life anything is possible—even what seems impossible. And the woman I've chosen has taught me that you don't need to know someone forever to know they're the one you were made for. You just have to know your own soul. And through her, being around her, I've gotten to know my soul pretty well."

The silence outside the tent was deafening. At that moment, not even the sounds of cars distracted them.

"Well, who is it!" a voice that sounded strangely like Nancy's asked.

Markos didn't turn to find out. He only gazed into the most beautiful eyes he'd ever seen and said, "I want to share my life with you...Justine...if you'll have me."

"Justine?"

"Who the hell is Justine?"

"What!"

"No, no! You can't choose—"

Justine's mouth gaped open in stunned silence. She felt tingly and sweetened like sun tea that had been basking outside all day long.

"M-me?" she asked, mouth quivering. For someone who thrived on planning her life down to the last detail, she had no idea how to deal with something so unexpected and completely unplanned.

Markos took two long strides and he was standing before her. He took her hands in his and Justine felt her life change like the colors of the evening sky. Deepening. Growing richer.

"I—I," she stammered and swallowed hard. She gazed up into his handsome face. "Me?"

"Who else?" he said, eyes the brightest points of light in the darkening sky. "You couldn't possibly think I would choose anyone but you? Right?"

He searched her face, waiting for a response.

Just then Justine caught a glimpse of her father. He was looking on intensely with surprising calm.

She squeezed Markos's hands to keep herself steady. To remind herself that this moment was the real thing. Not the show or much of what came before it as far as relationships were concerned. This was it. Right now this moment was all she had.

And all she wanted.

"Justine?" Markos said softly. Expectedly.

"What about the show?"

"I don't care about the show. I care about us. But you've got to tell me, will there be an us?"

Video cameras zoomed in. Digital cameras flashed. And camera phones clicked. Like the sounds and images of a celebration that Justine hoped was just beginning.

"Yes!" she said, a surge of elation propelling her into his arms. "I choose you, too."

The soft sounds of clapping and calls of approval faded as Markos kissed Justine until she couldn't see or think straight.

CHAPTER 12

By the time *Marrying Markos* aired on Olmec Broadcasting, Justine and Markos had left the country to plan their wedding and get away from the demands of the media. Justine's success with the series had left other stores and organizations clamoring at her office door for a shot at the reality TV magic. Markos, on the other hand, had been bombarded with requests to appear on talk shows and for cameos on sitcoms. After a guest appearance on *Girlfriends,* he was seriously thinking about expanding his fifteen minutes of fame into half an hour on a semiregular basis.

Justine snuggled closer to Markos. They'd been lying on a private beach in Barbados for the better part of the evening and had spent most of the time trying to come up with a way to have a big wedding and keep it secret from the press.

In the last few moments, they'd both fallen silent.

"What are you thinking about?" Justine asked.

Markos's eyes had looked distant for a second, but her question seemed to bring him back.

He bent closer. Kissed her forehead. "I was just thinking how crazy the past six months have been. Crazy, fast, almost out of control. It's good to be here. To slow down for a minute."

"Yeah," she said in complete agreement. "Feels good to just catch my breath."

Markos drew closer. Covered her legs with one of his own. "I don't know if I want you to catch your breath," he said, brushing his lips over hers. "I like you breathless."

A shiver of desire moved through her body and Justine knew she would never get used to the effect he had on her.

"Remember what I said about doing you slow?" he asked. Desire deepened his voice and darkened his eyes.

"Yes," she said, barely above a whisper.

"Well, I always keep my promises."

Markos kissed Justine deeply. Thoroughly. And she knew that she wanted to spend the rest of her life being the most important promise in Markos's life. A real promise. One he would keep forever.

MY PROMISE TO YOU

Natalie Dunbar

This novella is dedicated to my husband, Chet.
I will always remember my promise to you.
Love,
Natalie

CHAPTER 1

Charlimae Watson sat in the second row at the Red Oaks Christian Fellowship tent revival clapping her hands and singing her heart out. Several other choir members sat on folding chairs close by, filling the tent with music so bursting with spirit that it made her eyes water. In the front row, Mother Maybelle Carmichael sat in a white silk suit with pearl buttons, clutching an exquisite lace handkerchief and smiling through her tears. Looking distinguished in a tan summer suit, Charli's father, Chuck, sat next to Mother Maybelle, solicitously patting her hand. Some people stood, testifying and thanking the Lord.

A bead of sweat dripped down Charli's neck. Her white cotton dress was already damp in a few spots. Lifting her fan, she waved it back and forth to create a cool breeze. It was a hot Georgia night. The electric fans moving the air and fluttering the flaps of the white tent could only do so much. Still, several people crowded the area, enjoying the revival.

As the song ended, she checked her program. Reverend Avery had already delivered a stirring sermon. Reverend Danforth was scheduled next. The organ's inspirational music occupied the audience while Danforth stepped to the podium and prepared to speak.

Charli glanced at the entrance to the tent. Should she step outside for an ice-cold bottle of water? The tent flaps opened. Like the answer to a prayer a familiar chocolate-brown figure stood in the opening. Charli's breath caught in her throat as a mix of strong emotions gripped her.

Starving for the sight of him, she let her hungry eyes drink in the vision of deep brown eyes, a straight nose, full mouth, and square chin. Her gaze fell to note the drape of the white golf shirt over his wide shoulders and trim waist. His runner's legs were encased in a tan pair of slacks. He looked better than anything she'd imagined. Hers. Her husband. Would she ever get used to it? Better still, would they ever get things right between them?

Charli wanted to run to him, but pride, self-respect, and a sense of decorum pressured her to turn back to face the podium and pretend she hadn't seen him. *Let him come to you.* Rooted to her position in the seat, she could only watch, trapped by emotion, as he scanned the crowd, looking for her. His eyes brightened, a look of such naked longing changing his face that she blinked fast in an effort to stop the tears forming behind her lids. He'd found her.

Her head tilted up like a flower seeking the vital rays of the sun as he strode up the narrow aisle between the folding chairs.

A man who runs off is worse than no man at all. Ignoring the voice at the back of her thoughts, she felt faint. He was the other half of her soul. The tent, Reverend Danforth speaking in the background, and the rapt faces in the crowd faded with an air of unreality. This was like something out of her dreams. She forced her throat to work as he neared, her hands twisting in her lap.

"Charli," he whispered, ending his journey at her seat. He eased past her knees to the miraculously empty seat beside her.

"Sam," she whispered back, glad that she couldn't say more. She felt much too vulnerable. *Sam, my friend, my love, my lover, I was afraid you didn't love me anymore.*

His big, warm hand engulfed hers. She tightened the grip, intent on proving that this was real. A current of electricity went through her. She tried to listen to Reverend Danforth's message, but there was a roaring sound in her ears. Charli couldn't think. Abruptly she realized that she was trembling. With a conscious effort, she made it stop.

They sat through the reverend's sermon, sneaking glances at one another and respecting the silence of the audience. When Reverend Danforth ended his sermon Charli stood on shaky legs.

Briefly she noticed that her father had turned in his seat and was frowning at them. He'd been certain that Sam had left her for good and would be sending divorce papers any day. That's why he'd been urging her to hurry and divorce Sam first. Now it looked as if he didn't want her to talk to Sam. She didn't need the additional conflict and she wasn't going to let her father into their reunion.

Her gaze found Sam's. Their love and the sight of him filled her so she could think of little else but him. Still anger, hurt, and resentment at what he'd done simmered at the back of her thoughts, gathering heat. That he could do this to her without a word meant things that had been haunting her thoughts for months.

Sam didn't look away from her the entire time they traversed down the crowded aisle of legs, knees, purses, and walking sticks.

"Well, would you look at that?" someone whispered under her breath. "The nerve!"

"I wasn't expecting him to come back," another remarked.

"Shhhhhh!" a third person interjected mercifully.

Charli felt herself blushing. She kept her head up and pretended not to hear the rude comments. Sam's hand tightened on hers. She could have sworn they were shaking. Was she imagining the note of pleading in his eyes? The urge to kiss him warred with the urge to slap his face as they left the tent.

Sam walked her to her car, standing close to her.

She turned to face him, unable to hold things in any longer. "*Where* have you been? Why haven't I heard from you? I've been worried sick," she managed, finding her voice and pushing against the solid bulk of him. She'd been depressed, too, but it wasn't the time to go into that.

"Shhh, we can't talk here. Let's keep this private." Sam put his hands on her shoulders. "I'll tell you everything when we're *home* alone. No sense giving them any more to talk about. Can you drive? I can't leave my hoopty here."

Home. The word had a new meaning now that Sam would be there. "I can drive." Her voice sounded a lot stronger than she felt. He opened her door and saw her settled in the seat. Then he closed the door and went to get into the truck.

Automatically placing her key in the ignition, she started the car. *People argued all the time,* she reasoned, *but love kept them together.* The sooner she got home, the sooner she could hear why he'd gone and stayed away so long.

Turning out of the lot, she checked the rearview mirror to see that he was following in an old Ford truck.

The drive seemed to take longer than usual. She was a nervous wreck and glad to be alone in the car with all her doubts, fears, and insecurities. Finally she pulled into the narrow dirt drive of their little house and parked close to it. Opening the car door she stood on fluid legs, the squeaky sound of crickets filling her ears. A warm breeze moved her dress and soothed her skin, but her thoughts were bits of paper scattering with the wind.

As his truck turned into the drive, she let her glance stray to the house. She'd left the porch light on, but other lights were on, too. It meant that Sam had come here first, looking for her.

Turning back, she watched him get out of the truck. He was a tall, tightly built man who walked with the confident air of one who could handle himself in any situation. She'd been sneaking glances at him since junior high, but he'd never seemed to notice or have an interest in her until her last year of high school. Then he'd come on strong with a fierce passionate interest that fascinated her. As her daddy often pointed out, he'd come from the worst section of Red Oaks, but he'd always been like a prince to Charli.

"Let's go inside," he murmured, putting a gentle arm around her shoulders and letting it drop to her waist.

She stared straight into his brown eyes and swallowed.

Why hadn't she summoned the nerve to divorce him? She still loved him, but trust was another issue.

"Charli," he said, a plea in his voice.

She went along with him, going up the stairs and waiting while he opened the door.

"New steps," he remarked, glancing back at the cement stairs.

"They had to be replaced," she answered.

Stepping inside she placed her purse on the rectangular table and held on to the edge for support. "So, tell me now. Where have you been?" she said, her voice growing sharp and ugly with demand.

"I've been working at the automotive plant in Silver City, what did you think?" he asked. His tone sounded much too calm and reasonable for a man who had been gone for so many months.

She shook her head. "But you didn't call or write. You didn't even leave a return address on the envelope of those checks you sent."

With an impatient sigh, he shifted his feet. "I was angry and frustrated when I left. I felt like a loser. You know how much we were fighting. I couldn't handle any of it. I loved you, but I had to go."

"Loved?" she repeated, her eyes going wide at hearing the past tense.

"Charli, I love you. Always will."

"You left me...." The words came out on a sob. Mortified, she drew in a deep breath and continued. "I thought it might be for good."

"No. It'll never be over between us. Never," he

declared, pulling her into his arms to cover her face with warm kisses and promises of forever.

A tear ran down one cheek. She put her hands on his chest and pushed him away. "This isn't the answer," she cried, choking back another sob. "How can you say you love me and expect me to believe you after this?"

"Because it's true," he declared, coming back to stroke her face and cup her chin.

She twisted away and stepped back. "Is it? I could never voluntarily leave you for so long. I couldn't bear it. Sam, you *abandoned* me."

"No," he insisted stubbornly. "Didn't Reverend Avery come and tell you I was all right? He let me know how you were doing and told me when you needed anything."

"I'm not married to Reverend Avery," she argued, raising her voice. "Why couldn't you tell me that you were all right?"

Guilt, frustration, and righteous anger warred in his expression. "At first I was too depressed to do anything but work. Then I realized that I'm weak when it comes to you," he said finally. "You would have convinced me to come back to Red Oaks."

Charli swallowed hard. "You're damned right I would have. You belong here with me."

Sam shook his head and came at her with his hands spread. "Not when I can't find enough work to take care of you. Not when we're in danger of losing our home."

Her voice rose sharply. "Your home is with me. What's the use of being married if we can't be together?"

He wiped the moisture from her face with a fingertip.

"Charli." His voice dipped low with a note of aching sadness. "I know what it's like to lose my home. When my father died it was all over. I wandered from foster home to foster home and nothing was mine. This is our home and I'm not going to lose it. I never want you to have to go through that."

Reminding herself that she was the wronged party, Charli bit her lip and squashed the flash of sympathy running through her. She knew how deeply he'd been affected by his father's death and the loss of their home. He sometimes drove by the old place, over and over again, looking at it with a sadness that never seemed to ease. Still, she was no shrinking violet, wanting to sit at home and wait to be taken care of. She was an equal partner in this marriage. "I thought we were partners," she explained. "Don't I have a say in this?" she asked, trying to penetrate his determined expression. "Don't I get to say whether I want to be left here all alone?"

"A man takes care of his family. You know that. It's the way I was raised and so were you," he insisted. "I did what I thought was best for us."

"Sa-am," she began, drawing out the syllables, "we should be taking care of each other! You know how much I want to be a doctor. I'll get there someday. Right now I know that we're more important than that. Why else would I quit school to work two jobs?"

"I hate that you quit school. Being with me shouldn't be the end of your dreams."

"It's not the end of my dreams," she protested. "I'll start back as soon as we're caught up on the bills."

"Isn't it? There will always be bills. That's life. That's why I made a sacrifice for us, for our future."

"What about my sacrifice? What happened to getting married so we could work together and build our dreams?"

He drew a frustrated hand through his hair. "I'm doing the best I can."

"Are you?" she screamed back. "Because you haven't talked to me. What about your promise to me? For richer, for poorer, for better or worse?"

He blinked, his jaw tightening. "Charli, I'm doing everything I can to keep us from losing everything. Can't you understand that?"

"No, I can't." She wiped away fresh tears and lowered her voice. "Can you understand that without you this marriage doesn't exist?"

He stared at her, dumbfounded. "Charli..."

"I'm so mad at you, Sam Watson, I just want to shake you. I can barely speak, let alone look at you!"

With a quick maneuver she went around him and ran into the bedroom. Slamming the door behind her, she quickly turned the lock.

She heard him on the other side of the door.

"Charli, I'm sorry...."

Stretching out on the bed, breathing hard, she was suddenly dry-eyed. She couldn't remember having such a hard time communicating with him. The man she'd fallen in love with had all but disappeared. Sam had finally come home and she was still alone. Had she romanticized their relationship and their love?

CHAPTER 2

Charli dreamed a scene that had actually happened a number of times since Sam had gone. Her father sat across from her at the dinner table, that sympathetic look on his lined face. "Sweetheart, I hate to see you so unhappy. I hate Sam even more for doing this to you. Now, you know there is a solution. Maybe you can't contact him directly, but you can divorce him and start healing right now. My lawyer can draw up the paperwork and get things started."

"Daddy, I can't divorce Sam without talking to him first. I want to work things out with him. I love him."

"But does he love you?" her father asked in a remedial tone. "Men who love their wives don't leave them alone for months on end. In a few months it'll be a year. That's desertion in anyone's book."

At a loss for words, she shook her head. She'd meant it when she told Sam she loved him and she believed that he loved her, too.

The loud, urgent sound of her alarm wakened her. Still half asleep, Charli pushed herself up from the bed and crossed the room to turn it off. She was fully clothed. The events of last night came rushing back to her. Sam had come home and they'd argued. Then she'd locked herself in their room.

Suddenly wide-awake she unlocked the bedroom door and hurried to their tiny guest bedroom. Early morning sunlight filtered in around the sides and corners of the miniblinds to touch the flowered bedspread. The room was empty.

Footsteps slowing, she checked the living room. At the sight of him, asleep on the couch, she let herself breathe. Relief eased the choked feeling in her chest. There was still hope for them.

Charli checked the clock on top of the television. Time to get moving or she would be late to work. If Sam was awake she knew he would do his best to keep her home. The ugly truth was that despite his feelings about her working, their finances hadn't fully recovered from him being out of work.

Stepping fully into the room, she hovered over Sam, wishing they could communicate and that she could enjoy a relaxing day at home with him.

He was sprawled on the couch, naked except for the blue sheet he lay on and the corner he'd folded over his hips. His face showed no trace of the anger and frustration he'd shown last night. Lying there, with his thick dark lashes against his cheeks, he actually looked innocent.

Despite lingering anger, she felt love, pure and simple, filling her as she gazed down at him. He'd said he loved her. It that was true, she knew that he'd never leave her again. Gently, she ran her fingers through his thick hair, something she wouldn't have dared if he were awake. He didn't move. Finally she pulled herself away and headed back to the bedroom to shower and dress for work. With any luck she could be back before he awakened and got himself together.

Charli unlocked the door to Dr. Burk's office at ten to eight. It was a little later than she usually managed, but her job didn't really start until eight. Hilda Collins, one of the regulars, was standing in the hall waiting. Charli noticed that Hilda was breathing a little hard and had a light sheen of moisture on her forehead. The woman was sick.

If she had been a doctor, she'd have taken Hilda straight back into one of the examining rooms for some emergency care. Ignoring Hilda's sharp glance, Charli stepped into the cool office with the woman on her heels. Charli did what she could to make her comfortable.

In no time Charli had the lights on and the examining rooms ready for patients. Dr. Burk's nurse, Ann, hurried in about fifteen minutes later in her formfitting uniform. Checking the rooms, she thanked Charli for covering for her. Then she ushered Hilda to one of the examining rooms and took her vitals.

At her desk, Charli checked appointments, pulled the medical records, and prepared billing statements. Despite their argument and her insecurities she was still coasting on the joy of having Sam home again. Nothing was going to spoil it for her.

When Dr. Burk arrived his sharp blue gaze focused on her for several moments. "You're looking well, Charli," he said, a smile adding new creases to his wrinkled face. "Looks like you finally got a good night's sleep."

"Yes, I did," Charli answered, trying her best not to blush.

"Good morning, Dr. Burk," Ann said from the doorway. "I've got Mrs. Collins ready for you. Her blood pressure is up and she's complaining of chest pains."

"Morning, Ann. I'll be there in just a minute," Dr. Burk said, moving on to his office with added purpose to his step.

With a hand on one hip, Ann threw Charli a sly smile. "I'll just bet you got a good night's sleep!"

Charli worked at blanking her expression. If Ann only knew how she'd really spent the night. "What do you mean?"

"Girl, I was at the revival last night. I saw your Sam show up in the middle of Reverend Danforth's sermon. Talking about fire. The two of you were all but sparking off each other. Then both of you nearly ran out of there."

Despite the argument Charli's body had responded to Sam; it had been all she could do to push him away till they settled things. A tiny smile escaped her. "You do love to exaggerate."

"Do I?" Ann's wide smile was contagious. "I know how much you love that man."

Charli's smile widened. "I won't argue with that."

Ann slung an arm around Charli's shoulders and gave her a little hug. "I'm so happy for you, girl. We've all been concerned for you. And I'm more than a bit surprised he let *you* come in to work."

Charlie felt some of the joy in her smile fade. "Who's next for Dr. Burk?" she asked, changing the subject.

"Sorry. Didn't mean to pry." Casually leaning against the counter, Ann took the next patient's file off the stack Charli had prepared. Reading the name on the label, she grinned. "It's Bill Casey, ol' cutey pie himself. I can hardly wait."

As the morning passed, Charli found herself staring at the clock from time to time. She fought the urge to call Sam to see how he was doing. If he was asleep, she reasoned, she'd be disturbing him. If he was awake, he surely knew where she was, whether he liked it or not.

As the clock moved toward twelve, she realized that she'd forgotten to pack a lunch. For emergencies, she kept five dollars in her purse, but with their restricted finances, she hated to use it. Deciding to stay at her desk, she worked on the files. She declined an invitation to lunch with Ann and one of the town's most eligible bachelors, Bill Casey. Ann had been chasing him for months, and Charli didn't want to horn in on Ann's time with him.

Charli's stomach whined. In the empty office she giggled and told herself that she could well afford to skip a meal. She'd been riding the line between voluptuous and plump for years.

The office door opened. She realized that she should have locked the door.

"We're closed for lunch," Charli called, placing a file back into the cabinet. "We'll reopen at one o'clock to see patients."

Heavy muffled footsteps sounded on the carpet.

Charlie glanced up.

Sam stood there dressed in a summer T-shirt and jeans. Looking like a dream, he held a picnic basket in his arms.

"I thought you might be hungry. It didn't look like you fixed anything to eat at the house."

"I don't like arguing, so I was still a little upset this morning and forgot," she confided, scanning his face. He looked calm.

He shifted his feet, meeting her eyes with an obvious effort. "I love you, Charli. I'm sorry about everything. We were both unhappy when I left, but I still had your best interests at heart. I knew you would be angry, but not like this. I don't want you to do anything crazy or permanent. I—I know I should have talked to you first and I realize that being apart like that was a sacrifice for both of us. Do you want me to get on my knees and apologize?"

Charli shook her head. "No, but I'm still hurt by what you did. We lost so much time together. We can never get it back. And I don't feel secure anymore. I still feel like I could wake up tomorrow and find you gone."

He set the basket down and stepped forward to pull her into his arms. "I won't leave again without talking to you first, I promise."

With her face against his shoulder she closed her eyes. "If you ever leave me again we're through," she declared. She felt his body tense. Fear shivered through her. Was he planning to leave again already? "Did you hear me, Sam?"

"Yes, and it's going to be all right," he whispered, stroking her head and pressing his lips to the side of her face.

Charli reveled in the scent of soap, Sam, and his aftershave. While he stood there holding her she felt warm and safe and loved. Gradually she made herself move away from him. This was where she worked after all, and anyone could come in and see them.

"If we hurry, we could have a quick picnic at our favorite spot. I could have you back before one," he promised.

"No. It's too soon," she explained, backing to her desk and taking a seat. "We have to talk about what you did while you were gone and things that have happened."

Sam scanned her face. "I've done nothing to be ashamed of," he said boldly. "Can you say the same?"

"Yes," she answered, not flinching under his critical gaze. "But we still need to talk about it."

With a tired sigh he threw up his hands. "Are you going to be mad at me forever? Because if we can't get past what I did, our marriage is already over. There's nothing to fight for."

She tilted her head. With few exceptions, he'd never been a patient man. "I won't be mad at you forever. That's not me and you know it, but it'll take a while before I can truly feel and accept your sincerity in my heart."

Moving closer, he stared at her hard. "Can I kiss you? It's one of the things I missed the most," he said softly.

"Yes," she breathed, suddenly needing the kiss as much as she needed air.

Sam drew her into a deep embrace. His mouth fastened on hers for a dizzying dance of lips, teeth, and tongues. Butterflies fluttered in her stomach and rushed upward. Charli moaned softly. This was the Sam she knew and loved.

He released her gently. She pried her fingers from the curve of his bicep, one by one.

"Should I leave you a sandwich and some fruit?" he

asked, going back to the basket and rummaging through the contents.

Still dazed from the kiss she wanted to change her mind about the picnic, but she refused to be a doormat for anyone, even Sam.

"Yes, I'll take the sandwich and fruit, thanks," she managed, wetting her lips and tasting him there. "Is that lemonade? Leave me some of that, too."

After he'd gone she sat at her desk and ate the ham and cheese sandwich. She washed it down with the lemonade and told herself she'd done the right thing. Still, it was lonely in the deserted office. She reminded herself that this time she'd made the choice.

Afterward, Charli buried herself in the routine office work and her interaction with the patients. She knew all their medical histories by heart and prided herself on her observations. Dr. Burk had assured her that she would make a fine doctor someday.

CHAPTER 3

Sam hated to see Charli crying and upset. It hurt even more when he was the cause of it. He'd been in love with her since she was ten and had been the only classmate to attend his father's funeral and check on Sam afterward. She was a beautiful girl with a good heart and a lot of spunk. She'd also been one of the most popular girls in school and too rich and smart for the likes of him.

Once he'd learned to accept his father's death, he'd decided that Charlimae Greer would someday be his. It had taken years, but he'd made it happen. He was living one of his dreams, but it had become a nightmare when the local meatpacking company closed its doors. He hadn't planned to pack meat for the rest of his life, just long enough to get Charlimae and himself through school.

Thrusting his thoughts away from the fear he'd seen in Charli's eyes, Sam drove home in his old truck, forcing his thoughts on the list of things he needed to do. At the top, the grass needed cutting and a few of the doors in the house were sticking. Several windows needed screens, too and the neighbor down the street had asked him to try and fix her car. Despite the work, it felt good to be home and with his wife.

Parking the truck in the yard, he got out and put the contents of the picnic basket in the refrigerator inside the house. Then he rummaged through the shed for the old lawn mower. The ornery thing wouldn't start. Wiping the sweat off his forehead, he bent down to check the gas. The reservoir was empty. He walked back to the shed, looking for the can of gas he kept there.

The sound of an engine and someone pulling into the yard grabbed his attention. He looked out the door of the shed. A green Jeep was parked in the yard. It was his father-in-law's car.

Sam felt himself tensing. Gritting his teeth, he rolled his shoulders and rubbed his neck. Determined not to throw the first salvo, he stepped out the shed. Chuck Greer was getting out of the car. "Afternoon," Sam called politely.

"Afternoon," Chuck called back, touching his hat and steadily approaching. "It's kind of hot out here. Got something to drink?"

"Sure. Come on in," Sam said, speaking out of a sense of duty. He didn't like Chuck and Chuck didn't like him. He led the man into the house. "Beer or lemonade?"

"Beer," Chuck said gruffly, softening the tone with a grin. He helped himself to a chair at the kitchen table.

Sam grabbed a cold one from the refrigerator and handed it to his father in law. He poured lemonade for himself.

"I saw you at the revival," Chuck said conversationally. "How long have you been back?"

Sam sipped lemonade. "I just got back."

"You back for good?" Chuck asked, his nose wrinkling with distaste.

Sam set his glass down. "I'm discussing that with Charli this evening."

"Land sakes man, you've been back home since yesterday. You two aren't newlyweds anymore. You've had more than enough time to talk."

Folding his hands across his chest, Sam kept silent. He chomped down on the urge to tell Chuck just where he could go with his nosy observations.

"Charli wasn't happy with you gone, but she did a lot of growing up. I knew you were working at that new plant in Silver City," Chuck confided, "but I didn't say anything to Charli. With the way you two were fighting I thought you might decide to make a clean break."

You hoped. Sam shot him a warning glance. "What do you want, Chuck?"

Chuck's eyes narrowed. "I want my little girl to be happy. I want her to finish school and follow her dream to be a doctor."

Sam's hands fisted. "She's not a little girl but I want those things for her, too."

Chuck all but sneered. "Really? How's she going to get there married to you? You're a loser, Sam. You don't have any real skills and that job in Silver City is only as good as the next hard time in the auto industry. You're pulling her down."

Sam stiffened his back and swallowed a boatload of pride. He needed something from Chuck Greer. "If you know what I was doing in Silver City, then you also know that I took some business and automotive classes."

Chuck nodded. "I'm aware that you don't have nearly

enough credits for a degree. Those auto mechanic classes were a waste of time and money."

"Before I took the job in Silver City, I made some money from auto repairs," Sam reminded him. "Not everyone can afford to drive over to the next town to get their repairs. I was thinking that Red Oaks could use its own auto repair shop. If I had some start-up money I could get a place and all the equipment and tools needed to service the cars in the area."

Chuck's gaze sharpened. "Are you asking me for money?"

"I'm asking you to help me and Charli. I could sign a note and pay interest. It would be a way for us to stay together. It wouldn't be much of a risk because I always pay my debts and I'll be able to take the more expensive auto repairs if I have the equipment."

"To tell you the truth I don't want to help you stay with my daughter," Chuck said callously. "Without you, she'd still be in school. Besides that, I don't like you. I shouldn't have let her go out with you. What makes you think I'd risk some of my retirement money on you?"

The barbed comments hurt, but they weren't anything Sam hadn't already told himself. Once and for all he wanted to see where Chuck stood as far as helping them. In the past he'd always given Chuck a ready excuse with arguments and the fact that they didn't get along. History aside, he asked himself why anyone would expect Chuck to help him. "Charli says we're all family and family helps family," Sam quoted, meeting Chuck's gaze head-on.

Chuck's face looked flushed. He expelled a noisy puff

of air. "With Mary dead, Charli's all I got," he admitted. "I'd sooner pay you to go away."

Sam was on his feet in an instant. "I love Charli and she loves me," he grated out.

"She could get over it," Chuck assured him. "You've made that easy. Plenty of good men around here hated to see her marry you. She could learn to love someone else."

"Get out of *my* house," Sam said between clenched teeth.

Chuck's laugh was ugly. "You mean the house you were only able to get because I gave you two the down payment as a wedding present?"

Balling up a fist, Sam took a menacing step toward him.

Chuck's eyes widened. "You wouldn't hit an old man with heart trouble, would you? Charli would never forgive you."

What he said was true, but it didn't stop Sam from physically nudging him toward the door. "Don't come back without a personal invitation."

"Ask my Charli girl. I'm always welcome in her home," Chuck said as he reached the door.

Sam took his arm and walked him out. Then he used his key to lock the door. "I won't give Charli up for you or anybody else, so you'd better get used to me," he ground out in a voice rough enough to blister.

Chuck stood blinking at him in the sun.

Stepping past him, Sam made his way back to the shed and retrieved the gas can. When he came out, Chuck was already pulling off.

Dr. Burk's last patient was Maybelle Carmichael, one of the mothers in Charli's church, Red Oaks Christian Fellowship. As usual, she was dressed to the nines. This time she wore a pink Chanel suit with a matching purse and sandals. Her short, silver-gray hair was immaculately coiffed in the latest style. She drew Charli into a warm hug. "How ya doing, child?"

Charli put everything she had into her trademark smile. "I'm doing just fine, Mother Maybelle. How about you?"

"I'm doing good for a woman my age, but ya don't really expect me to believe ya doing good, do ya?"

"Excuse me?" Charli swallowed hard, glad that the waiting room was empty.

"I saw ya and your Sam at the revival. Y'all lit up the tent like a miracle from heaven. Now your lip is dragging the ground. Ya in big danger of picking up some real dirt. Now tell me what happened."

Charli sighed and shrugged her shoulders. "Seems like we can't do anything but argue. He's only been back since last night and I can't shake the feeling that he's already planning to leave."

"Ya don't know that for sure, do ya?" Maybelle asked with an astute glance.

"No." Charli's answer was barely audible.

Maybelle Carmichael put a well-manicured hand on her hip. "Ya gotta stop whining and crying and find a way to *make him want to stay*, baby. That man is crazy 'bout ya. Why would he wanna leave?"

"He can't get a job here that pays enough for the house and school and then he wants me to quit working," Charlie confessed. "I'm not losing my house and going back to being Daddy's little girl."

"Ya always gonna be Daddy's little girl, honey," Maybelle observed with a gentle smile. "Since ya mama passed, you're all he's got. But it sounds like your man wants to take care of his family. What's wrong with that?"

Charli fought to keep her voice down as she gave her passionate answer. "I didn't get married to be by myself while my husband works in another town. I want us to be together."

"So why didn't ya go with him?" Maybelle asked politely. She was still making a point.

The pitch of Charli's voice rose so high that she was sure something inside her would break. "He never even asked me!"

Charli winced at the wounded and desperate sound of her own voice. She'd been wallowing in the pain of what she thought Sam had done to her and their relationship for much too long. Maybelle's words resonated with her. She needed to do something to change things. She was going to find a way for them to stay together.

Pity rested in the depths of Maybelle's kind eyes. "So he didn't ask ya to come with him," she said softly. "I wonder why."

Charli was having the same thought. Sam had barely mentioned job opportunities at plants in other cities and towns before he took off. He'd called Reverend Avery and asked him to tell her that he was all right and working hard to get the money they needed, but would not be coming home for a while. Charli turned at the sound of footsteps behind her. It was Ann, coming to escort Maybelle to the examining room.

"I hope I'm not interrupting anything, but we're ready for you, Mrs. Carmichael," Ann quipped with a cheery smile. She glanced back at Charli. "Are you all right?"

Charli forced a believable smile. "Yeah, I'm fine. I was just having a word with Mother Maybelle."

Maybelle Carmichael took Charli's hand and squeezed it gently. "Come and see me sometime, child. I'm gonna look for ya."

"I sure will," Charli assured her. Inside she was trying to remember the day Sam had come home excited about new opportunities in Georgia. He'd asked her how she felt about moving, as long as they stayed in Georgia. She'd felt a rush of sadness at the thought of leaving her daddy. With no sisters and brothers she was very close to her father. He had been a lonely man ever since her mother died of a heart attack, four years ago.

As he'd watched her face, some of the hope and excitement had gone from Sam's face. He'd been silent when she confessed that she couldn't imagine leaving her father and her friends behind. Then he'd dropped the subject. *He never asked you*, she assured herself. Still, she couldn't ignore the odd sense of guilt that lingered in the back of her mind.

Burying herself in her work, Charli finished the filing and worked through a number of billings. When all the patients were gone, she hurried home.

CHAPTER 4

Charli turned into the drive and parked her car behind Sam's old white truck. She saw him beneath the old elm in the backyard, tinkering under the hood of one of the neighbors' cars. He was so involved in the repair that he didn't look up as she approached.

Stepping across red dirt and fresh-cut green grass, she stopped right behind him. "I see you've been busy," she remarked.

Startling, he nearly hit his head on the raised hood of the car. Bending down, he eased himself out. There was black grease on his hands and a dark smudge on one cheek. Still, he was the most striking man she had ever seen.

"I was so deep into this old car I didn't hear you come up," he remarked a little sheepishly.

Charli tilted her head to look up at him. "I guess ol' Miss Lawson is as glad to have you back as I am." She lifted a hand to one of the elm tree branches to brace herself.

"I'm almost done," he said. "Why don't you get out of your work clothes? I'll be in in a minute and we can talk."

Charli carefully lowered her lashes. The words he'd just used had special meaning for the two of them. They were almost always followed by an extended session of lovemaking.

Sam blinked in sudden realization of what he actually said. His Adam's apple moved up and down as he did a slow perusal of her from head to toe.

Charli felt his gaze like his hands on her skin. She fought her body's heated response. It was still too soon. At the very least, she didn't plan on getting physical until she heard what he had to tell her. "I'll go change," she murmured, leaving him no doubt.

Inside the house she hurried into the bedroom and shimmied out of the flowered top and white pants she'd worn to work. From experience, she knew that if Sam made it to their bedroom before she'd actually changed, they wouldn't be able to talk. She drew her favorite T-shirt over her head and stepped into an old pair of jeans.

Sam entered the bedroom just as she zipped and buttoned the jeans. He'd already washed his hands in the kitchen sink. Somehow he'd missed the smudge on his face. "I need a shower," he mumbled, dropping down to sit on the neatly made bed and running a hand across his forehead.

"What do you need to tell me?" she asked, taking the place beside him on the bed.

They faced each other.

"You know that I was working at the new auto plant in Silver City," he began tentatively.

She nodded, waiting for the rest.

"Did you know that the plant is on a two-week shutdown for equipment changeover?"

"No." She shook her head, still trying to make the connection. *He wouldn't be here now if the plant hadn't shut down*. She nailed him with a sudden realization. "You didn't quit."

He spread his hands uneasily. "How could I? Employment around here hasn't changed much. We're still behind on the bills, and you're not taking any classes this semester."

"You wouldn't even be here right now if it weren't for the shutdown, would you?" she asked, voicing her thoughts.

"It had to be done," he insisted, his brows drawing together. "Add up the bills and see for yourself. We would have lost the house already."

Charli's voice rose. "Answer the question, yes or no?" she vented. "The only reason you're here now is that the plant is having a shutdown."

"The answer is no." Sam clasped her forearms. "Charli, the reason I'm here is that I love you. How many times do I have to say that?"

"If you love me you should never get tired of saying that," she answered, studying him and wishing she could read his thoughts. Sam had physically been away from her. Now she was afraid that distance had affected their love for each other. "But if the plant was still open and operating right now, you'd be in Silver City, wouldn't you?" she asked softly.

Something burning in the depths of Sam's narrowed eyes gave in the face of her stare. Was it guilt? she wondered.

Sam's gaze fell. "Yeah, if it was open, I'd be there."

His reply was barely audible.

Sam, her love, was becoming a stranger, she realized. He obviously saw himself as some sort of benevolent dictator in their marriage. "I don't know how to get through to you anymore," she said in sharp, brittle voice.

"Charli…" He tried to pull her closer and into his arms.

Feeling hurt, she twisted away and stood close to the bed, holding herself. This time she was determined not to cry, scream, or run away.

Sam watched her with a mixture of wariness and regret.

"Where did you stay in Silver City?" she asked, determined to plow through the questions that had been bothering her.

"I rented a room from an elderly woman on a fixed income. She gave me a deal in return for looking out for her and cooking for both of us every once in a while."

Charli narrowed her eyes. His answer sounded like something she'd read in a book. It was so innocuous she didn't know whether she should believe him or not. Sam had never been a liar, but he'd never left her before, either. She'd steadfastly defended him all these months, but her mind had conjured painful images of him partying down with a bunch of wild women in his free time.

"It's the truth. I can give you the address and you could talk to her," he said quickly, apparently gleaning something from her expression.

Charli shook her head, but there was one question she just had to ask. "You love sex almost as much as eating and breathing and you get more than your share of attention. It's hard to believe you could hold out for almost a year without sleeping with someone else."

"You accusing me of screwing around on you?" He looked a little hurt that she'd even asked. When she merely looked at him he continued. "No, I'm not screwing around. I know I shouldn't have gone off like that, but I take my vows seriously. I don't want anyone but you, Charli. Believe it. It's been hard being without you all these months…"

Tell me about it. She knew that her father and friends would call her a fool, but she believed him.

"So why didn't you ask me to come with you to Silver City?"

His chin dipped even lower. "You've spent your entire life here in Red Oaks and you're real close to your father. With your mother gone and no sisters or brothers, he's all you've got. I asked you how you felt about moving away from Red Oaks and closer to where there are more jobs. You said—"

"I said that I couldn't imagine being away from my father and my friends," she interrupted. "I said that, but I didn't know you would use that to justify taking off like that. You never asked me to go with you. I never had a chance to even consider it. I love you, Sam. What makes you think you're less important than my father and my friends?"

He studied her silently for several moments. "So if I'd asked, you would have come?" His eyes held a hopeful, almost pleading note.

"I—I don't know," she replied honestly. It hurt to see the disappointment in his expression, but she'd never been one to sugarcoat the truth. She tilted her head. "Are you asking me now?"

"Yes," he said, coming to a decision. "If I can't find a decent job here in Red Oaks, I'll have to go back to Silver City in a couple of weeks."

Charli nearly choked. Recovering fast, she forced her dry throat to work. "Give me some time to think about it," she said, leaning against the wall for support.

She'd gotten her wish. Sam had included her in the decision of whether she stayed in Red Oaks or went to Silver City with him. Far from being pleased, she worked at squashing the fear building inside her.

She'd heard a lot about Silver City. The people were mostly transplants from the North and none too friendly. It was a city that had sprung up around the automotive plant and it was an eight-hour drive from Red Oaks. She'd never driven more than an hour straight. Still, the alternative she'd already experienced for nearly a year was bleak and demoralizing.

"What would we do with the house?" she asked, glancing around the bedroom they'd painstakingly furnished.

"We'll have to talk about it, but we could rent it out till we come back—"

"No! I don't want someone else living in our house," she interrupted.

"Or we could close it up, save on the utilities, and come back on weekends when it gets warm enough."

Charli drew in a ragged breath. Nothing he'd suggested was remotely acceptable. She'd have to think of something fast or life as she knew it would be over.

Suddenly Sam was there, drawing her into his embrace, covering her face with soft kisses. "We'll think of something," he whispered, his warm breath tickling her ear.

Closing her eyes, and letting him comfort her, she wasn't so sure.

Sam hummed a few bars from his favorite song and danced her around the bedroom. Dipping her back over one arm, he leaned in and kissed her lips with a dramatic flair.

Staring up into his handsome face she found herself smiling.

"It's going to be all right," he promised.

Was it? Charli wasn't so sure, but she let him fill her with hope.

CHAPTER 5

Almost ready for work, Charlie came out of the bedroom to find Sam in a pair of gray boxers at the kitchen table with a pocket folder full of papers. Bands of morning sunlight from the kitchen window striped his naked chest and arms and his thick black hair. He'd been increasingly restless since he'd been home sleeping on the couch.

Swallowing, Charli forced her glance away from her view of his padded brown chest and muscular arms. She was restless too and she needed her husband, but she didn't plan on letting him back into their bedroom until she got over the pain of what he'd done and knew that she'd forgiven him in her heart.

"Good morning," he said, his voice rumbling low in his chest.

A sensual heat flashed through her, rooting her to the spot. She returned the greeting.

"Don't I get a kiss good morning?" he asked with a wolfish grin.

Almost dreading this test of her defenses and her resolve, Charli pushed herself forward, trying to look natural.

Sam eyed her quietly, then drew her down onto his lap.

Curving his fingers around her face, he fastened warm, gentle lips on hers.

With a small sigh, she relaxed into him. Her fingertips massaged the soft mat of dark hair on his nape.

Opening his mouth, Sam deepened the kiss, bringing on the heat, bit by bit. She matched him quarter for quarter until the chair tipped precariously, threatening to dump them to the floor.

Charli jumped to her feet, smoothing her clothes and fighting the urge to head back into the bedroom. "I've got to get to work."

"Want some breakfast?" he asked, getting up too. "You've still got a few minutes. Let me take care of you."

She dropped back down to the chair, a molten mass of nerves, needs, and emotions. Her hands shook beneath the table while Sam prepared French toast, microwaved bacon, and tea.

"I miss you, Charli," he whispered as he set the plate in front of her.

She gazed into his warm brown eyes and forced herself to breathe. "I miss you, too."

He drew out the other chair, pushed it close, and sat on it backward. "It's driving me crazy to be this close and not really be with you."

She gripped the edge of the table. "What do you want me to do?"

He scraped the chair a bit closer. "Do you really *have* to ask? If we're going to be together, we should be together."

She shot him an exasperated look. "We've talked about this. Waiting means something very special to me, and you should understand. You were gone for months and I had to do without. Are you threatening to leave me again if I don't sleep with you?"

"No," he said, looking shamefaced and a little bit hurt. "I don't want to ever leave you again. I—I just wanted you to know how miserable I was and how much I regret hurting you."

Charli cut her eyes at him and frowned. Holding the line against Sam wasn't easy. She felt pressured. Even worse, deep inside she was fighting a losing battle with herself. The plain truth was that she desperately wanted her husband. How could she expect Sam to respect her if she couldn't respect herself?

Sam massaged her back and rubbed her shoulders. "I just want us to be together. I know you have to do what you think is best. I'm telling you how I feel about it." After a few moments he added, "If you're not hungry, at least take a bite of the French toast and drink the tea."

She managed a couple of bites of the toast and several swallows of the tea. Then checking the clock, she stood. "I've really got to go now."

Sam got up to retrieve the folder he'd left on the other end of the table. "Can you take this with you and see what you can do about filling out the forms?"

"What's this?" she asked, scanning the front and recognizing the *Georgia State University* logo. In smaller letters she saw the words *Red Oaks Campus*.

"I went down to campus to talk to the financial aid officer yesterday. When you applied last time, we hadn't been married long so they were assuming that your dad would pay some or all your tuition like he did before. Now that we've been married a while, they'll use our income. With our income and your grades, you could qualify for enough grants and student loans to go back to school."

The prospect made the cloud she had been walking under disappear. "And if...we have to leave Red Oaks?" she couldn't help asking.

"You could probably get the money transferred to the campus near Silver City."

Charli accepted the folder and gave the contents a quick scan. It was filled with grant and loan application forms. She smiled, appreciating his thoughtfulness. "Thanks for looking into this for me, Sam. I really want to go back to class. Every day I go to work I see what I could be and how I could be helping others and it gives me strength."

"You've got what it takes to be a good doctor," he said, kissing her cheek. "Have a good day at work."

CHAPTER 6

It was evening and Charli and Sam went into the kitchen to cook dinner together. Sam had apparently learned to cook while he was away.

"I had to," he explained as he seasoned and coated the chicken drumsticks and dropped them into hot oil. "I couldn't afford to eat out. Some of the recipes I remembered from watching you cook."

Working alongside him, Charli cooked a quick batch of fried collard greens and made corn bread. Afterward, they sat at the little table in the kitchen and ate.

Sitting across the table from Sam, Charli relished this time with him. Her house was alive again. They talked and laughed. Except for the occasional awkward silences, things seemed almost the same as before he left.

Glancing across the room, she caught sight of the clock. It was twenty minutes to six. Charli dropped her fork. "I've got to get to work," she exclaimed.

Sam looked like she'd hit him upside the head. "You're not going to work now!"

"Yes, I am. I don't have a choice." She emphasized each word so he'd know she didn't plan on backing down.

"My contract with them is for another month and I'm going to stick to it."

"With the money I've been sending, you really don't need to work," he continued.

Charli stood and pushed her chair into the table. "Actually, we're still a little behind. The furnace went out and I had to have it fixed."

His eyes widened. "Reverend Avery didn't tell me about that."

"Reverend Avery doesn't live here," she replied, coming on a little stronger than she'd expected. "I didn't exactly run out and tell the world, you know. I went and stayed with Daddy for a few days and then I found someone at church who used to work for a big furnace company. He does odd jobs now. Anyway, he gave me a good deal on the repair. The parts weren't cheap, but I saved on the labor."

Sam let out a frustrated sigh. "I really hate that I wasn't here when you needed me. I'm sorry about that."

Charli met his gaze.

She saw sincere regret and remorse in his brown eyes, but she didn't have it in her to tell him that his being away was okay. She tried to think of something comforting that she could say and mean at the same time. Nothing came to mind, because despite their warm camaraderie, she was still angry with him. She acknowledged his apology with an incline of her head. "I'm got to get my things and get out of here," she mumbled.

Sam's mouth drooped downward. "Where's the job?"

"Downtown. The Winston Bank on Oakview and Paddock."

"I wish you could stay home with me." Sam's voice and his choice of words hit her with a sense of irony.

Charli set her teeth. "I wish you'd stayed home with me all those months you were gone."

Pain flashed in his eyes and quickly disappeared. He nodded calmly. "I know I deserved that and more, but I'm here now. I know you're still mad. Would it be better if I just left?"

"No," she said quickly. The thought made her chest hurt. "The truth is that I—I wish I could stay home, too, but I've got to go." With an abrupt turn, she hurried to the bedroom for her purse and keys.

Minutes later Charli headed for the door. Sam was at the kitchen sink washing the dishes.

"Let me drop you off," he offered, stopping to dry his hands. "You don't need to go alone."

"It's not necessary," she protested. "You'll just have to wait up to come back and get me."

"I want to wait for you, Charli," he said in a husky voice. "You're worth it and I don't want you out there alone at night."

Charli fought a wave of frustration. She could see straight through his delaying tactics. Harsh words tumbled from her mouth. "You haven't been worrying about me being out alone at night all this time. Why start now?"

Sam simply stared at her for a few moments. "I did worry about you, Charli, but I convinced myself that you'd quit working and start back to school. I even took some business and automotive classes to make it easier for me to get a job."

Charli bit her lip. She didn't like the way she felt or the way she was acting, but she couldn't seem to help herself. He was not getting an apology.

Sam dried his hands and took the keys from her numb fingers. "I'll drive."

Charli got into the car, frustrated, angry, and a little ashamed. She couldn't go on like this. She needed to forgive him and move on or let her daddy's lawyer draw up the divorce papers. Despite her tough talk, there was really no decision to make. She loved Sam and she didn't want to give him up. As she'd said before, forgiving and forgetting would be her biggest problems.

By the time Sam dropped her at the bank he knew the time she got off and had promised to come back and get her promptly. He'd asked detailed questions about what she did and whether others worked with her. "See you at eleven," he said and drove off.

Mo, the one of the bank's night security guards, let Charli into the bank with a friendly greeting. Going to the maintenance closet, she quickly got to work. Because funds were short at home, she hadn't bothered to hire someone to help her clean the premises. The money helped, but the biggest benefit was that working hard kept her too tired to spend a lot of time thinking about being home alone.

While emptying wastebaskets and vacuuming and dusting the cubicles and offices she thought about going with Sam or staying in Red Oaks alone. Her hands shook. She was no closer to thinking logically about this. He'd mentioned taking automotive and business classes to make it easier to get a job. That meant he had a plan. She spent the rest of her cleaning time trying to come up with ideas.

At eleven Sam was outside waiting. A green Jeep was just turning the corner. That's when she remembered that she hadn't told Sam that her father followed her home from work at night to make sure she was safe.

"Tell me you and Daddy weren't arguing just now," she murmured, getting into the car and closing the door.

Sam flashed her a wise look. "Not this time," he murmured.

"What does that mean?" she shot back, fiddling with her seat belt.

His jaw tightened defiantly. "He came by to argue with me this afternoon."

"About what?"

"You and how I'm no good for you. What else?"

Sinking her head back into the seat cushions, she closed her eyes and sighed. "It's been hard for me all these months, Sam. Daddy just wants me to be happy."

"Hold on to that thought," he replied, taking off. "But that man won't really be happy until you're free of me. No matter what I do, your father is in the middle of our business, our life," he bristled.

"*You* hold on to this thought," Charli said, turning her head to give him a meaningful look. "I'm married to *you* and I've been doing everything I can to stay that way, but you've got to help me. We have to talk more and you can't just run off without me, even if it's for my own good. We have to love each other and work together—"

"And you have to forgive me," he interrupted.

Nodding her head, she ran a hand over her eyes. "Yes, I do."

That effectively killed their conversation for the rest of the trip home. There, Charli showered and got ready for bed. Sam hovered around, a hopeful look on his face until Charli finally told him that it was still too soon.

CHAPTER 7

Dressed in his best suit Sam sat in the Winston Bank parking lot for several minutes, gathering his nerve and going over what he would say. He had a lot of ideas and little money. Hopefully he could convince Winston's loan officer to part with enough money to start his business. He knew more reasons why he shouldn't get the loan than why he should, but as Charli had said when she gave him the pep talk this morning, what did he have to lose?

At home he and Charli had settled into an uneasy routine as the week wore on, but the future was never far from their thoughts. Charli continued to work her night job, but Sam went, too, and insisted on working the cleaning jobs with her. It made the work go faster and freed her to spend more time at home. During the day, Charli worked for Dr. Burk and Sam split his time between repairing cars and day work as a laborer.

In the evenings they cooked and ate together. Then they discussed their plans for the future. Sam had found an old building in town that was up for lease. With it and a loan, he was certain he could get the equipment he needed to make a go at a local auto repair shop. Since the nearest big city was more than an hour away, the town sorely needed an auto repair shop.

Shutting the engine off, he stepped out of the truck in the searing summer heat. He'd barely taken a couple of steps when the sweat started dripping down his face. Speeding up, he hurried into the bank's heavy glass doors.

Air-conditioned cool surrounded him, enabling him to take a breath and look around. The place was a modern showpiece of wood, chrome, glass, and open spaces. It looked different from the place he'd helped Charli clean.

Except for three people in line for the tellers, it was virtually empty. In an area off to the side a toffee-colored man with waves and a navy blue suit sat behind a glass door. The sign above the door read Loan Officer. A notebook hung on a hook outside with a pen attached.

Loosening the jacket on his tan suit, Sam pushed himself forward. The man didn't look up as Sam took the pen and wrote his name in the notebook with shaking fingers.

After signing in, Sam took a seat on the leather couch outside the loan officer's door. This loan meant too much to him and Charli for him to be thinking of failure, but it lingered at the back of his thoughts. If he didn't get the loan, he would have to go back to Silver City and he didn't think Charli would come with him. Sure, she said she was thinking about it, but he'd seen the crushed, hopeless look on her face. If he went back to Silver City, he would be alone and it wouldn't be long before Charli's father talked her into signing divorce papers.

The loan officer got to his feet and opened the door to

his office. Lifting the notebook, he read Sam's name aloud and invited him into the office.

Inside, Sam settled into the leather guest chair and forced clean air into his lungs. The loan officer introduced himself as Ossie Davis Turner and put Sam at ease with the story of how his grandmother had been so in love with Ossie Davis that she'd insisted on the name for him.

"So how can I help you?" Mr. Turner asked.

Sam detailed his need for a fifty-thousand-dollar loan that would cover his lease of a building for a year, the utilities, and the lease or purchase of the automotive diagnostic equipment and tools needed to run a repair shop. He talked about the need for a shop in Red Oaks and how many repairs he had done within the last few days. Then he added how he would dispose of waste and get the supplies needed to run the place.

Turner made notes on a pad of paper while Sam talked. "It sounds like you've got your business plan in your head. We need to see it in writing, but you can bring that in tomorrow if the committee seriously considers your loan. What sort of training do you have?"

Feeling woefully inadequate, Sam kept his head up and infused his voice with confidence as he described the licenses and certifications he'd obtained to be a mechanic on the various parts of cars. Then he talked about the courses he'd taken on running a small business. It gave him hope to see Turner still making copious notes.

Turner reached into a drawer to pull out an application. "You need to fill this out," he explained, "but before we waste any more of your time and mine, do you have any collateral or assets?"

"Our house and cars," Sam answered, his hope fading.

"Do you fully own both? How much do you think they're worth?"

Sam's shoulders tensed as he rattled off the numbers. "We own the cars. The house is worth about seventy thousand, my truck, six hundred, her car, eight thousand..."

"How long have you been in the house?" Turner asked, tapping his pen against the pad of paper.

Sam wiped a sweaty palm against his pant leg. "Two years."

Turner shook his head. "Do you have a job?"

"Yes." Sam was glad to be able to say that he worked at the factory in Silver City.

"I see that you're wearing a wedding ring. What about your wife?"

Forcing his shoulders to relax, Sam talked about Charli's two jobs and added that she was a premed student.

Lips tightening, Turner gave Sam a hard look. "I'm trying to help you out here, man, but there's not much to go on. We sometimes give business loans without collateral, but the business plan has to be good and a return on our investment virtually guaranteed. Give me your name, address, and Social Security number."

Sitting across from Turner and writing the information was one of the hardest things Sam had ever done. He wanted to get up and run out of the bank. There was no way they would give him a loan once they looked at his credit. What had he been thinking?

"This won't take long," Turner promised with a polite smile. "Would you like something to drink while you wait?"

Sam nodded and accepted the ice-cold bottle of water. Turner took the information and stepped out of the office.

Sam sat fidgeting in the chair and waiting. He eased the painful dryness in his throat with the water and struggled to maintain his dignity by not falling apart.

Turner returned to the office with a sympathetic expression on his face. "I'm sorry, Mr. Watson, but you don't meet the requirements for the loan you're applying for."

Sam's ears rang in the silence following Turner's statement. "How much of a loan do I qualify for?" he managed.

"We'd have to have the house and the cars appraised of course, and adjustments made for the amounts owed on your mortgage and on the loans, but I'm guessing about ten thousand."

Sam's chin fell. It wasn't enough. Besides that, he'd have to risk everything he and Charli had. He couldn't bring himself to even consider it.

"Thanks for your time and consideration," Sam murmured, getting to his feet.

"My pleasure, Mr. Watson," Turner said, offering his hand.

Sam shook Turner's hand, nodded, and started for the door.

"You could always try another bank," Turner said helpfully. "Of course you should have your business plan in writing when you do."

Thanking him again, Sam made his escape. Ovenlike heat blasted him in the face as he stepped outside the bank and hurried to his truck. Once he'd cooled the interior, he started the drive home.

Down the street from the Winston Bank, he stopped in front of the Stone Morton Bank. It was one of those banks that bragged incessantly on the air about their friendliness and service for small businesses. Gathering his courage, Sam went in.

Forty-five minutes later he left the bank with his spirit at an all-time low. He knew of another bank two streets over, but he'd had enough for today. Besides, he knew that he needed to put his business plan on paper.

Sam drove home, certain that his life was falling apart.

CHAPTER 8

Charli got home from the office to find Sam gone. For just a few moments the old fear gripped her. Had he taken off again? No matter how tough she talked, she knew that she still loved her husband and wanted him with her.

Glancing around the living room, she caught sight of his gym shoes under the coffee table and his favorite shirt on the arm of the couch. No, Sam was still somewhere around.

The doorbell rang. Wondering who it could be, she went to answer it.

Built like a man on the cover of *Men's Health* magazine, the very handsome and ultraeligible bachelor Alphonso Wright stood on her doorstep. He had a growing heating and cooling business and did some plumbing work. Charli had been grateful for his services when the furnace went out. Now he was back as promised to service the air-conditioning. With Sam's return she'd forgotten her appointment with Al.

Charli opened the door, noticing for the first time how his gaze caressed her warmly. Had he always looked at her like that? She couldn't remember doing anything to lead him on. She hoped she was imagining things.

"Since you didn't call, I'm assuming you haven't had

any problems with the furnace," Alphonso said with an engaging smile that reflected his sunny outlook on life.

Her lips curved upward in response. "It was fine. Thanks, Al, you did a wonderful job. Come on in."

He stepped in with the good-natured male swagger she saw in most of the guys and set his toolbox on the floor. "You can't be too careful when it comes to taking care of your house," he added.

"That's for sure," she agreed. "It's so hot outside, can I get you something to drink?"

He rewarded her with a flash of his perfect teeth. "Water, or lemonade if you've got it."

"I've got some homemade lemonade," she said, heading for the refrigerator.

"I know that's gotta be good!" Al bent his long legs to retrieve his toolbox. "I'll get started on servicing your air conditioner. Is it okay if I go out the back door?"

"Sure, help yourself." Charli opened the refrigerator and drew out the pitcher of lemonade. Then she found a big cup in the cabinet and filled it with ice. By the time she walked out the back door with the lemonade he'd replaced the filter and was checking the condenser and the lines running to and from the house.

"Everything okay?" she asked, watching him check the rest of the unit.

"It's fine." Al finished his maintenance and put the top back on her air-conditioning unit. Sweat dripped down his forehead.

"Here, this will cool you down a little." She handed him the lemonade.

He tipped his head back and took a long draught. "This is good!" he exclaimed.

Charli heard the sound of a car. Sam was pulling into the drive. Soon he got out of the car, fully dressed in his best Sunday suit, walking like he was carrying the sins of the world on his shoulders.

Just looking at him she figured that he'd applied for the loan and been turned down. A sudden sharp pain pierced her heart. Blinking, she looked down to hide the quick stinging tears that threatened to fall. She didn't want to leave the loving life she'd known among her family and friends in Red Oaks.

Sam walked along the side of the house until he reached them.

Charli threw him a sympathetic glance. Moving from foster home to foster home, he'd had a lot of rejections in his life. From watching him she knew that it never got easier.

Sam's gaze slid past her to rest on Al. A note of hostility flickered there. He was jealous.

"Sam, this is Alphonso Wright," she said brightly. "He repaired the furnace when it went out." She turned to Al. "Al, this is my husband, Sam."

The stunned look of surprise in Al's eyes made Charli want to sink through the red dirt and disappear. If she hadn't known better she would have suspected herself of screwing around.

Both men stared at each other for a moment, sizing each other up.

"You thought she was single?" Sam asked gruffly.

"I hoped she was a widow," Al confessed, "not that I

made any moves, understand. She just seemed sort of sad all the time, so I tried to cheer her up."

"She's right here and getting a little upset with two men who talk about her like she wasn't here!" Charli interjected angrily.

Both men apologized.

Sam stepped forward, a serious look on his face, his hands fisting at his sides. "So you're here about the furnace?"

Al shook his head and laughed. "No, no, man. When I took care of the furnace I promised to come back when it got warm to do the maintenance on the air-conditioning. You see, the old man who runs Finner Cooling in town has been sick for a while. His customers have been calling me."

"Oh." Sam's hands dropped to his side.

"My company operates in Harwell," Al explained.

Another "oh" from Sam and then the men shook hands cordially.

Al lifted his glass and finished his lemonade.

Charli let herself relax.

"How much do we owe you?" Sam asked as Charli took Al's empty glass.

Al looked surprised. "Oh, uh, give me thirty dollars."

"You only charge thirty dollars for a maintenance call?" Sam asked incredulously.

"No, but Charli's special," Al explained. He smiled in the face of jealousy leaking back into Sam's eyes. "Charli was my very first customer."

"Oh." This time Sam's tone was very low. The jealousy dissipated. "Charli is special for a number of reasons.

That's why I love her so much. It was nice meeting you, Al. If you'll excuse me, I'm going to get out of this heat and this monkey suit."

"Of course," Al said, echoing Sam's sentiments. "Nice meeting you, too."

Once Sam had gone into the house Al turned to her and said, "I'm glad your husband is home. You seem a lot happier. Now feel free to call me if you have any more problems with the furnace and Finner is still not accepting any jobs, you hear?"

"Yes, of course." Charli offered him her hand.

He shook it gently and went on his way.

Inside the house Sam had taken off the suit and changed into a T-shirt and a pair of shorts. He was coming out of the bedroom.

"You were jealous," Charli said flatly.

"Yeah." With that he headed for the kitchen.

Charli followed. "I can handle myself. You really didn't have a reason to be."

At the sink he pivoted to face her. "Yes, I did. You were alone here for months. I bet Alphonso wasn't the only man to look at you and think you were single and fair game. I left you vulnerable like that and I didn't even realize it."

She met his gaze and held it. "No one laid a hand on me, I swear."

"I know that. Otherwise you would have told me. I trust you."

Relief washed through her. She didn't know what she would have done if he thought she'd been cheating.

Opening the refrigerator, she took out the ground beef and placed it in a bowl. "Meat loaf or hamburgers?"

"Hamburgers, and let's do a salad." Turning back to the sink, he washed his hands. Then he found the salad ingredients and began to wash them.

"I saw that you had on your suit today," she remarked, mixing chopped onion, spices, and bread crumbs into her ground beef. "You must have gone in for the loan."

"Yeah." At the cutting board he was already chopping carrots and slicing cucumbers.

Mashing balls of hamburger mix into burgers she asked, "When will we know?"

"I know now." He scraped the vegetables into a bowl. "We got turned down for the money we need by Winston Bank and the Stone Morton Bank, too. Both offered about ten thousand with a lien on the house and our cars."

Charli set the hamburger in the bowl, wiped her hands, and dropped down into a kitchen chair. She hated being right. Suddenly there wasn't enough air in the air. She forced air in through her mouth. Ten thousand wasn't nearly enough money. She'd been hoping that there was still a way of making things work in Red Oaks.

"I really wanted you to have a chance at a business here. Maybe we could ask Daddy for a loan," she mumbled.

Sam expelled a harsh breath of air in a painful parody of a laugh. "Do you think I didn't? What do you think we argued about?"

The bleak look in his eyes did her in. "I didn't think much about it since you and Daddy don't get along," she admitted. "Maybe it would be different if I asked."

"Maybe," Sam affirmed in a flat voice, but she could tell that he thought she would be wasting her time.

She sat in the chair with her thoughts cycling uselessly. Time was running out on them. It wasn't fair that she should have to choose between her father, her friends, and the only life she'd ever known and Sam. Guilt ate at her conscience, too, because she'd married Sam with promises for better or worse, richer or poorer, and forsaking all others.

She felt the weight of his gaze on her and glanced up.

His eyes narrowed. "You're thinking about leaving Red Oaks," he murmured.

She nodded, unable to say a word.

He laid the knife on the counter and crossed the room to lift her out of the chair.

Pulling her close, he locked his arms around her waist. "You are my family, my love. I'd do anything for you, Charli, do you know that?"

"Yes." She laid her head against his chest, breathing in the exciting mix of aftershave, deodorant, and Sam and closing her eyes. "I'd do anything for you too."

He looked down at her, stroking her face with his fingertips, rubbing his face against hers in a tantalizing caress.

Bending his head, he fastened his mouth on hers in a hot, passionate kiss. Then his hands were on her, slipping beneath her clothes to touch and caress her skin while she trembled with pleasure. His tongue curled around hers, sliding and dancing in her mouth with an intensity that sabotaged all thought. It had been too long since they'd loved one another.

Forgiveness was the last thing on her mind. Instinct and need took over as her fingers caressed the smooth, well-toned chest beneath his shirt and eased down to cover the smooth plane of his abdomen. She slipped one hand lower to caress him, and rid him of the belt and pants with the other.

Gradually she realized that they were moving. The kitchen tile beneath her feet faded into the soft rug that filled the hall and then the thick bedroom carpet her father had given her for her birthday.

Sam tossed the blue dress onto a chair and removed the rest of her clothes in the sensual storm generated by his hands and mouth. Before she knew it he'd drawn back the covers and placed her on the bed.

"Charli?" The question was in his eyes, too.

This was her chance to step back, to deny him. But how could she deny herself the love of her life? Anger and hurt still simmered somewhere within her, but her love for Sam was a force to be reckoned with.

"Yes." She was still his. Charli met his burning gaze, curling herself around him and welcoming him warmly with her body and her heart.

Sam was so gentle she could feel the tension and strain of him holding himself back. He didn't want to hurt her. She urged him on with her voice, with her body and her intimate knowledge of his, until his control snapped. Then they came together with a wildness seated in the knowledge of just how close they'd come to losing each other. Afterward, Sam held her, kissing her over and over again. They made love once more.

Hours later she awakened with him holding her beneath the sheets. Sometime during the hours they'd spent making love she'd slipped out to put the food in the refrigerator and freshen up. Now she reveled in the sensual feel of his warm body enveloping hers.

"Who needs food when I've got you?" he growled close to her ear.

She wasn't hungry for anything but Sam, either. Turning in his arms, she whispered something sexy in his ear.

He stared at her, intrigued. "Can you do that? Would you do that?"

Laughing, she pulled the covers over their heads.

CHAPTER 9

Charli spent a good part of Saturday morning cleaning while Sam worked on cars in the yard. Afterward she got into her car and headed for the market with her grocery list since their supply of food was getting low.

It felt good to go up and down the aisles knowing that Sam would be there when she got home. Some of her friends and several members of Red Oaks Christian Fellowship were in the market and stopped to chat. She found herself promising that she and Sam would be in church on Sunday and would also come out for the last night of the revival. Her friend Lexy invited her and Sam to an end-of-the-month Sunday dinner with another friend, Selma, and her husband, Jake.

As Charli waited in line to pay, Mother Maybelle came to stand in line behind her in a green designer sundress that complemented her mature figure. "Ya never did come to see me," she stated in a teasing voice.

Charli smile sheepishly. "Sorry, Mother Maybelle, I meant to."

Mother Maybelle lowered her voice. "Ya just got caught up in all the love and drama at home, huh?"

Charli nodded. Mother Maybelle had always been good at sizing up a situation.

"Well, now ya got to have lunch with me to make it up," the older woman said, still smiling.

"Okay," Charli said agreeably. "When?"

Mother Maybelle began to place her items on the counter behind Charli's. "Well, right now, child."

"I'd like to, but I've got ice cream and milk that would spoil in this heat," Charli countered as the clerk began to ring up her purchases.

"Uh-huh," Maybelle Carmichael said gamely. "My refrigerator and freezer work just as good as yours."

Charli reached into her purse for her billfold as the clerk started bagging her groceries. "Oh, you're inviting me out to the house?"

"Sure am," Mother Maybelle confirmed with a curt nod. "I just made potato salad and decided I wanted some fresh tomatoes to go with it."

"It sounds good. Maybe I could just drop the groceries at my house along the way," Charli suggested.

"By the time you put all the cold stuff up and explain everything to Sam we could be halfway through our lunch," Mother Maybelle teased. "Does that man keep you on that short of a leash?"

Charli laughed out loud as she paid the clerk and accepted her change. "No, he doesn't. I'm going to load my stuff into the car and then I'll wait for you in the parking lot, okay?"

Mother Maybelle nodded. "Fine. It won't take but a minute." Then she stepped up to greet the clerk.

Charli followed Mother Maybelle home. She was surprised to find the table set for lunch out on the covered-screen porch next to the little pond. Fine china plates, green napkins, and place mats that matched Maybelle's dress and delicate crystal decorated the table. Mother Maybelle had sliced tomatoes and cucumbers, and set them on a crystal platter alongside a large bowl of potato salad and a covered silver tray of fried chicken. A crystal platter of bread and crackers was there too. Mother Maybelle certainly knew how to entertain.

"Who else is coming?" Charli asked, noting that the table was set for four.

"Just us," Mother Maybelle said as she came out of her kitchen with a big pitcher of sweet tea and another with lemonade. "Ain't we enough?"

Charli shrugged. "I was just counting the place settings, that's all."

Mother Maybelle flashed her a wonderful smile. "Sit down, child."

Charli sat and the two women went about the business of fixing their plates. The food was delicious. Charli ate like she was starving and lavished Mother Maybelle with compliments.

"So, are you keeping Sam Watson?" Mother Maybelle asked when they were nearly done. "He's a nice young man."

"Of course I'm going to keep him. I love him," Charli said honestly.

"Just asking," Maybelle said kindly. "In a town like this we all in each other's pockets. If you're thinking about a divorce, everybody gonna know it."

Charli set her fork down. "Things were really bad when

he left and he wasn't off cheating on me, Mother Maybelle. He was working and sending a lot of money home for the bills and getting some education and training, too. I can't stay mad at him for that. He should have talked it over with me and he should have kept in touch better, too, but if I'd known where he was I would have gone there and brought him home."

"Even if it meant you would lose your house and everything?" Maybelle asked softly.

"What good is a house if you have to stay in it by yourself?" Charli countered and then caught herself for being rude. Mother Maybelle lived alone in her grand mansion.

"It's all right, child," Maybelle chuckled. "I know I live alone. Lord knows I've tried many a time to find the right man, but after five husbands I'm afraid to go too much past Sunday dinner and a lot of talk. That's enough about me. If you two got love and want to stay together, that's wonderful. What's the problem?"

Charli sipped her sweet tea. "Money and making a living is the problem. He was hoping I'd quit working and go back to school, but we're still behind on our bills and the job situation around here hasn't improved much. He's been trying to get a loan to pay for a lease on a building and to get the diagnostic tools and equipment to run a repair shop here in town."

Maybelle's head bobbed up and down. "That's good. I know Sam is real good with cars and this town needs someone local. We shouldn't have ta have our automobiles towed over to the next town to get fixed."

"Sam's been turned down by Winston Bank and Stone Morton Bank for the amount we need to get started," Charli added. "I'm about at my wits' end. I was going to ask Daddy, but I hate to ask him to dip into his savings again."

Maybelle sighed. "Times are bad. Have ya thought of asking the church? My late husband, Thaddeus, before he died set up a big charity foundation down at the church to help folks. They give business loans and invest in the community. They could invest in your business, too."

Charli glanced up, hope building once more. "Do you think they would do it?"

Maybelle smiled. "I'm on the board of trustees. What do ya think? No guarantee, but ya have got to do what ya can ta keep your family together. Ya hear?"

Charli nodded, feeling much better than when she'd walked into Maybelle's mansion.

Sam was out front looking up the road and waiting for Charli when she got home. "I got worried when you were gone so long," he explained, opening the trunk and grabbing a couple of the grocery bags. "I was imagining all sorts of tragic things."

"Sorry. I probably should have called," Charli said. The irony of the situation wasn't lost on her as she helped him with the bags. He'd taken off for months without calling her. She threw him a testy look. "You know—"

"It's okay," he said quickly.

"I saw Mother Maybelle in the grocery store and she wanted me to have lunch with her," she added.

Sam hurried to the door with his bags. "How's she doing?"

Charli followed him up the steps with the last of the bags. "Mother Maybelle's fine. She thinks we should ask the church for the loan."

He pushed the door open and didn't stop till he reached the kitchen table. "I didn't think of that, but I'm sure a whole lot of others did." He set the bags down. "We have to give it a try."

"Yes, we do." Charli placed her bag in front of the refrigerator. Opening it, she began to unload.

"What's for dinner?" he asked, coming up behind her to help place the cold stuff into the refrigerator and freezer.

"I don't know, Chef Watson," she teased. "What are you whipping up?"

"We could cook those hamburgers from yesterday," he suggested in a light tone.

Their gazes met and held for several moments as they remembered starting to prepare the dinner that never was. As if by agreement they resumed placing the last of the items in the refrigerator. Sam reached past her to close it. Then he backed her into it so that the full length of their bodies touched.

Their lips met in a searing kiss that set her body on fire. Sam's hands were all over her; touching, kneading, caressing, and teasing. She gloried in his scorching kisses and the feel of his strong muscular body beneath her fevered fingers. When she could take no more she leaned against him with a single whispered "yes."

Lifting her in his arms, he carried her to the kitchen table for a sensual session of sweet satisfaction.

Later Charli cleaned the kitchen and made a fresh salad

while Sam cooked the burgers. They ate together at the kitchen table. Afterward, Sam called Reverend Danforth and asked for loan consideration from the church's loan committee. By chance, the committee would be meeting that week. Reverend Danforth told Sam he needed to come in to do the paperwork as soon as possible since the committee would pick up their copies of the applications after church the next day.

Insisting on going alone, Sam went down to the church office to fill out the loan application form.

CHAPTER 10

At home alone, Charli worried about the future for her and Sam. Coping with an attack of nerves, she did the laundry. She didn't like any of the choices facing her and Sam. It was rapidly coming to the time when she would have to tell Sam that she would go to Silver City with him, and she didn't know if she could do it. It wasn't a decision she'd made, but given her love for Sam and the promises she'd made when they got married, she felt as if she were being pushed into a corner.

When her father called and asked her to return the premium MP3 player she'd borrowed, Charli was glad for something to take her mind off her situation.

At the mansion, Chuck Greer was packing his suitcases when Charli arrived. Looking dapper in a white silk shirt and matching pants, he was in a cheerful mood.

Hugging him hard and kissing his cheek, she gave him the MP3 player. "Sorry I had it for so long."

"Don't worry about it," he said, placing it in his carry bag. "There'll be one just like it in your Christmas this year."

"Where are you going this time, Daddy?" she asked,

"Just taking a little side trip to Paradise Island, Charli girl," he quipped with an affectionate grin. "I need to get away for a while. Want to come along? My treat? It could be just like old times."

Charli took the two shirts from his hands, smoothed and refolded them, and placed them in the bag. "You know Sam just got back. We need to spend some time together. That's why I couldn't go without him," she murmured, knowing what her father's response would be. She didn't know why she tortured herself like this.

Her father frowned and tilted his head. "Now, Charli girl, having Sam come with us wouldn't be like old times, would it?"

Steeling herself, she pushed the words out. "No, I guess it wouldn't."

His gaze hardened. "We've been through this before. Come home and whatever you want is yours. Helping my child is a lot different than financing her misery with a man she shouldn't have married."

"It's done. I'm married. Daddy, Sam is my husband," she said, studying him intently to gauge his expression. "He's family. Except for you, he's all I've got."

He expelled a tired breath. "What happened to the divorce you were getting?" he asked, looking up from dropping a pair of slacks into his open suitcase. "This could be the perfect opportunity to put some distance between you."

She shook her head. "I—I agreed to think about a divorce, Daddy. I never said I'd get one. I don't want more distance between Sam and me. I love him and it's not going to change."

Her father's brows went up. His voice went low and

cutting. "So you've actually forgiven him for taking off like that? Where's your backbone, girl?"

The words hurt. Her loving father had never spoken to her like that before. She recoiled as if he'd slapped her. "I'm...using it to save my marriage," she managed, standing up to him for Sam and for herself.

"Maybe there's nothing to save," he said, giving her a hard look. "He's a loser. Do you think a few business and automotive classes are enough for him to get a job any place other than a burger joint or that factory in Silver City?"

Charli froze. "You knew where he was?" she gasped, her face burning with the pain of his betrayal.

"Damned right I knew." His lips twisted. "It was the best thing he ever did for you. If he'd stayed away, it would have been better for everyone."

"Not better for me." She backed away from him, one hand covering the hardness in her chest as the truth of his betrayal sank in. "Daddy, you saw what I went through, how miserable I was." Tears slipped down both cheeks. She wiped them away with the back of her hand. "How could you keep it from me?"

"Baby, don't cry. I didn't do anything," he grumbled uneasily. He extended a hand. "I let him take himself out of the picture. It's no secret that Sam and I don't get along. It's because I always wanted the best for you. You married him and all your dreams fell apart."

Charli swallowed back a sob. "That's not how I feel. Sam is smart and kind and he's good with anything mechanical. He has a good heart and he makes me happy. He's my dream, too, Daddy."

"Is he? Well, I can't just stand by and watch you throw your life away," he snapped. His lips formed a straight line.

"Well—well, I can't stand here and let you talk about Sam like that." A few more steps and she reached the door. "We all make mistakes. I'm not perfect and you aren't either. I'm not giving him up. If you can't find it in your heart to accept me and Sam being together, then I can't be around you."

She wrenched open the fancy front door.

"Charli girl!" he bellowed, turning red. "Don't you go out that door like that. You know I was doing what was best for you."

"No, you were doing what was best for you." With that, she shot out the doorway and ran down the steps.

"Come back here. I'm not going to just forgive you for leaving like this," he shouted after her.

Openly crying now, she turned to face him. "What makes you think I'm going to forgive *you?*"

The tears stopped before she got home, but she was still mad. Her daddy had always been honest and forthcoming with her. So had Sam. Somehow both men had chosen the same time to let her down.

It's okay, she told herself. *You knew Daddy hated Sam and you knew Sam was desperately unhappy with losing his job and not feeling like he could take care of you. Something had to give....*

Outside the car, trees and bushes hugged the road, giving it an unfamiliar, cavelike appearance. Steeling herself, Charli drove through it, knowing that she was just going to have to push through this hard patch in her life.

* * *

Charli was on the couch with a romance novel when Sam got back, but she wasn't reading. She jumped up and came to meet him. "How did it go?"

Sam tried not to show the dark depression drawing him into its depths. "Times are bad, so they had a lot of applications. Some people are homeless, others losing their houses, and some want to start franchises here. I filled out the form and talked to Reverend Avery about what I wanted to do. He said to come back on Tuesday so I could talk to the committee. He says that the committee uses their heads and their hearts when it comes to loans. After that, I stayed to help them feed the homeless."

Charli gave him a quick hug and a smile. "I'm glad you did."

Despite the smile, he knew something was wrong with her. She was upset. He could see it in the pink tinge to the skin around her eyes and on her nose and her swollen eyelids. She'd been crying. "What's wrong?" he asked, noting how she didn't quite meet his gaze.

She shrugged, but he could see the tension in the lines of her body. "Daddy and I had an argument. That's all."

"It *was* about me?" he asked, knowing the answer but needing the confirmation. Charli and her father rarely argued about anything unless it concerned him.

"Yes." Her head came up. "You know I was angry and upset with you for taking off and staying away so long. I've never been so miserable in my life. Daddy was a real comfort to me. I—I thought he was doing everything he could to help, but tonight he admitted that he knew where you were all along."

Sam nodded. He felt her eyes boring into him, but he felt like he was in a lose-lose position. He couldn't talk too negatively about her dad because she'd never forgive him or forget what he said. The only way she would see her dad the way he really was would be through her own experience.

"I've never known Daddy to stand by and let me suffer," she said softly, her tone ringing with hurt and a bit of sadness. She assessed him with a look. "You're not surprised. Why?"

"Things he said before I left, things he said when I got back," he mumbled, deliberately vague.

"If I had listened to him, we'd be divorced by now," she confided.

No surprise there. He'd always known exactly how Chuck Greer felt about him. If Chuck hadn't been so deep into the church Sam thought he might even have arranged a timely accident for Sam, to get rid of him.

Taking her soft hand in his, Sam led her to the couch and pulled her into his arms. "You're a grown woman, Mrs. Watson," he whispered. "Nobody can make you do anything you don't want to, not even me."

With a small sigh she relaxed against him. "I'm praying for that loan."

CHAPTER 11

Charli and Sam dragged themselves out of bed on Sunday to make the eleven o'clock service. They ate salmon patties and grits on the back porch, then washed and dressed for church.

They arrived at church a little early, so many of the members were socializing and finding their seats while the organ played. There was a noticeable hush among several members of the congregation as Charli walked in with Sam. Charlie knew it was because Sam had been gone for so long and she'd been considering a divorce. Still, the rudeness startled her. To combat it she spoke first.

Mother Maybelle broke the ice by rising from her seat to give both of them a warm welcome. "Hold your head up high, child," she whispered to Charli in the middle of a hug. "Ya ain't done nothing wrong."

Charli hugged her hard.

After that, several others came forward to greet them. They chatted until Reverend Avery signaled that the service was about to start. Together, they took in the service, clapping, singing, and praying. After Reverend Avery's stirring sermon on "Being the Person God Wants

You to Be" they wandered down to the classroom for a brief meeting on the church's upcoming anniversary.

Outside, a short, attractive woman with long, reddish brown braids and a short green skirt made her way over to them. She greeted Sam by name with an engaging smile that lit up her ginger-colored face. Beside her, Charli felt Sam stiffening, but he politely returned the greeting, calling the woman Tanya.

"Hi, I'm Tanya Bynes," the woman said, her smile gone saccharine as she faced Charli.

Charli extended her hand. "Hi, I'm Charlimae Watson."

"I worked real close with Sam in Silver City and he really helped me," the woman continued. "Are you his wife?"

"Yes, I am." Charli tried not to stare at the woman, but she couldn't help feeling that there was more here than it appeared.

"I swear I was hoping he was yo' brother," the woman exclaimed, moving closer, talking to Charli, but letting her glance stray to Sam every few words or so. "Girl, you so lucky. Yo' husband is a dream. He's such a *fine* gentleman."

Charli felt her blood starting to boil, but she flashed the hussy a sweet acid smile. "Thank you. I sure think so," she cooed back. "I don't recall seeing you around. Are you from Red Oaks?"

The woman shook her head. "No, I'm from Pimperton, but I'm visiting my cousin, Geanetta, who lives here."

Now Charli had an idea of what was really going on. She and Geanetta hadn't gotten along since junior high, when they'd liked the same boy and he'd chosen Charli. Then there was the teacher in high school who'd given Charli the better grade, and then the job at the clinic that they'd both applied for, but Charli had gotten. The biggest question in her mind was, what truth, if any, was there in the poison these two women were trying to put in her mind?

Heels sounded on the hardwood floor. Right on cue, Geanetta White, one of Charli's main detractors, peeped out from behind Tanya with a wide smile. "Hello, Charli," she said. "It's so good to see that you and Sam have patched things up. All things considered, the Christian spirit must have touched your heart for you to be so forgiving."

The Christian spirit kept Charli from knocking Geanetta flat. Charli set her teeth, holding her bottom lip and her temper in with a heroic effort. She stared at the woman, her mind racing toward thoughts that were much too violent for a Christian woman in church on a Sunday morning.

Sam eyed both women with a furious glare, but beneath the surface of it Charli detected elements of uneasiness. "Just what are you trying to say, Geanetta? I ain't done nothing to be ashamed of."

Charli's glance went from Sam to Geanetta and then to Tanya. The unspoken question was, *What did Charli have to forgive?*

Geanetta laughed and pulled her lips into a parody of a smile. "Why, Sam, everybody knows that you been gone. How else could you have met Tanya?"

Sam narrowed his eyes. "We're coworkers."

"Why, Sam," Tanya tittered, patting his arm, "that's exactly what I said. I love working with you. If it weren't for you and all that *on-the-job training*, I wouldn't even have a job."

Sam glanced down at the hand patting his arm so pointedly that Tanya removed it.

Charli's gaze went from Sam to Geanetta to Tanya once more. She didn't like the snarky little game they were playing or the way people on the sidelines of their conversation were sucking up the drama. She was fighting it, but deep inside she felt a little hurt that there had been enough in what they'd said to inspire some level of guilt in Sam.

Straightening her shoulders, she looked Geanetta and Tanya in the eye with all the dignity she could muster. "Well, ladies, it has been interesting. We'll have to chat later because Sam and I have to get on home."

Sam drove as they went home. Charli was unusually quiet. She was still digesting all the innuendo Geanetta and Tanya had put out and trying to decide if there was any truth in it. "So, tell me how you know Tanya," she began, scanning his face to gauge his reaction.

"I was already working on the assembly line when she got hired in. She had trouble learning her job and keeping up, so I helped her. End of story."

"That's it?" Charli asked. This seemed too cut-and-dried for the show Tanya had put on.

"That's it," he confirmed with a nod. His eyes were clear and shining with the truth.

"You never even saw her outside of work?" she asked, trying to find something to explain it all.

Sam twisted in his seat. "No, I didn't," he said in an irritated tone. Turning his attention back to the road, he drove on for several tense minutes. Then he turned back to add, "Unless you add the fact that she was in the same burger joint when I was eating once or twice and I saw her walking across the campus where I took those classes, too. Does that count?"

At a loss for words, Charli shook her head. She didn't know a way out of this. "Geanetta has been my enemy since sixth grade," she remarked, "so I can understand her trying to make me miserable, but I don't know Tanya. You do. Sam, she couldn't take her eyes off you."

"So she wants me. This isn't the first time we had that happen to us." Sam pulled the car over to the side of the road. "Does that mean I'm guilty of something?"

Charli turned to face him, narrowing her eyes. "No. Are you?"

Sam shot her an angry look. His volume went up considerably. "I already told you that I wasn't."

Charli stared at him, not liking this side of her husband. "Don't talk to me like that," she snapped.

"Like what?" he asked, still bristling.

"Like I don't have a right to be asking these questions. Like I'm a little kid you can put off the problem with a few harsh words."

"I'm sorry. Real sorry." Sam heaved an exasperated sigh. "I get mad when people try to make it look like I did something I didn't do. What do you want me to do?"

"Just drive us home," Charli said, looking down in her lap at the wedding ring glinting in the light.

"I know I've been gone and I know it looks bad. You really think I was carrying on with that girl?" Sam restarted the car.

"I don't know what I think," she admitted, twisting her

hands in her lap. "But I don't like what happened in church today and I don't like how you're acting right now."

Sam's foot hit the accelerator, jerking them forward and back onto the road. He smoothed it out and continued the drive home.

When they arrived home, Charli got out of the car as soon as it stopped moving and went into the house. There, she went into the bedroom and locked the door. Her heart told her to trust Sam, but her mind kept replaying the scene at church and the threads of guilt she detected in Sam's expression. She knew her husband enough to know that something had happened, but what?

She paced the bedroom, stepping around the bed and ignoring the puffy-eyed woman staring out at her from the dresser mirror. The two people she loved most in the world had let her down and it had weakened her emotionally. She felt betrayed. She resented the fact that she had tough decisions facing her that would affect the rest of her life.

In her head, she went through everything that had been said in church. She questioned her heart about Sam and what it meant to really love him and continue to be his wife. Then she prayed for the faith and strength to get her through this and the decision she would have to make if Sam did not get the loan.

Outside the bedroom, she heard Sam moving around the house, but he didn't try the bedroom door. Finally she stretched out on the bed and let herself drift into sleep.

Much later, she got up and made herself a sandwich. Through the kitchen window she saw Sam working on a car in the yard. Hurrying, she took the sandwich and a glass of lemonade back to the bedroom and locked the door. She knew she wasn't ready to talk to him.

On Monday, Charli arrived at the clinic early as usual and began her routine with old Mr. Clemmons, a senior who came to the clinic often. His nutmeg-colored skin was wreathed with wrinkles and his hands shook, but his amber eyes sparkled with intelligence and charm and he still had most of his hair. He'd timed his arrival so that he and Charli walked into the building together.

He greeted her, his smile transforming his face to what must have been a shadow of the handsome man he'd been in his youth.

Returning the greeting and the smile, she was glad she had work and the people who came to the clinic to bring her out of herself and her problems. She noticed that he was walking slower than usual, even though Mr. Clemmons had his cane. "Feeling a little under the weather?" she asked as they started down the hall toward the clinic.

"Chest pains and gas," he said, rubbing his chest and stomach. "I shouldn'ta ate that chili with the habanero peppers last night."

"Where's your chest hurting?" she asked, noting that he looked a little pale beneath his coloring.

"In the center," he answered, rubbing his hand up and down over the area. "Stomach's upset, too." His breath came out with a wheezing sound.

Charli studied him in alarm. From what she remembered in the medical books she read in her spare time, he had the symptoms of a heart attack. She stopped short. "Maybe you should sit down."

Mr. Clemmons glanced down at the gray carpet and back at Charli. "I made it this far. I reckon I can make it to the office. If I get down that low, I ain't getting back up."

Charli took a hold of his free arm, silently helping him walk. She saw the sheen of sweat on his forehead. She didn't think he was going to make it to their office. In her head she prayed.

Several yards from the clinic's suite, Mr. Clemmons pitched forward and fell. Down on her knees, she leaned over him, calling his name. He didn't respond.

Forcing down rising panic, she felt his neck for a pulse. It was barely there and it was erratic. Whipping out her minute phone, she called 911. Assuring them that she knew CPR, she then called Dr. Burk.

By the time the ambulance arrived, Charli was doing CPR on Mr. Clemmons. She didn't breathe a sigh of relief until the emergency team arrived, hooked him up to their equipment, and took him away on a stretcher. Seeing that he was still alive made her feel like she'd won a marathon. When the emergency tech told her that she'd probably saved his life, she felt as if she could fly.

Charli floated through the rest of her morning, dreaming and looking forward to the time when she would finish school and become an intern. Her dream beckoned to her, just within reach.

At lunchtime her daddy showed up and brought her back down to earth. All the things he'd said and the way he'd acted replayed in her mind. "Daddy, I don't want to argue," she said under her breath as the last patient before lunch went in to see Dr. Burk.

"We can talk over lunch," he said quickly. "Come on, Charli girl, I'll take you to that new restaurant out on the highway."

"I—I'm not that hungry," she managed. "Maybe some other time."

"No, now," he insisted. "I want to explain myself and tell you how sorry I am for what I said, what I did, hell, just for being a sorry parent to you. The least you can do is come along to hear it."

Charli looked at him with tears glistening in her eyes. Chuck rarely made apologies for the things he did. "Okay," she managed.

With his usual flair, Chuck got the smaller banquet room in the restaurant so he could talk to Charli in private.

She pushed fried chicken salad around on her plate and snuck glances at him, waiting to hear what he would say.

"I didn't enjoy Paradise Island," he began, laying his fork down.

"Why not?" Charli's asked in a low voice.

"'Cause I kept thinking 'bout you. I knew I was wrong in what I said and what I did. I always knew you weren't going to always do and say the things I wanted, but you did for so long that I just couldn't take it when you decided to grow up and think for yourself. I should have told you about Sam, but he shouldn't have left either. I know that I should stay out of your business, but you're gonna have to help me with that and be patient. Understand?"

Charli nodded. "Yes."

"You're all I got in this world and I don't want you running off and never coming back because I did something stupid. I'm sorry and I'm trying to change. Think you can forgive me?"

"Yes, Daddy!" She pulled him into a big hug and kissed his cheek. "Daddy, I love you."

"That's my girl," he murmured, patting her shoulder. "Love you, too." When they'd gotten past the emotional moment he looked at her and asked, "What's this I hear about you saving a patient's life at the clinic this morning?"

Exhausted from the emotional highs that had brightened her day, Charli went home. She hadn't called Sam all day and he hadn't called her. In her mind they'd had a cooling-off period. It didn't take much to figure that he was still angry about the way she'd reacted to the drama at the church on Sunday. Well, she was angry that his taking off had put her in the position for someone like Tanya to get in her face.

Sam was in the yard with the top half of his body under the hood of an old blue Ford. He stuck his head out briefly, as if to gauge her mood. "Hi."

"Hi," she responded with the same tentative lack of enthusiasm.

Charli won the prize for holding the other's gaze the longest, but she didn't feel lucky as she went into the house alone. She'd had a life-affirming day at work and she couldn't even talk to her husband about it.

The light on the answering machine was blinking, so she pushed the playback button. The upbeat voice on the other end informed her that she had been given several grants and loans based on her GPA and her finances. She had more than enough to start back to class in the upcoming semester. "Woo-hoo!" Charli squealed and did a happy dance around the living room, whooping it up all the way.

When she calmed down enough to sit down, she saw Sam watching her from the doorway. "I hope you didn't just get divorce papers in the mail," he quipped with a straight face.

Charli laughed out loud; a wild crazy sound that made her giddy with happiness. "No, Sam, I've decided to keep you. A call from the financial aid office was on the voice mail. I've got enough grants and loans to go back to school next term!"

Sam whooped and hollered.

On impulse, she crossed the room to hug him, greasy T-shirt and all. Sam lifted her into the air, swung her around, and held on to her, rocking her from side to side like he'd never let her go.

"I missed you," she whispered. "I can't stand it when we're apart like that."

"Me, either." Sam's lips grazed the side of her face. They stood together, holding each other for a long time. "I've got to take a shower, get all this grease off," he said finally. "Want to come?"

Making more space between them, she met his gaze. "Not until we talk about yesterday."

Sam shifted his feet. "What do you want me to say? It comes down to my word against Tanya's."

"I—I believe you about Tanya and I'm sorry about how I acted earlier," she began slowly in a strained voice. "It sounds crazy, but for just a moment or two, you actually looked guilty. I didn't believe what she was trying to make me think, but I just knew that something had happened."

He eased down to the kitchen floor, drawing his knees to his chest. "Something did happen," he admitted, shifting his feet.

Getting down on her knees, Charli drew in a quick breath. She felt her stomach drop.

"It's not what you're thinking," he said quickly. He paused, searching for the words.

She studied him, wanting to pull the truth out of him in one violent swoop. "Tell me."

"I fell asleep in the break room one night and when I woke up she was all over me. I made her stop, but several people saw what she was doing and they thought we were making out."

"That's it?" Her voice came out unnaturally high.

"That's it."

Stunned, Charli shook her head. This was something she hadn't even imagined. That the hussy could be so bold boggled her mind and stirred a deeper anger. "Sam, what you've described…you didn't do anything to be ashamed of. She was taking advantage of you. She didn't have the right to touch you like that. It's considered assault. Did you report her or something?"

Sam inclined his head. "Discussed it with my supervisor, but he wasn't much help. He did talk to her, though, and it hasn't happened again." Sam extended his hand. Charli crawled over and took it. They sat on the floor with their backs against the wall. "I love you, Charli," he whispered simply, slipping an arm around her shoulders.

"Love you, too, Sam." She rested her head on his chest, enjoying his scent and the feel of his arms around her. She savored the feelings, reminding herself that they faced an uncertain future and she could be without him again.

A few minutes later they stood and headed for the shower.

CHAPTER 12

Driving to the church early the next morning for the loan committee meeting, Charli was too nervous to concentrate on any one thing. She caught Sam watching her silently. "What?" she asked, challenging him.

"You never said whether you would come to Silver City with me if the loan falls through."

She hadn't. One of her worst habits was putting off crucial decisions until they were overcome by events. "If you get the loan, I won't have to make a decision," she said lightly.

He glanced back at her and he wasn't smiling. "I need to know if you're with me or not."

"I'm with you. How can you even ask that?"

"Stop kidding around," he said, sounding a little annoyed. "You know what I mean. You're with me here in Red Oaks, but what if things don't happen for us today and I have to go back to Silver City? I need you. Are you coming with me then?"

Her throat froze. There it was. She had no wiggle room left. Charli massaged her forehead with her fingertips. She didn't want to leave Red Oaks where she had Daddy and her friends and a life that was safe from radical changes. But she didn't want to lose Sam, either.

Her fingers curled tight around the armrest. A decision meant picking the degree of unhappiness since she would be miserable, no matter what she decided. Balling her hands into fists, she looked down at her lap. Hadn't she promised to be at Sam's side, no matter what?

"Charli?" Tension and a bit of hurt feelings vibrated in his voice.

Something squeezed her heart. She reached out to touch his arm, needing the contact. "I'm coming with you."

Charli caught her breath and sucked back air. She hadn't consciously said those words.

"You're coming with me?" Incredulity and pure joy lifted his voice.

"Yes," she answered, smiling now, abruptly aware that for better or worse she'd made the right decision.

He gripped her hand and shook it like it was the most precious thing in the world. "We're going to be all right. You'll see."

She hoped she would see. Inside she was actually trembling with the impact of the decision she'd just made.

The car turned onto the church's street. For days, she'd been praying for Sam to get the loan. As they pulled into the church parking lot Charli prayed again.

The lot held a number of cars. A few people were on the sidewalk heading toward the church.

"Reverend Avery said that the committee reviews the paperwork and then they talk to each of the people wanting loans and ask questions. They want to do the right thing," Sam explained.

Getting out of the car, they made their way into the

church. Sam held on to her hand. She could tell from his tight grip that he was nervous and worried.

People sat on folding chairs waiting in the basement classroom. Someone had made coffee and provided hot water, tea bags, and doughnuts. Seeing that the coffee was out, Charli busied herself making more. It took her mind off the long faces of the people filling the room.

The church secretary, Betty Ann, came and got people one by one. The tension in the room rose as the crowd dwindled. Through the circulating conversation all knew that some loans had been refused outright. A few applicants had been given the option to wait upstairs until the committee finished meeting or to go home and wait for a call.

Sam's turn came next to last. Charli went with him, taking extra care not to stumble on the steps.

"Maybe I won't hold you to your promise," Sam murmured as they reached the landing.

"I meant what I said," she assured him. "I'm with you no matter what."

Inside the main office, the loan committee filled the room. She knew all of them, as she'd been a member of the church since her father had her baptized as a baby.

Mother Maybelle Carmichael sat close to the end. Charli focused on her kind but solemn face. Once the door closed, the committee asked Sam to summarize what he would do if he got the loan.

Standing, he outlined his business plan and told them about the buildings he'd scouted out, and the suppliers he'd contacted. He even detailed a number of price quotes and talked about his class work and certifications, and the mechanical work he'd done since he'd been back in town. Sitting there, Charli was so proud she thought she would burst.

Afterward, the committee thanked them and asked them to wait for the final decision and paperwork with the group in the front parlor. Charli went silently. She couldn't take much more of the drama and excitement. Being here meant too much to her. She and Sam sat on a love seat, holding hands and returning the tentative smiles of the others in the room.

Soon Reverend Avery came back with Betty Ann, and the waiting was over. Everyone got a packet of papers to review and sign. Opening theirs and checking the amount, Charli and Sam shared a joy-filled hug of relief. They'd been given a loan for the entire fifty thousand dollars. Both had tears in their eyes.

As their papers were being processed and they were given the check, Betty Ann gave them one of Mother Maybelle's business cards. "She say she own that old gas station down on Turner. She'll lease it to you cheap if you'll run the station for her. It's got a garage for ya to fix them cars, too," Betty Ann confided.

Neither Charli nor Sam could speak. They were too filled with love for Mother Maybelle, Red Oaks Christian Fellowship, and most of all, each other.

To my dad, Billy Brooks (1928–2004)

Daddy, you *were* and *still* are my hero. I miss you so much that words can't say. If only I had five more minutes that day, I would've said, "I love you," if I had had any idea I'd never see you alive again. I will always love you, and I am hoping you can read these words up in heaven. I may not have gotten the chance to say those words one last time, but please know that I carry you in my heart. When you left, you took a piece of me with you. There is a hole in my heart that nothing can fill. Rest on, Daddy; you fought the good fight. You were the greatest father any daughter could have had!

First, and foremost, I thank God for blessing me with the gift of words. I thank Him for giving me the strength to write this novella—I only hope that the readers "get" the message that's imparted in the plot. Thanks, Mommy, for being my rock and inspiration. After all you've been through, you're still standing. Your strength and fortitude inspired me to keep writing when things got rough. I love you much. Thank you. Thank you to my editor, Evette Porter. You're the best; it was great working with you. To my agent, Sha-Shana Crichton: Thank you. You're one in a million. We make a great team. To my coauthors Janice Sims, Natalie Dunbar and Kim Louise: We did it again, ladies. It was a blast. Thank you for being so wonderful to work with and for your great novellas. Let's work this book like "nobody's business!" I could not have written this work without the support of some very good friends. A big hug and thanks to my peeps: Darlene Mitchell, Maureen Blain, Patt Mihailoff, Robert Powell, Alvin C. Romer, Kaia Alderson, Kimberly King, Katherine D. Jones, Maureen Smith, Tonya Hopkins and Louré Bussey. Y'all pulled me through one of the roughest periods of my life, and told me I could when I thought I couldn't, and I will never forget it! Your friendship, pep talks and late-night chats were the medicine I needed. I cannot close without thanking RAWSISTAZ Book Club and Tee C. Royal, The GRITS Book Club and Marlive Harris, Prolific Writers and Dominique Grosvenor, SORMAG and LaShaunda Hoffman, APOOO Book Club and Yasmin Coleman, the *Romer Review,* Shunda Leigh and Ms. Emma Rodgers at Black Images Book Bazaar. Y'all have been there for me since the beginning and I am so very grateful. A huge thank-you to The Brooklyn Writer's Space for providing me with the perfect sanctuary in which to gather my thoughts and write this work. To all those I didn't name, it's only in the interest of time and page space. You are in my head and in my heart. Last, but not least, an extra special thank-you to Tony Cooper. Thank you for being the wind beneath my wings. I couldn't have done this without you!

CHAPTER 1

Philadelphia, Pennsylvania, Present

Gabrielle Regina Talbot paced the perimeter of her office at Temple University hospital like a caged panther in heat. Feeling more uneasy than usual, she knew only that she wanted *out*. Out of Philly. Out of her job as a urologist. Out of range from her family—who, although they meant well, were too overbearing, and were getting on her last nerve. All she wanted was to get as far away from her life as she now knew it. She wanted—no, needed—a break, and she needed it *fast*. Gaby's mind didn't usually wander, but today, she was fidgety and couldn't focus. The best thing she could do at that moment, she figured, was to sit at her desk and take a long-overdue coffee break. The shrill buzzing of the phone startled her out of her musings. The department secretary prescreened the call and told Gaby who was on the other end. She told her to put the call through.

"Good morning, Dr. Talbot, how may I help you?" she said to the caller, running her hand through her natural light brown hair.

"How are you, Dr. Talbot?" a mature male voice answered, a hint of a southern twang peppering his words.

"This is Dr. Whitfield from Mercy General Hospital in Red Oaks, calling with what I hope you'll find to be good news."

"I'm doing…well…just fine." Gaby hesitated, knowing that perhaps he wasn't the person to whom she should complain or be anything but her best—or what *he* thought to be her best. "It's nice to hear from you. I sure didn't expect it to be so soon." Gaby thought about how she'd only flown to Georgia less than five days ago for a one-day series of interviews at that hospital. She said a quick silent prayer that this call would, in some way, change her life.

"Glad to hear it, Dr. Talbot," he said. Dr. Whitfield cleared his throat and continued. "Let me get right to the point. Since you left, you're *all* we talked about. I met with the board of directors and the vote was unanimous. We want to make you an offer as the second in command at Mercy General."

Gaby shot upright in her chair upon hearing that. Her eyes blinked with incredulity, and she gawked in disbelief. It was all she could do not to scream her delight in his ear, but she took a quick intake of breath and composed herself. Surely, she was more of a professional than that. "Thank you. I'm listening," she said in a calm voice.

"Yes, Dr. Talbot. You're *everything* we're looking for in our second in command. Your record and credentials are impeccable, you're a fine doctor and surgeon, and you're making some nice strides in research as well," he began. A smile was evident in his tone. "You'd be a fine asset to our staff, and our patients need your expertise. We're prepared to offer you a lucrative benefits package. Part of it includes moving and relocation expenses. Is that acceptable to you?"

Gaby's heart leapt with joy. She felt a warm glow flow

through her body. Acceptable? He had no idea just *how* acceptable that offer was to her. With everything she'd been through in the past three years, it was like the answer to a prayer. It was exactly what she needed. Like her father used to tell her, sometimes for one's luck to change, a person needed to put some rivers between her and her hometown. And if the money was right, she intended to be on the first thing smoking to Red Oaks, Georgia. "It sounds good so far," she told Dr. Whitfield.

"That's not all, Dr. Talbot. You'll be moving into a home in a new area of Red Oaks at the hospital's expense. Plus, you'll receive a generous stipend for furniture and basic necessities you'll need to make yourself comfortable. Whatever you need, just ask, and I'm sure we can work something out."

Gaby sighed, not believing what she'd heard. "Dr. Whitfield, this seems highly unusual. Isn't this a bit over-doing things?"

"My dear Dr. Talbot, you are worth every penny and more," he said, chuckling. "We realize that you work for a major university hospital in a big city. We're sure you're well paid and have a lucrative benefits package to match. If we want you to leave all of that, we'd be remiss if we didn't offer certain incentives. We're located in a small town, but once you've adjusted, I believe you'll come to love it here. But we will talk about all that when…if you accept our offer."

Gaby sat on her desk and crossed one chestnut-brown leg over the other one. She tapped her neat French-mani-cured nails on her desk. What Dr. Whitfield *didn't* know was he had her from the beginning of the call when he said they'd like to extend her an offer. She didn't need moving and relocation expenses or a house. Anything that would help her put Philly behind her was welcome. But there *was* the matter of the money. They'd discussed everything but the salary.

"Dr. Talbot, we didn't discuss the most important thing," Dr Whitfield reminded her.

Over the next hour, they discussed her salary, fringe benefits, and her official start date. Everything was more than she would ever have expected, and Gaby agreed to all of it—pending the contract that Dr. Whitfield promised would arrive by FedEx that next morning. When she finished the phone call, Gaby thanked God and exclaimed with intense pleasure. She felt bottomless peace and satisfaction.

Within ten days, Gaby was packed and moved into her brand-new 3,163-square-foot stately brick home in Red Oaks' newest exclusive gated community, Pine Ridge Estates, where the hospital kept several properties for its key employees. If everything went her way, the Liberty Bell and the clothespin near City Hall would be a distant memory.

Red Oaks, Georgia, August 2006

Gaby had just put the finishing touches on making her office functional and reviewing her new patients' charts when an attractive older women burst in, knocking as she walked inside, but not bothering to receive permission to enter. Gaby noticed that she had the prettiest salt-and-pepper shoulder-length hair. She also noticed that the woman sported a beautifully designed lavender linen pantsuit and contrasting shell that was perfect for the balmy August day.

"Good afternoon, Mrs. Carmichael," Gaby said, a smile lighting up her attractive face. "It's so nice to see you again." She couldn't help but think that she hoped to look half as fly as the feisty senior citizen when she was her age.

"You were what this hospital was missing, sugar," Mother Maybelle told Gaby. "We needed your big-city smarts down here to help heal some folks. I wore the board's ears *out* about you, and I wasn't going to let them rest until they offered you the position."

A wave of gratitude washed over Gaby as she wondered about the gorgeous woman standing before her. Sure, she'd been one of the members on the board of directors during her interviews, but there was something *else* about her. It was as if she wielded slightly more power and influence than the others. "I don't know what to say, Mrs. Carmichael—except thank you very much. I appreciate your advocating for me the way you did."

"Your credentials and experience in the field spoke for themselves, and when we saw you and had time to speak at length, we all knew you were the right choice for this position," she explained, gently touching Gaby's shoulder. "And, sugar, please drop that Mrs. Carmichael stuff. It's so formal, makes me sound so…old. Just call me Mother Maybelle. Everyone does, so you should, too."

Gaby smiled and nodded in agreement.

"I almost forgot why I stopped by. I want to invite you to our annual soul-saving tent revival. It starts tonight, so you're here just in time." Mother Maybelle smiled, her recent dental work evident from the gleam of her pearly white teeth. "Are you a believer, sugar?"

"Yes, I am, Mother Maybelle, and I'd like to know more about the revival. I haven't been to one of those since I was much younger."

"Glad to hear that you know the Lord. I am a proud member of the Red Oaks Christian Fellowship Church on South Green Fork Road. The tent will be set up on the church grounds, and it starts at seven-thirty P.M. sharp. We'd love to have you join us tonight and for the rest of the week," Mother Maybelle elaborated. Her pride was evident from the way she stood erect as she strutted like a peacock, showing off its beautiful plumage around Gaby's office as she spoke. "I'd like it if you'd be my special guest. When you come in, just tell the usher you're with me, and she'll know where I am. Oh, and since you're unchurched, why don't you consider making Red Oaks Christian Fellowship your church home? We have an anointed pastor, a lively service, and the members are like a family when they surround our newcomers with the love of the Lord. We have fun there, and for sure, we have *church!* I know you'll like it."

That didn't sound like a bad idea to Gaby. She did want to find a good church home in which to become a member, and she wanted to know someone there so she wouldn't feel quite so alone. She thought about how she'd attended church all of her life because that was one thing her parents had instilled in the Talbot children. Even when she attended college and medical school, she became a member of a local African Methodist Episcopal Church. Now that she lived in Red Oaks, searching for a new church home was most assuredly a priority. If Mother Maybelle's church could feed her spirit the way she wanted, perhaps she'd join. Until Gaby located it, she'd visit various churches until she found "the one."

"I accept your kind invitation, Mother Maybelle," Gaby said, walking toward the door, attempting to give her a hint that the visit should be ending. "I'll find my way there, tonight, before the service begins, and I'll look for you. Thanks for thinking of me."

"Sounds like a plan. See you tonight, sugar," Mother Maybelle replied, finally walking out the door, getting the hint. "Welcome to Red Oaks. I'm here if you need me, okay? Remember that."

With that, she was gone, and Gaby did everything she could to get settled in. The rest of that day, she familiarized herself with her most difficult cases before she made rounds until it was time to leave—barring any unforeseen emergencies.

Gaby was awestruck by how quickly the half-full tent filled up. She'd arrived at seven o'clock, and Mother Maybelle had given explicit instructions to the pair of burly ushers to get her there and seated comfortably in the least amount of time possible. And they did, putting her next to Maybelle in the second row. Gaby looked around the tent—which was one of the largest she'd ever seen—and reveled in how well everything was set up: chairs, the podium, and a makeshift choir stand. The praise and worship team was already in full swing, singing a contemporary praise song that she didn't recognize, but she sighed as it soothed her restless soul.

Soon, everyone stood as the team invited the congregants to join in with them as they sang a medley of songs and made a joyful noise unto the Lord. It wasn't long before the tent became an array of sounds as cries of "hallelujah," "thank You, Jesus," and "we praise You, Lord" were heard—punctuated by the powerful chords of the Hammond B-3 organ. By that time, Gaby made sure to keep her head out of the way of flailing and waving arms, as many of them became caught up in their praising—so as not to get hit in the head and possibly knocked out. The more the team sang, the more demonstrative they became. Where the praise and worship team left off, Witness, the church's popular 175-voice mass choir, took over, accompanied by the orchestra.

Gaby took it all in, never having seen anything quite so spirited in all of her years of attending church. A strange warmth penetrated her soul, and she felt tingling in her feet. She didn't know why, but she watched as the choir director, Norman Grant, directed the choir with the same precision as Otto Preminger would have directed a movie. She'd never heard anything sound so good. She closed her eyes to fully concentrate on the beautiful harmony they made. For a moment, she thought she'd died and gone to heaven, because for sure, those couldn't have been mortal men and women singing like that; they *had* to have been angels!

"Sing to Him, children. That's all right," the tall pastor said, rubbing his bald head. "Worship Him with all your might!"

The choir sang and worshipped for the next hour, leaving the attendees who danced around the tent, physically worn out but feeling spiritually renewed. Even Gaby joined them but didn't know why this church was having such an effect on her. Mother Maybelle sensed the questions in her mind, so she pulled her to her bosom and hugged her until she felt better. The sound of Reverend Avery's booming voice broke the hug.

"I love the Lord and I lift my voice, to worship You. Oh my soul, rejoice. Take joy, my King, in what You hear. Let it be a sweet, sweet sound in Your ear," Pastor Avery sang, inviting everyone to sing along with him. Praise Him, saints, any way you know how!"

In minutes, the tent was transformed from a mere structure into a cacophony of sights and sounds as the attendees praised the Lord with song, shouting, hand clapping, and foot service. Gaby's eyes became big and round as she watched the commotion and unabashed praise with the curiosity of a small child. In all of her years of attending church, Gaby had never seen anything like that. Sure, she'd heard of churchgoers shouting and praising to the point of unconsciousness, but until today, she'd never witnessed it this close. Gaby opened her mouth to ask Mother Maybelle a question, but quickly closed it when she saw her in a trancelike state talking to Jesus. For sure, this was *not* the time to ask her anything, Gaby thought. So she bowed her head and prayed that God would take away the hurt and animosity she had in her heart over what had happened to her.

She listened intently as Reverend Avery continued

speaking. "Beloved, God laid it on my heart to have this revival now to help our youth who are just returning to school and to bring in the lost," he began, walking from one end of the podium to the other. "The Internet, videos with half-naked women shaking what their mamas gave them, and games filled with demonic images take up the majority of their time, and they don't make time for God. Let's not forget about the lure of making quick and fast money at every turn. He told me to get back to basics, where we came from—praying, singing, praising His name, and the unsaved tarrying and sitting on the mourner's bench to get their religion. There's someone here who can't find his way. Someone who strayed away. Someone who just needs to get back in communion with God. So this week, there won't be any big-name preachers or guest choirs coming in to minister to us. We're doing what thus said the Lord and keeping this in the Red Oaks Christian Fellowship family. Amen?"

Under a chorus of "amens," the choir began to sing "Get Right with God and Do It Now," a standard that flushed out lost sheep who'd strayed away. "If that's you, come on up to the altar and let's talk to God. He'll forgive anything you've done and welcome you back home in His loving arms. Don't let Him speak to your heart and you put it off for another day, because tomorrow's not promised to anyone. All you have is today, right now. So to that person to whom God's speaking, come on up and let us pray for you," Reverend Avery admonished.

At that moment, an elaborate, casual expression crossed Gaby's face. Her eyes widened, and her face settled into a sheepish grin. She looked over at Mother Maybelle, who recognized guilt when she saw it and gave her a gentle nudge. Gaby stood and made her way to the altar before it was too late.

Reverend Avery and the elders prayed for Gaby and the other congregants who had strayed away from the church for one reason or another. He anointed her with blessed oil and laid hands on her as he prayed. Gaby felt as if she were the only person in the tent, right then. A warming sense of peace started at her head and traveled down to her feet. Nervous, she smiled at the inner fulfillment she felt—similar to the way she felt when eating Godiva chocolates. It felt so good, so gratifying, so satisfying. Soon, she began to shake uncontrollably, and the tears that fell freely blinded her. Sobbing, she rocked back and forth, deep sobs racking her from inside out. It was as though everything she had inside her was being purged before her eyes. Gaby began calling out Jesus' name, again and again. Mother Maybelle ran to the front to help the elders who held her, and she continued to pray in the spirit for Gaby's redemption.

By then, the choir was singing "Stand," and there wasn't a dry eye in the tent. As quickly as she was saved, Gaby was hurtled back to the here and now. She glimpsed Mother Maybelle, who continued to hold and rock her just as she would a restless infant.

"It's all right, sugar, let it out. We've all been there. Give your life to God. He's there for you and never left you," Mother Maybelle told her in her soft, comforting, almost motherly voice. "Gon' get you some pain medicine. Jesus is good for whatever ails you!"

After she felt better, the hospitality staff led Gaby to the back, where they signed her up for baptism and gave her an information packet of scriptures to study.

Reverend Avery took his place at the lectern on the podium, but something was wrong, judging from the deep lines creasing his brow. It was almost as if he'd gone from a hundred to zero in seconds. Just a few minutes ago, he was praising God for the number of backsliders who had found their way back to Him. Now, it seemed as if he had the weight of the world on his shoulders. "May I have quiet, please? I want everyone to be still, and stop wherever you are," he said in the tone of a parent chastising his errant children. "The Bible says where two or three come together in Jesus' name, He will be in the midst of them. Please come quickly and quietly and gather at the altar for a prayer of healing for our own assistant pastor Danforth."

Low rumblings were heard, from many wondering what was wrong. "Please...gather around, brethren, and I will explain everything!" Reverend Avery told them. Quiet abounded, and the obedient members stood up in all of the aisles.

"Pastor Danforth, please come stand next to me." Looking haggard and worn, he did as instructed. His usual clear café au lait skin looked ashen, and he moved gingerly as if every step was measured. "You all probably noticed that Reverend Danforth has been quiet tonight, and not participating in much of tonight's service. He's been *very* ill. He has been undergoing tests because it's suspected that he might have prostate cancer. But I know a man…hallelujah…who can heal every infirmity—if you believe and have the faith the size of a mustard seed. Let the church say amen."

The church exploded in a chorus of amens, agreeing with Reverend Avery. "I want every eye shut, every mouth sealed, and every hand joined with your neighbor's. Let's form a prayer chain around our brother and believe God for his healing. The doctors may say one thing, but God will say another, and it's His will that'll be done. Norman, would you please play 'Sweet Hour of Prayer,' and, Valerie, please minister to us in song as we pray? Let's talk to our Father about our dear brother."

They prayed for Reverend Danforth for the next forty-five minutes, and after that, the revival service seemed to have a black cloud hanging over it. It no longer had the fervor it did several hours ago. Everyone loved assistant pastor Danforth, and although they believed God would heal him and make him whole again, they were human. They were worried.…

A wave of acid rolled around in Gaby's belly as she went into work the next morning, armed with notes from some of her more difficult cases as well as several tapes she'd dictated for the transcriptionist. Something made her uneasy. But she didn't know what or why. Something just didn't sit right with her. By the time she came into her office, she was also laden with her daily oat bran muffin, a fruit cup, a cup of gourmet coffee, the *Atlanta Constitution*, the *Red Oaks Post-Gazette,* and an assortment of other daily papers. Entering the office carrying her load,

Gaby didn't look up right away until she heard a familiar voice. "Good morning, sugar. Let me help you," Mother Maybelle suggested, taking some of the packages from her arms and setting them on her desk. "You're loaded down like a government mule."

"Good morning, Mother Maybelle. I didn't expect to see you, today. What are you doing here?" Gaby looked around to see that she didn't come alone. She had an attractive, hazel-eyed young woman and a preteen boy dressed in baggy hip-hop clothes in tow. The boy must have had some kind of problem, she thought, judging by the way he touched everything in her office—knocking magazines off the table and an array of medical books off the bookshelves.

"We're here on serious business, sugar, on behalf of Reverend Danforth," Mother Maybelle began. "This is his wife, Sasha, and his nephew, Kevon. I'm sure you can see he's in need of a good whupping." Mother Maybelle cut him the evil eye, thinking that would stop him.

Sasha verbally chastised him, then said hello to Gaby and shook her hand, while Kevon replied, "Yo, what up, Doc?"

Gaby smiled at Sasha, who invited them to have a seat to get right down to business—wishing they'd come back later so she could enjoy her usual morning jolt of caffeine. Her thoughts were disrupted by Kevon's sudden desire to run around her office and turn her magazines into missiles. She shot Kevon a blank stare, a look of both wonder and amazement at his disrespect. She'd deal with him, later. Now, there was a more important matter at hand that perhaps she needed to deal with.

Even Sasha's reprimanding him did no good. That seemed to motivate him to get worse, because while he had run around Gaby's office quietly, this time he was noisy.

Mother Maybelle rolled her eyes at him—mostly in disbelief about his awful behavior. "That boy needs to be introduced to a switch! I'd set his tail on fire!" she said to Sasha, who nodded in agreement. Mother Maybelle had to grit her teeth so she wouldn't say anything more. For now, there was something more important that needed to be taken care of. She spoke on Sasha's behalf as per the agreement they'd made before they came in to talk to Gaby.

She squared her shoulders and stood up straight and erect as a soldier. "There's no need to beat around the bush. Let's get right to the point. We'd like you to become the lead doctor on Reverend Danforth's case."

Sasha continued. "Dr. Talbot, God has blessed your hands, and Mother Maybelle and some of the other members of the board of directors filled me in on your credentials. You've been making great strides in the field. Why wouldn't I want someone with *that* kind of track record treating my husband?"

Gaby took a seat behind her desk. She allowed her subconscious thoughts to surface. She'd only been in town a couple of days, and already they were putting her in a tenuous situation. What about his doctor who was currently treating him? How could she come in and just take his case, usurp his authority? It didn't seem right to her. It wasn't proper, she thought.

"This is most unusual," she said, trying her best to

ignore Kevon—who by then was looking down her throat at every word she said. Didn't the boy know that it was bad manners to stare and be right in the midst of adult conversation?

"Kevon, why don't you go sit down on that sofa and wait for us until we're done?" Sasha screamed, wringing her hands. "Stay out of grown folks' business. Now, I see why they sent you here with us. You need some home training!"

"I don't want to!" he shouted in response, not paying any of them any attention. "And I'm not going to—until I get good and ready!"

When it became obvious that Kevon was unruly and just plain bad, Mother Maybelle implored Sasha and Gaby to ignore him because without them as an audience, he'd stop.

"As I was saying before we were so *rudely* interrupted," Gaby said, giving Kevon a black, layered look, "this is unusual and highly unethical. Reverend Danforth already has a doctor treating him. I'm sure that he is capable enough to handle this case."

"If I may butt in here—not that I don't already do enough of that—we figured you'd say that, so we've spoken to your boss. That nice Dr. Whitfield," Mother Maybelle began.

"And he thought that was a fine idea," Sasha explained, a hint of arrogance ringing in her voice. "He had a consultation with Hunter's doctor, who agreed that your reputation preceded you, and he'd give you the case if you wanted it. He thinks you can do Hunter far more good than he can, being fresh out of med school. Furthermore, Dr. Whitfield feels you're best, so it's his call to make."

Gaby sighed and crossed her arms, walking the floor of her office. Her mind went on alert, thinking in overtime. "Yes, it is Dr. Whitfield's call to make because he's chief of staff. I respect that, but it's also up to *me* to take this case or not."

"Ooh, forgive me, Dr. Talbot, if I was out of line and perhaps a little too high-handed. I meant nothing by it. I just want my husband to have the best possible medical care, and I want you to at least consider taking his case," Sasha begged. "I don't want you to say no. I'd do anything. Just name it."

Gaby looked at the sincerity in Sasha's hazel eyes. She saw love in them, honesty, a look that said she loved her husband and really would do anything to make sure that he had every opportunity at life. To live and be made whole again. How could she say no to possibly saving his life? After all, wasn't that why she became a doctor? Wasn't that what she agreed to do when she took the Hippocratic Oath?

"Okay, Sasha, Mother Maybelle, I'll take Reverend Danforth's case," she said through a smile, taking Sasha's hand in hers. "Of course, I'll double-check and make sure my boss is okay with this, and if he is, I will get started immediately. Reverend Danforth is my pastor now, so I will do everything in my power to get him well."

Sasha was so overcome with emotion that she hugged Gaby, then realized what she'd done. She jumped back. "I...I...am—"

"Don't worry about it, that's okay," Gaby reassured her. "I understand you're happy. Thank you for believing in my ability that I should be the one to help the reverend."

"We both know he's in more than capable hands now that you're overseeing his case," Sasha told her, looking at Mother Maybelle, who nodded in agreement. "We'll just leave you now so you can get started. We've taken up more than enough of your time. But before we do, here's a little peace offering so you won't be too mad at us being that we met you at the door and didn't give you time to breathe," Mother Maybelle said, handing her a small basket.

"Thank you, but that was unnecessary. That's what I'm for," she said, accepting it. She unwrapped the red and white checkerboard cloth napkin to reveal several still-warm banana pecan muffins, a couple of slices of smoked ham, and a tiny jar of peach preserves.

A hearty smile ruffled her mouth. Maybe it *was* true what she'd always heard about southern hospitality.

"One thing you might as well learn early is that Mother Maybelle will feed you." She laughed, revealing a set of healthy teeth—one of them encased in gold. "I love to cook and love to see smiles like the one you just gave on people's faces when they see or eat my food. Enjoy, and we'll be in touch."

She gave Gaby a hug, and Sasha smiled at her—thanking her again. "Oh yeah, sugar, you're in the South now, and we're huggers. Wear your day well."

As soon as they left, Gaby put her muffin and fruit cup in the fridge for tomorrow and ate Mother Maybelle's homemade breakfast. She couldn't resist the smell of the items that reminded her of eating breakfast at home with her family. One bite into the muffin and the ham made

Gaby think she was in heaven. They were delicious, and the preserves made them taste even better.

As soon as she finished breakfast, she met with Dr. Whitfield, who confirmed what Sasha and Mother Maybelle had told her. Then, she sent for Dr. Danforth's medical records. When she got them, she thoroughly reviewed the series of charts, tests, and procedures. By noon, she had a battery of tests ordered, and had charted a tentative plan of action for his healing—pending the results.

"Are you comfortable, Reverend Danforth?" Gaby asked, taking his blood pressure. "I can have a nurse come in and give you more blankets or prop your bed up if you need it. Anything you need, just ask, okay? We're here to help you."

Although he was in pain, Reverend Danforth managed a slight smile. He was happy with Gaby's "bedside manner." It was obvious to him that she was concerned about him as a person and a patient. "The only thing I need right now is to know what's wrong with me. Do I have the big C?"

Gaby wrote some information in the chart in her hands, then began to leaf through it. "The tests you had in the past were inconclusive. That's why I ordered some new ones and some different procedures. When the results are in, I will study them, and you'll be the first to know as soon as I have some answers. Fair enough? Now, if you're asking if you're going to die, the answer is no—not on *my* watch!"

At that precise moment, a sudden change came over Reverend Danforth. Although he was very ill, his features became more animated. Gaby looked at him, puzzled as to what was going on. She turned around and looked up into the dark brown eyes of the most handsome pecan-tan man she had seen in a long time. She studied his neatly barbered hair and his muscular physique—evident under the summer shirt he wore.

"My brother, what are you doing here?" Reverend Danforth asked. "What a pleasant surprise!"

He went over and gave the reverend dap, then a hug. "I heard you've been under the weather, bro. What's up? Talk to me."

"Well, I think you better have some words with my doctor," he said, pointing at Gaby. "Dr. Gabrielle Talbot, this is my favorite brother, Marcus Danforth."

His eyes raked boldly over her, but his dimpled smile told her that he was well pleased with what he saw. Big pretty legs, an attractive face, and a brick-house figure that was made for his good loving. To his way of thinking, it didn't get any better than that. And this fox was his brother's doctor? Couldn't be; no way. "Great to meet you, Dr. Talbot. I see that Hunter's in good hands with you." He extended his hand for a handshake.

Gaby couldn't help but enjoy the tall man offering her his hand. She had a thing for tall men, and this one fit the bill perfectly at about six-three. She stared at him with boldness, assessing every bit of his hard body. A strange tingling began in the pit of her stomach and ended in her head. She had to fight the need she felt within to be close to this man who looked like he had everything she needed and then some. "It's nice to meet you, Mr. Danforth," she said in her most professional tone. "How do you know that he's in such good hands?"

"I came here straight from the airport and was told that I could find you because you'd cut your dinner break to come to check on Hunter," he said, his pulse pounding. He couldn't deny that being in this woman's presence disturbed him in every way. "I watched you interact with my brother for a few minutes before I made my presence known. It's clear that you're a doctor who cares about her patients, and aren't here just for the money or to buy an expensive sports car. Your warmth and compassion were very evident to me." That second, he so wanted to feel that warmth and be encased in it any way he could.

"Thank you very much for your vote of confidence, Mr. Danforth," she said, feeling that tingle and her blood pressure rising by the moment. "I'll give you a few minutes to speak with your brother, and then I want to see you outside."

Marcus pulled up a chair at his brother's bedside and caught up with what had been going on with him. They discussed various topics, but the one that the reverend was stuck on was what brought him to Red Oaks. "Your wife is what brought me here, bro. She called and said you were sick and that Kevon was bad as hell. Sasha said she needed me, she's family, and I'm here. So what else do you want to know?"

Reverend Danforth couldn't argue with that. As always, Marcus gave it to him straight, no chaser, and got right to the point. He hadn't changed in all these years. Hunter was glad that Marcus cared enough to come and see about his big brother.

Marcus excused himself and went outside to speak with

Gaby. "What's the *real* deal with my brother, Dr. Talbot? We might as well be straight about this, don't you think?"

"That's the only way I know it to be when it comes to my patients," she said, running her hand through her curly natural reddish brown hair—something she did when she was deep in thought or had something heavy on her mind. "I don't have very much to tell you because I just became Reverend Danforth's doctor this morning. But I will tell you this: his previous doctor suspected that he might have prostate cancer. I don't believe that because there are other diseases that mimic cancer, so I ordered more tests to know for sure. Once they come back, I will know more to tell you. Your brother's a *very* sick man, and he needs you right now. Please stick close to him. I will do everything in my power to make him well when I find out the nature of his illness."

Marcus thought of everything that was good and made him happy at the sound of her words. *My kind of woman. A straight shooter.* He believed her and would do whatever he could to help his brother and his family. In the midst of their conversation, Gaby licked her lips, and that was almost his undoing. Every sinew in his body went on alert. If he weren't careful, his lower body would reveal an embarrassing reaction that she didn't need to see.

Everything Marcus was feeling, she felt, too. Something unexplainable happened between them. They fixed their eyes on each other, and their gazes locked. They stood spellbound, not thinking about Reverend Danforth or anything else but each other. As far as Marcus was concerned, he'd *finally* found the woman who was capable of completing him. Gaby didn't know it yet, but he would move heaven and earth to make her his. And nothing would stop him!

CHAPTER 2

Gaby felt the heat steal into her face the closer she stood to Marcus. She didn't understand why she felt that way. Was it seeing a gleam of interest in his sexy, chestnut eyes? Was it how they seemed to bathe her in admiration? Or was it those kissable lips with just the right thickness she liked? Whatever it was, she couldn't stop looking at the gorgeous man who stood before her. *Stop it, Gaby,* she willed herself. Going after any man right now was the *last* thing she needed at this point in her life. She had promised herself that she was going to totally concentrate on her career. Love wasn't on the agenda for her. Been there, done that, and it failed. In the meantime, she had a patient whose life hung in the balance, and he needed her help.

"May I speak candidly to you about a personal matter?" she asked, looking as though she were weighing the question.

Lady, you can ask me anything if it means that I'll get to spend more time in your presence, he thought. "Sure, ask away," he told her, shooting flitting glances up and down her body. The other part of the truth was that his curiosity was getting the best of him, and he wondered what she had to say. Whatever it was, he wanted to hear.

"Well…it's about your nephew, Kevon," she began. "He was in here earlier with your sister-in-law, and he's a handful! No, let me be blunt. That boy is bad and needs some home training! Please forgive me for talking bad about one of your family members, but I think he can benefit from a positive male influence to help straighten him out. He's at that impressionable age, you know, and to be quite honest, he's out of control!"

"And you think I can help?"

"Yes, I do. Anyone could see that he's taking full advantage of Mrs. Danforth," Gaby began to explain. "She can't do a thing with him. I watched as he made mincemeat of her when they were in my office. With your brother being so ill, there's very little that he can do. His priority will be following whatever course of treatment I prescribe."

Marcus wished that he could freeze that moment in time. He looked at her with reverence. He heard the caring in her voice, where someone else would have heard her sticking her nose where it didn't belong. Her intentions were all good—he just felt it. "How can I help him? What can I do?"

"Maybe that's a question you shouldn't ask me. The sister-girl in me would say that you should get a switch and whip him like he stole something. But the professional in me would tell you to mentor him, do things with him. Find out what's making him act out like he does," she suggested. "There's something eating at him. Find out what it is so he doesn't become a statistic and another lost black male. There's hope for him with your help. Most important of all, keep this away from Reverend Danforth. The drama and stress of dealing with an unruly child can have a negative effect on him, and possibly cause him to have a relapse—and I won't have that. I don't allow anything to interfere with the progress of any of my patients!"

Marcus's eyes glinted with pleasure, and he couldn't stop the smile that played across his face. His admiration of Gaby grew by leaps and bounds, listening to what she said. That woman had a good heart. She was an old-school kind of doctor who didn't just dispense pills and send her patients home. She had a comforting, nurturing bedside manner. She was concerned about her patients as *people,* not as *numbers* to be rushed in and out of the hospital to free up the bed for others and make a new batch of money. She was going to stick by Hunter until the end—whatever that meant. She was the kind of doctor he remembered having as a child: one who healed the sick, but also doled out advice and any pearls of wisdom that would help his recovery. Marcus *liked* that. He liked Gaby more and more by the minute. He wondered if there was any chance that she felt the same.

With a shiver of vivid recollection, a round of painful memories flooded Gaby's mind. Her face became a study of desolation as she revisited the images of her younger sister, Carolyn, in bed with her fiancé, Sean—the day before the wedding. Dazed and in total shock, Gaby cussed both of them as if she were in a bar, then pulled them apart and slapped her sister so hard, her handprint was left in her face. Then she threw him, naked, into the night. She had been shamed and humiliated, so why shouldn't he be treated the same? All of his begging to let him get dressed and his words of remorse didn't faze her. She was a woman scorned, and the last time she checked, those women got revenge on the ones who hurt them! Too hurt to think past that moment, all she knew was that she wanted both of them to feel her pain. At least, Sean had some shame—whether he was for real or not. Carolyn had none, and as far as Gaby was concerned, she thought her sister needed to put the shame back in her game.

Gaby gritted her teeth as she thought about that night. She was so angry that the veins in her neck stood out in livid ridges. Tears flooded her eyes, and she sobbed so much that her chest heaved in deep, gut-wrenching sobs. How could her sister—her own flesh and blood—betray her with the man to whom she was about to pledge her life and fidelity? How could he have slept with her, knowing that they were very close? Was he thinking about Gaby while he was doing the wild thing with Carolyn? Those were some of the many thoughts that played through her mind. Gaby remembered feeling that she was on the inside looking in at the scenes of someone else's life unraveling. No way could it have been her life that exploded around her with that one vile act of lust and betrayal.

Marcus noticed how her countenance changed from happy to sullen and sad. Did he *do* or *say* something to precipitate such a change? "Are you okay, Dr. Talbot?" he asked, not wanting to seem too personal as if he were dipping in her business.

Gaby was too deep in thought, still haunted by the events of that awful day to hear him. She recalled how she expressed her disappointment to Carolyn about her betrayal, hoping that talking to her would make her feel some sense of regret or shame. Something that Gaby never realized about her sister suddenly became clear: Carolyn had a heart of ice. She didn't care about anyone but herself and about whatever benefited her. Gaby didn't know how or when Carolyn had become such an ice princess, but she didn't want to be around her another second. She told her to leave her apartment by the time she'd get back and to have a nice life. That was the *exact* moment that Gaby fixed in her mind that she only had one sibling: her big brother, Gerald. Carolyn Talbot ceased to exist for her, and Gaby hadn't spoken to her since that day—and she wasn't trying to!

The beeping of her pager brought Gaby back to the present. She walked to the nurse's station to use the phone to answer it. She learned that one of her patients was in crisis, and she was needed immediately. She looked up at Marcus, who had an odd, unreadable expression on his face.

Although he liked everything he saw about Gaby, his nephew wasn't the only one with something bothering him. Gaby was a woman of mystery, and that intrigued the scorpion in him. He didn't care if it took him a year; he was going to find out what that was!

"I'm needed, Mr. Danforth, so I really must go," she said to Marcus, not missing the heady scent of his favorite Armani Black Code cologne that wafted past her nostrils, or the cut of his arms and the corded chest under the summer linen shirt that fit him just right. Gaby couldn't quell thoughts of wondering how he could put those muscles to work in the throes of passion. She'd been hurt, yes, but she was still a woman with needs—who, although she wouldn't admit it to herself, missed the touch and feel of a man. The dog days of August temperature seemed to soar to two hundred, because a hot flash overtook Gaby, and she began to sweat. She reached into an ice bucket and grabbed a big cube of ice and rubbed it all over her face.

Marcus looked at her and became undone. Seeing Gaby in heat turned him on more than if she'd grabbed him and given him fifteen pounds of tongue right there in public. It wasn't a full second later that a rush of heat invaded his body, stopping at his loins. Everything below the belt throbbed, and there was only one way to make it stop: He *had* to have Gaby. He had to get Gaby in his bed or bust!

"Thanks for filling me in about the situation with Kevon, Dr. Talbot. I will look into what's going on and do all I can to help. Don't worry, we'll keep this away from Hunter. We won't let anything impede his healing. Oh, and by the way, I want to be involved in every facet of Hunter's care. Call me if you need *anything*—no matter what time it is or how trivial it might seem." He smiled, handing her his business card on which he'd written his local number.

He began to walk away because if he didn't, she might've wound up in one of the broom closets or stretched out somewhere. So it was best he left while he still could, he thought.

"Thank you, Mr. Danforth, I sure will," she purred, knowing a flirt when she heard one.

CHAPTER 3

Gaby summoned Sasha to her office to discuss Reverend Danforth's condition. Then she called Marcus, requesting that he join them. An hour later, they sat in Gaby's office, discussing Reverend Danforth's condition. She positioned herself behind her desk and put on her reading glasses—giving herself an intellectual, rather interesting look. She leafed through a pile of notes, charts, and reports that she'd stickered with Post-it notes. Her furrowed brow indicated that she was deep in thought. Gaby stopped at a specific page and began to speak.

"As you know, I've performed a new battery of tests on Reverend Danforth. The results are beginning to come in," she said, pursing her lips. "The problem is that the tests, so far, show that he may have prostate cancer or benign prostatic hyperplasia, which is caused by an overgrowth of prostate cells. What makes it confusing is that BPH looks so much like prostate cancer. So he will have to undergo a biopsy of the prostate to know for sure."

The blood slid through Sasha's veins like cold needles. She could feel the roaring of blood in her ears. "I don't understand all of this medical-speak, Dr. Talbot. Is there anything good in all of this?"

"Will my brother pull through—no matter what it turns out he has?" Marcus asked, saying what Sasha didn't or couldn't. A strange but sheepish grin was plastered across Marcus's face as his eyes widened whenever he glanced at Sasha.

"Let's hope it's BPH, because it's completely curable once the right treatment is prescribed," Gaby said, her tone laced with confidence. "However, if it does turn out to be cancer, there are different types, and we will do all we can to make him well. Cancer does not have to mean a death sentence. Whatever's wrong with Reverend Danforth, we will deal with it quickly and aggressively."

Gaby noticed the look that Marcus had given Sasha, wondering what was up. But it wasn't important at that moment. Reverend Danforth was her priority. Everything else would have to take a backseat to that until his condition was treated and he recovered.

Sasha broke into Gaby's thought when she asked a question.

"I hope that I'm not being too impertinent, but may I pray for you and with you?" she asked Gaby.

Gaby smiled in response. "Yes, Mrs. Danforth, I'd like that very much. A prayer would be very welcome."

"Good. Let's all please stand in a circle and join hands," Sasha requested. "Let's go to our Heavenly Father and intercede on Hunter's behalf."

The three of them stood in a circle and joined their hands as Sasha had asked. Gaby reveled in the way Marcus's warm hands met hers in a warm clasp. He had a gentle touch although his hands were callused and rough. *A hardworking man. I like that,* she thought. She wondered how he could make those manly hands make her feel like a desirable, sexy woman. *How well can he wrap me up in those big, muscular arms and find my special spots? How long will I let him work me before I beg him to stop?* she thought.

Bowing their heads, they closed their eyes as Sasha prayed. "Father God, we come humbly to You today to ask You to guide Dr. Talbot's hands as she works with Hunter. We ask that You please give her revelation knowledge as she determines his condition. We're believing You for Hunter's total healing and renewal. This we ask in Your most holy and precious name. Amen."

I'm going straight to hell lusting over this too-fine man—whom I don't want or need—during this prayer. Stop it! What's wrong with me? she asked herself, feeling scandalous. She willed herself to come back to the present and focus on Sasha and Marcus and their prayer. By the time she did, they were unclasping hands.

"A little extra insurance won't hurt—and frankly, we need *all* the help we can get," Sasha said, winking at Gaby and Marcus. "From this point on, I'm believing that Hunter is already healed—like the Bible instructs us to do."

Sasha and Marcus thanked Gaby for the update about Hunter, and then they left to visit with him.

All of the tests results finally came in and just as Gaby had suspected, Dr. Danforth had BPH. His prostate was very enlarged, so she decided to treat him with surgery and drugs. After calling his family to his bedside and discussing his treatment plan and prognosis with them, Reverend Danforth gave Gaby the go-ahead to operate. He told her that God had his back and hers, too, so she should do whatever was necessary to heal him. Gaby was happy that he had a strong will and was a compliant patient. That would make both doing her job and his recovery so much easier and would free her up to take on other cases as they were assigned to her.

The day of his surgery, Reverend Avery and Mother Maybelle led a group of members in forming a prayer band to pray with Reverend Danforth before the orderlies came to wheel him to the operating room. They said an extra-special prayer for Gaby, who was scrubbing in the surgical suite, awaiting the arrival of her patient. They didn't know it, but she had already prayed and asked for God's guidance as she'd done before she performed any surgery on a patient.

When the surgery began, the prayer band moved to the waiting room, where they began an intercessory prayer of healing and kept vigil until it was over.

Gaby's eyes were moist with joy, and there was a look of delight on her face when she came to the waiting room to meet the Danforth family and Reverend Danforth's church family. "Mrs. Danforth, all, God indeed is still in the healing business, and He does answer prayers. Reverend Danforth came through surgery fine, and he's in the recovery room now. His prognosis looks excellent. Mrs. Danforth, come with me. I'll take you to him," Gaby said. "I'm sure he'd like nothing better than to see you, right now."

After a five-minute visit with Reverend Danforth, Gaby escorted her out and came in to get Marcus; then she called them into her office for a consultation about his condition.

She closed the door and invited them to sit down. Then she began, referring to Reverend Danforth's chart as she updated them. "I don't mean to throw too much jargon at you, but I want to explain a little about what was done to Reverend Danforth. If there's anything you don't understand, please tell me, and I will elucidate. Fair enough?" she asked.

Sasha nodded her head, while Marcus admired how good she looked even in green scrubs. He noticed that she had an air of calm and self-confidence—which he liked. She took charge with a certain quiet assurance that made him know that she was a consummate professional who enjoyed her work. It was plain that medicine wasn't just her *job;* it was her *calling.* The sound of her voice startled him back to the reality at hand.

"In ninety percent of cases, men with BPH improve after having this surgery," she explained. "That's the *good* news. The bad news is that just as with all surgeries, there can be side effects and complications—including his semen passing into his bladder during ejaculation and reducing fertility. Some other complications can be urinary incontinence, damage to the urethra, difficulty passing urine, or penile erectile dysfunction. Of course, I will monitor and treat any of these conditions to the best of my ability. However, any or none of them can happen. We'll just have to watch and wait. Watch as well as pray."

Sasha asked a series of questions to clarify what Gaby told them, as she didn't quite get some of it. Gaby answered all of them with patience and as much knowledge as she could impart. She did the same as Marcus interjected with a few of his own questions about how to care for Reverend Danforth at home.

On a sigh, Gaby replied, "Reverend Danforth needs your total love and support. His emotional state of mind must remain positive and stress-free in order for him to have the most successful recovery. I'll begin him on a regimen of drug therapy, as well as work in tandem with a nutritionist to get him on a very strict low-fat diet that'll be full of fresh fruits and vegetables. There'll be a definite change of lifestyle for him, and that is one major area in which he'll need your help—especially yours, Mrs. Danforth, as I'm assuming you prepare the meals for your family?"

Sasha thanked Gaby and left, hoping to spend some more time with her husband in the recovery room. The idea of her husband regaining his health began slowly germinating in her mind. Almost as soon as she left, Marcus came in and took a seat.

Searching her eyes for answers, he looked as if he were weighing a question. "Doctor, are you giving it to me straight? Is my brother really going to be okay?" he asked.

Her face was full of strength, and shone with a sense of steadfast and serene peace. If Gaby didn't know anything else, she was confident in her medical abilities. She knew that she was a good doctor and had a high success rate with her patients. Of that, she was proud. "Yes, Mr. Danforth, I told you *everything* I know so far.

I promise to give you regular updates on your brother's condition," she said. "As you get to know me, you will find that I am a straight shooter. When you're dealing with patients' lives, there's no other way to be."

Marcus didn't respond verbally right away. Once again, he searched her eyes, hoping to find truth in them.

Gaby let out a breath of frustration because she didn't know what more he wanted to know. She'd already told him all she could until she received the report from the pathology lab reconfirming her findings. "Quite frankly, Mr. Danforth, I am rather offended that you would question my integrity. If I am to be the lead doctor on this case, you must *trust* my judgment—if you expect me to help your brother. Before I make a treatment plan, I research and explore *all* the options, and have a clear idea of what I'm dealing with. I don't just make recommendations without considering all of the angles first. Do you understand?"

Marcus wished that the floor would swallow him whole. A shudder of humiliation passed through him as he looked into Gaby's chestnut-brown eyes that had now become glittering ovals of repudiation. "I didn't mean to offend you or make any negative implications about your medical skills. I'm only making sure that my brother is all right. I'm sure you can understand that, am I correct?"

"Yes, that is right, but you must have trust in me and my abilities if I'm to continue working on this case. That's the only way I can help your brother. Now, think about *that*, Mr. Danforth."

Marcus noted the hint of censure in her voice. His first

instinct was to kiss it away and make her understand what he meant, but his better judgment told him that he'd said enough. Saying anything more, he felt, would have further incensed her, and he definitely didn't want that to happen. But he still wanted to kiss her—especially when he saw how luscious her sexy, bow-shaped lips looked. They called him to give them his full attention. That wasn't an option, so he'd get back to the subject at hand: his brother.

"I am willing to do whatever's necessary to help speed up my brother's recovery. I'm ready to become totally involved—if need be."

The musky, masculine scent of Marcus's cologne wafted past Gaby's nose and she reveled in it, enjoying it for a moment. He was a man's man, for sure, she told herself. He was one who could get her in a lot of trouble that she didn't need, she noted. Gaby willed herself to get back on task quickly—not to have unclean thoughts about this finer than fine man that she didn't know from Adam's house cat. "That's good to know, Mr. Danforth, because Reverend Danforth will need you and all of the other members of his family in order to make a full and speedy recovery. I trust that you will do your best."

"That I will," he chuckled, shaking her hand. "Thank you for all you've done, and I'm hoping you won't get sick of me because you'll be seeing a *lot* of me around here in the future, Dr. Talbot."

Every sinew in her body went on full alert when she

CHAPTER 4

"I know you must be tired of being poked and prodded, Reverend Danforth, but your fever and some other symptoms indicate you have an infection," Gaby said, instructing the nurses to draw blood and perform several other vital tests.

He groaned, telling them to go ahead and do whatever they needed to so he could get well and return home to his church and his beloved family.

"That's why you're my favorite patient, Reverend, because you're so cooperative," she said, giving him a smile and a gentle hand squeeze. "This looks like a staph infection. We're going to find out the strain of bacteria that's infecting you so it can be treated."

"Why is this happening to me, Dr. Talbot? Is this serious?" He sighed, frustration evident in the tone of his voice.

"There are any number of reasons why this is happening, but let's begin with the fact that you're a patient in the hospital," Gaby explained. "That is reason enough. But to answer your other question, yes, this *can* be dangerous. If the particular bacteria is resistant to the drugs it's usually treated with, that's a problem. Also, you're recovering from surgery, so that makes it especially dangerous. In addition to that, a staph infection can cause sepsis, or an infection of the blood, and that can make you very sick or worse. But we won't even address that because we're catching it early enough, and if the tests confirm what I suspect, this is very treatable."

Reverend Danforth grunted and said he'd heard enough. He'd put his healing in God's hands, so he wouldn't worry anymore about it.

"That sounds like the best thing you can do. Leave your healing to God and your treatment to me. Together, we make a good team, I'd say."

With that, Gaby excused herself and went back to her office to await the results of the tests. She intended to wait—no matter how long it took. It was already after her quitting time, but her patients came first. In the meantime, she dictated some case notes for the transcriptionist to type up tomorrow, and she went over some test results for some of her other patients. She was also able to answer a few overdue e-mails and return phone calls. A knock on her door startled her. "Come in," she yelled out, asking the caller on the other end to hold on.

"Good evening, Dr. Talbot," Marcus said, extending his hand. "I didn't realize you were on the phone. I can come back later."

Gaby met the smile and the hand that was offered. "No, stay. Sit down. I'm just winding up my call. I'll be with you in a moment."

Gaby concluded the call, hung up, and focused her attention on the tall cutie who sat before her—resplendent in a casual goldenrod linen suit. The scent of his signature Black Code cologne assaulted her senses, making her feel slightly off-kilter. The sight and smell of him disturbed her in every way she could imagine. "What can I do for you, Mr. Danforth?"

"Wow, I thought you had left for the day. I'm *so* glad I caught you. I just came from seeing my brother, and he told me there's a problem—"

Gaby explained about the staph infection, and just as she finished, her computer dinged. The results had finally been sent to her, and she studied them carefully, then once again to be sure of what she was reading. "It's just as I suspected, Mr. Danforth. Your brother has a staph infection, but the bacteria that's causing it can be treated with a regimen of antibiotics and cream on the infected site. If all goes well—and it should—the infection will be cured in a week or two at the most."

It was as if everything in Marcus's body relaxed when he heard that, because Gaby saw relief cross his face. "That is good news, and I am so happy to hear it. I was about to think the worst."

"Oh no, please don't. I am writing a script for some antibiotics to be started immediately, and I will hang around awhile longer to make sure that he's tolerating them," she said, thinking about how much she'd like to be in his arms, with her nose pressed against his firm chest, inhaling the scent that made her want to do the most unladylike things to him. Her heady thoughts were interrupted by the loud rumbling of her stomach.

"When was the last time you ate, Doc Talbot?" Marcus asked, a wicked gleam in his eye.

Gaby thought about that because she didn't quite remember eating anything for a long time. "Well, I had breakfast, and I stopped after lunchtime and ate a cup of soup and a couple of crackers not long ago." Before another word was spoken, her stomach growled again—and this time, it sounded like the beating of a drum because it was so loud.

"Well, that won't do," Marcus said with conviction. "Allow someone to take care of *you,* Dr. Talbot. You take care of my brother and others, but obviously neglect your most basic needs."

Boy, do I ever—if only you knew which ones I really neglect, she thought. "I didn't have time to eat. Today was crazy!"

"I don't want to lecture you, but maybe I should. How will you be any good to others if something happens to you because you don't take care of yourself? You really must do better." He gave her the gentlest smile that warmed her heart.

Gaby opened her mouth to speak, then closed it. She didn't have any excuse that made sense, so she decided to say nothing. Some things were better left unsaid.

"I haven't eaten either, so allow me to take you to dinner."

"Mr. Danforth, I am *not* going out on a date with you!" Gaby exclaimed, a bit upset that he'd dared to presume that she'd agree to such an outlandish notion.

"It's not a *date,* it's just dinner. We both need to eat, so why not do it together?" he asked, hoping that she'd say yes. He imagined himself sitting across from her, looking into her lovely orbs, and touching her buttery soft skin from time to time while deep in conversation. And oh, how he wanted to hear the hearty sound of her laughter. No, it wouldn't be a date; it would be a *treat!*

"I don't think that's a wise idea, but thank you for the invitation—"

Before she could continue, it sounded as if someone were sawing a block of wood in her stomach. Gaby felt an unwelcome blush creep into her cheeks. This was as bad as when her stomach growled in church—during the quietest moment and everyone turned and stared at her—*knowing* where the unwelcome noise came from. She thought about how he said it was just dinner and that they both needed to eat. Perhaps he wouldn't be a bad dinner companion, after all. He would certainly be a handsome one. And she did detest eating alone if she had a better choice. Gaby couldn't think of any better one than the fine man who sat before her. "Maybe you do have a point, Mr. Danforth. I am awfully hungry. I'll have dinner with you."

His eyes sparkled with happiness and joy—much like the kind that little children experience after they'd open their presents on Christmas morning. Nothing would make him happier than having dinner with the prettiest doctor in Red Oaks, Georgia. "Fantastic, Dr. Talbot. I'm ready whenever you are."

Gaby gave Marcus a lovely, warming smile as she scanned the exposed bricks, high ceilings, terra-cotta tiles, open-grill kitchen, and candlelit tables as they walked through the El Gaucho Grill restaurant—located in the downtown section of Red Oaks. The hostess led them to a cozy table in the outdoor patio area. A few moments later, a waiter handed them two menus and recited the specials of the day.

"I hope you don't mind eating here," Marcus said. "I'm a steak man, and they make a pretty mean one."

"I like it so far, and if the food's as good as you say, it's a winner. Plus, I'm too hungry to be particular," Gaby said, thinking about how glad she was that she was having dinner with a companion, rather than alone.

They looked at their menus, and Marcus took the liberty of making several suggestions. Gaby was feeling adventurous, so she told Marcus to order for her. In a few moments, he placed their orders and two small plates of beef empanadas (patties) were served.

"We need to change something, Dr. Talbot. You don't need to call me Mr. Danforth. Please call me Marcus."

Gaby sighed and looked at him for a moment, then back down at her well-manicured pastel coral fingernails. "Okay, Marcus. Then, it's only fair that you call me Gabrielle or Gaby."

Marcus nodded in agreement, then asked Gaby some questions about her previous job and general topics in an effort to get to know her better. She answered them very generically between taking bites of her empanadas.

Marcus smiled and thought that she had no idea how happy he was to have her sitting across the table from him, having dinner on that sweltering August evening. Although he'd come to Red Oaks to help out his sick brother, there wasn't anywhere else he wanted to be at that moment.

Marcus was pleased to see Gaby unwinding by bobbing her head to the tango music that played in the background. It was as if he had a hand in helping her stress disappear. He knew she'd had a long, hard day, and he was glad to bring some degree of normalcy or relaxation to it. Before his thoughts got away from him, the scent of the dinner the waiter set before them refocused his mind on eating.

"Umm, this looks absolutely delicious, Marcus," Gaby purred, licking her full lips. "I've never had Argentinean food before. Can you explain what I'm eating?"

It needs to be my tongue licking those sexy lips, lady, he thought before speaking. "Sure, Gaby. You have a skirt steak that's grilled Argentinean style with other meats like sausages, beef kidney, and beef liver, a side of pasta, and some lightly grilled vegetables. What looks like pesto sauce is called chimichurri sauce, and it's for spreading on your meat and veggies."

Gaby chuckled in response. "You sound like a chef. How do you know so much about that cuisine?"

"Oh, I can do a little something something in the kitchen." He laughed, the sound of which was marvelous, catching. "As I said earlier, I am a steak and potatoes man, so I make it my business to know which cuisines incorporate a lot of beef in their diet. Argentineans eat twice the beef as Americans, and have one of the highest consumption rates in the world. I'll go out of my way to find a restaurant featuring that cuisine."

Gaby sampled some of everything on her plate and let the flavors kiss her tongue before she commented. She'd had grilled food before, but nothing like what she was eating, she thought. "This steak is cooked to perfection. I've never had any so moist and tender."

"If you don't mind, let me tell you why," Marcus added, touching her hand ever so gently with his.

"Not at all, I'd like to hear it."

"Well, it's because the meat is cooked slowly over a low charcoal fire to seal in the flavor and maintain the moistness. Salt and pepper are the only spices used so that the natural beef flavor isn't lost," he elaborated. "That's why this is some of the best beef in the world and beef lovers gravitate to these restaurants and this style of cooking."

Gaby ran her hand through her curly hair, her mouth curving into an unconscious smile. "That's very interesting, Marcus. I had no idea. You're a wonderful dinner companion—after all, I'm getting a scrumptious meal and a cooking lesson. Can a girl ask for more?"

Marcus threw his head back and laughed, both amused by her comments and happy to see that she was cool. "So you got jokes, huh?"

"I get off some good ones every now and then—especially when I'm being well fed."

"Hang with me, Gaby, and I'll have you in all sorts of restaurants with food from all cultures." *And I'll keep you well loved, too—if you let me,* he thought.

Gaby kept eating her meal and flashed him a quick smile. She looked at him as if she were looking through him and trying to figure him out. "I hope you don't think you're getting away without telling me something about yourself. Tell me the basics, where are you from, what kind of work you do, and anything else you want to share."

Marcus's body stiffened in apprehension. He swallowed a lump in his throat, so uncomfortable with her questions. He tapped his foot under the table—not to the rhythm of the sensuous tango beat, but out of tune, more from nervousness than anything else. "I live in Charlotte, North Carolina, and I am a building contractor," he offered in a rushed tone, as if he wanted her questions to go away.

Gaby noticed his obvious discomfort and wondered what was up with her gorgeous dinner companion. Was he hiding something? If so, what? Was she breaking bread with a serial killer, rapist, or ax murderer? she wondered. If he were any of those things, he'd better not try her, she thought, because she was a Philly girl. She was tough and could hold her own. Although she hadn't had a good fight in years, she'd always been scrappy, and she wouldn't mind showing off her skills on him. However, she couldn't resist asking him one more question. "What exactly do you *build,* Marcus?"

The way she called his name sent chills up his spine and excited him. That took the edge off the uneasiness he felt talking about himself. "I build homes, businesses, churches, and anything else that needs building. There's not much else I will say about my job or anything else, Gaby."

"Touché. Since you won't talk about yourself, I'd like to know more about how Kevon came to live with Reverend and Mrs. Danforth. Consider that a question I'm asking for medical reasons. I can help your brother better if I know what kinds of personal stress he's up against."

"Now, *that* I can answer, Gaby," Marcus said. "As I said before, there's nothing I wouldn't do to help my brother. Let me start from the beginning...."

Maybe you'll say something that'll help me to understand why you're so cagey when it comes to talking about yourself, Gaby thought. "I'm listening, Marcus."

"You may not be aware of this, but our father is the Reverend Cecil Ambrose Danforth, the pastor of the Word of Faith Tabernacle in Macon."

"No *way,* Marcus! You're *kidding,* right? I know exactly who he is. I've watched his ministry on TV and listened to him on the radio. He's one of the most popular ministers in this country," Gaby said, spearing her last piece of steak.

"Good, then you'll understand some things when I explain them to you." Marcus sighed and continued. "Kevon found out that my father had an outside child by one of the ex-members of his congregation. The monthly support checks and his good name or connections couldn't keep that secret once Kevon somehow got hold of it. He figured that was leverage for my dad to take care of him and welcome him into his home. But he didn't know his grandfather very well. Dad doesn't take kindly to blackmail—from anyone, including his own grandson. Let me back up. Kevon's mother—my sister—is a crackhead, and she couldn't properly take care of him. He was getting sick and tired of not having anything and fending for himself. He figured that since his granddad was so well off, had a huge church, a television ministry, an estate in Macon, and all of the trappings of success, why not ask to be raised there? It made sense to him, and it makes sense to me. As I said, my dad refused him and sent him packing."

"Why did he turn his own flesh and blood into the streets, Marcus?" Her tone carried an edge of indignation.

"From what I was told, it had everything to do with the fact that Kevon had information that could destroy his ministry if it were to get out. The only reason I'm trusting you with it is because of doctor-patient confidentiality. I do believe this falls under that umbrella?"

"Yes, it does. You don't have to worry, I won't say a word of this to anyone. But why didn't your mother help or try to intervene on her grandson's behalf?"

"She didn't know about this. Kevon is a very bright boy. He's very enterprising and savvy, so he figured out how and when to get his granddaddy alone. Trust me, if Mama knew about that, Kevon would've been straight. She would have taken him in and given him the keys to the kingdom without question. She's all about helping family whenever she can—especially the children."

Gaby's brow furrowed as she pondered the situation. She figured that it must have been difficult for Kevon to be turned away by such a wealthy and powerful man who certainly had the means to help him. It must have been equally as hard for him to start over again in a new town with his uncle and aunt. *That poor baby,* she thought. *No wonder he acts out so much.* "So how did he come to live with your brother and his family?"

"Kevon knew his uncle, but hadn't seen him much since he took the pastorship down in Red Oaks. He knew the name of the church, and when he contacted him and explained the situation, Hunter went down to Macon to see what was going on. The situation was even worse than Kevon had explained it. There was no way he'd leave him in it. So after trying to talk to our sister who wanted nothing but her crack pipe, Hunter took Kevon in and became his foster parent."

Gaby's jaw dropped at hearing about Reverend Danforth's generosity. He had a family of his own, and he surely didn't need another mouth to feed—especially an unruly nephew who could possibly have a negative influence on his own children. That was proof positive, in her mind, that Reverend Danforth practiced what he preached—literally and figuratively. "I'm happy that Kevon made out so well and found a good, loving home," she said, a bleak, wintry feeling sweeping over her. Her eyes seemed haunted by some inner pain. "I can't tell you how many kids I've seen who weren't anywhere as lucky. All they wanted was to have love and the basics that any child deserves. I am hoping that one day he'll appreciate how fortunate he is, and not take it for granted."

"Yes, I agree with that, Gaby. In time, Kevon has to know that he could've ended up in a group home with a bunch of thugs who'd terrorize him in every way imaginable just because. My brother's a good man, and he'll raise Kevon right, and he'll put him on the path to success."

At that moment, Marcus's eyes fastened on Gaby's. Their gazes met and held. If one knew what the other was thinking, their thoughts would have been similar.

Gaby felt the magnetic pull of his masculinity. Try as she did, she couldn't deny the attraction she felt toward him. Yes, he was secretive about *something,* bordering on being downright circumspect, but there was something she liked about him. If only she knew how he felt about her.

Marcus hoped he hadn't turned Gaby off by not being

forthright when he answered her questions. If only he could make her understand that he was a typical Scorpio who was more comfortable getting her to tell him her business than he was to reveal his. But no matter, he felt an intense physical awareness of her. He'd become so aware that if he'd stood right then, he'd embarrass himself. A certain part of his anatomy would give away exactly what he wanted to do *with* her…*to* her…if he had the opportunity. He looked at her with something much deeper than a man enjoying a woman's company. Marcus felt a tenuous link between them, and it was one he wanted to explore. Or did he?

Just as quickly as he wanted Gaby, the next minute he was reluctant—figuring that she couldn't hold up to the only woman who'd ever meant anything to him: Sasha Danforth—now his brother's wife. He remembered that night so many years ago when they were thrown together because of Hunter's church and school obligations.

There was a terrible snowstorm on that cold January night. Sasha had stopped by their home looking for Hunter. They knew he was very late, but had no idea that he was stranded in the first freak snowstorm to hit that area in decades. It was freezing, Sasha was crying—afraid that something bad had happened to Hunter—and Marcus had fallen madly in love with her, despite his efforts to stop those feelings. He comforted her, and before they both knew it, one thing led to another, and he made love to her—right in the Danforth family's great room!

Realizing it was wrong, the two of them admitted they'd made a big mistake, and vowed it would never happen again. And it didn't. The *only* time that thoughts of her ever came up was whenever he was getting ready to become involved with a woman. He wondered—as he did with Gaby—if she could compare in terms of class and sophistication with Sasha. She had always been the yard-stick by which he compared all women. In his book, she was a first-class, stand-up kind of woman. If he were to date anyone, that woman would have to be on that level, or else he wouldn't even consider her. He'd dated plenty of women—usually thinking with his heated loins, instead of with his head. Those dates never went anywhere, except to the bedroom or wherever else they decided to take care of business. But something was different about Gaby, he thought. Not only was she an intellectual, but she was also a perfect combination of class, sass, and compassion. She was just what he always wanted. She had the same qual-ities as Sasha had and more—and she didn't belong to another man. She was single and free.

Excitement mounted within Marcus as he thought about the fact that he hadn't had *real* feelings for any other woman since that incident because he felt so guilty and so hurt that he would do such a thing with his own brother's fiancée. He wouldn't or couldn't forgive himself long enough to pursue a love of his own. He immersed himself in his work, tiring himself out so that dating was nothing more than an afterthought. But meeting Gaby had changed all that. He realized what he was missing. He wanted love and a special beautiful woman in his life. Because he hadn't had such a relationship in many years, he'd take things slowly with her. Gaby was a top-shelf woman—a lady—and he knew he couldn't come at her as he would a hootchie from around the way. Plus, he recognized the hurt he saw in her eyes. Someone had hurt her *badly,* and if he had his way, he'd remove every bit of her pain and replace it with total joy and happiness. He had to savor Gaby like a fine wine, court her, and let things happen one step at a time. When they did, he was going to make Dr. Gabrielle Talbot his woman and prove to her that there was one good man left, and he'd love her as no other woman had ever been loved. He'd give her a love to remember—one way or another!

CHAPTER 5

Gaby had just finished her morning rounds and went to the cafeteria for a much-needed cup of coffee. Not a minute after she fixed it to her liking, she was startled by a sexy and very resonant male voice.

"Good morning, Gaby, and how are you?" Marcus beamed, his eyes sparkling.

Sparks of unwanted electricity shot through her. His presence unbalanced and disturbed her in every way. It had been a long time since she noticed a man in anything but a platonic or professional way, she thought. "I'm well, thanks. How are you, Marcus? Have you been in to see your brother, today?"

"You're looking lovely as usual," he commented, his gaze steadying on her luscious lips. Oh, how he wanted to lock his around hers and explore her mouth. But it was too soon, he convinced himself. He'd only scare her off, and he didn't want that. "Yes, I just came back from a quick visit with Hunter."

"Good, I was in with him earlier, and he's responding well to the antibiotics for the staph infection. He'll be just fine, real soon. I'm sorry, where are my manners? Won't you join me for a cup of coffee?" Gaby asked, blowing on the steamy brew.

Everything in Marcus's body seemed to ignite at once, being so near to the pretty doctor who not only looked good, but *smelled* good. He inhaled her feminine scent—which was accentuated by the faint but fresh smell of Egyptian Musk. *First, dinner the other night, now coffee. How can a man get so lucky to have dinner with a gorgeous woman twice in one week?* he thought, as he lost himself in the scent that was capable of making him lose his mind if he stayed around her too long. He'd hoped to run into her because there was something he wanted to do, and there wasn't any time better than the present to do it. "I appreciate the update on Hunter's condition. Frankly, though, I know he's in good hands," Marcus responded to Gaby. "Between you and the good Lord, y'all have Hunter covered. I *know* he'll make a full recovery."

He excused himself to get a cup of coffee, then quickly rejoined her. They engaged in light banter and shared their memory of eating at the restaurant the other night. But Marcus began to rub his tapered fade haircut several times. There was something on his mind, but he didn't know how to get it out. Finally, he decided to be straight up and just ask her. He'd figure it out as he went. "Gaby, I'm taking Kevon to the Red Oaks Theme Park on Saturday, for him to get 'buck wild' as he calls it. We're talking rides, water slides, games, junk food, and hopefully lots and lots of laughter. We'd both like it very much if you were to join us," he said, a look of longing evident in his eyes.

Gaby smiled and laughed. "Asking me out on another date, huh, Marcus?" She couldn't help but rib him for some reason she didn't understand.

"No, Gaby, it's not *really* a date," he said, trying his best to not make it look like a date, but something she needed to do. "This is a good way for you to get to know Kevon in an informal setting. And doing so might help you to help Hunter better."

Marcus knew he had the gift of gab. He'd always been able to talk himself out of any situation—from a low grade to a higher one, a behind whipping, or even getting into many girls' most private sanctum. He hadn't had to go into his arsenal lately, but he knew he had it in reserve if he needed it. This was one of those times. More than anything, Marcus wanted to spend time around Gaby somewhere that she could get stupid and act like a girl and have some good, clean fun. If it was the last thing he did, he was going to make that happen.

"You do have a point, Marcus. You know I'd do anything to help Hunter recover as quickly as he can." With that, she pulled a BlackBerry out of her lab coat pocket and keyed in something. She scrolled through several screens and mumbled as she did. "You're in luck, Mr. Danforth. I happen to be free on Saturday. Yes, I'll join you and Kevon. Thanks for thinking of me," Gaby said, finishing her cup of coffee.

Yes! he thought. "That's great, Gaby. You will have a good time, I promise. I'll get back to you with all of the details before Saturday."

Gaby told him that would be fine and she went back

to her patients, and Marcus went to spend the next several hours with Hunter—a big schoolboy smile plastered on his face.

That day came sooner than either Gaby or Marcus expected, and the weather was perfect. Shafts of sun dropped through the clouds. The sky glared hot and was the crispest shade of blue. Had they put in an order for the day, it wouldn't have been any better. After admonishing Kevon to be on his best behavior in front of Gaby because he'd already made a bad impression on her, Marcus told the youngster to do everything he could to try to change the negative image Gaby had of him into a positive one. He frowned when Kevon shot him a blank look, unsure of whether his request had gotten through to him or not. Marcus stepped up and rang Gaby's bell, admiring her huge home and the golden daylilies framing her beautifully landscaped lawn. It wasn't long before she answered the door.

"Good morning, gentlemen," she crooned, admiring the cut and rippling of his muscular arms, accentuated by the sleeveless Bolero Guayabera shirt he sported over a pair of jeans. The rich outlines of his shoulders strained against the fabric of the shirt, pointing up what a beautifully proportioned body he had. Gaby's eyes scanned every inch of him, and her face became aglow with happiness the more she saw. She knew that Marcus had no idea how tempting and handsome he was or how unladylike she felt in his presence. She invited them in, but Marcus shook his head, declining the invitation.

"Thanks, Gaby, but I think it's best that we get going and beat the crowd," he said, thinking of how well her derriere filled out her jeans. He'd seen other women in simple denim outfits like she wore, but this sister was working it. If only she knew how good and delectable she looked, or what he wanted to do to her. "By the way, this is my nephew, Kevon—Kevon Danforth. And this is Dr. Talbot," Marcus said, formally introducing him.

Kevon smiled at Gaby and stood back hip-hop style, tilting his head. He folded his arms and nodded his head up and down. "Nice to meet you," he chimed. "Yo, you're a dime!"

"*Excuse* me, Kevon? What did you say?" Gaby wasn't sure if he'd just cussed her out or complimented her. She wasn't up on kidspeak, thinking it had changed as quickly as the current gas prices.

"Chill, Dr. Talbot, yo. That means you're phat," Kevon attempted to explain.

Oh no! Now he's calling me fat! He has some nerve, she thought. Now Gaby really began to panic. She was comfortable in her own skin as a size 14, but *fat* was something she never wanted to be. She figured that she'd put on some extra pounds since she'd moved to Red Oaks. Between the fresh food and the unexpected treats that Mother Maybelle always brought by her office for lunch, Gaby's hips had probably widened, and her waistline had gained a few extra inches. But did it take a precocious preteen to bring it to her attention? She stared at the cute chocolate-brown boy who stood five-six and was already 105 pounds—although he was only eleven. She looked to Marcus for answers.

Noticing that her usually bright eyes showed the tortured dullness of disbelief, Marcus intervened. "I'm learning quite a lot from being around Kevon. Maybe I can help him take his foot out of his mouth. He's not saying you're fat weightwise. That word is spelled p-h-a-t, and it means 'you're the bomb.'"

Gaby remembered hearing that word a lot in Philly, and she recognized it as something good.

"Unc, please, let me handle this." Kevon smiled, the deepest dimples piercing his cheeks. "Dr. Talbot, I said you're all that and a bag of chips. You're fine. And, Unc, 'the bomb' is *old*. It's played!"

Gaby couldn't help herself. She was so taken with how cute he was that she hugged him.

Kevon purred with contentment and reveled in her soft, feminine smell as he pressed his head against Gaby's bosom, wishing that his mother would've hugged him just once. "Thank you, Kevon. You can call me that if you want. I don't mind."

Everything finally fine between them, Marcus ushered them all to his SUV, and they rode to the theme park—laughing and joking all the way. Marcus only had eyes for Gaby, and she for him. Kevon had developed an instant crush on Gaby that he was quite open about, and she became quite fond of him as well. She had to be, because she endured his gangsta rap music and his bending her ear about his music and what his favorite celebrities were doing.

Gaby heard a myriad of sounds when they arrived at the theme park...voices, children's laughter, the roar of the rides, and balloons bursting at some of the game stands.

There was a ceaseless hum of human traffic in the huge park that had several roller coasters, water rides, many game stands, a funhouse, spooky house, sideshow, kiddie park, tunnel of love, sidewalk café, and drive-through zoo.

"Can we ride the roller coaster, Unc?" Kevon asked, leading Marcus and Gaby in that direction. "All the kids say that ride's cool."

Gaby and Marcus looked at Kevon, who was different than the first time she'd seen him. He still looked like a thug in training with his sagging pants and BVD underwear showing, but he was calmer. Gaby thought her eyes deceived her, because he was anything but calm before, and he certainly couldn't stay still. She wasn't a roller coaster type, but she wasn't going to look like a punk in front of the guys, so she'd grit her teeth and bear it—if Marcus agreed to get on the metal monster.

"We have a whole roll of tickets, so we can go on anything in here, Kevon," Marcus said. "Even that killer roller coaster."

After waiting in a line that snaked around the mass of metal at least twice, they finally got on the ride. As soon as their car got to the top of its trail, it dropped at least ten feet. "Oh, Lord Jesus, help me!" she screamed. "This boy got me up here, trying to kill me!"

Before she knew it, tears of fright, joy, and laughter rolled down her face. She'd been on coasters before, but this one was the worst of all. She didn't know it, but the 450-foot-tall ride was referred to as "one step before death" because it went from zero to 150 miles per hour in 3.5 seconds, and had a two-hundred-foot drop. People with any type of health ailments were barred from riding it. Riders had to be young and in great physical shape. Which she was, but by the end of this so-called thrilling experience, she knew her *mental* status would be questionable. As if it were the most natural thing in the world, Marcus put his arms around her, blanketing Gaby in a cocoon of warmth and security. He hoped that that would help ease her fright or whatever she was feeling.

Kevon was busy trying to stand up in the car, but couldn't because riders were strapped in for their own protection. He stopped wiggling when he remembered that, and at that point he focused on Marcus and Gaby. He was only eleven, but was very mannish and astute. Not much got by him. He had great instincts and street smarts. Right then, they told him that his uncle had a thing for the fine doctor. After all, he thought, he'd have to be blind to miss the way his uncle acted "brand-new" and giddy like a young man who had gotten his first kiss around Gaby. Or the way he looked at her like he could grab her and kiss her crazy in the middle of that crowded theme park. And Kevon knew that if he wasn't anywhere around, his uncle would be trying to get some of her sweet stuff. Kevon was no one's fool. He knew what time it was, but did his uncle realize that he had a thing for Gaby?

The next ride they rode was the Zipper—a conglomeration of metal that turned them up, down, side to side, and every which way but loose. By the time they got off that ride, they were dizzy and held on to each other to prevent falling down and hurting themselves. That was the exact moment that they bonded.

"Unc, why don't we chill with the rides and let's go play some games so you can win one of those big teddy bears for your shorty?" Kevon laughed. "Must I tell you how to mack a honey?"

"Shorty...honey?" Marcus asked, his eyes getting big and round. Surely, Kevon wasn't talking about what he *thought* he was. He was wise and intelligent beyond his years, but not *that* grown. "What are you talking about, young man?"

"Buy a clue, Unc!"

"Boy, you better watch your mouth and show some respect around Dr. Talbot," Marcus chided him. "Don't show out, because if you do, I'll have to do the same—and that *won't* be a good thing."

"Sorry, Unc, but I'm saying—"

"Yes, what *are* you saying? Speak English to me, not street."

"I'm saying that Aunt Doc is your shorty, oh, I mean...your love bone. That should be old school enough. You're feeling her, and you want to get with her."

Gaby stood by, amused that Kevon—although putting it crudely—had perhaps seen through his uncle. The little man saw something she'd missed, she thought. She also observed that where Kevon was wild and rough, he was tamer, but still with a street edge. She saw vital differences that indicated that Marcus was having a positive influence in Kevon's life.

"Back up that train, young man," Marcus said. "What's up with this 'Aunt Doc'? Her name is *Dr. Talbot*. Now you apologize and show her some respect, or your behind is going to be mine!"

"You can do whatever you want to me, Unc, but I know you're checking for Dr. Talbot. And if you're not, you should be," Kevon said, leading them to a concession stand, pointing at his throat. "She's gorgeous, fun, and she's a doctor. Oh, and she gives great hugs. What's not to like? You better step to her before someone beats you to it."

"You hold it, and right now. You ought to stay out of grown folks' business and stay in a child's place."

"Maybe I'll do that…but not before I tell you that I'm calling Dr. Talbot 'Aunt Doc' because something tells me she'll be my auntie soon!" Kevon joked.

The three of them spent the rest of the afternoon having fun all over the theme park. Although they weren't a family, they sure looked like one. Both Gaby and Marcus thought about what Kevon said. Gaby wondered if Marcus was "feeling her," and Marcus wondered if he had a chance with Gaby if he wanted to date her regularly without using the pint-size pimp as an excuse. Time would tell, they both thought, but right then wasn't the time to think about it. There was a more important issue at hand.

"Marcus, I sure would like one of those big teddy bears," she teased in a cute, little girl voice. "Think you can win it for me?"

Gaby's eyes were so fixed on Marcus that she didn't see Kevon giggling and clapping, so happy that they were now beginning to "kick it" together. Nothing would stop him from working on his uncle when they got home, he thought. It was only a matter of time for both of them to come to their senses….

Marcus bowed to her as if she were queen of the court

and chuckled. "Lady, it would be my pleasure. I'll win that for you and so much more."

It was late evening before they finished riding many of the rides in there. What with the rides, the extreme heat, the ride through the zoo, and eating all manner of greasy junk food, they were exhausted—especially Gaby. Her eyes felt sandy, and her bones ached. The malaise she felt nearly choked her. Marcus insisted that he take her home, and she didn't argue. She didn't have the strength left anywhere, so she got in the SUV, and rested her head on the back of seat. The next thing she knew, Kevon was announcing their arrival at her house.

Kevon bade her a good-night, and Marcus helped her out of the vehicle and escorted her to her door. "Thank you for one of the best days I've ever had, sleepyhead," he teased and grinned. "I can't remember *when* I've had more fun."

Gaby yawned and excused her manners. "I should be thanking you and Kevon. I haven't had the chance to go anywhere socially since I've relocated to Red Oaks. I've been to work and to the revival every night, that's about it. This is the first place I've been where I could get loose, and it felt good!"

And you looked even better being relaxed, letting it rip, lady, Marcus thought. "Let me say good-night, Gaby, and thanks again for a wonderful day. Thanks, also, for bringing some joy into a little boy's life. Kevon might talk a good game, but he's been through a lot. He just hides it well with the tough guy act."

"I know. He's a pussycat posing as a big, bad lion. You're welcome, Marcus."

Marcus asked her permission to hug her because he didn't want to startle or upset her. Everything in her demeanor and body language said she was shell-shocked and hurt when it came to matters of the heart. He told himself that he'd take it slowly with her, and he meant it. He hugged Gaby and kissed her gently on the cheek. "I'll call you, and I hope to see you again real soon."

"Back at you, Marcus Danforth," she said, hugging him back, then loosening their hug.

Marcus smiled and watched until she was safely in the house and closed the door behind her. Then, he went back to his vehicle and drove away with memories of his day with Gaby rippling in his mind. He wanted to stay in that place and never come out, but that was hard because Kevon pelted him with a bunch of questions about his feelings for Gaby. He told his nosy nephew that he thought she was the best thing since sliced bread and that, yes, he *was* feeling her. However, something told him that it wasn't the time to step to her. Kevon "advised" him to make Aunt Doc his shorty—and fast—because someone else would jack her right from under his nose! Marcus burst out laughing at the young matchmaker because that was his plan, and had been all along. *If only you knew, little one, I'm way ahead of you.*

Gaby's days at the hospital got longer and more exhausting. It seemed that half of Red Oaks had urological problems that needed treatment. With dictating reports and letters, making chart notes, studying test results, and examining patients, thoughts of Marcus snuck into her head. She couldn't believe all the fun she'd had with him. To her, Marcus was an exciting challenge. Something about him didn't add up. It was clear that there was something he didn't want to talk about. He didn't mind finding out anything she had to say. Was it that he was a private person, or was he hiding something that could harm her by not knowing?

She'd been there, done that when it came to things being kept secret. And she had her fill. The memories were so vivid, so clear. Her mind floated in a sepia haze as she recalled that fateful night three years ago when she discovered her fiancé's cheating and betrayal. Months later, her sister tried to talk to her and apologize, but Gaby told her to get lost and stay out of her life.

It took a lot of prayer and looking within herself for Gaby to go on living. She immersed herself in her work, working long and crazy hours. She worked until she was near a breakdown and was so tired back then, that she passed out as soon as her head hit the pillow. She put the thought of romance, dating, and relationships out of her mind. That was something she never wanted again in life, she tried to convince herself. As far as Gaby was concerned, anything having to do with men had nothing to do with her. Until Marcus.

As much as she tried to think bad thoughts about Marcus and imagine all of the wrong he was doing, for some reason, she couldn't. Something held those thoughts back, and she didn't know why. There was some good in him, her mind told her. That was enough to make her feel a tingling delight when she thought she could feel his arms wrapped around her, pulling her into the sweetest kiss in Georgia. Thoughts of his sexy body, kissable lips, and strong confident gait haunted her. And he was articulate and could be an excellent conversationalist—if he put his mind to it. Working with his hands did his body right because Marcus had muscles for days—big, well-defined ones. Those were arms that she wanted to be held in and never let go. Marcus Danforth was everything Gaby wanted in a man, but it was too soon. She wasn't ready for a relationship on any level other than a professional one, she convinced herself. It wasn't time to embark on love, because he'd turn out to be a cheater or liar like any other man. Never again would she suffer *that* kind of hurt—the kind that almost debilitated her—at the hands of any man. That's what her lips said, but her heart said differently.

CHAPTER 6

When Gaby arrived at the revival service that night, the church was ablaze with the sounds of dozens of tambourines shaking, a chorus of "hallelujahs," and the now two-hundred-voice choir—Witness—singing a contemporary version of the old standard "Leaning On The Everlasting Arms." Many attendees danced and shouted in the aisles and let loose in the name of the Lord. Gaby dug her nails into her palms—unsure what to make of the very *loud* service. Sweat trickled from her armpits as she waited for one of the ushers to look her way and find her a seat somewhere in the crowded tent. To say that everyone was caught up in the spirit would've been an understatement, because some kind of activity was happening everywhere. But the ever watchful eye of Mother Maybelle was on the lookout for Gaby. As soon as she spotted her and got her attention, she waved Gaby down front. Meandering through the worshippers, Gaby made her way to the coveted second seat of the second row—right beside Mother Maybelle.

"Praise Him like you mean it, church!" Reverend Avery exclaimed. "Don't hold back. If God has been good to you, *say* so! Choir, help 'em out with some shouting songs."

Choir director Norman Grant didn't need another invitation to show off his huge, award-winning choir. One was enough. At the directive, he reassembled them quickly and eased them into a medley of songs. He went three-quarters the way up the aisle, then to the back of the church as he admonished and directed the choir to sing so pretty, the angels would cry. Gaby watched him as he waved his arms left to right, right to left, and danced out directions for them to follow as he led them in an extended version of the favorites: "Victory Shall Be Mine" and "Lord Help Me To Hold Out." Then, they ended their medley with a version of "Looking For You" that even Kirk Franklin would've enjoyed.

Gaby began to sing along with them, and before she knew it, her body warmed and she felt as if she were floating. Heat radiated from her head to her toes, and soon Gaby's feet began to tingle. She couldn't help herself from breaking into a holy dance, shouting and praising God as she never had before. She thought she had lost her mind, because she was usually more sedate in the way she worshipped. *Something* had most assuredly gotten inside her, but she didn't have a clue what it was.

"That's right, sugar, get your praise on. Give yourself to Jesus," Mother Maybelle said, encouraging Gaby. She smiled widely. "That's all right, give Him all of His due."

Gaby continued her shouting for the longest until she couldn't dance anymore. When she was worn out, Mother Maybelle helped her back to her seat, where she put her head down and cried tears that seemed cathartic—making everything wrong right again. She was so into that special zone of rededication and getting right with the Father that she didn't even notice Marcus and Kevon—who were now also seated on Mother Maybelle's row.

The nurse came over to Gaby to see if she needed attention, but Mother Maybelle waved her away.

"I got this, honey. She'll be okay after she gets right. Let her be," the matriarch ordered, adjusting her favorite lilac hat on her head, setting it at the angle that best suited her. That was the nurse's sign that her word was the last one, and it was indeed time to go.

When Gaby felt better, she participated in reading the scriptures along with Reverend Danforth, who was getting around much quicker than before, but he still wasn't his usual self. He led the congregants in responsive readings, a prayer, and read several announcements.

Gaby felt a sense of peace and contentment that she couldn't ever remember feeling before. All she could think was that she'd found her center, an unspoken joy she hadn't had since before her sister's and her ex-fiancé's betrayal. It was a feeling she didn't want to lose, but she didn't know how to keep. Until then, she'd keep her mind on the revival service that had changed her life. She smiled as Reverend Danforth took his place at the makeshift pulpit.

"Church, I just have to say thank You, Heavenly Father, for the precious gift of healing. I'm so much better now because of Your healing powers and Dr. Gabrielle Talbot's blessed and gifted hands. Look down on her, Father, and grant her favor. I'm a witness that she has healing in those hands," Reverend Danforth shared with the church.

Cries of "Amen" and "bless her, Lord" rang out across

the mammoth tent that had finally quieted down enough for the evening's message to be heard.

At that moment, all eyes were on Gaby—especially Marcus's—whose chestnut-brown orbs were fastened on every inch of her that he could see from the pew.

Feeling his eyes boring into her, Gaby couldn't help but return his gaze—giving him a thorough dustup and a sunny smile. It was as if there were no one else in the tent at that moment but them. She continued her visual assault of the handsome suit-clad gent, thinking about how much she'd like to be enfolded in his arms, being kissed senseless until her lips were swollen beyond recognition. Similar thoughts pervaded her mind until the sound of Reverend Avery's voice stirred her out of her romantic musings.

"I want everything to stop, right now. Every eye shut, every mouth closed. All movement shall cease because I have a word for *someone* from the Lord," Reverend Avery said, as he adjusted the microphone on the podium for maximum sound quality. "Can we receive it?"

"Amen" rang out in unison from his obedient flock.

For the next few minutes, he prayed for all of the attendees to soften their hearts to hear, understand, and discern what was in the message. He said an extra few words for the person for whom the message was meant to act on it without haste. Then, he began speaking the words that he said God had laid upon his heart.

"The Word gives us sixteen specific things to love— God, neighbors, strangers, brethren, wives, husbands, and children among them," Reverend Avery began, tugging on the stole of his summer robe as he paused. "It tells us to love with all of our heart, soul, mind, and strength, and to love exceedingly. The Bible tells us to love without hypocrisy, with a pure heart fervently, not in word but in deed, and without fear. Most importantly, love as Christ loves us. Saints, the Lord says for me to tell someone to forget the wrong that has been done to you by people you loved. He says that *He* will deal with them and their wrongdoing. The battle is His, not yours. He also wants me to share this scripture with you. 'Love is patient, love is kind. It does not envy, it does not boast. It is not rude, it is not self-seeking. It is not easily angered, it keeps no records of wrong. Love does not delight in evil, but rejoices with the truth. It always protects, always trusts, always hopes, and always perseveres. Love never fails....'"

It was all Gaby could do to sit still. She *knew* that God was speaking to her spirit. The problem was that she wasn't ready to love again. In her mind, it wasn't time. When she tried, she failed, she thought. Her leg pumped up and down like a piston, and she wrung her hands—which had grown clammy. Her stomach knotted, and she hoped that Reverend Avery would get off the topic of love and continue the normal order of the revival service. The more he spoke, the more nervous she felt.

"Saints, love is all around you, and is right in your midst, thus saith the Lord," Reverend Avery continued. "If you don't reach out, grab it, and pursue it, you'll lose it. Now, take heed, because that's a word in season for *someone*. Amen?"

Cries of "Amen" and "thank You, Jesus" were heard all over the tent. After a prayer thanking God for that message, the revival resumed, and went on until the wee hours of the morning. Gaby wanted to leave when everything in her body began to ache, but one look at Mother Maybelle's pursed lips and furrowed brow was enough of a warning to make her stay.

The next night at Mother Maybelle's invitation, Gaby went to her home for dinner. She arrived at the sprawling ranch house with a bottle of rose wine for her thoughtful hostess. She rang the bell and waited.

In seconds, Mother Maybelle answered the door. She hugged Gaby and invited her inside her beautifully decorated home. Gaby commented on the beautiful artwork and lavish furnishings she saw on the way to wherever she was being taken. On that journey, Gaby handed her the wine.

"That's so sweet of you. Thanks, sugar. This'll come in handy when I feel the miseries coming on. Mother Maybelle likes to take a little nip every now and then." She winked at Gaby.

"Well, enjoy it."

"I will. Hang out here with Marcus, while I finish up dinner. Maybe *you* can show him how to shoot pool, because he wasn't doing too well last time I looked. You know it takes a woman to get a man right and keep him from messing up."

"Let me help do something, Mother Maybelle," Gaby offered, remembering one of the basic rules of etiquette her mother taught her. "I don't mind working for my supper."

"Not in *my* house on your first visit, you won't! You're a guest, so do as I said, young lady." Mother Maybelle laughed, her gold front tooth showing. "I'll be back directly with some sweet tea for both of you."

They nodded to the feisty matriarch who looked ten years younger in a pair of lime green cotton pants with a matching floral shell. Her salt-and-pepper hair was pulled up and secured with a tortoiseshell comb. Gaby hoped to look as good when she was Mother Maybelle's age.

Gaby and Marcus shared a good laugh because they knew full well what Mother Maybelle was trying to do by sequestering them in her well-equipped game room. They chatted, saying how they thought it was cute. They played one game that Marcus won. He was strutting his male prowess, and was finishing up the last sip of Mother Maybelle's tasty sweet tea. They had started on the second game when they were called to dinner.

Upon entering the large recently renovated state-of-the-art kitchen, Gaby noticed the gorgeous, formally set table that was laden with food. There were steaming platters of barbecued spareribs, macaroni and cheese, collard greens, corn bread, corn on the cob, potato salad, three-bean salad, coleslaw, oven-fried and baked honeyed chicken.

"Oh my, Mother Maybelle, everything looks absolutely delicious"—a sentiment to which Marcus agreed. "I can feel the pounds sticking to my hips," Gaby teased.

And *what lovely hips they are. Hips that I would love to caress, feel, love…*he thought, licking his lips at that wicked thought and the array of food before his eyes.

"Nonsense, gal. There's nothing wrong with your having a little meat on those bones. More for your man to love. Ain't that right, Marcus? I've always heard tell that although a dog wants a bone, he wants some meat on it!"

"Yes, ma'am...I guess you have a point, there." His lips parted in surprise as he looked at Mother Maybelle, wondering why she had drawn him into that particular conversation.

She popped him upside the head with her cooking spoon and chuckled.

"Ouch! What was that for?" Marcus asked, rubbing the stinging spot.

"Ma'am me again, and you'll find out. Mother Maybelle will do *just* fine."

With that, she invited them to sit down for dinner. After she blessed the food, everyone fixed their plates.

"Everything's just as delicious as it looks. You're a fantastic cook, Mother Maybelle," Gaby complimented her. "I hope to learn how to cook this well, one day."

"Thanks, sugar. But I suggest that you better get to getting in that department so you can pull a good man," she said, eating a forkful of greens, then spearing a piece of macaroni and cheese. "Last I checked, food was still the way to a man's heart. Along with good loving, that'll keep him home every time!"

Gaby's body stiffened in shock and a soft gasp escaped her lips. "Mother Maybelle! What—"

"Gal, please. I know what time it is when it comes to getting, keeping, and pleasing a man. I've certainly had enough experience, but that's not the issue. You have to be about your business in the kitchen *and* in the bedroom these days, because if you're not, some fast-talking man that's sweeter than Dixie Crystals sugar will steal the fellow you have your eyes on. You better get hip, girly-man, because this 'down low' stuff is no joke. I never thought I'd live to see the day when men kiss on other men right in the middle of the mall, the supermarket, or wherever they're grown enough to do it. Mother Maybelle knows *all* about it! If you ask me—and I know you didn't, but I'm going to tell you anyway because I'm Mother Maybelle, and I can do that—they need to put some shame back in their game and go back in the closet they came out of!"

Marcus shook his head, shocked that the attractive old sage would say anything that came on her mind. It was clear to him that she didn't care what she said or whose business she minded. The woman was downright nosy to his way of thinking, and he didn't know how to take her. He studied Gaby's face for a moment, to see what he could discern from her. He made a mental note to himself to enlist her for a partner in his next card game because he didn't have a clue what she was thinking. Their eyes locked, and she looked away at Mother Maybelle.

"You're not getting any younger, Gaby, so I'd say you better get busy with those cooking lessons so you can bait a prime catch and reel him in—if you know what I mean," Mother Maybelle told Gaby, still on her mission to help the couple in need of her "services."

She shot Gaby a conspiratorial wink, then studied Marcus as if she were looking straight to his soul, letting him know that everything that had been said was meant for his benefit.

He bit into his oven-fried chicken leg, and took another

piece of the crispy golden brown, slightly sweet bird that made him think of his mother and how well she cooked. He wondered what Mother Maybelle's secret for cooking chicken was, because if she hadn't said it was cooked in the oven, he would've sworn it was fried in lard in an old-fashioned cast-iron frying pan! No matter, because something he couldn't quite figure out about her made him nervous, so he kept his eyes on his plate when he wasn't looking at Gaby.

The sound of Mother Maybelle's voice stirred Gaby and Marcus out of their reverie.

"We're all grown folks here, and since I don't see any bushes to beat around, I'm going to have my say. What's up with the two of y'all?" she asked, standing over them, with her hand on her hip.

In fear of another lash from her cooking spoon, Marcus remained mum—so he wouldn't accidentally say the wrong thing. He looked at Gaby with a sad, doe-eyed look, for help. He wasn't sure how to answer that question, and if he did, would he say the right thing that would make the newsy elder back up off them?

"I have no idea what you mean, Mother Maybelle," Gaby said, biting into her corn and mopping the dripping butter from her mouth with a napkin. "Far as I know, we're both fine."

Mother Maybelle got up from the table and went to the stove to refill several of the empty bowls. "Listen and learn, okay? Y'all need a checkup from the neck up, as the kids would say. Anyone with eyes can see that y'all are feeling each other in a major way. I see the way you look at each other when you think no one's looking. It's like y'all could butter each other up one side and down the other. The chemistry's so strong between you, it can be cut with a knife. In no way am I stuck on stupid, so remember that. You have to get up mighty early in the morning to fool *this* old doll!"

"I'm not looking for a man, Mother Maybelle," Gaby said, staring past the gleaming appliances, retreating into her own thoughts. She tried as hard as she could to convince herself more than Mother Maybelle, who already knew the deal. "I came to Red Oaks to heal the sick, not fall in love."

"Honey, you don't have to *look* for love. It'll find you when you least expect it. Plus, your work can't cuddle with you after a long, hard day. Nor can it make love to you all through the night and make you feel like a woman. You better pay some attention to taking care of those needs now before you grow old and wind up being alone. You'll regret it later when you see your life passing you by and there's no one to share it with," Mother Maybelle said on a sigh. "The Lord saw fit to call all of my five husbands home before me, and I'm *alone*. But don't feel sorry for me, because I've known what it is to love and be loved so hard that our two hearts beat as one. I've been blessed to have had more love in my lifetime than one person deserves. My greatest wish is the same for you— that you find and grow old with *your* one true love."

Gaby and Marcus looked at each other, both noticing the elder's set face, her clamped mouth and fixed eyes. Gaby had a feeling that there was something more that she wanted to say, but didn't. Everything in Mother Maybelle's body language said that she knew what she talking about—that she was talking more about herself, but didn't. One nosy person in that kitchen was enough. Gaby wasn't going to add to it. She'd leave those duties to the feisty elder who she was sure was just beginning to grill her and dip into her business.

"And as for *you,* Marcus," Mother Maybelle continued, "you better be on top of your game and step to this gal. A pretty, educated, and full-figured woman like our Gaby doesn't come along every day. She's the best catch in Red Oaks right now, and if you don't make hay while the sun is shining, some other man will snatch her right from under you. If you let that happen, I have a switch with your name on it, and I'll whip you good! You've already felt my cooking spoon. My switch is way worse!"

Marcus led the laughter, but he heard her words loud and clear. She was right in every way, and he knew if he didn't make a move soon, some other man surely would. Maybe the elder's unsolicited advice was just what Marcus needed to make him take things with Gaby to the next level, he thought.

"If you need a refresher course on how to court a woman, let me learn you, Marcus," Mother Maybelle teased as she loaded the scraped dishes into the dishwasher. "As for you, Ms. Gaby, I'll expect you over here next Sunday after church for your first cooking lesson. Stick with me and I'll have you cooking in no time! And, Marcus, you'll come to sample her food, and you'll like it!"

Before long, Mother Maybelle quizzed, picked, and

probed so much that she learned that Marcus had been a player. She also learned that his sister, Kevon's mother, was a crackhead, and he had another brother named Oliver, who was a twin to Reverend Danforth. According to what little she could pull out of Marcus, Oliver owned a popular nightclub called Heat, in Atlanta, and their father was the minister of a famous megachurch. She found out that Marcus was cagey—very adept at discussing other people's business, but kept his a top secret. She wondered why.

Mother Maybelle moved their dinner party outside to the deck so they could enjoy the cool night air under a blanket of stars. She gave a tray to Marcus to carry for her, then made a beautiful arrangement of coffee and dessert on the table. Candlelight completed the soft look she wanted.

Before they could be seated, a handsome couple walked up, hand in hand—very obviously in love. They both kissed Mother Maybelle on the cheek and sat down.

A big smile came to her lips, curving them like a snake. "Good, y'all are right on time," she said, introducing them to Gaby and Marcus.

"This is Norman and Valerie Freeman, my son and daughter-in-law. By now, I'm sure you've seen them at the church. And these are my new friends, Gaby and Marcus."

"We're glad to meet you both," the couple said, happiness in their tone. "By now, I'm sure Mother Maybelle has given you 'the business,'" Norman added.

"And you see where it got *us*, don't you? So be careful!" Valerie told them, unclasping her hand from her husband's and showing off her glittering diamond wedding ring set. The pride she felt was evident from her glow.

The four of them reeled with the laughter of revelers. Mother Maybelle nodded in the affirmative as she witnessed the beginning of a brand-new friendship and a night of fun.

Gaby and Marcus complimented the talented newlyweds on their musical contributions with Witness's and Valerie's emotion-filled solos. Mother Maybelle smiled, knowing they'd get along well together because they were close in age and were all professionals who needed to widen their social circle with like-minded, positive people. She was glad that she had followed her mind to personally introduce them. Red Oaks Christian Fellowship wasn't unlike any other church in that people formed cliques and found friendships within them. Had they not been introduced, they might never have met—unless they joined the music ministry. To that end, Mother Maybelle figured that she'd just "help things along."

Mother Maybelle fixed everyone a cup of coffee and invited them to dig into the lemon butter pound cake— her signature dessert—and a cobbler made with fresh peaches from her tree. She set down a bowl of whipped cream that she'd made earlier, saying that that store-bought stuff in the can was full of sugar, air, and was made out of "light" milk—not fit to eat.

"See, right there—as Steve Harvey says on his morning show," Norman joked, pointing at the cake. "When my mama breaks out the lemon butter pound cake, you're *really* in for it! There's bribery or a lecture *somewhere* in the mix."

By the time their evening ended, Norman and Valerie had exchanged numbers with Gaby and Marcus, and

Mother Maybelle had Marcus promise to do minor renovations on some of Red Oaks Christian Fellowship's "seasoned citizens'" homes at a reduced rate under a new church-sponsored program. He agreed without too much coaxing, saying that he missed working with his hands and doing something constructive. He told her that business was booming back home, and he wasn't needed back there because with modern technology, he could oversee the operation from anywhere in the country.

Mother Maybelle stepped back, folded her arms, and admired her handiwork. She knew in her soul that she had "helped" another couple and planted another seed in the garden of love. *It's a matter of time before Gaby and Marcus get together...dang, I'm good!* she thought.

Driving around getting more familiar with Red Oaks, Gaby found herself in the Magnolia Heights area of Red Oaks, so she decided to stop in on Reverend Danforth and make a house call. Part of it was to check on his progress, and the other part was because she wanted to see a certain tall, fine, pecan-tan man. To her way of thinking, *any* excuse was a good one to see Marcus. She rang the bell and was granted entrance.

Sasha hugged her and led her to a tastefully appointed living room that was decorated in beige and maroon tones. African art and wood sculptures adorned the walls and added to the homeliness of the space. Green plants completed the look, making the room inviting. When she came in, Reverend Danforth, Sasha, and Marcus were enjoying a thriller movie, *One Night Stand,* on their mounted LCD TV and home entertainment system. "Come on in and join us, Dr. Talbot. You're always welcome in our home," Sasha said, touching her hand.

Gaby greeted everyone, but her eyes lingered on Marcus. The fact that she found him so handsome disturbed her. She noticed that he couldn't take his eyes off her, either. His look traveled up and down her curvy body, taking in the round-ness of her breasts and the swell of her hips. Her heart pounded as it never had before, reacting immediately to his scrutiny. "Thanks, Sasha. I won't be long," Gaby explained. "I was passing through the area, and thought I'd come and check the reverend's vitals and see how he's doing."

"That's mighty thoughtful of you, Dr. Talbot," Reverend Danforth said, enjoying the sight of his brother falling in love with Red Oaks' most beautiful physician. "I'm doing great since I've been back home with my family."

"It seems as if you are, but let's have a look," Gaby said, taking his wrist to feel his pulse. She made several sounds, then went into her black physician's bag to retrieve several instruments with which to complete her examination.

"Where's Kevon?" she asked Marcus. "I'd like to see the little guy before I leave."

"You'll probably miss him because he's at the church at a youth club meeting with Mother Maybelle," Marcus explained. "There's no telling how long he'll be there, because she keeps them quite a while with all kinds of ac-tivities, tall tales, and her good home cooking that seems to be legendary in this town. Kevon doesn't like much, but he loves that club!"

"That's great, Marcus. Maybe that's what helped to

calm him down from the kid who tore up my office the first time we met."

Gaby put her instruments back in her bag and stood up. She told Reverend Danforth that his vitals were excellent and that she was pleased with his progress.

"Don't be so modest, bro. You had a lot to do with Kevon's new attitude," the reverend interjected. "Between having to deal with my own very young kids, my illness, church duties, and keeping my Sasha happy, I didn't spend the kind of quality time that a troubled boy like Kevon needed. He came right at the end of the school year and was forced to adjust to a new school, a new town, and make new friends. He didn't have a positive male role model—until you came."

"I can't say that I did anything special except stay on his behind, making sure he did the right thing."

"You did more than you may realize, Marcus," Sasha said. "That young man was a terror when he first got here, and I'm not ashamed to admit that I couldn't do a thing with him. You offered him the discipline he needed and did what I couldn't. He made mincemeat out of me, but you weren't having it!"

Just then, their discussion about Kevon was interrupted when a chubby toddler ran into the living room in front of the TV, right into her mother's arms. Sasha picked her up, planted a kiss on her cheek, and bounced her up and down before passing her to her husband.

"Dr. Talbot, meet our little dumpling, Lindsay Danforth," he said, beaming with pride. "She's a twin to our son, Lamar. They're three and are quite a handful."

"What an angel, Reverend. May I hold her?" Gaby asked, a tinge of sadness shadowing her face. "I hope to have one just like her, one day."

Both Reverend Danforth and Marcus took notice of that statement—especially Marcus, because he wondered if Gaby was satisfied being a successful doctor, or did she want more? He wondered if she ever thought about having a family or a man. Her actions, holding and loving on baby Lindsay, and her statement gave him his answer.

The baby began crying, obviously cranky, and ready for bed. "Floretta, come put Lindsay to bed, please," Sasha called out.

In a moment, a tired-looking middle-aged woman ran out and took the sleepy baby in her arms. "You're off to meet the sandman, little one," she said, holding her up for a kiss from everyone in the room. "Let's say your prayers and get you settled."

"We're so blessed to have found her. She's terrific with our children," Sasha told Gaby.

"How many children do you have, Mrs. Danforth?"

"Three—the twins, and our youngest, Solomon, is six months old. Let me make that four because Kevon is our foster child now."

"They're all very young. I can see why you have a nanny."

"I couldn't survive without her. See, I work from home, and before Floretta, I was going crazy. At least three days a week, I need to work six hours. The other days, I'm out in the field. So when I saw Floretta and how good she was with kids, I had to have her."

"What do you do, Mrs. Danforth?" Gaby asked,

curious how she could balance being a pastor's wife, mother, and entrepreneur and look so sane.

"I plan events and see them through from the setup to the breakdown, as well as cater them."

"And she's the best in the business," Reverend Danforth dipped in, so proud of his enterprising wife. "Any Sasha Danforth event is a first-class affair, every time. Every client leaves her events well pleased with her and her staff's work."

Impressed with Sasha the more she learned about her, they talked a few more minutes about her business. Then, she excused herself—thinking that it was time she let the family get back to their Blockbuster night. Everyone bade her good-night, but Marcus insisted on seeing her out.

"Gaby, it was great seeing you again, tonight. What a nice surprise," Marcus said to her when they got to the door.

"Nice seeing you, too, Marcus. But this wasn't a social visit. This was strictly professional."

I don't care what reason you stopped by, Gaby. The point is that you did, and I could spend some time with you, Marcus thought. "I won't hold you up, but I have two tickets to see the symphony tomorrow night. I'd be honored if you'd join me."

"Thanks, but I don't think so, Marcus."

"Are you busy?"

"No…but…I don't think—"

"Don't think so much, Gaby. You do enough of that at work. Enjoy life. Enjoy yourself. I know you'll like this concert. The tickets were hard to get because everyone wanted a seat. Please don't force me to go alone."

This concert must've been important to him if he was willing to beg her to go with him. She did love the symphony, and spending time in his company wouldn't be a bad thing. She could think of worse ways to spend an evening. At least, she wouldn't have to eat another micro-waved dinner alone, planted in front of her DVD in her big, empty house. Some male company—especially Marcus Danforth's—just might be a welcome change. "Okay, Marcus, you've talked me into it. What should I wear?"

"The dress code's classy, but I know you won't have a problem finding something fierce. Thanks for agreeing to be my date. The curtain's at eight, so I'll pick you up at seven."

Gaby fanned herself as she walked away from the man who warmed her heart and sent her blood pressure soaring to new heights. If she weren't careful, Marcus Danforth could be very hazardous to her health, she thought.

Gaby had put the finishing touches on getting ready and was through by a quarter to seven. She did some last-minute straightening up so her home would be spotless and ready to receive visitors—namely, Marcus. She didn't have much to do because the hospital sent in Maritza, a housekeeper, to clean every other day. She was excellent, and enjoyed cleaning Gaby's home because she was a neat freak who didn't mind picking up after herself. And that suited the young Mexican girl quite fine, Gaby thought. At that moment, the doorbell rang and she spritzed on some Diva cologne, looked at herself once more in the mirror, and declared herself ready. She opened the door and her mouth formed a perfect O. Her eyes became as big as fifty-cent pieces at the sight of Marcus. He looked tall, lean, and sinewy—resplendent in his eggshell-white designer suit. His posture was as strong and straight as a towering spruce, and he stood there as if he prided himself on his handsome looks.

"Good evening, Marcus," she managed to get out through the wide smile she couldn't stop. "Please come in."

He kissed her on the cheek and accepted her invitation. "These are for you, Gaby. I hope you like them." He reached out and gave her an arrangement of bright flowers. "They so reminded me of you."

Something went off inside Gaby, making her fully aware of his deep masculine appeal. The heady scent of his Hummer cologne didn't help matters, because it seemed to make her dizzy with desire. She sniffed it in, as well as the scent of the asters, spray mums, monte casinos, daylilies, and assorted perennials that were arranged to perfection in an oversized coffee mug. "These are beautiful, Marcus. Thank you."

"You're very welcome, Gaby. I know how much you enjoy coffee, and as I said, they reminded me of you. The arrangement is called 'Radiant Java Jive.'"

She sniffed them again, thinking that not only was he fine, and smelled delicious, but he was also considerate in an old-school kind of way. She set the floral arrangement on a table in the foyer. They looked as if they were made for that spot.

"You're *gorgeous*, Gaby," Marcus said, his heart almost skipping a beat at the sight of her. He shot a flitting glance up and down her body, smiling everywhere his eyes stopped to enjoy. She wore a peach linen pantsuit that she accessorized with a keyhole-front blouse, high-heeled sandals, and gold bangles on her wrists. She didn't know it, but her scent was calling him to her—making him want to grab her and kiss her until she begged him to stop. It was as if she were wearing some kind of aphrodisiac because he couldn't get past the urge to mate with her. "I think we better go so we won't walk in late after the curtain goes up."

She thanked him for his compliment, and they left for the short ride to the Red Oaks Arts Center and Concert Hall.

During intermission, Marcus led Gaby to the lounge area of the venue, where they sipped white wine and rehashed the performance they'd just seen.

"Wow, Marcus, Clazz-Soul is wonderful!" she gushed. "I've never seen an all-black symphony that plays classical music with a touch of jazz, soul, Dixieland, and ragtime thrown in for good measure. What a concept!"

"My sentiments exactly, Gaby. I try to catch their performance whenever I can."

"How did you learn about them?" Slipping a foot out of her sandal, she let her naked heel relish the feel of the plush carpeting beneath her feet.

"Well, I had nothing to do one night, so I got the paper. I looked through it for something that interested me. That's when I saw an ad for their performance that evening. I rushed down to the box office, got a ticket, and went."

She looked at him with indignation. "A *ticket*, Marcus? Surely, a handsome man such as yourself could do better than sitting up in a concert hall alone, watching this caliber of a performance. Why didn't you try to find a date?"

Marcus sighed, not yet ready to share that part of himself with her. To appease her, he'd throw her a proverbial bone, he thought. "At that time, I wasn't with anyone seriously. There wasn't enough time to find someone who could go out on such short notice."

Gaby recognized a snow job when she heard one. She had a feeling that there was more, and that he wasn't giving her the full story. *That's okay, I'll get him later,* she thought, remembering their first date when he wouldn't share much about himself. "I see, Marcus. The main thing is that you went and saw this great symphony. I'm sure they were well worth every penny you spent on getting a ticket at the last minute."

"For sure, Gaby. After seeing them that first time, I was hooked, and I went to see them any time they came to Charlotte or anywhere nearby. I even joined their e-mail newsletter list to keep up with them."

Gaby had the wide-eyed wonder of a child as their discussion continued.

"They're calling for us to be seated, Gaby. The second act is even better than the first. I know you wouldn't want to miss it," he urged her, instinctively reaching for her hand. As before, their gazes met and held. But this time, interest and intensity radiated from them.

The evening was still young, so they decided to have dinner. Not knowing Red Oaks as well as he would have liked, he asked Gaby to suggest what she'd like to eat and where.

"I don't want to go anywhere especially fancy, Marcus. Truth be told, I could do with a good blue-plate special somewhere."

Marcus excused himself and retrieved his cell phone. He called his brother, Reverend Danforth, and asked for some suggestions. It was a short call because he suggested Big Roscoe's Café on the other side of town. After getting Gaby's approval, they headed there, where it felt so homey they thought they were sitting in Big Mama's kitchen.

Over two smothered turkey wing blue-plate specials, they discussed the concert; and by the end of the meal, they were comfortably holding each other's hand.

"I can see that living in Red Oaks is going to make me as big as a house, Marcus," Gaby quipped, laughing. "The food was so good, but I can't eat like this too often. I need some exercise to burn off all the calories and carbs I just consumed."

Marcus's eyes glinted with pure masculine interest, a hungry, seductive look in them. "Gaby, my dear, you have *nothing* to worry about. You're the kind of woman that'll make a man hurt someone over you. Everything you have is perfect, and is in the right place. I'd say leave well enough alone, and let me enjoy you as you are. Don't lose even an inch!"

His remarks took her off-guard because she didn't know that Marcus paid her any real attention—at least not on *that* level. "Well...thanks, Marcus. That's nice to hear," was all she managed to string together with some semblance of intelligence.

"Come, Gaby, I know the perfect place for us to go that'll take care of that exercise you claim you need."

Skeptical, she tried to get out of going because she was afraid to go anywhere that she would possibly be alone with him and out of the public eye. He wouldn't have any of it, and assured her she'd be safe. Before she had any real time to protest, they had arrived at a local club in the entertainment area by the waterfront. She looked at the sign, on which the locals said was a club that catered to "the grown and sexy."

Marcus paid admission and led her inside where everyone was indeed grown, over thirty, and dancing to soul and classic R&B tunes. Looking around the space, she saw couples dressed in their summer finery as they swayed, dipped, and turned in rhythm to the music. The dance floor was a flurry of bodies in motion, and everyone seemed to be having a good time based on their smiles and partying noises. Just then, R. Kelly's song "Stepping in the Name of Love" came on, and Gaby pulled Marcus to the dance floor. "Dance with me, Marcus?" she asked tentatively, realizing she might have made a serious faux pas. "Do you know how to step?"

"You better know I do!" he exclaimed. "They call it hand dancing in Baltimore, where I first learned it, but I can hang with the best of them."

With that, they danced the night away, doing some fancy footwork that showed them how in tune they were with each other. Every turn, twist, and step was in perfect time and alignment. In reality, they were two bodies dancing together, but their movements translated as one body that interpreted the music with its own brand of rhythm and passion. They were hot, and they knew it! Everyone gathered around to watch the couple who had that certain dance floor magic, hoping some of it would rub off on them.

The rest of that night belonged to them. Despite the sticky Georgia heat, they laughed and joked like old friends. They didn't think twice about the fact that they were both drenched in sweat, or that their clothes were sticking to them. Their successful dancing stint at the club had left them high and giddy, and that was a feeling that neither of them wanted to let go of just yet. Gaby was more animated than usual, and she was in a more relaxed mood than he'd ever seen her. So he decided to seize the opportunity to take things a step further right at her front door.

Pulling her into the circle of his arms, Marcus bent his head down and slowly pressed his lips to hers. She met them, accepting the invitation. His mouth moved over hers with exquisite tenderness. Gaby's lips opened fully, like a budding flower. His tongue entwined with hers, beginning a deep exploration of every corner of her mouth. Marcus's tongue made love with Gaby's—caressing its sweet walls. The thrusting of his tongue pushed her toward new sensations and made her feel things in her nether regions that she hadn't felt in years. He explored her mouth in an attempt to taste every bit of her brown sugar. She tasted him with a new kind of wanting. Together, their tongues danced a silent melody that only they understood. That was only the appetizer, she thought. He pulled Gaby closer to him in an effort to make them one body. Then he *really* kissed her, and she kissed him back with everything she had inside her. Her body betrayed her, because she couldn't deny that Marcus had kissed her and was still kissing her in such a way to end all kisses she'd ever had. Her words said one thing, but the real power was in her tongue, because it said something totally different to Marcus. It didn't or couldn't deny what her heart felt for him, and that was all he needed to know!

CHAPTER 7

Over the next few days, Gaby and Marcus were insepa-
rable. One wasn't seen around town without the other.
Being with Marcus felt like home—warm, comforting, and
peaceful, she thought. She'd enjoyed every minute of their
being together, laughing and joking, and sharing their
hopes and dreams for the future. He was more fun than
she could ever have imagined as she found out from their
spending so much time together. They took in an exhibit
of indigenous aboriginal art at the Red Oaks Art Museum,
dined at the grand opening of a new eatery, saw the auto
show, went to a gospel play, took in a movie, and watched
a visiting dance troupe called Cuba Libre perform at the
Arts Center—complete with an accompanying concert of
native Cuban music. Marcus was a man of many myster-
ies, she thought, as she enjoyed the various types of places
he took her. Indeed, he kept her guessing because she
couldn't figure him out. When she thought she was getting
to know him and what he liked, he flipped the proverbial
script and exposed her to something else. And that was fine
with her. She didn't like predictable. She liked breaking
away from the traditional, and she liked all things unique
and spontaneous. The only traditional thing she had any

use for was stability—someone to be there for her and offer her the long haul. From everything he'd shown her thus far, Marcus could fit that bill, but something within her kept her from reaching out for it. It also kept her from even seeking what he had to offer, or going after it.

On the other hand, things were different for Marcus. He was well aware that his feelings had intensified to mammoth proportions for Gaby, and he was ready to act on them. As the old folks would say, he "had it bad" for the good doctor. His feelings for her were unlike how he felt when he dated for the sake of not being alone or keeping his bed warm. But he couldn't let her know how he felt, because he didn't want to spook her and scare her off. He wanted as much as he could get from and with her, but all in due time, he figured. *I'll let her know in my own way, in my own time, but only in a manner in which I can maintain control over it,* he thought. *Dr. Gaby Talbot will be mine— whether she knows it or not!* But there were more important matters at hand—namely, the job he was completing.

"Kevon, pass me that large roller over there," Marcus requested, pointing at an assortment of paint rollers in the corner, while trying to balance himself on the ladder. He admired the significant change in his errant nephew's behavior.

"Sure thing, Uncle Marcus." He passed his uncle the roller and continued painting the walls in the home they were working on that day.

"I'm impressed to hear you call me Uncle Marcus instead of 'Unc.' *I hated* that, it sounded so disrespectful."

"I didn't mean that," Kevon said. "Thanks for hiring me as your assistant. I'm learning a lot helping you out fixing up these old people's homes."

"Don't thank me, thank Mother Maybelle. It was her talking you up to the pastor and getting him to loosen the purse strings that made it possible," Marcus explained. "When she presented the idea of offering you this opportunity—and we can't say 'job' because you're not old enough to get legal working papers—and said the church would pay you, we both agreed it was a good idea. It made no sense for you to sit around bored all summer with nothing to do when you could be helping me, learning some new skills, and making a little spending change. It was a win-win situation for everyone."

"And I'm enjoying it, too, Uncle Marcus. Thanks. I didn't know I'd like working with my hands so much," he said, painting a large area on the side of the room. "I'm willing to learn whatever you want to teach me—if you have time to show me some things."

Marcus beamed with pride at that statement because he loved being a contractor. He loved renovating old homes and making basic living spaces into showplaces, instead of keeping them ugly and substandard. He thought of how happy he'd made his clients over the years when they saw how he improved their living space. If he could impart even the smallest amount of his love for that to Kevon, he was willing to do so. Who knows, maybe Kevon could come and work for his company one day when he was older and had taken several apprenticeships and/or courses at an appropriate school. He would be honored to teach Kevon the contracting business from the ground up, he thought, because it had certainly grounded him. Where he was wild and uncontrollable before, he had turned into a much calmer, better behaved, hardworking preteen—a vast improvement over how he was when Marcus had first arrived in Red Oaks. If he could help him stay that way, he was game! Now, if he could only get Gaby to feel about him the same way he was beginning to feel about her...Marcus would be ecstatic.

Gaby couldn't get herself together—no matter how much she tried to concentrate on her work. She drummed her fingers on her desk, tapping a furious rhythm she didn't recognize. She crossed one leg over the other several times in rapid succession—plain nervous and fidgety and she didn't know why. The growling of her stomach announced the fact that she hadn't eaten since she'd had a light continental breakfast that morning. She'd had a full schedule with several surgical procedures, rounds to make, and a class to teach some visiting medical students requiring a lecture on urology. She didn't have a moment to spare, or to think—much less eat. She looked at her watch and saw it was nearly 1:00 P.M. Gaby was hungry, but desired a *real* lunch besides in her office or eating on the run. She wanted to hear the sound of the human voice, engrossed in a conversation or even a debate with her. *Any* human voice would do, she thought. No, it would have to be a man's voice—but not just *any* man, a special man: namely, Marcus Danforth.

At that thought, Gaby went online and pulled up the

Red Oaks Gourmet Palace and Deli and typed in an order. She went into her private bathroom and refreshed herself after her long, hard morning. Removing her lab coat, Gaby was on her way to have a real lunch outside the hospital with the person she wanted to see most.

When she arrived at the shop, a young clerk handed her a large wicker picnic basket. She scanned the well-stocked emporium where food of every sort lined the walls, and foot traffic was brisk with shoppers picking up various items for lunch, and others shopped for larger meals.

Gaby told the young, blond sales clerk how pleased and impressed she was to get her order so quickly after just having placed it online.

"We aim to please, ma'am," the clerk crooned in a deep, pleasant Georgia accent.

Smiling, Gaby thanked her and left the store. *Now to find Marcus,* she thought. It's a good thing she'd already had her earpiece in, because all she had to do was hit the speed-dial button for Mother Maybelle, who answered by the third ring. Gaby asked her where Marcus was working that day, and of course, Mother Maybelle wasn't going to make it that easy.

"Why do you want to know where Marcus is working, Gaby? What's up?" she quizzed, hoping that some progress was being made with their impending romance.

"I want to see him," Gaby said, keeping her plans secret for fear that Mother Maybelle—meaning well—would accidentally let it slip if she knew.

Disappointed, Mother Maybelle gave her the address to the home that he was working on that day and bade

Gaby good-bye—saying she had to get to her sewing studio to work on a quilt to hang soon in the church.

The unsolicited directions Mother Maybelle had given Gaby came in handy because they helped her get there quicker. In a short while, Gaby found the address and rang the doorbell. The workmen Marcus had hired that day whistled catcalls and teased him. "I'm sure that Marcus will be glad to see anyone who looks as good as you," one of the carpenters sporting a brand-new initial gold grill, quipped. "Go on in, he's in the back."

She announced her presence so as not to frighten Marcus, who was totally immersed in putting up some tiles and caulking in the bathroom.

Marcus blinked several times, thinking his eyes deceived him. When he was sure that Gaby stood before him—real and in the flesh—his smile was as bright as the morning sun as he looked up and saw how beautiful she looked in her floral-print summer sundress. It hugged her ample curves and showed enough leg to let him know how shapely they were, without overexposing any part of her. And her smell, he thought, was so fresh and feminine that it reminded him of the way clothes hanging on the line smelled after a good rain. It was clean, refreshing, and a scent for him to lose himself in if he weren't careful. It was a scent on which he could build memories and call up later after she had gone. There wasn't anything better—except her being in his presence at that moment. "It's great to see you, Gaby. What a lovely surprise."

"You, too, Marcus. Have you eaten lunch yet?" she asked, holding the picnic basket in front of her.

"Come to think of it, I haven't," he said, a strange, almost imperceptible tremor going through him as he moved closer to her. "I'm a hungry man right about now. What you got in that basket?"

"I'm hoping you'd say that. Come on outside with me. Let me fix you something." Just then her eyes met his, and her body filled with desire. Even dirty from hard work and dressed in work clothes, Marcus radiated a sensual vitality that excited Gaby—although she didn't want it to.

Marcus sighed with contentment, thinking it didn't get any better than that. "Let me wash my hands, and I'm all yours."

If I were you, I wouldn't make promises you can't keep, she thought. *This man makes me crazy!*

Marcus gently took Gaby's hand in his and led her outside to a shady pine tree. There, she removed a thin blanket from the basket and spread it out. "Will you join me for lunch, Marcus?" she asked, flashing him a warming smile that reached to the bottom of his heart.

"It would be my pleasure, lovely lady."

With that, she arranged plates of cold fried chicken, sliced country ham, water crackers, potato salad, coleslaw with blueberries, soft rolls, and fresh Georgia peaches on the blanket—along with plastic spoons, forks, napkins, and two glasses. She fixed Marcus a plate, then one for herself. He said grace, and they began to eat.

"Thank you for this treat, Gaby," he said, eating a bite of the ham and a forkful of potato salad. "It's as if you were reading my mind about wanting to eat, but I kept putting it off to get one more thing done. Before I knew it, time got away from me."

"I know exactly what you mean. I do it every day and wind up eating at my desk, on the run, or sometimes not at all," she said, chewing on a peach slice, then pouring them each a glass of sparkling cider.

"So you followed my advice and decided to mack Aunt Doc, huh, Unc?" Kevon asked, plucking a fat chicken wing off the plate.

"Hey, Kevon," Gaby said. "There's plenty of food. Why don't you join us?"

She looked from him to Marcus and back to Kevon, her eyes saying he was more than welcome. She noticed the look of longing and begging in Marcus's eyes, asking her to send him on his way so they could spend some time alone.

Kevon turned his cap from the back to the side and took a napkin to wrap the chicken bones. Taking another one and wiping his hands, he said, "Never that, Aunt Doc. Y'all go on and do your thing. I'm going right down the road to Mickey D's for a burger or something. Go on back to whatever you and Unc were doing."

Kevon sauntered away, snickering—just knowing that if they hadn't made out yet, they would. For sure. He didn't need to be around to witness that. In his mind, there wasn't anything worse than seeing two adults kissing and slobbering all over each other.

"Later," Gaby and Marcus called out as he left them.

"Now, young lady, you were saying..." Marcus eyed Gaby with a scorching intent, drinking in every inch of her. He crushed her to him, claiming her lips. Marcus kissed with words right out of Gaby's mouth—his kisses slow, deliberate, and drugging.

Spirals of wild ecstasy invaded the pit of Gaby's stomach as Marcus's surprise assault of her mouth overtook her. She returned his kiss with everything she had inside. The more he took and gave, the more she opened up—welcoming it. She was shocked at her hungry response to his lips. But Gaby couldn't resist, she had to taste as much of him as she could. His tongue explored, tasted, teased, taunted, and made love in every possible way to her mouth. Then, he seared a heated path down her neck, shoulders, and was working his way down to her cleavage—which peeked out of her dress. His lips re-captured Gaby's demanding even more—his tongue dancing, mating with hers, in the oldest dance known to man. As they enjoyed each other's nectar, white heat shot through Gaby's loins, and she felt as if every one of her senses had short-circuited. The blood pounded in her brain, leapt from her heart, and made her body and wom-anhood spasm with tremors she'd never felt before.

As Marcus ignited her passion, his spiraled out of control—making him senseless. They kissed and made out like two lovesick kids on prom might for the next hour, when Gaby remembered that she had to review one of her patients' test results. She broke away from Marcus—not because she wanted to, but she had to. Every sinew in Gaby felt alive, her consciousness ebbed and flamed more distinctly than she ever remembered. She didn't know what to make of what had just happened between her and Marcus. Her thoughts said one thing, but her body betrayed her and said another. So did her heart. Could she be falling in love with him? Or was it a physical reaction from not having had a man for so long? That was something she had to think about long and hard. She'd have her answer soon, she convinced herself. There was no room in her life for love, Gaby thought. She didn't need or want it, and to her way of thinking, it would only complicate things. She'd had enough drama in her life, and wasn't setting herself up for more!

CHAPTER 8

Gaby didn't realize it, but as she and Marcus were spending lot of time doing positive things with Kevon, he was becoming the well-rounded kid everyone knew he could be—as well as the fact that she was becoming very close to Marcus. The ice cream outings, trips to Dave & Buster's to challenge him in a few hours of games, and several more jaunts to the amusement park made them look like the typical, happy American family. No one knew that they were only friends who'd met each other not long ago and just two of them were related by blood. Both of them stood back and admired how far Kevon had come in a short time. He still had a smart mouth and quick wit, but what new millennium kid didn't? He'd polished up his manners and showed way more respect to both of them, and other adults in general, than he had before. He wasn't perfect, Gaby thought, but he showed a vast improvement over who he'd been. Although she didn't want to admit it, she enjoyed the closeness she and he had developed, and the little imp was beginning to feel like her son. She liked that, but she was just as afraid of moving to that level with him, as she was of her growing feelings and relationship with Marcus. She decided to ride them both out and let come what may—unless things got too crazy, she thought.

"What's up, Aunt Doc?" Kevon crooned, as he walked into Gaby's office. "Can you explain what you're doing with me today, again?"

Gaby took a few minutes to answer him because all she could see was Marcus—all six-three of him—looking so sexy in his cornflower-blue linen walking shorts and sandals—as if he were a gift for her. The smell of his signature Black Code cologne wafted across the room, sending her sensibility reeling. She felt like grabbing him in her arms and burying her head in his strong, corded chest to fully partake of his manly scent. The scent that had invaded her thoughts—even when she didn't want it to. But she'd never do that—at least not around mixed company. Right then, it was all about Kevon and his future. It was *his* day.

"This is Shadow Day, and I'll be taking you everywhere I go so you can see what I do—except for places where you're not allowed like in the OR or in the recovery room," she explained. "Who knows? One day, you might consider medicine as a career choice. I talked to your uncle to find out it was okay that I do this. I figured that I would give you a personal tour and spend time with you showing you what being a doctor is like, so you will get a firsthand look for yourself. You seem to like working with your uncle Marcus, so I wanted to give you something else to see and consider, one day."

"Cool, Aunt Doc, this is going to be fun!" he exclaimed.

"I want you to also learn some things while you're having fun." She smiled, looking at Marcus, and bidding them good-bye until he came to pick up Kevon at lunchtime.

During that morning, Gaby took Kevon on rounds with her, with the patients' permission, and he attended Grand Rounds as well. He didn't have a clue about what was going on during the presentation of some of the most difficult and unusual urological cases or their treatment. Gaby saw the puzzled look—that translated to boredom—on his face, so she took him back to her office and explained some of what was going on, as well as some of the more common urological conditions she treated. Then, she explained what chart notes, giving dictation for the medical transcriptionists, and studying test results entailed. It seemed as if Kevon was most fascinated about some of the tests she performed on patients, as well as the various diseases men got. By that time, their lesson and question-and-answer sessions were over when Marcus interrupted them and reminded them it was time for lunch.

Because Kevon requested burgers and fries, they wound up in a local hole-in-the-wall eatery called Mama's Burgers, where the burgers were huge, homemade, and calorie-laden but delicious. Gaby could feel the grease clogging her arteries, as well as the burger sticking to her already ample hips. But to make Kevon happy and to keep him as good and calm as he'd become, she'd make that sacrifice. Then, her mind drifted to Marcus, and she caught him regarding her with an intense but secret expression on his face. Her cheeks flushed at his scrutiny.

Before she could collect her thoughts or get her

for some reason? Did I do something wrong? she thought, wondering what could've gone wrong in the short time she had worked at the hospital. She made herself presentable, took a deep breath, and went to his office. Better to face whatever it was then, than to put it off and let it escalate into something worse, she told herself.

"Come on in and have a seat, Dr. Talbot," Dr. Whitfield told her. He pointed to a comfortable-looking leather sofa. Then, he took a seat at the other end. "I'm elated to give you some news, Gabrielle," he said, preferring to call her by her full given name.

Gaby exhaled at the word "elated." "Yes, and what is that?" Still nervous, she played with her pager in the pocket of her lab coat.

"You've been chosen to be the MC at our annual charity auction and ball. It's always quite fun and raises lots of money for the hospital. After all, this is a private institution, and we depend very heavily on donations from generous benefactors and other sources," he announced as easily as if he were telling her that she had to see a new patient.

"When is this event, and how did I become the MC?"

"Well, the event is tomorrow—"

"Oh no! I can't get myself together overnight! That would be like pulling off a miracle."

"Not to worry, Gabrielle. I'm giving you the day off so you can go and get yourself something gorgeous and have a day of beauty—on the hospital, of course—since you'll be our ambassador, so to speak. Now, about how you were chosen—"

"Thank you, Dr. Whitfield. It will help having the time off to shop and prepare. I'm sorry, I cut you off. Please continue."

"Gabrielle, since you've been in Red Oaks, you've made some mighty powerful friends. Mother Maybelle and Valerie Freeman Grant are both board members, and they recommended you very highly. The final vote was unanimous," he explained. "We're happy to have you represent the hospital and we're all confident you'll do a fine job. Now, enough talking. Get going, young lady, and we'll see you tomorrow night in the atrium of the Financial Center. Not a minute before that, you hear?"

Gabrielle raced back to her office to collect her things so she could get to the mall and the day spa before they became too crowded. To her surprise, arrangements had been made for her. The spa expected her, and would service her as soon as she arrived. The only detail left undone was the fact that she didn't have an escort. She knew whose arm she wanted to be on more than anyone else's, and she set out to make it happen.

Gaby had spent the better part of the next afternoon getting ready for her big night. She intended to look stunning that evening—for more reasons than one.

Before she knew it, she was letting Marcus in to pick her up that evening. She hoped she didn't make a fool of herself, because the sight of him, resplendent in his black tuxedo with tails, made her pulse skitter at an alarming rate. The air electrified around her. The man was exquisite, like a handsome and chiseled brown Adonis made for loving. She couldn't stop staring at the man who was finer than he'd ever looked since she'd known him. All she wanted at that moment was just one taste of him—any way she could get it!

"These are for you, lovely lady," Marcus said, handing her a corsage of rare tropical flowers, speaking where she couldn't. "They reminded me of your beauty. Exotic and unique." He found himself very aware of her sensual appeal, his gaze riveted on her face, drinking in every inch of her. *What an incredibly gorgeous woman. She has no clue what she does to me or what I'd like to do to her,* he thought. Never in his life had he seen a V-necked evening gown with a beaded plunging neckline look that good on any woman. Gaby had it going on in his book!

"Thank you, Marcus, this corsage is absolutely beautiful. Would you pin it on me?"

Marcus couldn't think of anything he'd rather do right then—except maybe pull her into his needy arms and kiss her until daybreak. But in the meantime, he'd settle for relishing the sensuous scent of her as her perfume wafted past his nose, causing his stomach to ripple and his heart to beat a little faster. *You got it bad, man. Chill,* he thought, pinning on the corsage.

He extended his arm and led her to a waiting chauffeured Lincoln Town Car. The chauffeur let her in and gently closed the door before Marcus got in beside her.

"Marcus, this is too much. It's totally unnecessary."

"Woman, don't tell me how to spend my money!" he teased. "Seriously, Gaby, I was honored when you asked me to escort you to this event. So I figured I'd better do it right."

Mister, so far, you've been doing everything right. Does that cover all areas? she thought, as they talked and laughed, and made out kissing and touching all the way to the charity auction and ball.

Almost as quickly as their making out began, it ended. Her breath quickened and became raw in her throat. She heard her pulse roaring in her ears, and she felt a cold fist closing over her heart. "Stop it, Marcus. Get away from me!" Gaby pushed him away with every ounce of strength in her body. "Things shouldn't have gotten this far!"

"What's wrong, Gaby? Did I do something?" Marcus quizzed, wondering what spooked her so badly and if he was the cause of it.

The thought of the most awful day of her life three years ago froze in her brain. It was the day before her wedding, and she was the happiest woman in the world. She'd been at her bridal shower and was feeling on top of the world from the champagne, the beautiful gifts she'd received, and dancing with the fine stripper her girls had hired for the occasion. She expected to go home and get the rest she couldn't get running around from one wedding-related event to another. But that wasn't to be. When she got home, the sight that greeted her was the most shocking in all her life!

There was something different about her normally quiet house…something didn't seem quite right. After a few minutes, she heard noises—the sound of a man and woman moaning. She followed the sounds and found they led to the bedroom—*her* bedroom. She fell backward, flinching as she threw open the door. Before her in living color were her fiancé and her sister, engaging in loud sex in her bed! Between the primal lovemaking noises they made and a Maxwell song playing in the background, neither of them heard her come into the room. Neither did they see her standing over them.

Gaby's jaw dropped, and she felt the blood drain from her face. "I can't believe this, you no-good, cheating bastards!" she screamed, tears streaming down her face. The veins stood out in livid ridges along her temple and throat. She grabbed the closest objects she saw and flung them at the cheating couple. "How *dare* you do this—and in *my* bed! Both of you need to have some shame!"

They were so in the throes of passion that they barely moved to avoid being hit with the missiles Gaby threw, but even that wasn't enough to stop them. They kept right on until they'd achieved ultimate satisfaction.

Gaby remembered calling them every foul name she knew, trying to push him off her sister, and running out in frustration when nothing she did fazed them.

That was a time in her life that she didn't want to revisit, and she shook her head from side to side in an effort to rid herself of the unpleasant images that flashed before her eyes. It had been three years since she'd seen them. Sure, both of them later tried to apologize, plead ignorance, and cited a lapse of bad judgment, but Gaby didn't fall for any of their excuses. They were two grown people who made a bad choice, and they'd have to live with it.

The sound of Marcus's voice jarred her back to reality.

"Hey...what happened? What did I do? Can I help?" Marcus asked, not giving her a chance to answer any of the questions. He regarded her with bewilderment, experiencing a gamut of emotions about what had just happened. He'd never seen anything like it.

"I'm fine, Marcus," she deadpanned, her tone icy. "Forget it, please. Don't ask any more questions." With that, she moved over to the far end of the backseat, away from Marcus, and crossed her arms across her chest. They rode to the event in silence, both unable to voice what was going through their heads.

Gaby had never seen anything so beautiful in her life. She scanned every inch of the medium-sized space at the Financial Center. It was a mere atrium; she never would've thought it could be transformed to the splendor that was before her eyes. Tapered candles arranged in floral displays of white, yellow, and pink roses adorned each table, along with the finest crystal stemware and bone china. Matching luxury pastel linens completed the look. The sights and sounds of the band playing soft jazz and R&B tunes in the background brought a smile to Gaby's lips. She looked up at Marcus, who she didn't know was thinking that she was every bit as beautiful as the atrium. She studied him from head to toe, admiring the handsome, virile man standing with her, beside her. She couldn't help but wonder if she had been unfair to him pulling back as she did. Her head told her no, but her heart said yes!

Gaby mesmerized the room as the event's MC, paying attention to detail, professionalism, and quick wit when it was called for. Several hundred people were in the room, but she only saw one of them: Marcus.

Her boss thanked her for doing a great job as the hospital's ambassador, and told her to enjoy the rest of the evening: Eat, drink, and dance until she'd had enough—because she'd earned every bit of that enjoyment. Then, he disappeared into the crowd.

Marcus stood nearby and heard every word he'd said to Gaby. As if it were his cue, Marcus swept Gaby into his arms and urged her to the dance floor. His arms circled her waist, triggering primitive yearnings within her. She wrapped her arms around his neck and surrendered to the crush of feelings that drew them together. She laid her head on his firm chest, inhaling the heady scent of his cologne, and thought that just as the vocalist was singing, Marcus Danforth was as right as rain. The tingling effects of their closeness spread through her like wildfire.

Simultaneously, Marcus steeled himself against the tide of pleasure that threatened to transport him to another place, another dimension in time. To his way of thinking, Gaby was all woman—hot, stimulating, and sexy beyond belief. The contours of her curves complemented his body, and when they moved they looked as if they were one body. They were a perfect fit in every way, he thought, as he felt their hearts beating as one. He looked down into her eyes, sparkling in the candlelight, noticing from her gently tightening the hold around his neck that she was just as caught up in the moment as he was.

Without thinking, he pressed his lips to hers, finding her hungry tongue, and kissed her as if his life depended on it. It was a kiss full of passion and need. His tongue entwined with Gaby's—sweeping, caressing, and exploring every nook and cranny in her warm mouth. Marcus gave her a preview of what was to come—the way he made love to her mouth, his tongue mating with hers.

Their tongues danced together in a silent melody that only they understood. Gaby's lips throbbed with desire and urgency as she familiarized herself with the taste of Marcus, enjoying the feeling of his hard steel against her body. Wishing the kiss would last forever, she felt every one of her senses reeling from the touch, scent, and feel of him. As she had imagined, Marcus Danforth was indeed her undoing, but she couldn't get enough of him. Although she refused to admit it to herself, she was a goner. Gaby knew she was caught up and lost in love.

Pressing every inch of her body to his, Marcus gazed into her eyes and with gentleness, tilted her chin up. "I love you, Gabrielle Talbot."

Then, he tightened his arms around her and kissed her as if he were trying to pour every bit of that love into her needy body that was weakening to him by the millisecond. Theirs was a kiss that spoke volumes to them and everyone in their midst.

Continuing to dance—almost in celebration of the moment—Gaby didn't hesitate, nor did she think about her past or her future, only about all that gorgeous man in whose strong arms she was enfolded.

"I love you, too, Marcus," she breathed, almost instinctively.

Everyone in the atrium broke into a hearty applause at the sight of their celebratory dance of love—never having seen anything so romantic happening to one of their own.

Of all of them, Mother Maybelle was probably the most joyous—because finally they gave in to what they knew they felt, but were too afraid to pursue. The smile that stretched across her face told it all. Even at the height of nosiness, she couldn't say anything at that moment. *My work is done for the time being. Let nature take its course with them,* she thought.

Gaby and Marcus didn't care who saw them, because this was something they never expected, nor asked for; but now that it happened, they were all about it. From that point on, the evening belonged to Red Oaks' newest couple. Gaby and Marcus danced the night away—kissing and declaring their love for each other.

CHAPTER 9

Hand in hand, Gaby and Marcus strolled into the tent revival service. They headed straight to Mother Maybelle's row. Beaming at that sight, she let them pass and welcomed them to sit with her. They recapped the events of the ball the previous night, and caught up on general gossip until the service began that evening.

The praise and worship portion of the service was shorter than usual, and Reverend Avery took his place in the pulpit. "Saints, tonight there's something pressing on my heart, and it's heavy. When God has a word for us, we're compelled to listen. Amen?"

Roars of "amen" filled the tent. "There was once a shepherd whose pasture held a hundred sheep. One of them must've had the hot foot because he couldn't stay put, and every time the poor man looked around, he'd 'broken out' as the kids would say. Well, the shepherd still had ninety-nine sheep left, but you know what? He'd spend hours on end chasing after that one straying sheep until he found him and brought him home. You're probably asking why the shepherd would spend so much time going after him when he had so many more to whom he could've given his attention?"

"Why, Pastor?" several voices asked in unison.

"Let's make a parallel here. The shepherd is God, and the lost sheep is one of you—a backslider—who has strayed away. In Luke fifteen, three through seven, it says that heaven is happier over that one sinner who was lost and returned to God than the others who haven't strayed away. That lost soul just has to ask for forgiveness of his sins, church, and he will be forgiven. But as with everything else in life, God's forgiveness doesn't come so easily. He requires two things of us as His conditions of forgiveness. Repentance and forgiveness of others," Reverend Avery said, holding up his Bible. "If you will, turn with me, and let's see what thus saith the Lord...."

Gaby's eyes widened the more verses the pastor read. The deepening hue of shame crept through her veins because she felt as if he were speaking directly to her. Squirming in her seat, Gaby kept crossing and uncrossing one leg over another. Nervous flutterings pricked her chest. She looked away from Marcus (who she hadn't a clue was also easy) as she hid a thick swallow in her throat. A creepy uneasiness settled in the bottom of her heart.

"In the Word, Jesus said we must be willing to forgive people who sin against us, and our ability to forgive them must be limitless. It's on us to have a forgiving spirit—even if the offender doesn't repent and ask for forgiveness. If we don't, we damage our relationship with God and harm ourselves if we stay angry or hold a grudge," she heard Reverend Avery say.

At those words, hot tears crept down her face. She stained the church fan she held in her hands with her tears. Gaby bit her lips to quell her sobs—which by then had overtaken her.

Marcus wrapped his arm around her shoulders and rubbed them in his attempt to take away whatever pain she was feeling. He had no idea what demons were plaguing her, but he wanted her to know that she could lean on him for support through that which was bothering her. The one issue he struggled with would have to wait, because his lady's need came before his own, he thought. Together, they listened as the pastor continued.

"According to Matthew six, fourteen, 'If you forgive those who sin against you, your Heavenly Father will forgive you. But if you refuse to forgive others, your Father will not forgive your sins,'" he said, tapping on the side of the pulpit as if he were deep in thought or in that zone he often spoke about going into when the Holy Spirit was speaking to him. "Along with forgiving others, we have to forgive ourselves, saints. I'm feeling that some of you are holding on to past transgressions that you can't let go. Let it go, let it go if you want forgiveness from our Lord! As the Word advises us, boldly approach the throne of God for His mercy and grace, and cast all of your burdens to Him. Give Him all of your guilt associated with your past sins. It gets even better, church, because the Word makes us a promise. It says that when we do that we have an advocate in Jesus for any of our sins we repent for before God, the Father. And guess what? When we repent and are converted, our sins aren't even remembered—according to the Word. There's no condemnation to those who are in Christ Jesus, amen?"

By now, it was Gaby who comforted Marcus—who was getting rid of or dealing with something that she wasn't privy to. She didn't know that he had never forgiven himself about what had happened with Sasha so long ago. She'd since gone on and built a life for herself with Hunter, and put it past her, so why couldn't Marcus? he wondered. They were, after all, family, and had to be around each other—especially now that Marcus was in Red Oaks. Avoiding her would be stupid and would raise questions and open up old wounds that had long been healed. He looked over at his precious Gaby, who seemed lost in her own reveries. He wondered what made her look so pensive.

Before hearing Reverend Avery's lesson on forgiveness, Gaby hadn't even considered addressing Carolyn's and Sean's betrayal. She figured it would be best to let sleeping dogs lie, so to speak, figuring they deserved each other. They were two of a kind, cut from the same cloth. But she hadn't counted on having the act of forgiveness broken down so plainly and laid at her feet to examine as she never had before. She had no choice but to listen and she heard every word. Most importantly, they got into her heart....

Pastor Avery continued the message, and a short time later, the tent exploded into a cacophony of noises: shouting, praising, and a medley of good shout-'em-up songs.

As the old folks often talked about, the reverend had torn the church up with his brand of starting a sermon calmly so everyone would "get it," and once they did, it was on and cracking. At that point, he became more animated and demonstrative in his preaching style and gave a sermon similar to the fire-and-brimstone types he gave every Sunday morning that his congregation loved so well.

After he got everyone to calm down, he opened the doors of the church and invited the unsaved or those who had strayed for one reason or another to come down front to the altar and make Jesus Christ their personal savior. A throng of people came forth. Almost instinctively, Gaby went, then Marcus—each for different reasons. Reverend Avery asked the deacons, deaconesses, elders, and other ministerial staff to come and lay hands on them. They did as asked, and Gaby was one of the first people they ministered to.

The minute the elder's hands touched her, her body was filled with a mixture of peace and Holy Ghost fire. The next thing she knew, she danced in the spirit and was praising the Lord—something she'd never done before. "Thank You, Jesus, I want to do Your will!" she cried as she danced. Deep sobs that seemed to come from her belly shook her, purging her of everything that was wrong in life. She cried as she came out of it, and thanked the Lord some more. A deaconess came over to her and prayed for her and over her. "I forgive you—*both* of you!" she screamed, eliciting everyone around her, including Marcus, to look at her with understanding.

"That's okay, my child," Reverend Avery said, a soothing tone in his voice. "Let God deal with you. He'll never lead you wrong. Purge it all out of your system until you get right again."

And that's what Gaby did. She asked God for forgiveness over having shunned her sister and her ex-fiancé—despite what they'd done to her. She knew that she wouldn't ever move forward in her Christian walk if she didn't let her negative feelings go. Then, she asked God to forgive them their transgressions. Next, she forgave them publicly—not caring who heard or witnessed her transformation.

Simultaneously, Marcus finally forgave himself for his tryst with Sasha so many years ago, realizing that they were young and had both made a terrible mistake. He would never be able to properly love anyone until he let go of the ghosts from his past. If there were anything he wanted to do, it was to love Gaby with his whole heart—without anything from his checkered past preventing him from doing that.

"Can I get an amen, church? This is exactly what was supposed to come out of tonight's lesson," Reverend Avery explained. "Our resident urologist seems to have gotten it and she came and did what she had to do. Now, her walk will be that much stronger and meaningful because she has learned how to forgive. Give her a hand, saints."

Gaby felt renewed, rejuvenated, and like a giant weight had been lifted off her for the rest of the service.

Basking in the glow of newfound love and the lightness of letting negativity go, Gaby and Marcus left the church with a new spring in their step. They both commented on how refreshing the gentle breeze that cooled off the hot August day felt. It was a clear night view; the dazzle and glitter of the many stars shone above. But the stars weren't any brighter than the love emanating from their eyes when they looked at each other. It wasn't too late, so they decided to go for a short walk. They wound up at an all-night old-fashioned ice cream parlor—complete with a soda jerk and as many flavors of homemade ice cream as they could imagine.

Over an ice cream sampler plate from which they fed each other several different flavors of the delectable dessert, they talked, laughed, and kissed. They were like two silly schoolkids who were experiencing their first love. It didn't matter that they were full grown, and had been in love with others before. To Gaby and Marcus, their love was all they were concerned about.

Marcus broke the spell that had developed between them when he spoke. He took her hands in his and fastened his eyes on her. "Gaby, how do you feel about what has happened between us...about our being together—finally? Are you okay with it?" he asked.

Gaby's expression stilled and grew serious. It became intense as she became aware of Marcus's eyes scrutinizing her. Yes, she was happy, she thought, but his question caught Gaby by total surprise. She couldn't voice the joy her heart felt—not just yet. The concept of loving and being in love was new to her. She had to get used to it before she could talk about it—even with Marcus. "Yes, Marcus—"

The word "yes" was all he needed to hear, because at the sound of it he coaxed her to him and covered her lips with his—kissing the rest of the words right out of her mouth. The tenderness and white heat of Marcus's kiss were exactly what she needed at that moment to make her feel safe, and that she had been blessed to find love twice in her lifetime.

Gaby's body warmed, and her eyes were alight with the glow of love as she looked into Marcus's chestnut-colored orbs, almost becoming lost in them. "Honey, I didn't mean to fall in love, but I did—and I have *no* regrets. You're all the man I'll ever need...."

CHAPTER 10

Gaby was more than aware that she didn't skate very well, but there was no way that she was going to turn down an invitation from Marcus to go skating with him and Kevon. The clincher for her was that the event was a skate party featuring classic soul and R&B music. She was an avid fan of Felix Hernandez's popular Rhythm Revue dances in New York, and she'd often go with a carload of her girlfriends whenever she could. Skating to her favorite music was something she wanted to do!

"Okay, Aunt Doc, show me what you got," Kevon said, putting on his old-school metal skates with four wheels.

Marcus threw him the key and reminded him to tighten the fit to his comfort level.

Gaby took in the scores of skaters of all ages whizzing around the Skate Key rink, located in the Red Oaks Entertainment complex. Most of them were excellent skaters and demonstrated some fancy footwork on their skates. Dips, twists, twirls, flips, and steps from every possible dance between the 1960s and the present weren't too much for many of the skaters who enjoyed the classic music as much as her. There was an intense level of noise, and she heard a myriad of sounds: fantastic music, whoops and hollers, lots of laughter, and groups of skaters verbally challenging each other. They were wonderful sounds to her ears, and Gaby wondered if she could keep up. She didn't want to look foolish in front of Marcus and Kevon, so she kept her lack of skating skills to herself. It was then or never, so she willed herself to skate slowly around the length of the rink.

"Okay, young man, you're on," she told Kevon, beginning to skate. The skates were the ones she'd worn while growing up, so she was familiar with them, she thought. She moved with the swiftness and fluidity of a great buck. In midskate, Gaby executed a playful pirouette, gave a whirling salute, and stamped her feet in a left turn in beat to the classic tune "Double Dutch Bus." She moved lightly, with enough hip sway to pull her skirt in alternate directions, then wrapped it up with expressway speed.

"That's right, Aunt Doc," Kevon said. "Drop it like it's hot! Those are some mighty mean moves."

Yes, right now they are, but how long will I be able to keep this up? she thought. *The Lord is with me so I won't make a fool of myself in front of y'all. Thank You, Jesus!*

"Now show me what *you're* working with, Uncle Marcus," challenged the pint-size mischief-maker.

As Gaby watched Marcus, all she could think of was the phrase "poetry in motion." His movements were full of vigor and grace, with a touch of sass, and some of the hottest dance moves she'd ever seen.

"This is old school, nephew. You can't mess with this," Marcus bragged as he glided around the rink as if it belonged to him alone. He winked at Gaby as he passed her several times.

Not to be outdone, Kevon did his thing in the rink and wowed them with his new-school hip-hop moves, bounces, rolls, and shakes. Both Gaby's and Marcus's mouths formed a perfect O. They had no idea that a preteen boy could move like that. Marcus made a mental note to encourage that talent, and help him develop it. One never knew where it could lead with the right training and professional connections—aka a hookup.

"You go, nephew. That's what's up," Marcus said, speaking Kevon's language and giving him dap. Then he gave Gaby some, too.

They spent another two hours skating and enjoying the old-school jams that played that evening. However, whatever magic Gaby had earlier was wearing off because she fell a few times, but managed to get back up and start over. One of those times, though, she couldn't get up fast enough.

A tall, shapely bombshell, sporting a mane of bouncy auburn hair and big legs, sashayed by them, stopping long enough to talk to Marcus. Talking was obviously *not* what she had in mind, because she sidled up to him and ran her long red talons through his hair and rubbed his chest as if it were something she was used to doing.

Who is this witch, and why is she all over my man? Gaby thought, jealousy washing through her. Her lips puckered with annoyance, and her lower one began to tremble the more she watched the scene unfold before her eyes. Struggling through anger and being unable to get up, she finally righted herself and strode over to where they were.

Gaby grabbed Marcus's arm, then his hand, sending an unspoken message to the hoochie-looking woman to back away from her man. That move was in vain, because the mystery woman kept touching Marcus, and judging from the slight smile on his face, he liked it and didn't want her to stop. Nor did he ask her to!

"So what brings you to Red Oaks, Sandra?" Marcus asked with a ring of familiarity in his voice. "Last time I saw you, was back in Charlotte. You're a long way from home."

"I'm here on business and went online to WhatsHot-RedOaks dot-com to find out what was happening and found out about this old-school skate party," she purred, "so I thought I'd come and shake my groove thing for a few hours. Looka here, I ran into the man I wanted to see most. We have some unfinished business...."

Gaby looked at Marcus's reaction, and not once did he even try to stop the woman who had hands like an octopus. He didn't even tell Hands Almighty that Gaby was his woman. Gaby's face became a glowing mask of rage. She rolled her eyes at them, her lips thinning. *I've had enough of this sideshow. She can have him if she wants him that badly,* Gaby thought as she skated away.

Her ex-fiancé's betrayal with her sister flashed through her mind like a movie montage. That was the most hurtful thing to ever happen to her, and what she'd just witnessed seemed like yet another man would betray her—and she wasn't having it. Her body quaked from the sobs she could no longer control. Tears blinded her as she ran aimlessly into the hot Georgia night. "All men are dogs...and Marcus is no different!" she screamed into the air, still crying. "I shouldn't have been taken in by his good looks and sweet talk. He's no different from any other man...."

Gaby continued her tirade about how no-good and trifling men were—not caring who saw her or who had something to say. To her way of thinking, that's what she got for falling so hard for *another* man after one had dogged her so badly. She was only getting what she deserved for letting her guard down.

She was having such a good time at her pity party that she didn't hear Marcus, who had left Sandra immediately after Gaby ran out, and he ran behind her. He was in great physical shape, but made a vow to himself to work out more, eat more Wheaties, and perhaps lift a few weights along the way because his Gaby could *run!* He didn't know that she could run like that and make such a quick getaway, or that she'd ever want to! It was clear that she was in the better shape between the two of them, and she could get ghost when she wanted to. This was one of those times.

A tight place of anxiety entered Marcus's heart that evening when his phone remained silent. There was no nightly call, talking, and laughing with Gaby for hours while he chilled in bed at the end of a long, hard day. There was no impromptu IM session when either of them saw the other online checking e-mail. He was going to do everything in his power to change the situation—starting *that* moment.

Marcus became a man with one mission in mind: to get his woman back and make her understand what she saw. Replaying the situation in his mind, he figured out that she was upset about his talking to Sandra. Sandra Hylton wasn't like most women—she came on strong, and made wives and girlfriends think something was going on when it wasn't. That had to be what happened tonight, Marcus told himself. *If I'm right, that's about to change!*

Marcus logged online to see if Gaby was out there, and she was. He attempted to e-mail and IM her, but neither one worked. He realized that she had blocked his e-mail address from having any communication with her. If that didn't work, he knew other ways, and as soon as day broke, he'd put them in motion.

Over the next couple of days, he sent Gaby flowers with cards apologizing, sad-faced teddy bears with pitful notes attached, a classified ad in the local paper, and he even took out a billboard in Town Square proclaiming his love for her. The craziest thing he did, though, was having Hunter "page" her during the revival service. None of it fazed her. Gaby ignored his every attempt to communicate with her. What Marcus didn't realize was that once she cut her ties with a man, they were cut—forever. If he didn't know that, he would!

Marcus lay on his sofa, his face twisted in a pained expression. *Why is that woman so stubborn and pigheaded? All I want to do is to tell her about Sandra and explain that Gaby is the only woman I'll ever love,* he thought. His eyes were clamped shut, and his brows were deeply furrowed. The presence of overgrown whiskers shadowing his face indicated that he hadn't shaven in several days. There were take-out containers and plastic microwave platters strewn all over the floor, as well as beer cans. In a space that sat catty-corner to the sofa was a half-empty wine bottle. Everything inside his body ached without Gaby in his life. His every thought was of her. It seemed as though everywhere he looked, he could see her face or that full womanly body he'd come to love so well. Nothing he did could remove her from his system: drinking, eating badly, sleeping, or not sleeping. In his mind, soul, and body, Gabrielle Talbot remained—and she wasn't going anywhere! He'd finally found the woman who made his heart sing and made him feel alive. Just like that, she was gone out of his life—over her having jumped to conclusions about something so totally innocent. Without her, Marcus was a miserable someone, and he just wanted to be left alone to self-destruct.

No matter how much Marcus's heart was shattered and hurt, he still had a responsibility to Red Oaks Christian Fellowship. He'd promised to do repairs and minor renovations to the church, and he fully intended to keep up his end of the bargain. He dragged himself out of bed, washed up, and threw on the first thing he found. Within minutes, he arrived at the church, and the first person he ran into was Mother Maybelle—the one person he hoped not to see.

She looked him up and down, shaking her head. "Umph, umph, umph, Marcus, what's wrong, sugar?" she asked, noticing that his eyes looked vacant, and he was spent, all of his emotions were smoothed away. "Say the truth, because you know you can't hide anything from Mother Maybelle."

"I'm okay, Mother Maybelle. It's nothing that I can't handle myself." Marcus tried his best to perk up, but couldn't because he felt as if whole sections of his body were missing and torn away.

"Bull, Marcus! You look terrible, tore up from the floor up—if you understand that better. Look at you. Your clothes are mismatched, your five o'clock shadow is now at high noon, and you smell like you need to become re-acquainted with a bar of soap and water! That plain enough for you?"

"Mother Maybelle!" Marcus exclaimed. He felt humili-ated and deflated, knowing that every word of what she said was on point. The problem was without Gaby, he didn't know how to change it and do better.

"Don't Mother Maybelle me, young man," she scolded him. "Something's up, and I want details. Now, spill it!"

Marcus felt uneasiness, tinged with irritation, creep through him. All he wanted to do was get to work and be left alone. He could hide his pain by immersing himself in hard work. He knew he wouldn't be allowed to do that unless he threw the wise but nosy sage a bone. So he did. He gave her an abbreviated version of what had happened with Gaby, and told Mother Maybelle that it was all a big misunderstanding.

Mother Maybelle looked off in the distance for a few moments; then she studied Marcus—looking deep into his eyes as if they held the answers she was searching for. Soon, she broke the uncomfortable silence and spoke. "I believe you, sugar. I have a plan and know how to help—if you don't mind."

"Thanks, Mother Maybelle, but I don't need you to fight my battles. I'm a big boy and am capable of doing that by myself," he said, tempering his tone so he wouldn't sound as if he were defensive.

He didn't know her very well, because she felt that her sole purpose on earth was to "help." Mother Maybelle wasn't complete unless she was helping someone, and help Marcus was what she intended to do—with or without his permission. "Sugar, you're not doing so well alone from the looks of you, so you might as well let me help."

Maybe I can benefit from your wisdom, because I'm fresh out, Marcus thought. *Maybe you know something I don't.* "Okay, Mother Maybelle. You can help me, this *one* time."

Mother Maybelle smiled as bright and pretty as the torrid Georgia sun that shone that day. "Good choice, Marcus. I got this. Don't you worry about a thing."

For some strange reason, he believed she did have his back, and could in some way help to remedy the situation between him and Gaby. He felt a little better, and went right to work restoring Red Oaks Christian Fellowship to its usual standard of beauty and grandeur.

Mother Maybelle went downstairs to a back area of the Fellowship Hall for privacy, and she made a call on her cell phone. "Hi, my dear, I need a favor…" she said, cut-and-dried, no-nonsense.

"Well, let me hear what it is first, because I commit myself," said the Honorable Hezekiah E. Jackson, her very close "friend."

"I want you to summon Dr. Talbot to the courthouse

about some unpaid traffic tickets—and tell her she'll do jail time if she doesn't show up."

The judge's heart warmed and skipped a beat at the sound of Mother Maybelle's voice. He knew her well, and knew that she was cooking up another zany scheme, but that was what he loved most about her: her big heart, and her willingness to help others—even if it did border on nosiness. She didn't know it, but there wasn't anything he wouldn't do for her. "Let me run her name through the system and find out if she even has any traffic tickets. She is an A-1 model citizen, you know," he told his woman, running his hand through his curly black hair that was the prettiest shade of silver at the sides.

"If she doesn't have any, *create* some. Just get her there, and I'll handle the rest...."

He couldn't have been any more in love at his age than he was when he was thirty years younger. As with any man in love and his woman needed something, he obliged, knowing that if she made such an outlandish request, there was a good reason. Plus, he owed her a favor.

"I need to see someone, immediately!" Gaby roared to the security officer stationed inside the Red Oaks District Court. She wondered why she was summoned to the courthouse so abruptly for two traffic tickets. She had intended to send a check and pay them off, but had become distracted, and they'd slipped her mind. They could've at least given her a written warning, she thought, or shot her a quick reminder e-mail. She had better things to do than to come to the courthouse in the middle of the afternoon. But when the caller told her if she didn't show up she'd be put in jail, she had Gaby's full attention. So she came as requested. She only hoped the process would go quickly, so she could return to work to the patients who needed her.

"Oh yes, Dr. Talbot, place your things on the belt and walk through the metal detector," the guard said, smiling, examining the ID she presented. He waved a wand over her body and found that she didn't have any weapons. "Go into courtroom three. Judge Jackson is expecting you."

Gaby had never heard of personalized service, and figured that was the kind of treatment she could expect living in a small town. Gaby was sworn in almost as soon as she arrived in the courtroom, and then the judge asked her to approach the bench.

"Young lady, I have no intention of keeping you here any longer than necessary," Judge Jackson said, his voice booming across the small courtroom. "Communication— especially listening to what others have to say—is a very good thing. In fact, it's an art that you and many other people need to learn," he lectured, holding up his hand in a stop motion so he could finish. "However, hearing what someone says isn't enough. You must listen, and just nod your head to acknowledge that you are indeed listening and processing what is being said. Another thing, no one's perfect and everyone makes mistakes. Learn to allow others a second chance, Dr. Talbot. Do you understand what I'm saying?"

She lowered her gaze in confusion. "Yes and no, Your Honor," she replied. "I'm not quite sure why you're saying these things to me. I came here to pay traffic tickets and leave."

"You can settle your tickets, later. Now, all you have to do is promise me that you will think about what I said, and when the time is right, you'll act appropriately. You'll understand better in a little while. Can you do that?"

Still confused and feeling like a blind person driving down a steep cliff with no one to rely on but herself, she felt uncomfortable. But Gaby was a team player, and she knew enough not to rock the proverbial boat.

"That's the wise answer, Dr. Talbot. Follow the bailiff, and the rest will be revealed to you, shortly," the handsome elder judge ordered.

When Gaby arrived in the judge's chambers, she could not believe what she saw. Her eyes blinked with incredulity and became as big and round as fifty-cent pieces. The chambers had been converted into a romantic café—complete with candlelight, fresh-cut peonies, roses, magnolias, and baby's breath everywhere. The sound of Sarah Vaughan singing Brazilian bossa nova tunes played softly in the background. But the sight that took her breath away was Marcus in a blue linen short set and sandals, smelling delicious. The scent of his Hummer cologne wafted through the air and mixed with that of the seafood pasta creation that a waiter had just uncovered.

"Have a seat, Gaby," Mother Maybelle ordered. "You'll be here for a while, so enjoy yourselves. Dominick will attend to your every need."

With that, she winked at Marcus and mouthed "good luck." She and the judge started out of the door, but he doubled back. "Oh, by the way, bailiff, I want you to lock this door, stand outside, and guard it. I order you to arrest this woman if she tries to bolt! She may use my facilities for her personal needs. You got that?"

The bailiff nodded affirmatively, and the judge and Mother Maybelle left.

"Would you like some wine?" Marcus asked, telling Dominick that he would pour it for her.

"I have no other choice, so why not?" A twinge of anger was in her voice. She was ticked off that she was sequestered in a locked room, forced to listen to whatever tales Marcus decided to tell.

He poured the wine for both of them and proposed a short toast. "To *understanding*."

As they clinked glasses, their eyes met and held. But it was Gaby who broke their gaze, too afraid of what could happen if she looked into his hypnotic and sparkling depths too long. Something was happening, and not even Dominick's serving their seafood pasta, tomato and fresh mozzarella on arugula, and fresh-baked garlic rolls disturbed the moment.

Marcus drew in a breath and decided to take charge; it was then or never for him to make things right between them and get his woman back. He'd fight for her or die trying, he told himself. He said a quick silent prayer, then began. "Gabrielle, I'm not going to mince words. I know why you are upset with me. Putting myself in your shoes, I can understand how things must've appeared. Let me assure you, Sandra Hylton meant nothing to me—now or ever."

"It sure didn't *look* that way, Marcus," Gaby said, sighing. She wound her linguine around her fork, using a spoon, then ate the delicious pasta.

"It sure didn't. I knew her because I renovated her home a few years ago," Marcus explained. "She was a recent divorcée, and once she saw I wasn't fat, bald, and ugly, she made every play in the world for me. But she would've done that with any man. After all, she was lonely, needy, horny, and very alone without her husband or children. I refused her advances and let her know I wasn't interested in her. You see, she had made her way through all of my buddies, and they kissed and told. Believe me, what they said about her would've made that Superhead woman look tame! That wasn't the kind of woman I wanted in my life. Sandra began to follow me everywhere I went, and I wound up talking to the sheriff—who was a friend. I went to her and told her that if she followed me one more time, I'd press charges against her for stalking. Finally, she got the message and stopped. She realized that I was serious, so she staked out her next victim and left me alone. The next time I saw her was at the skating rink that day. And I was as shocked as you were!"

Gaby's body finally began to relax. Her body language stopped being defensive as it had been. "If all that's true, why couldn't you tell her not to touch you, Marcus? She was all over you, and that was uncalled for."

"I guess that came from being in shock and the fact that everything happened so quickly, I wasn't thinking clearly. Charge it to my stupidity, Gaby. All I know is that we need to stop this silent treatment. Let me out of the doghouse.

I've been in there long enough, and I don't like it," Marcus pleaded, giving her a sad-eyed look.

She looked at how precious he looked when he begged. Her heart was softening a little more each time she thought about how happy he'd made her thus far. She knew she had trust issues and if her relationship with Marcus was to work, she had to trust in him. If he were truly her man, she had to believe in him, believe what he told her, and that he would never hurt her. After all, he wasn't Sean. Until that day, Marcus had never done anything wrong to her or hurt her in any way. He was secretive and not too forthcoming at first, but she couldn't hold that against him. She would wait a few more minutes before she let him off the hook. No matter what, she loved Marcus Danforth with all of her heart, and it was high time he knew that, she thought.

Marcus finished his food and gently took her hands in his. Staring into her eyes and getting lost in their chestnut-brown depths, he said, "Gaby, I love you so much that my words aren't enough to express what I feel. I hurt when you're not around. I cannot live without you because you're everywhere. In my heart, in my mind, and in my soul. Lady, you've gotten to places no other woman has, and that's almost scary. But it's most welcome. I love you, and I don't care who knows it—as long as you do."

Gaby couldn't stop the smile from lighting up her face. She couldn't hide her feelings another minute for fear she'd burst. "Marcus, I love you more than I ever thought I would. I never dreamed I'd love this way again, but then you came into my life. You're more than I deserve."

Marcus wiped the tears that streamed down her face, kissing them away. "No, baby, things happened the way they were meant to," he said, reassuring her. "We deserve each other and are just right together. If I have my way, we'll get even better as time goes on. You'll see."

Taking her hands, he coaxed her up. "Dance with me, baby?" he asked, hearing George Duke singing "No Rhyme, No Reason." "This is one of my favorite songs."

Gaby sighed with the utmost of contentment as Marcus wrapped her tight in his arms. Pressing her head against his firm, corded chest, she felt as if she were home. The scent of him, and his soft kisses on her neck and ears, made her feel safe, loved—as if nothing or no one would ever harm her again. The aggressor finally, she found his lips, and kissed him with every drop of love she felt for him. Her tongue mated with his as they moved ever so slowly with the music. Gaby felt as if she were being transported to another time, another place, and that this world was careening off its axis as she became lost in Marcus's kiss and in Duke singing so sensually.

"Baby, may I ask you something?" Marcus asked, so as not to spoil the magic between them.

"Yes, my love, ask me anything," she breathed, purring like a fat, contented cat.

"I have to go to Savannah on business this weekend. Will you come with me?"

She thought about it for a few seconds so she wouldn't seem anxious; then she responded. "Yes, Marcus. I'd go with you to the ends of the earth."

Marcus grabbed her tighter and kissed her until her lips

CHAPTER 11

Marcus took Gaby's hand and led her through a huge Victorian home with a lush garden in the back. Gaby oohed and aahed as she toured the historic building with the gingerbread trims, stained glass windows, and beautiful architecture. She thought of all the kids they could have and the fun they'd have making them. Desire shot through her body as one thought after another invaded her mind.

"What do you think of this house, honey?" Marcus asked, kissing her hand, then her lips.

"It's absolutely lovely, sweetheart. The owners should be quite proud to own a property like this."

"I so agree with you, except this won't be a home that anyone will *live* in. My company is renovating this into an upscale southern and Low Country restaurant downstairs, and the upstairs floor will be a bed-and-breakfast," he explained. "In fact, my meeting with the owners will begin in a few minutes."

"I know you and your men will turn this building into a place of splendor." She smiled.

"That's my intention. The owners were in Charlotte and saw a similar restaurant and bed-and-breakfast combination that I'd built, and begged the owners there for my contact information. We talked, the terms were right, and I wanted the job. So we're here."

"I don't want to hang around, then. I need to get lost."

"No, take the car, honey, and go shopping. You can go over to River Street where there are many interesting shops, or check out the Oglethorpe Mall on Abercorn Street. There's a street map in the glove compartment," Marcus urged her. He went into his wallet and pulled out several bills and handed them to her. "Have a good time. Get a facial, or something relaxing. Your man will be waiting when you get back."

She thanked him and handed him back his money, but he refused it, saying he was happy to give her some spending change to fund her shopping trip. She kissed him good-bye, thinking she could get used to having such a thoughtful man in her life.

A few hours later, the reunited couple took a romantic walk in Savannah's Historic District. The day was perfect because the sun was a peaceful burst of light across the beautiful tree-lined streets, and it shone brighter than Gaby ever remembered seeing it in Philly. There wasn't a cloud in the sky. Like two kids, Gaby and Marcus strolled down the street, hand in hand, kissing each other, laughing, and giggling. A feeling of glorious happiness sprang up in her heart. Everything in her laugh, smile, and demeanor said that she felt blissfully happy and alive.

Sniffing the azaleas, magnolias, and camellias, she thought about how they were some of the most refreshing scents she could remember in a long time. She enjoyed the sight of the live oak trees dripping with Spanish moss, and the sturdy antebellum mansions—some with wrap-around porches. She scanned the area, totally immersed in every sight and sound around her until she saw the cutest little man cross her path.

"Peanuts, boiled, parched, and roasted," a street vendor sang as he pushed a cart down the street looking for customers. The sound of his voice and the bell he rang made Gaby avert her gaze from her gorgeous new surroundings to regard what he had to offer.

Wanting to expose Gaby to an age-old southern treat, Marcus bought two bags of boiled peanuts from the old, rheumy-eyed man who boasted a toothless smile.

"Honey, you haven't had a real taste of Georgia until you've tasted salty boiled peanuts," he said, feeding her some of the delicious snack.

"Umm, tasty...but they're pretty salty."

"That's the fun of them. That what makes them taste so good," Marcus said, continuing to feed her more of the morsels she was beginning to enjoy.

The doctor in Gaby made her open her mouth to remind him about how salt could run up their blood pressure, and how hypertension was out of control in their community, but she closed it—thinking she'd just live in the moment and have fun for once. That one time surely wouldn't kill them!

Before the day was over, they took the "Midnight in the Garden of Good and Evil tour" to see the various locations where the movie that brought increased tourism to Savannah was made. They were lucky because they got to take photos with Lady Chablis—one of the stars of the movie who happened to be at home and in town. They continued on to take the Savannah Riverboat Cruise, visit the Riverfront, the Savannah National Wildlife Refuge, an art museum, and to enjoy chopped barbecue sandwiches at Roscoe's. But Marcus insisted that they cut their fun short and return to the hotel. "Work with me, baby, and I promise I'll make it worth your while,' he whispered to her, gently rubbing her face. "Trust me."

And she did. In another hour, they had showered and changed into summer linen attire, both matching in coordinating shades of sea green: Marcus in a casual suit and Gaby in an above-the-knee bustier dress with a short-sleeve jacket. Despite her fifty questions, Marcus wouldn't tell her where they were going. It wasn't long before they arrived at their destination, and he led her inside.

"Here we are, my love," he said, giving the hostess their name.

Gaby's face lit up like a neon sign on Broadway as she read the sign: THE LADY & SONS. "Marcus, this is Paula Deen's restaurant! I watch her on the Food Network and I have all of her cookbooks. How did you know that I'm one of her biggest fans?"

Marcus struggled with the urge to take her, right there in public, the more he thought about how sexy she was: her looks, her scent, her voice, her curiosity. He drew in a sigh and willed all of him to behave and not show out in public. There would be plenty of time to do what he had in mind. "I've observed your huge cookbook collection and noticed which chefs you favored. I figured that this restaurant would be the perfect choice for us, and a great surprise for you."

"Thanks, honey, I love it here," she said, admiring the simple, tasteful décor and the throngs of people enjoying their food. Gaby thought about how Marcus couldn't know her any better because this was a perfect choice, and she looked forward to dining with him there.

They were seated quickly by the window in a romantic spot as Marcus had requested. It wasn't long before they had drinks and shared the popular seafood dip and fried green tomatoes. From the closeness they shared and the way they touched each other, no one would have known that several days earlier they weren't speaking. They looked like a couple as in love as any had ever been. Their spell was broken by the sound of a resonant male voice.

Gaby looked in its direction and saw the solidly built six-foot-seven man who stood before them, working a Stetson hat and alligator boots.

"Hey, man!" Marcus greeted the handsome stranger whose very presence upset several of the women who practically salivated at the sight of him.

"Let me introduce you to my lady. Gabrielle, this is Chase Thomas, a dear friend of mine. And this is Dr. Gabrielle Talbot. We go *way* back!"

"Glad to meet you, ma'am," Chase said, tipping his Stetson in the Texas tradition. "We'll just keep talk about our checkered past to ourselves. That was a long time ago, and I'd like for this fine woman to respect me."

"It's my pleasure, Mr. Thomas," Gaby said, extending her hand to shake his.

"My friends call me Chase. Mr. Thomas is my father." He laughed.

"How is your family—Alex, Lizzie, and your parents?" Marcus inquired.

"Everyone's fine, thanks. They're doing well. Daddy's still raising plenty of cain, you know how he does. They're all working on some special promotions at Panache and restocking inventory."

"What's Panache, may I ask?" Gaby wanted to know.

"Only the baddest jewelry emporium in Texas…maybe in the world!" Marcus exclaimed. "It's by invitation only, and you won't find the exquisite quality of jewelry sold there anywhere else."

"Thanks, man, I appreciate that. You're too kind. Look, y'all, it's been nice, but I'll let you get back to your supper. I didn't mean to take up so much of your time," Chase said, giving each of them a hug. "Come on down to Texas for a visit so we can show y'all a good time, okay?"

"We'll be down that way soon, buddy. Can I holler at you a minute, Chase?" Marcus asked, walking him to the door. Marcus excused himself for a moment while Gaby waved good-bye to Chase.

Marcus returned quickly, not keeping Gaby waiting too long. She noticed that a sly grin shadowed his face as if there were something he knew and she didn't. Her curiosity didn't let it rest. "What's up with you? Why the little wicked smile?" she asked.

"Oh, nothing. Just glad to see Chase. We used to have so much fun back in the day," he said, giving her a safe and generic answer. Only Marcus knew the real reason behind his smile.

The glow of their love continued through their seafood and crab cake dinner, and spilled over into dessert and coffee. Marcus couldn't wait another minute. He had to get a certain something off his mind, right then. At that moment, Marcus's heart hammered, and his insides ached with an inner longing in anticipation of what was to come. He ran his tongue over his lips and spoke. "All of my life I've hoped and prayed to find one special woman—one who'd be my soul mate and complete me," he began, clasping her hand in his. "Little did I know that I would come to a small town and meet a woman who would change my life in such short time! But they say when you find 'the one,' you know, and there are no time limits on what the heart feels. I did just that—find the right woman. Gabrielle, I fell in love with you the moment I saw you. I don't want to ever spend another moment without you. I need you, I want you in every way a man could want a woman, and I love you with all my heart."

Gaby sat stark still in total shock, not answering.

With that, Marcus walked around to where she was seated and knelt on one knee. He reached into his pocket and pulled out a small green velvet box. He gently removed a yellow three-carat, pear-shaped diamond surrounded with Colombian emeralds in a yellow gold setting and took her hand. "Gaby, all the love I have and more is represented with this ring. You're the woman I want in my life for the rest of my days to love, to have our children, and share everything I have as well as my every hope and dream. Will you do me the honor of marrying me?"

Gaby's face flushed with happiness, and her breath caught in her throat. Her eyebrows shot up in surprise. Her face glazed with total shock. Then, came the tears of joy streaming down her face. She tried to wipe them, but Marcus did the honors, telling her it was okay—to go with what her heart felt and to let them flow.

"Yes, Marcus...yes, yes, I'll marry you! I love you, too!" she exclaimed, grabbing Marcus and kissing him like crazy. This time, she didn't let the onlookers bother, distract, or discourage her. In her heart, mind, and soul, the only two people in that restaurant were she and Marcus. "Oh, what a beautiful ring! I love it—almost as much as you," she said as she admired the glittering gem.

"It's a rare stone that reminded me of you. You're the type of woman who's one in a million and can't be found every day. But I was the lucky man who did," he said softly, kissing her hand. "And I've been thanking God every day."

The restaurant patrons were romantics at heart and appreciated a good love scene when they saw one, so they broke out in a hearty applause. Several people who were leaving passed by their table, congratulated them and wished them well. A waiter came over and brought them a bottle of champagne to celebrate the occasion and two hefty slices of cake that he described as "a little something Paula made." They thanked the waiter, and then Gaby questioned Marcus about the ring.

"My darling wife-to-be, I worked with Chase by phone

and e-mails, and he designed this ring. Since he was in Savannah on business, he decided to bring it to me and we could catch up, and he could meet you. He gave me the ring when I walked him out earlier," Marcus elaborated.

"Ah, you *sneak!* So that was why you had that slick grin on your face?" Gaby laughed.

"I won't start our engagement with secrets between us," he said. "Guilty as charged."

They shared a hearty laugh over how well Marcus had pulled the whole thing off. "Honey, are you ready?" he asked, the light of love glinting in his eyes. "I want to spend some quality time with you, my lovely fiancée."

Her toes curled with ecstasy at the thought of being alone with Marcus. What she didn't know was that he was growing more feverish with desire by the minute.

The moment Gaby and Marcus arrived back at the hotel and got to the room, he pulled her into his arms. His mouth moved over hers in a sensual exploration of desire, wanting, and need. Horny as he was, his kiss was urgent, deep—moving his tongue with strong, impelling strokes. Gaby understood what he meant—and she answered in kind, mating her tongue with his, accepting his invitation in every way.

Intense wanting invaded Gaby's weakening form, and her womanhood throbbed from the feel and heady scent of Marcus. What he had was hot, exciting, and she wanted all of what he had to offer!

"Gaby, I love you so much…I want you. Let me make

love to you," he breathed. The scent of the lavender candle he lit radiated the room with a pleasant, romantic scent.

She didn't know if it was the feel of Marcus's body and pulsating manhood pressed against her, or the smell of his cologne, or his kisses that threatened to drive her out of her mind, but she felt as if she were being transported to another realm, another place, another time. All she could do was nod her response.

That was all Marcus needed because with that, he scooped her up in his arms and carried her to the bed. Quickly, he pressed Play on a portable CD player he'd placed on the nightstand next to the bed. Peabo Bryson invited them to "Feel the Fire," and that is exactly what they did.

In record time, Marcus undressed Gaby with speed and control, throwing her clothes in a heap on the floor. "Beautiful...so beautiful," he said, kissing and admiring her naked body.

Gaby undressed him almost as quickly as he'd done her, and her hands began an exploration of their own. In that moment, she totally surrendered to the feelings that drew them together, and moaned her approval of the sensual assault Marcus was perpetrating on her body. Her stomach twisted with the hard knot of need, and a painful ache built between her thighs. "Um, Marcus...yes...lower. Don't stop, please don't stop," she whispered, her response shameless, primal.

And he didn't stop. He savored, slurped, sucked, and satiated everything on Gaby's body from head to toe— wanting to unleash her hunger and satisfy it. The magic of his mouth and fingers overrode every one of her inhibitions. He turned Gaby into a babbling, writhing mess. Turnabout was fair play that evening because Gaby had given Marcus as well as she'd gotten.

"Baby...Gaby...yes! Do it! Oh—"

Exultant sensations wafted through Gaby's body in heated, fiery waves. "Marcus...honey...now, I need it..." she begged.

Marcus reached over on the nightstand and retrieved a black foil packet. Sheathing his thick length, he used two fingers to test Gaby's readiness, and gently parted her thighs with his knee. He buried himself in her dewy warmth, reveling in her softness. Marcus moved against Gaby, fanning the sparks of arousal she felt into a full-blown flame.

The untold delight of his throbbing massive manhood was too much for Gaby, who was overcome with waves of ecstasy. She understood Marcus's rhythm, and arched her hips to meet it. She clenched her vaginal muscles with the instinctive movements of a woman who knew how to please her man.

"Marcus...sweetheart...so good! Give it to me," she moaned, trembling with each thrust. Suddenly, she thought Marcus had given her all he had, but he lifted up, worked his hips, and gave her every centimeter of the total joy with which he'd been blessed.

By this time, the sound of raw, primitive sex was the only reality in the room—along with the sound of Luther Vandross singing in the background and the scent of the fresh-cut tea roses encased in a vase on the dresser. Gaby wrapped her legs around Marcus's back and put some loving on him—the likes of which he'd never experienced from any woman. "Gaby...my Gaby...that's right! Oh my...I love you!" he moaned, meeting her thrusts with slow and measured ones of his own.

At long last, their bodies mated with the reverence of true love and that passion of seduction and animalistic lust that only they could satisfy. Molten shafts of desire crept from the depths of her stomach to her toes, and uncontrollable spasms quaked her tingling body. "Marcus... I'm—" she screamed.

"Let it go, my baby," he urged, a starburst of ecstasy starting deep inside him. "Come for me."

Gaby gave in to a spiraling climax that utterly consumed her and took her to a special place of rapture, transporting her to the stars. Sighs of satisfaction shook her body, and in a few moments she felt Marcus jerk inside her with a fevered groan. The passion and unconsummated bond they'd felt for each other was finally satisfied, and a sense of completion washed through them.

"I love you so much, lady, my beautiful wife-to-be," Marcus whispered to Gaby, who was spent after the workout he'd given her.

"And I love you, Marcus Danforth," she responded before his mouth covered hers with a kiss that sang through her veins.

He pulled Gaby into his arms, and they fell into the easy sleep of sated lovers. They awakened, and they made love again and again and again throughout the night until dawn.

* * *

Gaby and Marcus returned to Red Oaks with a new spring in their step, exchanging the knowing looks of a couple in love. Their eyes sparkled every time they regarded each other, and it was clear that *something* was up. But no one knew what that was. Before she could tell anyone, her boss, Dr. Whitfield, outed her secret.

"Oh my, look at that rock!" he exclaimed. "*That's* what I call a ring. Who's the lucky guy?"

"Marcus Danforth, Reverend Danforth's brother," she said, beaming with pride at the mention of his name.

"Congratulations, Gabrielle, I wish you and your fiancé every happiness. No wonder you can't stop smiling. When's the big day?"

"We're working on that and haven't set a firm date yet. Don't worry because when we do, you'll be invited."

He couldn't wait to get back to his office. He called Mother Maybelle and told her Gaby's good news. He was like an old refrigerator and just couldn't keep it! He had to tell it or he'd burst. Plus, there was a little matter of a bet they had between them that they'd be engaged before the year was over. As badly as he didn't want to admit his wise old friend was right, he had to. He also had to pay her or risk her embarrassing him about not paying his debts. He didn't play anyone challenging his integrity or character in any way.

That Sunday, the service was especially hard. Gaby felt as if all eyes were on her, because people she didn't even know congratulated her. She saw that one of the women cut her eyes at Marcus, despite the fact that he was standing right by her side, his eyes fastened securely on her. She was confident in their love. She knew that he'd be hers forever, and no other woman would ever come between them.

One thing she didn't count on was Mother Maybelle officially outing her in front of the whole Red Oaks Christian Fellowship congregation. Although Mother Maybelle had gotten the 411 about how their engagement happened, when, and all of the particulars, she couldn't resist having one formal opportunity to put her stamp on things. She got it during the morning announcements.

Dressed in a coral and brown outfit, with a matching hat tilted in her signature way, she sauntered up to the podium. "Giving honor to God, Reverend Avery, pulpit associates, and saints, good morning," she began. "I am proud to officially announce the engagement of Dr. Gabrielle Talbot to Marcus Danforth—the brother of our own beloved assistant minister, Reverend Hunter Danforth. Ladies, don't be jealous when you see that rock she's wearing! She'd better walk around town with a bodyguard by her side—but make him old, fat, and bald. Marcus darling, you have excellent taste in women, and you couldn't have found a finer one than Gaby Talbot. You also have wonderful taste in jewelry because as the kids would say, that ring is working! On behalf of the Red Oaks Christian Fellowship church family, we would like to extend our congratulations and best wishes on your engagement. Would y'all please stand. Church, show them some love."

The church broke out in applause and cheers from most of the members. A few of the single and matronly women were too jealous to clap and rolled their eyes at them, as well. Even at that happy news, the devil was good and busy. Gaby saw them and ignored them, fighting the temptation to roll her eyes back at them. She had a good man, at last, and was the winner in the situation—not them. She owed them nothing, and refused to step down to their level.

Hunter had them come up to the podium, where he hugged them both and officially welcomed Gaby to the Danforth family.

After the service, Gaby and Mother Maybelle used Reverend Danforth's office and turned it into wedding central. Armed with fabric swatches and bridal magazines, Mother Maybelle, Sasha, and Valerie brainstormed with Gaby about her wedding. The planning was officially in full swing from that moment on.

That Saturday night, Sasha called Gaby and extended an invitation on behalf of the Danforth family to come to dinner. For Gaby, it was a no-brainer because she liked Sasha and all of the Danforths. So she accepted right away. A great sense of joy filled her heart at the thought that they wanted to host her in their home, and that she would soon be a part of that wonderful clan.

When Gaby arrived at the Danforth home, Sasha greeted her with a kiss on the cheek and a big hug, then led her into the formal living room reserved for special occasions. In Sasha's mind, the upcoming nuptials of her brother-in-law to Gaby indeed qualified for a special occasion.

"Welcome, future sister-in-law," Reverend Danforth said, smiling brightly. He hugged her. "Who would've ever guessed that first your gifted hands saved my life, and now you're going to be family? Wow, He does work in mysterious ways, huh?"

They all shared a laugh—especially Marcus, who was seated at Gaby's side, and held her hand like a true man in love. "I had no idea this was coming, bro, but I cannot say when I've ever been happier."

"I can vouch for that, Marcus, because back during the time when you two were at odds, pardon the expression, you looked like hell!" Sasha said. "I—we—were so worried about you because you were slowly sinking into depression, and that wasn't a good thing. I'm thrilled that y'all could work out your differences and get back to the love."

By this time, wine was poured in all of their glasses, and Sasha had served a round of hot hors d'oeuvres. "I can't think of a better toast than what my Sasha just said, so hear, hear! Be happy and be blessed," he offered, clinking his glass with Sasha's, urging everyone to follow suit.

Immediately after their toast, Sasha called them into the dining room for dinner. Hand in hand, Gaby and Marcus went in, and Gaby's jaw dropped when she saw the beautiful table. It was adorned with an ecru lace cloth, matching linen napkins, sterling silver utensils, bone china, and the finest Waterford crystal stemware. And the food was in a class by itself. There was turkey, ham, dressing, string beans mixed with potatoes, collard greens, potato salad, and a yam casserole. "Sasha and Reverend Danforth, this is way too much. You didn't have to put yourselves out like this for me. This looks like Thanksgiving."

"Gaby, nonsense! I was too happy to cook this special meal in your honor." Sasha smiled. "I am ecstatic to have you as my future sister-in-law. We'll be as close as blood sisters, and hopefully, do all the girly-girly things sisters do. I liked you from our first meeting—although I was tripping about Hunter's illness and everything else. It was no trouble at all."

"My Sasha can throw down as you can see from this table and the few extra pounds I've put on since I've been released from the hospital," Reverend Danforth added. "Now, I've got a bone to pick with you, young lady. Please call me *Hunter*. We are family now, and that's appropriate."

"But...but—"

"But nothing. As far as I am concerned, you are my sister, okay? Enough said. Let's bless this food," he began. "Lord God, we want to say thank You for finding two good people and bringing them together. In Your word, it says that the man who findeth a wife findeth a good thing. We believe this to be true. We ask that You bless their union, give them the strength to withstand any trials and tribulations, stand with them through the good times and bad. We ask that You look down upon them and give them favor and every desire of their heart. We also ask that You make their union fruitful in any way You see fit. Bless this food, Father God, and the hands that prepared it in Your most holy and awesome name. Amen."

A chorus of amens rang from around the table—even from Kevon, who'd now joined them.

"One more thing," Reverend Danforth said, standing. "As the head of this household, I would like to officially welcome you to the Danforth family, Gaby. We're not perfect, but in all things we have each other's back—unconditionally. With the Lord and the Danforths with you, behind you, and around you, you're part of a winning team!"

"Thank you...uh...Hunter, Sasha, and children," she said, looking at the babies for whom Sasha had fixed and cut up a mini meal. "I will be proud to wear the name Danforth. Thank you all for this food and the hospitality."

Marcus grinned a huge Kool-Aid–size smile. "You see why I love this woman so much?"

"We do," they said, and began eating their food—not knowing what to eat first.

For the next two hours, they ate and drank the delicious fare that Sasha had prepared. They got to know more about Gaby, her medical career, her life in Philly, and her likes and dislikes. She shared her hopes and dreams with them, as well as how she never thought in her wildest imagination that she would meet a man, fall in love, and entertain the idea of marriage. Reverend Danforth told her that the best-laid plans are often waylaid by God because He has the Master Plan—a better one—because it's His will. For reasons only He knew, they were put together, and it would be revealed in time, Hunter said, donning his ministerial hat for a moment. In mere seconds, the laughing, joking, and revelry stopped when Kevon said he had something to say.

"Go on, nephew," Hunter urged, pleased that he sounded so grown-up. "We've been wondering why you were so quiet, this evening."

"I've been thinking about a lot of things. I'm not surprised that Auntie Doc's going to marry Unc. They've been feeling each other from the beginning," he began. "And their hooking up is what's up. I want to be in the wedding!"

He couldn't help getting in a good joke, but the slight lines furrowing his young brow told them that something was still on his mind.

"I would like to live with Unc and Auntie Doc—if that's okay," Kevon announced.

Utter astonishment crossed Reverend Danforth's and Sasha's faces. Gaby and Marcus looked at him as if he'd grown another two heads.

"Don't you like it here, Kevon?" Reverend Danforth asked. "Did we do something to run you away?"

Kevon sighed, wondering how to say what he felt without hurting anyone's feelings. "I like it here fine, and I'm happy you didn't send me to juvie hall when I first came here. I know I was tripping. But Unc and Aunt Sasha were there for me. You too, Uncle Hunter—after you got better from your sickness. Before that, you were always at the doctor's or away on church business, so you didn't have time for me. See, if I live with Unc and Auntie Doc, he can teach me the contracting business. I like it, and think I want to grow up and be a contractor. We have a lot in common, and they have more time to 'mentor' me."

Reverend Danforth was thinking that Kevon could sell ice to an Eskimo in the dead of winter, because masterful persuasion seemed to be his style. Much of what he was saying was true—especially that part of his not having time for him. He thought that Kevon brought up some good points, and he spoke the truth. Reverend Danforth looked at Kevon, then Sasha, and Gaby and Marcus, shrugging his shoulders. He wasn't quite sure what to make of Kevon's request.

"Nephew, this is certainly a rather odd request, and one that I have to pray about. Such a decision that would affect your future cannot be made at the dinner table," Hunter began. "This is neither the time nor the place for it. I do need to explain something to you. It's unfortunate that you came when you did, because you were caught up in my illness and in one of the church's busy seasons. I'd just been diagnosed, and was running back and forth to the doctor's trying to get some answers about getting well. If I neglected you, I am so sorry. It wasn't meant that way. I love you and want the best for you. I hope you know that."

"I do, Uncle Hunter. But I still want to live with Unc and Auntie Doc. I require a lot of attention that you can't give me. You have enough kids of your own. They don't have any, so they could spend lots of time teaching me things I need to know and stuff like that. I would still see you and spend time with you and Auntie and my cousins, but I wouldn't *live* here. Please, at least think about it. Will you?"

"Hunter, the boy does make sense," Marcus cut in. "Doesn't he, honey?"

"It might not be a bad idea, but it's something we'd have to all sit down and discuss and come to an agreement before we could make a final decision."

"Let's join hands and give this to God. Let's see what He says about this and would have us to do," Reverend Danforth said, beginning to pray….

CHAPTER 12

At Reverend Danforth's insistence, Marcus picked Gaby up from work at lunchtime to take her to see him and Sasha. Neither of them understood what the great urgency was about. Soon they'd arrived and Sasha ushered them to the family room where plates of chicken salad, fresh-baked rolls, and tall, sweaty glasses of sweet tea awaited them. "Since Hunter summoned you over here so close to lunchtime, I figured it was the least I could do," Sasha commented.

Reverend Danforth and Kevon joined them and greeted them with hugs. "Let's eat while we chat. We're all family here, so there's no need to be formal," Hunter said.

He blessed the food, and they began to eat their lunch. "I know you both have to get back to work, so I'll get to the point. I've been thinking about Kevon's request and considering all of the options. I've even consulted with an attorney about this matter."

"Oh?" Marcus asked. "And what did you come up with?"

"Well, it's not as crazy as I first thought," Hunter began to explain. "There is plenty of validity to his request. He's a troubled young man who needs constant attention and support—mentoring as he calls it. With my schedule and Sasha's schedule, that might not possible. Don't get me wrong, we could spend some time with him, but not as much as he needs to really get him on the straight and narrow. Remember, we both travel a lot, and I am obligated to the church and its members. Then there are the kids, so where does that leave Kevon? Realistically, I can say that I am probably not the best candidate to raise a 'tweener' with so many needs. I do have the desire, but my time is funky."

Marcus deferred to Gaby. "Honey, what is your position in all of this? How do you feel?"

She uttered an indrawn gasp and smiled. "Sweetheart, if you want to take in Kevon, I'm all about it. I love him, and think he'd complete our new family."

"Okay, y'all, this is what I propose," Reverend Danforth elaborated. "My attorney will secure the legal paperwork, and you and Gaby can legally adopt Kevon—if that's okay with you both and him."

"It's more than okay with me, Uncle Hunter!" Kevon exclaimed. "I'd love that!"

"Consider it done, then. Here's one little condition, though. I am not letting you take my nephew unless I can be his godfather. I still want to be involved in his life and well-being," Reverend Danforth teased.

"That'll work! You'll be a good godfather, and I'm sure you'll give me everything I want, huh?"

"More—especially all the love you could want."

They ended their meeting with hugs, laughs, a prayer, and more of Sasha's delicious chicken salad.

Four months later, December 31

No one knew what to expect from a winter wedding held on New Year's Eve at the stroke of midnight, but everyone's jaw dropped at its beauty. A chuppah adorned with white satin, lace, and netting stood at the altar. Birch branches accented with strings of white cybidium orchids glowed under the flickering candlelight. White roses decorated each row of pews, and petal garlands and votives created an ice-storm effect. A string quartet, stationed in the back, played a medley of beautiful music to fit the occasion as excited attendees awaited the bride. Red Oaks Christian Fellowship had been transformed into a winter wonderland by Mother Maybelle, Valerie, and the bridal party.

Gaby arrived at exactly 11:55 P.M. in a white carriage, drawn by six white horses. Valerie, her matron of honor, gingerly removed the white blanket that covered Gaby on the unseasonably cold twenty-five-degree evening. Helping her descend, Valerie pulled down the long white mink that kept her warm during the ride.

Once they arrived inside the sanctuary and Valerie and the two bridesmaids helped Gaby out of her coat, everyone smiled at how lovely a bride she was in her bustier white Casablanca wedding gown with floral lace, pearls, and rhinestones. Moments before the organist began the first chords of Pachelbel's Canon, Valerie pulled Gaby's veil over her face and gave her a hug of support. Then, she handed her a beautiful white bouquet made of freesia, tulips, spray roses, narcissus, and dusty miller, accentuated with hyacinth petals, beaded pine leaves, and clear beads.

* * *

If an earthquake happened, Marcus would have remained locked in place at the altar. This was the day he dreamed about—he was marrying the woman who was perfect for him in every way. Tears streamed down his face as he saw his bride making her way down to him. Never before had he loved a woman so much.

Gaby looked in Marcus's eyes, seeing nothing but love in them as she listened to Valerie singing "So Amazing." Gaby thought that *amazing* was the perfect word to describe what had happened between her and Marcus. A year ago, she would've shot down the whole idea of her meeting Mr. Right—much less marrying him. She took another look around the crowded church, and saw that there wasn't a dry eye to be found. She watched as several women grabbed their spouses' hands, and a few of the single women sat sour-faced. The sound of Reverend Danforth's voice startled her out of her musings and brought her back to the splendor that surrounded her.

"It is my pleasure to join my brother, Marcus, to this fine young woman, Gabrielle Regina Talbot," he began. "Never was I more anxious to officiate a wedding, but this one is indeed special to my heart." His voice broke with emotion.

He led them through the traditional wedding vows, and invited them to recite their own. Marcus went first. Grabbing Gaby's hand, he began. "Gabrielle, I cannot put into words the joy my heart is feeling at this moment. All I've ever wanted was you, but didn't know it. I believe that God creates a woman who's perfect for every man. I know He did for me, and that woman is you. You're my friend, my lover, my soul mate, my life. I promise to be there for you however you need me—in sunshine and rain, in the midst of all storms. I will never leave your side. On that, you can depend. You complete me and make me a total man."

Valerie handed Gaby a tissue, then took one for herself. Gaby wiped her tears, then began. "Marcus, you are a miracle—my miracle. Just when I thought I'd never find love again, there you were. You made me believe in goodness, honesty, loyalty, and most important of all—love. You taught me to trust again, and for that, I thank you. I thank you for coming into my life and choosing me as your wife. I promise to be by your side, with you in every area of your life. When I think of everything that is right and good, I think of you. As you said, you complete me, and when our journey on earth is over, we will continue it in heaven. I love you, Marcus Danforth, and am happy to call you my husband."

They lit the unity candle and released a flock of white doves in the sanctuary. "With the power vested in me by the laws of the State of Georgia, I pronounce you man and wife." Reverend Danforth beamed. "Marcus, kiss your lovely bride—my new sister-in-law."

In front of a clapping and cheering congregation, Marcus whirled Gaby around and kissed her with every bit of the love and joy inside his heart. White heat crept through his loins, and Gaby's body became hot despite the frigid night.

Gaby broke with tradition and ran to her sister, Carolyn, and hugged her. "I'm sorry, Carolyn. No matter what happens, no man will *ever* come between us again. You are my sister, and I love you," she said, sobbing.

Their parents and Marcus looked on, also crying tears of joy that they finally reconciled. "No, sister, I apologize to you," Carolyn sniffled. "I was wrong, and I realize that. Give me another chance, and I promise that I'll spend the rest of my life making it up to you." Marcus let them talk for a few more minutes; then he took his wife's hand and led her to the back to begin the receiving line.

The guests adjourned to the Red Oaks Country Club and Golf Course, where the reception was under way. The large ballroom was decorated with snow-white amaryllis, fragrant eucalyptus, velvety lamb's ears, crystal, and the most pastel-blue accents. Candlelight softened the décor and made the room sparkle.

Gaby and Marcus glowed under the candlelight, but it was the light of their love that shone even brighter. They couldn't seem to break away from the photographers who snapped them at every turn, saying they wanted to capture one of Red Oaks' finest weddings—especially a unique winter one. They snuck away long enough to greet some of their guests at the cocktail hour, and to enjoy the band that specialized in playing classic soul and R&B songs.

"May we have the bride and groom to the dance floor?" Reverend Danforth asked.

Hand in hand, they sashayed to the dance floor and began their first dance as a married couple to Phyllis Hyman's song "Complete Me." The onlookers clapped as

Gaby and Marcus whispered sweet something somethings in each other's ear, and kissed throughout the song.

Soon it was time for the toast, which Mother Maybelle led. "I am full today as I stand here to toast this beautiful couple," she said, wiping a tear. "Y'all know that I'm a sucker for love, and they represent the kind of love authors write about in romance novels. Never before did I see a couple so in love, but tried everything to avoid and deny it—except maybe my Norman and Valerie. But when two people are meant to be together, nothing can keep them apart. I fell in love with Gaby the first day she came to work at the hospital. There was something special about her, and I am so glad that Marcus saw it, and chose her to be his wife. I wish you a lifetime of happiness and love, and may every desire of your heart be yours. Stay together and stay strong, because as sure as there will be good times, there *will* be bad. Look to God, and He will get you through them. You've found each other. Now hold on for the ride of a lifetime!"

She raised her glass of champagne and invited the guests to do the same. They toasted Gaby and Marcus and clinked glasses. Their toast was followed by Gaby's parents, Marcus's parents, Gaby's boss, Judge Jackson, and Reverends Danforth and Avery. Before the reception was over, there was the father-daughter dance, a seafood dinner, a dessert table, and a coffee bar ended the festivities.

Just before the bouquet was thrown, Gaby and Marcus wowed their guests when they joined the dancers doing the "Cha-Cha Slide," demonstrating their slick move to the crowd—giving each other a prelude to what was to come when they were finally alone. A wicked smile played across Marcus's lips at that thought.

Gaby threw her bouquet and her sister, Carolyn, caught it. But it wasn't an easy catch, because she had to push a large woman off her who tried to tackle her like a linebacker on the Atlanta Falcons.

Just then, they noticed Mother Maybelle and the judge dancing a little too close and looking a little too cozy on the dance floor. Something was up, and they wanted to be the ones to out her since she thought she had a monopoly on it. "Sugars, this is y'all's night, and Mother Maybelle got more sense than to try to upstage you." She grinned, her gold tooth shining. "Y'all are *so* right. Something is up, but now's not the right time to announce it. It'll keep till later, trust me."

"Oh no, you don't, Mother Maybelle," Gaby told her, dragging her to the front of the room. She instructed the band to stop playing. "Sorry to interrupt, but Mother Maybelle has something to share with us all," Gaby said, putting her on the spot as she had done so many times to members of Red Oaks Christian Fellowship.

"Okay, enough already. I might as well tell you because some of y'all got real loose lips and can't hold water. Judge Hezekiah Jackson and I are engaged, but we haven't set a date quite yet. Now, that's it. I don't want to spoil this occasion."

Gaby and Marcus were the first to congratulate them, followed by the ministerial and members of the church. The only thing that got her away from them was that she and Valerie grabbed Gaby and took her to the bridal suite changing area to help her get out of her bridal gown.

When she came back out, she had changed into a beautiful winter-white pantsuit, trimmed with white mink around the collar. Gaby and Marcus went around the room and bade their guests good-bye, thanking them for helping to make their wedding day special. The last person they spoke to on their way out was Mother Maybelle.

"Have a good time, y'all, and this is for you," she said, tucking an envelope in Marcus's tuxedo pocket. "This is a little nest egg to help y'all get started. Use it well."

What they didn't know was that she had made a sizeable financial investment in their names for them to use as a down payment on their first home together. They hugged and kissed her and thanked her for everything. While they admitted she was plenty nosy, she also had a heart of gold and meant no harm. She and Valerie saw them to the white limo awaiting them for the trip to a bed-and-breakfast in Atlanta, until it was time for them to catch their flight to Maui.

In the limo, Gaby let out a long exhalation of relief. Being Marcus's new wife was something wonderful, beyond her wildest imagination. She couldn't stop smiling, or kissing, or touching her husband.

"Happy, Mrs. Danforth?" Marcus asked, kissing her face and neck.

"The happiest I've ever been, my darling Mr. Danforth."

"So am I, honey, and will be as long as we're together—no matter what life brings us."

"That, too, dear husband, is my solemn vow," she said, pulling him into her arms for a kiss like none other.

Celebrating life every step of the way.

YOU ONLY GET *Better*

New York Times bestselling author
CONNIE BRISCOE
and
Essence bestselling authors
LOLITA FILES
ANITA BUNKLEY

Three fortysomething women discover that life, men and
everything else get better with age in this entertaining
three-in-one anthology from three award-winning authors!

Available the first week of March wherever books are sold.

KIMANI PRESS™
www.kimanipress.com

KPYOGB0590307TR

Enjoy the early *Hideaway* stories
with a special Kimani Press release...

HIDEAWAY LEGACY

Two full-length novels

ROCHELLE ALERS

Essence Bestselling Author

A collectors-size trade volume containing
HEAVEN SENT and HARVEST MOON—
two emotional novels from the author's
acclaimed *Hideaway Legacy*.

"Fans of the romantic suspense of Iris Johansen,
Linda Howard and Catherine Coulter will enjoy the first
installment of the *Hideaway Sons and Brothers* trilogy,
part of the continuing saga of the *Hideaway Legacy*."
—*Library Journal* on *No Compromise*

Available the first week of March
wherever books are sold.

KIMANI PRESS™
www.kimanipress.com   KORA0650307TR

Pleasure SEEKERS

Part of the Hideaway Legacy

A sizzling, sensuous story about Ilene, Faye and Alana—
three young African-American women whose lives are
forever changed when they are invited to join the
exclusive world of the Pleasure Seekers.

Rochelle Alers

NATIONAL BESTSELLING AUTHOR

"Fans of the romantic suspense of Iris Johansen,
Linda Howard and Catherine Coulter
will enjoy [*Pleasure Seekers*]."
—*Library Journal*

Available the first week of January wherever books are sold.

sepia™

www.kimanipress.com

KPRA0360107TR

**What if you met your future soul mate...
but were too busy living in the here and now
to give them the time of day?**

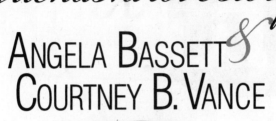

friends: a love story

Angela Bassett &
Courtney B. Vance

An inspiring true story told by the celebrities themselves—
Hollywood and Broadway's classiest power couple.
Living a real-life love story, these friends-who-became-lovers
share the secret of how they make it work with love,
faith and determination.

Available the first week of January wherever books are sold.